NORTHERNMOST
Hyperborea
odor's Anchorage
Old Ward Forest
Mainland
Little Bay
Imperial Summer Palace
Royal Island
Hinterland Farms
The Narrows
Griffon's Nest
The Jogga
Danilova Bridge
Mayoral Tower
House of Wisdom
lchemist's le
Naval Barracks
The Polar Sea
72°00'31"N 40°51'55"E
Severnayan Harbour
The Blossom of Boats
Bears Paw
Blackglass Beach
The Swans
Krjuchók Island

That Great Leviathan

By Tyler Kimball

CHAOSKAMPF PRESS

First Edition.

This is a work of fiction. All the characters and events depicted in this book are fictional, and any resemblance to real people or incidents is purely coincidental.

Chaoskampf Press

Cover art by Tyler Kimball
Edited by Jake Lueckler
Additional art: Blue Whale Skeleton (1832) by George Johann Scharf; the frontpiece of Hugo Grotius's De jure belli ac pacis libri tres (1704); Lithograph by Broussais after J.J. Grandville (1832); Belted Kingfisher Study by John James Audubon

Print ISBN: 979-8-3304-6449-4
eBook ISBN: 979-8-3304-6450-0

Also by Tyler Kimball

Bathwater
Whom Gods Would Destroy: An Occult History of the
First World War, parts I-III

Chapter 1: Down Dark Tides the Glory Slides

Although its dark red stains were simple paint, the wooden circle nailed to the mast testified to a grim maritime tradition of blood sacrifice. Something must lure the winds, the sailors will explain, and it is better that one man die by an opened throat than everyone aboard succumb to slow thirst and maddening sun. At the center of this primitive ritual site, a clean cross-section of a willow, a sacrilegious nail supported the modern miracles of a thermometer and an aneroid barograph.

Further up the mast, in the crow's nest, another assurance against a dead calm and starvation shivered in the evening air, awakened by the chunky tumult of the icebreaker straining to prove its name with the painful zeal of an inadequate heir.

Kingfisher Volganin stood up and let the bedding slide off her back. Her long legs, built to wade through shore and swampland, dug into the wood for balance as she adjusted her precious leather bookbag and pushed aside her cedar trunk. She sniffed and brushed the flaking skin from under her nose. The heavy air of Samyy Severnyy's vast port smelled different than most sea fronts, too cold for the pungent scent of rotting kelp, but the acrid winds spread the unctuous odor of the Alchemists' Isle whaling lots and the fish canneries of the Royal Island. The port was quieter than most, with the cawing gulls facing heavy competition from terns, white waders, and auks both great and little.

Volganin hopped from her barrel nest on the central masthead to the bow mast's top, and to the lowest spar of its square rig. She grasped a taught loading cable, avoiding the sailors' work routes as she descended to the deck with the crane hook. The aging, three-mast warship had been refitted into a cargo ship, trading armaments for a spacious hold, block-and-tackle loading mechanisms, and an ice-breaking grill empowered by emergency boilers and the thrust of a great steam screw. The *Imperator Dragomir*'s high center of gravity protected it from treacherous, icy scrapes but slaved it to pernicious Polar Sea weather and cursed it with a stomach-churning sway. The North's cruel wind chilled her bare legs and numbed her lips. She thought that the navigator's promise of warmer days ahead had fallen through, but the thermometer supported him. A horror gripped her as she realized that yes, this was indeed the warmth of the Severnayan Thaw.

She struggled to find a spot in the work detail as she regained her balance and warmed herself with pumped legs and quaking shoulders. She apologized for waking late, but the crew ignored her. It was the tightest ship she had ever witnessed.

The black-coated mariners brought down the sail with a song led by an aged and respected boatswain with a stunning *basso profundo* voice. She smiled at the brief show of warm humanity. After a week of long travel, their admirable professionalism shifted to an eerily, quiet solemnity. Their departure from Novoport was quite possibly the cleanest and fastest she could recall. Their discipline became off-putting, uncanny even.

"Have you ever been this far north?" she asked, interrupting the second mate's inspection of an sail painted with lucky stripes of ultramarine, sacred to the sea god Craethion. At night, the enchanted canvas darkened and twinkled with phosphorus star charts.

"Out west, once," whispered the thin man, without pausing his scan of the deck, "But we don't come to Northernmost, Dame Kingfisher."

"We?" she asked. "This crew?"

"Tsokiri," he said.

She tilted her head quizzically. Northernmost was, last she heard, part of the Homelands.

One heavy-set sailor, winding a rope around his forearm,

looked up at her and said, "They service foreigners from all over the Polar Sea, and further west and east. But they're enemies of Chernograd, even if they don't have the guts to act on it."

"How can they survive up here without the capital?" she asked. "It's frozen for more than a season."

"Northernmost has been dying slowly, for a century," said the Second Mate, "The port thrived, until the Vankiri armada tried to blockade. And its burning. After that, things went very...hush, hush. These Severnayans had ambitions, tried to break away from Tsokir...and then came the curse."

"Serves them right," said the heavy sailor. "To much of the Old Guilds in them."

Kingfisher visited many of the ports that once belonged to the Confederation of Maritime Guilds, who retained a common tradition of elected mayors, merchants' councils, and various laws and customs. But the league's promise of mutual protection faltered when the Septentrine Empire claimed Swanlands, Palantoke, and Ingeborg, and Tsokiri armies captured Lentora, the Timorats, and the Shankir. The Severnayan State, with Northernmost as its capital, was an even older alliance of northern cities and counties, absorbed into the Volgamazgan crown seven hundred years ago.

To the Throne of the Fallen, foreign rivals had always had a dangerous foothold in the empire's north.

"Curse?" Kingfisher asked. Something caught her eye through the inland fog, a thick shadow looming behind the amber haze. It was Northernmost's legendary tower of black iron, stretching at least half a kilometer into the sky. The natives say it was here before them.

"I've only heard rumors," said the second mate, and the sailor concurred with a nod. "Ask those foreign doctors in the hold. Like I said, we don't come up here."

Kingfisher had barely heard from them in their rickety

berths in the underdeck; one spoke good Tsokiri, and another decent Merovene, but they kept to themselves, and did no work above deck. She wanted to ask what changed, what drew this ship to Northernmost, but the sailor and the second mate turned from her, driven away by the First Mate's scowl.

In stretches of sea notoriously infested with mermaids and sirens, a woman called the Captain's Wife is brought aboard, with smelling salts and horns to break their enchantments. Wayland and Merovy send out entirely female crews through the worst of them, but this is vanishingly rare elsewhere. This dangerous task, more than any, was why ship insurers and captains sought out Kingfisher's services, despite the misfortune brought by her womanhood and the malevolent winds in her veins. She could break a siren song, fight off invaders, and even pull fish, flotsam, and castaways from the blue.

Still, men usually kept their distance from her for the first few days of a voyage. But by the end of the first week, that same femininity, at least until the span of her shoulders and the top of her knee, provoked prurient remarks and offers. Not these men.

A feral part of her wished to sing to them. To draw out that lust. It wanted to join the work song and transform these labors into a bacchanal. She smothered that bestial impulse under righteous disgust and got to work as the ship maneuvered to the dock under an odd combination of falling sail and steaming mechanical oar.

A pair of men pulled a heavy canvas cloth from the anchor, a heavy stone slab rather than the traditional bowed steel weight. She had never seen such a practice, but she assumed it had something to do with the Polar Sea's ice and hearty barnacles.

She grabbed the end of a heaving line, fluttered to the dock, and returned with a pair of bulky hawsers attached to mooring winches. The heavy hauling ropes fought against her legs like constrictor snakes, animated by the winds sweeping across the coast. After choking them down against the docks and looping them through the bridles' eyes, she returned to the winches to turn the crank. She gasped and recoiled from a steam-heated crankshaft. She laughed at herself in embarrassment, the mechanism was merely unexpectedly warm, not scalding, and she should have noticed that something had de-iced the device. She then gasped again as she slipped on black ice, and spread her wings wide, accidentally ringing a silver bell mounted on a dockside lantern. She drew up the air to catch herself, to the horror of a nearby longshoreman.

The old man clutched at his chest as he steadied himself against the dock's pylon. His hands quickly snapped up, pulling his cap down and cupping his scalloped ears. He struck at the silver bell, meant to break curses, hauntings, and enchantments. Volganin tried to calm the man, but quickly realized that her continued advance would have driven the old man into the icy drink of Seal Skinners' Head.

Kingfisher called herself an alkonost when she had to, but the old man called her by her people's common names.

"Siren..." he gasped in a soft, wheezy voice. "Harpy!"

She tried to say that she meant him no harm, but the automatic winch let out a clanking howl as it drew in the sixth-rate post ship, drowning out her reassurances. She instinctively entered a deferential stance, with wings covering a downcast face. The yard-man slipped, and she forced the air behind him to cough up a salty wind. She righted the old man, and clasped his right wrist with the bend of her wings. She curled the single digit on each wing to hide its fearsome claw.

"Everything is going to be fine," she said with a smile. "Let's unload this ship."

The crew was already at work, and the anchor sunk below the waves with an echoing splash. A gust pushed past her, bending a few pinions, as the ships' other passengers, a pair of foreign doctors, made their way down the dock.

Kingfisher flew back to the crow's nest. The boat roared and strained and broke. Kingfisher shrieked and turned, blind and deaf above an inferno that screamed across the water and warped the wharf. The rapidly-heated wood moaned and cracked, drowning out the breaking of bones and the gasps of lungs beaten flat by the pressure wave. Frothing water surged through the dockyards and workers panicked as flayed whales rose as vengeful revenants on blood-pink tides.

The shock and updraft tossed Kingfisher towards the clouds, with such force that she strained against an outright inversion of her wings. Above the graying mists, the sea and sky blurred into a tangerine nightmare. A second blast tore through the hold, and the aft of the sundered ship splintered. Kingfisher closed her eyes as the fireball expanded. They were met with a blinding pillar of smoke when opened, and she cried out. The crowd along the shore was a riot of madmen, and she could have sworn she heard gunfire. She fluttered clear of the pillar and turned her wings to sweep outward and circle back. A second smoking pillar swirled from the corner of the port market, the militia's powder magazine ignited by the pressure wave. After wiping her eyes clean on her biceps, she turned her keen gaze to the water, searching for men to rescue.

She circled twice and found only the dead. The torn-open, the headless, the charred and the broken... and limbs, limbs everywhere. She let out a hoarse cry of distress. The smell of blood and grease the sight of gore kindled a vicious hunger within her. Small flames danced across the rippling harbor. The orange tinge to the water cooled into a soupy, golden brown that Kingfisher recognized as half-melted blubber. The voices along the shore buzzed like horseflies swarming on carrion. She dropped her water-proofed dittybag on an outcropping, tensed her wings and tightened them towards her chest, straightened her spine, and took the plunge.

The ringing in her ears died down below the surface. She heard a brief hum from the water, eerie yet gentle, like whale-song. She tried to listen for an enchanting melody, as counter-singing undines was one of her duties. She ignored the strange tone upon spotting a young man floating, intact but for a superficial head wound. She hooked her head under his armpit and kicked towards the shore. She deposited the man on a beach of ice and pebbles, balled up a talon, and forced the water from his chest with a blow. She lowered her head towards his and felt his failing breath. She listened to his chest, placed her mouth over his, and set a vital wind whirling through his collapsed left lung.

Kingfisher gasped upon hearing the crack of a rifle and the cries of militiamen.

"Vulture!"

"Looter!"

"Harpy!"

She deflected the bullet with an exhausting blast of air and dove into the water. Each chilling dive was a stunning blow, with the thunderbolt alertness of arctic immersion clashing with mind-obliterating cold. She dove deeper and glimpsed the faint outline of something like a traditional bowed anchor in a broken crate swallowed up by the great darkness, her eyes easily picking up the contrasts in fields of gray and blue. Black swirls of bitumen leaked from two dozen barrels, grasping at the wreckage like a ghostly kraken. She took a quick count of the bodies, some thirty, obviously dead or hopeless. One seemingly intact man sent her panicking with the revelation of a skinless face with a boiled-away eye.

She breached the surface for another lungful and remembered her locker, tucked away in the crow's nest. She panicked again and searched for the mainmast. Its high construction saved the nest from destruction, but the search strained muscles and frayed her nerves, to the point that even a diving puffin sent her into a tizzy. The salty sea water ablated the insulating, waterproof oil on her feathers, and the universal cold suppressed her pores' capacity to replace it. The bone-deep cold came quickly, and her talons were not her own when she gripped them around her locker's handles.

She was not sure how she did it, but she found the strength to circle back and retrieve her book bag. She waded ashore on quaking limbs, and blew her nose, sneezing out a thick and bloody brine to the din of the dockside rabble. She snapped to attention as a blur of men in naval black and longshoreman's gray focused into rescue teams running chains and stretchers up the wharf and a firing squad standing dangerously still. The chill in her hollow bones fought a paradoxical war with the burning strain of back muscles as she fled from the local militiamen and the crack of their rifles. A wall of hot smoke met the icy fog, and Kingfisher dove straight into their firing line. Her glaucous wings matched their marengo coats, her pale underside, the rising smoke. Watchers along the shorefront market of Lukomorie Bay screamed and gasped. The irregulars parted and ducked as she had hoped, buying her enough time to fade into the haze of Northernmost.

She flew up the Inland Prospekt and towards the Mayoral Tower at the center of the mainland development, catching the thermal rising from the eerie heat of its black iron majesty and the mundane concrete and tar-pavement. In the harbor she acknowledged its size on an intellectual level, but up close, spiraling up a weather system created by its mere presence, the tower was confounding, terrifying. What intelligence, what forgotten empire, could have made such towers?

Kingfisher turned to the west over the fortified Merchant Court, pivoting outside the warm shadow of the Mayoral Tower. She hissed as a chilling wind rolled down from Hyperborea, the north pole's wrath impeded only by the shadow of a short mountain and the pines of the taiga. She passed over a fine set of houses in the neighborhood of Griffon's Nest, where people milled about outside, craning their necks to see the tower of smoke in the harbor.

Kingfisher came down on a scale-shingled tent-roof. She scanned her surroundings, watching for the flow of emergency traffic to the docks. In the Bereginya, a neighborhood along the Narrows that terminated in the smoldering charcoal kilns of Nine Bear Cave, she saw a tailor's shop and the Quill, a playwrights' café next to a trio of large buildings teeming with activity. The nearest, the wooden, wedge-roofed Driftwood Theatre; the furthest, a castle with a cluster of five great onion domes called the House of Wisdom, the greatest temple of the Severnayan region. Some sort of civilian rescue effort mustered here.

Between the house of gods and the arena of heroes, just a small hop across Ogre-Back Row and down Scheznik Avenue, stood a large stone building with a bochka roof, elevated half-barrels rising into a single bulky dome. Nurses stood outside, preparing triage, while runners carried supplies to shore. Kingfisher focused her eyes on its sign, "Blessed Kiril's Infirmary," unchanged from the aged sketches of the House of Wisdom. It had a somewhat melted quality to its stone edifice, common to the area, with creamy traces on its window frames. The Alchemists' and Royal Isles are ancient calderas from the Great Northern Volcanic Ring, rich in sulfur and cinnabar. Hot-melt sulfur forms the mortar of much of the stonework, and local carpenters decorate their woodwork with inlays of molten sulfur, poured into their etchings from tinker's tools and scraped away when scarred. In this land of ever-present cold and water, the natives clung to heat and fire.

Local alchemists and priests, shamans from the Pokinutin East, doctors, naturalists, and alienists toiled here for a cure to

Northernmost's medical crisis. It would be a good place, she thought, to save people.

As the hummingbird rush of her escape ebbed away, the exhaustion and killing cold ganged up on her. Her knees gave out, and her thighs rested awkwardly against her tarsi, taught and shaking like the great cables of a tall ship's mast. She shook the water from her wings, and cringed as whale oil dripped down her pinions. Wind-worn scales rubbed against each other, painfully overlapping in places, sloughing off a cheesecloth sheet of taupe skin. Her wickedly curved, syndactyl toes tightened their grip around the stony lip of a corbel decorated with a grinning gargoyle. She hopped up onto the roof and ducked tightly against the brick chimney. She nodded off, before feeling returned, and the soaked and freeing bandage on her ankle inspired a surge of panic that sent her scrambling to open her bags and trunk.

She breathed a visible sigh of relief. Her blouses were damp, but not damaged. Her cuirass and arming doublet were perfect, and the saltwater did not breach the leather case around her storybook, manual, and grimoire. More damage had been done by her talons frantically scratching into the clamps and straps. That was today's small blessing.

Kingfisher scanned for prying eyes, and quickly changed her chemise and put on the sleeveless doublet. All of her clothing had to be specially tailored; they snapped or laced together over the shoulder or side so she could dress herself by mouth and the hooked finger on her wing. She was rather embarrassed by her body; while clothed, her torso and head resembled a human woman, but a glimpse of her bare form revealed the subtle oddities. While most of her was thin and wiry, her biceps were comparable to those of a strongman's, and slabs of muscle covered her shoulder and back.

She finally slipped into the century-old cuirass and sealed its side with a slam against the brick chimney. For once, she was overjoyed that the metal plates retained heat like a smelter's kiln.

She was so cold, tired, and hungry that her eyelids appeared to have launched a coordinated effort with the stomach, torturing and blinding their foe while its ally rumbled demands. A trade mission had been dispatched to her toes, but they were halted and possibly lost on the winter march.

She peaked her head out as she finished fastening her cloak. Perhaps an hour had passed since the explosion, and the town had settled down once it was clear that the fire was confined to the waterfront. The sailor must have been brought here by now, if at all.

"Hey!" a voice cried out. "What are you doing up here?"

Kingfisher's head darted towards the source of the noise, an old, wiry man in a raggedy gray coat darkened by soot. He held a broom and a bucket in webbed hands.

"Are you the chimney sweep?" Kingfisher asked.

"I sweep the entire fucking hospital," the man said. "You can't be up here. Get back inside."

"Inside?" Kingfisher said.

She snorted and sneezed out another glob of sea salt and dried blood.

"I... Did a young man come in recently?"

"Young man?" he said. "What, your husband? Brother? Why'd you creep up here?"

"No, I didn't know him. A sailor, pulled up from the harbor," she said. "There was an explosion..."

"Yeah, heard about that," the custodian said. "Hell, I *heard* it. But no, I don't handle the patients, miss. Not the living ones, heh... The door is open. Get back inside. Looks like your hair's wet, you'll catch your death."

She didn't rise.

"Can you... run a message to them? About the sailor? He was blond, a score and five years, at most. Please, sir, I will pay you two prince-heads."

"See, I like the offer, but I don't like that you're hiding, miss," he said. "You're sounding more and more like an assassin. Stand up."

"I can't," Kingfisher said.

"Why?" he barked.

She looked down and tried to think of something that wasn't truly a lie.

"I am not wearing a dress. Or breeches," she said.

"Then get inside or you'll be dead by morning, you damn fool."

He shuffled towards her, and she instinctively skittered backward, but could not hide the blue-gray of her wings.

He sputtered and hurled the bucket at her and retreated, his broom pointed at her like a halberd.

She fluttered out of the way and landed on the lip of the chimney, ready to use its rising warmth for a quick getaway.

"Look, look, I know how this looks–"

"You won't be singing me off this roof!" he yelled. "Back! Back!"

"I just want to know if the sailor is safe!" she shouted back.

"So you can eat him?" he yelled in a strained, reedy voice.

"No!" Kingfisher spat. "Look, call the constables or the militia. If you want me dead... let them kill me. I'm too exhausted to fight back. I only... want to know if I saved one life today."

The old man pulled the broom back.

"I'll go ask about the matter. You stay here. Don't try any tricks," he said.

He backed towards the door.

Before he closed it, he added, "You eat fish?"

Kingfisher nodded.

She bode her time by opening up her old storybook,

Tarasov's *Tales of Great Deeds and Chivalry*, a thick volume of romances sung by troubadours and mistrals, legends of heroic virtue written by ancient philosophers, elfen-songs and retelling of primordial fables and titanomachies.

The old man crept outside again, with baked cod stewed with sour cream, onions, and potatoes, served on kelp in a trencher resting on a hospital blanket.

"Alright, girl, here you go, it's been steamed... the blanket, I mean. It was from a patient with a foot injury, so no need to worry... Eh, the cod's probably steamed, too," he said. "I don't know, that ogre nurse made it."

"Ogre nurse?" Kingfisher asked, perhaps too quietly to hear.

"Oh, your boy... I don't know, miss, he's not woken up," he said. "But give him time, just arrived."

Kingfisher lowered her head, shielding her face with a wing.

"He would have certainly died if you hadn't dragged him out," he said. "You gave him a chance, at least. That's all you can do."

Kingfisher peaked up from her fanned feathers.

"Can you eat this?" he asked.

Kingfisher mumbled aimlessly, before nodding. She cocked her head at the blade of kelp.

"Right, you sound Southern," he noted.

"I'm from the Grand Duchy Gulf," she said, somewhat in-dignantly.

A slight curl crossed the corner of his lip, and his tone soured as he asked, "Novoport?"

"Peresheyeka Derevnya," she said. "On the *north* shore."

"This is Northernmost. You're a Southerner. And that's kelp," he said. "It won't grow in the sea, so we grow it in caves. They burn it on Alchemists' Island, for glass and soap and gunpowder. And those tinctures, for the surgeries. I mean the, uh, soda ash. But it's good for you. Especially if you ever get pregnant. Or, er, egg."

"I will try to remember that," she said.

"Can I set this here?" he said, setting the blanket and trencher on a rooftop steam stack.

The harpy nodded.

"You'll catch your death out here, I think."

"Thank you," she said, as she carefully placed the folded trencher in a leather ration bag. She watched the suspicion in his eyes warm at her unexpected politeness. "We handle wet, cold... wetness...better than Urizen's folk."

"The blanket still has some steam heat in it," he said, closing the trunk for her. "If you want to roost up here, I won't tell nobody, but I'm not sticking around to protect you, neither. If you want a shelter, you might look over to Shura's Inn. Middle of the Staretsy's Prospekt, dead south of the Mayoral Tower. Some of the young doctors are there. And the innkeep will be good to someone like you."

He pointed to the southeast.

Northernmost was uncommonly easy to navigate, its roads planned from the bottom up by Imperator Svyatopolk II's builders, wide and straight for rolling lumber from the taiga or long-hauling loads from the ships. These thick roads cover and brace a network of subterranean rivers and aqueducts, carved by lime-rich water leaching out to sea from the inland karst, thaw after thaw. These bituminous, cement roads held in heat, serving as convenient thermal routes. A grid of bronze pipes allowed salamanders to pass through and warm the streets.

The necessities of logging also left Northernmost vulnerable. It was the first city she had seen without a wall or palisade, instead protected by a series of wooden towers, and raised bastions filled with ash and seashells. Kingfisher noted that all the other cities were messy whirls ebbing from a river, with streets like cracked glass.

It did, however, take her a three-lap run down the prospekt to find Shura's Inn, stopping to watch a cat with seven toes on its back paws writhe on the ground, mewling like a human infant. She'd seen many ship's cats in her career, crew mascots, and mousers, but she had never seen one behave like this. The closest she could remember was Pork N. Beans, a Waylander cat that had chimerized with a pig, who liked wallowing in mud and squealing.

Shura's Inn stood at the foot of that ancient tower. Its two-stories of brown wood vanished against its dizzying black majesty. The inn bore the typically elaborate signage of Severnayan businesses, curling thorn bushes of wrought iron and hinges that slough off the ice and cater to illiterate sailors with negative-space iconography.

It took Kingfisher a moment to puzzle out the silhouette of a troika stagecoach, as seen from the side. She usually saw them top-down. She had a twinge of anger when she read the sign. The Inn seemed to be properly called 'Eternal Flame,' or maybe 'Evening Will-o'-the-Wisp'; it was hard to read, a cursive, wiry tangle in a baroque style about two centuries out of fashion. The name was painted plainly beneath in Waylander, Merovene, Skeironic, Argaman, and Murmurish, but that was no help to Kingfisher. It was only a bit of eagle-eyed scanning that picked up the worn-down name of Shura above the door frame.

The inn had grown from a small depot, with a once detached livery barn for horses. A later overhang bridged the gap, with the added benefit of sheltering an insulated chicken coop set next to what looked to be a brick oven and smoker.

Kingfisher flapped up and down in front of the door, hoping to see through the closed slat in the window. Feverishly, she realized that midnight must be approaching, yet the sun had not set. She was going to miss the night sky, and the constellations, the halo of salt and iron, and the racing stars which flickered in their close circuit around the globe.

A woman in a white and red sarafan dress opened the door. Kingfisher noted that there was something vaguely familiar about her but couldn't place it.

"Hey," she said. "We have two rooms available, one grivenka a night, breakfast in the morning, meal at night included, tea all day. There's a banya next door, tell them you came by us. And we no longer have a hosteler on hand, but still supply horses."

"I'm a harpy," Kingfisher said, rather bewildered that she was the one to table the issue.

"I saw the wings and claws and pieced it together, yeah," the innkeeper said. "And I assumed you knew, so why bring it up?"

"Will it be a problem?"

"Perhaps not," the innkeeper said.

She spoke in an artificially clear, slow way, enunciating for travelers who may not be fluent in Tsokiri. While it slipped a bit, her accent resembled something closer to a school-taught Chernogradic.

Kingfisher noticed that the other Severnayans spoke like old people, or like the rustics in her books, pronouncing syllables that people in the Gulf or Chernograd long ago slurred together, and threw in nautical terms from Waylander, Murmurish, and Rannican. While Northernmost liked the mythology of the Kochniks, hearty seasiders in icebreakers and tall fur hats, the majority of Tsokiri in the port were descendants of the Shitikmen, settlers from the balmier, downstream marshes of the Otmel who paddled northwest in their riverboats to escape the Ölek Hordes. The accent of Northernmost ironically sounds more southern and inland than those they call "southerner" or "inlander."

The innkeeper looked at the harpy's talons. "You're not

going around snatching up sailors, right?"

Kingfisher shook her head and bit her lip. It was a lie if taken literally, but she was justified in the spirit of the concern and didn't want to spend time explaining the asterisk.

She wore a leather band around her left leg for easy access to a few coins for petty spending. Three grivenka around the ankle, thirty-four in her trunk. She pulled out a silver queen's-head and presented it with her right talon. The innkeeper looked at the face of the half-grivenka coin, frowned, and pocketed it.

She gestured for Kingfisher to step inside and spoke with an older man with a deep, raspy voice. Kingfisher assumed that they were daughter and father, separated by some thirty-five years. Both had a rustic look to them, with stocky builds, wide necks, and powerful hands. Their chests were notably broad; she was buxom, and he looked like a brawler. The knot in his nose hinted at a long-healed but brutal break. In his youth, a punch from him must have been devastating, and he could probably still lay someone out, well into his late sixties or early seventies. There was still some of her hair's copper in the old man's stubble, although any remaining hair on his head hid under a river flotilla cap. It matched the coloration of their eyes, not just a light brown, but a glistening bronze that shone through narrow, heavy lids.

Kingfisher's heart sank when she noticed a gray braid bound in a silver ring hooked to the wall, a charm of Incano's hair given to those who have lost a mother or wife. The gods of Aquilo embodied contradictions – kingly Urizen was bound in chains of law and discipline, while his kindly wife In-cano was the mistress of death, spinning fate with her with-ered left hand. Urizen was once said to be the Divine Centaur, a wild beast tamed and divided into Man and Horse by his mate, a hag who aged in reverse. Their parting, it was said, would send Urizen back into bestial madness and return Incano to the shape of an all-devouring spider. It was only the chains of civilization and the silk of life, that bound humans to their humanity.

The woman handed Kingfisher a matchbox and a hooligan lantern and said that it was complimentary, even if it wouldn't get dark out for another five fortnights. The wick hooked through the gills of the alcohol-soaked candlefish. Harvesting and preparing the invasive Thrascian eulachon was a minor industry in Northernmost, both straight from the ocean, and, preferably, out of the freshwater rivers when the larger, oilier males come upstream to spawn like salmon. Severnayan hooligan lanterns could be found far to the south, traded down the 'grease trails' along the White Meska.

The woman pointed out the mail lockers and the work board for job postings, usually teamsters, small-time laborers, and sailors. These menial listings hung below a two-tier wood-carving set with sulfur, a divine Titanomachy over a farce of pygmies fighting cranes.

The master of the house, seated and doing sums in a ledger, slightly rose from his work behind the bar and added, "If you sweep the roof, we'll give you a free night. Some snow and leaves up there... Lena won't let me make that climb any-more."

Kingfisher agreed with a nod and a tired "tomorrow" and looked at the faces around the common room. It was late enough that most of the crowd had dispersed, but a couple of older human men were leaving the bar, stumbling on their weak legs, leaving a twitchy gnome behind. Kingfisher noted that the barwoman, in her mid-thirties, may have been the youngest native she had seen so far. The merwoman playing the spring bagatelle cabinet could be anywhere from a score to centuries old, but the latter seemed more likely. One man in the corner looked to be in his twenties, but Kingfisher as-sumed that he was a traveler from the Septentrine Empire, with a waterproofed watchcoat and a top hat of felted black beaver fur. He read from a heavy book while drinking coffee. From across the room, Kingfisher could make out an anatomical plate demonstrating the dissection of a woman's swollen throat. He looked up to speak to the barmaid as she poured dandelion and burdock mead into a glass. He tapped on his own wrist to indicate her arthritic brace, but his voice quickly trailed off as he spotted the siren.

A hooded Acthnico sat in the opposite corner, marked by an Ouroboros armband. Kingfisher was a bit unnerved by the salamander's yellow, slitted eyes and serpentine scales, but decided that monsters in glass houses shouldn't throw stones. Although she did wonder why serpentfolk were so obsessed with the snake motif; humans don't typically shape everything they own into a humanoid pattern, and she had personally never seen a reason to sit in a siren-shaped chair. But perhaps once your culture settles on a footless form as the ideal, one feels the need to hammer the point home in the face of some persistent and obvious doubts.

A bluebird crafted from wood chips hung from a large black duct that rose from the ground and terminated through the ceiling. The bird of happiness had no glue; its split pine petals interlocked like an elaborate puzzle, light enough to spin slowly as hot air rose through the inn. Kingfisher interpreted it as providence, not knowing that similar 'sun doves' hung in almost every Severnayan household.

She walked past the gregarious old gnome and up the stairs to her room, setting down her trunk on a step before propelling herself up with the other leg. The staff and patrons of the inn watched her, everyone hoping that someone else would cut the tension and play porter for the handless bird lady. She was already up the stairs when the Waylander stood up and sighed.

Kingfisher closed the door of her room, set down her

bag, and opened up her trunk. She checked everything again, taking inventory of her blouses, file, comb, rope, pan, ration and coin bags, perfume bottle, a sling, her great inheritance, and her sword and armor. She took off her cloak, cuirass, and doublet, and set them by her greaves and a hoplite-style barbute. It was only then that she tore into her meal, heating the contents of the ration bag on a corner stove.

She grabbed the room's pitcher by the mirror and basin and dropped a spherical soapstone into her shallow pan. It was her childhood toy, and the sensation of skimming the water with her talon and snatching something warm soothed her nerves. It was her little egg, its blue-gray a near match for her topside feathers. But tonight, the skimming of water brought to mind thoughts of the young sailor, and his devastated crew. She wanted to save someone. She wanted to be the hero... for once.

She also thought of him... the unmet man who must have been her father, a sailor pulled from the sea or ship, tormented, ravaged, and devoured by her mother. She thought of him often, who he could have been. At ports, she asked companies and customhouses about lost or harpy-harried vessels from two decades ago – she wasn't sure of her exact age, but she estimated about twenty-three years – hoping to narrow it down, but it was to no avail. Perhaps he was a smuggler, a slaver, or pirate. Maybe it was better, she thought, if he had been a bad man, but that was a desire to shift blame. An attempt to justify her birth, and the death of an innocent man.

She would have traded her life for his, in a heartbeat.

She looked at the brass mirror and lowered her eyes in shame at her comb and perfumes, a foul creature of vanity and pride. She raked her central right toe across its sinister sister, wincing as blood clouded the water. After the punitive shock of pain ebbed, the smell of blood met her nostrils, and her stomach rumbled in anticipation, grinding with a primal frenzy. She ate that night's meal alone and weeping, as she often did.

Chapter 2: Halcyon Days

After days of planning and cloud-watching, the young harpy covered the sound of her break-in with the fall of heavy rain over marshland mud. She used a dried bulrush to undo the latch on the keep's attic window, and quietly crept inside. She shivered rapidly and forced a hot wind through her feathers, rapidly drying and cleaning herself, stripping the black filth to reveal the gray-blue below. This was part of her plan as well; humans had excellent senses of smell compared to harpies and despised the smell of the carrion-snatchers. She smiled at her cleverness and began to walk across the floor with long strides and half-hops. If she made footfalls, it would sound more like random creaking than the one-two stride of humans.

She clutched the rail of the loft's stairs and glided across the hallway. There it was, the master bedroom of Volganin Keep, as she predicted from the layout of the windows. One can generally tell how humans use their dwelling space by the windows, they sleep in places with flexible ventilation and work in places of illumination. She went quiet and listened for breathing, there was one human there, older by the rasp and labor. It was lying flat.

Her digitigrade legs let her stoop low and still walk, managing to hide behind the footboard of the bed. She readied herself to pounce and tear open the sleeping man's stomach with her talons. She hesitated and bobbed up to see his face.

"Katyusha?" he asked.

The man sat up and turned towards the harpy.

"Is that you?"

The harpy froze. He was looking right at her but did not notice her form. She figured he must be blind and calling for some kind of scullion or scrounger from his flock. She wondered if it could have been his mother; age crushed his shoulders, but maybe female humans live much longer than the males.

For some reason, instead of attacking, she said, "No."

"Are you a new girl?" he asked, his voice wavering and strained. "I'm sorry, I get a bit foggy."

For another reason, or perhaps a freak mutation of the prior one, she quietly said, "Yes, I'm the new girl."

"I see, new girl," he said. "Do you have another name I could call you?"

The harpy paused, fumbling for a name. She had heard a human name before - "Orlov" - the head of all their local flocks, an 'eagle clan.' An emperor or king. Humans were obsessed with names and titles, their cultures too large to identify each other by nicknames or voice alone.

"Orlov," she said.

"Orlova?" he said, quietly correcting the name's sex.

He chuckled and smile.

"Am I in the presence of a royal?"

"Oh, no," she said. "I'm not a king."

"And what is your given name, your highness?"

Human women, if she remembered correctly, were named after flowers. Chamomile came to mind, so she said, "Romashka."

"Hmmm... I've never heard of that name," he said. "But I like it. How do you know Katyusha?"

"Oh," the harpy said. "We met in the village."

"Ah," he said. "Can you be a dear and see if there's an open window? I felt a terrible draft. Oh, and pour some milk for the domovoy."

The harpy nodded. She then remembered that the man was blind.

"Yes!" she barked. "I will do that."

She left the room and pretended to search for the open window, instead searching for valuable items. A clock the size of a man stood at the end of the hallway, its face a complex astrological device mapping the paths of the gods and their children through the heavens. The crippled sun god Los sat at an anvil, hammer-strokes beating out seconds from the raw matter of time.

A chalky man trapped in a metal suit stood in a nearby glass-covered alcove. The harpy recoiled and raised her talons, remembering the tales of the subtle, pale lords and ladies of air imprisoned in chains of cold iron. But a slight turn of the head revealed the white figure beneath it to be nothing but fuzzy felt on some kind of wooden man-carving.

The sound of sweeping whispered from the floor below. The harpy walked down the stairs and found a room of cabinets, counters, and stores, where humans keep the base ingredients of their meals. One box housed cuts of ice. After struggling with the latch, she found a glass milk jug in the frost. Holding its handle in her mouth, she poured an offering of milk into a wooden bowl and rang a brass bell hanging from the ceiling. The oven's grass snake peeked its head out, before ducking back inside its warm home to feast on a rat.

The harpy hid and watched the domovoi. The creature hid its face under a thick burlap hood, but its body appeared to be humanoid in form but floral in matter. Its limbs were long despite its short stature, and its mossy skin a burnt orange, terminating in spindly fingers and toes the black of hearth-soot. The dust disappeared wherever those gnarled roots stepped. The Domestic set its broom against the wall and raised the bowl to its mouth. Its eyes shone green in the dark as it drank.

The harpy slipped away to the master bedroom.

"It is done," she said.

"Thank you," he said.

That gave her pause. Nobody had thanked the harpy before.

"What is that suit of metal in the hall?" she asked.

He chuckled.

"That's my armor," he said.

"Why did you wear it?" the harpy asked.

She did understand the concept of armor. A hard shell is better protection than flesh, but she had not seen humans wear such things.

"Do you not know who I am?" he said.

It wasn't said with indignation, but genuine curiosity.

"No," she said.

"I am Sir Eol Yelenovich Volganin," he said. "Knight of the Frog Marsh of Kekerekeksinsky, baronet of Halcyon Keep."

"What is a knight?" the harpy asked.

"Oh, dear," he said. "That is a question we've been grappling with for ages. A knight should be a warrior of valor, duty, and magnanimity. But too often he is simply an armed man in a keep."

"Were all knights men?" the harpy asked.

"Most, but not all. This keep is named after Dame Halcyon, the Kingfisher Knight, wife of the bogatyr Eol Eolivich. She would have been my... let's see... great-great-great-great-great... oh, I think there are seven greats here... grandmother."

The harpy was told that she descended from the bastard gods of the mistral wind and an Erinyes but didn't think she should share that information at the moment.

"See that tome on the shelf?" he said. "That's Timofy Tarasov's *Tales of Great Deeds and Chivalry.* She's in there, with the first Sir Eol, slaying the great Gar-Lion of Kalimo. They built a house and forged a sword from its mane of burning nails. It's an old book, my grandfather's, but you can read it if you're careful. And there's the *Toxotides* up there too, though its heroine was more of a noble archer, not a knight. There weren't knights then."

"I can't read," said the harpy.

"Neither can I," he said.

He gave a sad laugh.

"So what are we to do? If you stick around, I could teach you the letters. The book has some of the old ones, the ones the academies got rid of when I was a child, but they're easy enough to figure out, after a while."

"You would teach me to read?" she said. "What do you want for it?"

"Oh," he said, "Nothing more than what you're already doing, fetching things for me, maybe some deliveries into town."

"Why?" she asked.

Nobody ever did something for her, for no reason.

"Well… I was a warrior in the emperor's army," he explained. "Later, I enjoyed spending my time riding and reading–"

He stopped abruptly, but the harpy understood the back half of it. A woman had lived here, and likely two children. She had seen two rooms in this hall, in passing, abandoned but not emptied. An image of a woman hung on the wall in an oval of brass, decorated with a braid woven from fine silver.

"There was so much... chaos after the Cousins' War. Three decades of it. The war left behind bands of monsters, both man and chimera. The ogres and horsemen, mad salamanders burning with foul oil, twisted giants, and even horses clad in iron for flesh. But there was heroism, too. I won't lie to you, Romashka, there is great evil in the world. There are monsters. There is unfathomable cruelty. But there are also truly good people that will fight them. And be victorious. Good people who will rise up to heal the wounded and tend to the sick and succeed! The plagues pass. The doctors and nurses win out. I have watched people bring comfort to the dying for no motive, beyond seeing that someone truly needed that comfort in their final moments… Even when nothing can be done or won, people will help. Is there no other proof of a common decency than that?"

She had never seen such things. She had known only the destruction of the weak, the harrying of the wounded, the abandonment of the sick. She had watched her mother and sisters crush her grandmother's skull when the mad hag tried to eat the youngest of the brood. Her elder sisters enjoyed picking up dogs and turtles and watching them smash against the shore stones. Mercy was pointless. Tending to broken things only bound you to one place, a death sentence when the wind carries your world.

Perhaps that's why this old man gave her pause. She had never seen someone in his frail state treated with courtesy and some sort of prestige. She wondered why he hadn't been robbed and eaten by the other humans.

"Did you kill anyone?" she asked.

He must have been a killer, too. These were all justifications.

"Yes," he said in a strange way.

It was soft and weak, despite his obvious survival and victory. The harpy couldn't understand how that worked. He didn't revel in his triumph.

"I had to do it. I was left with no choice. But it had to be done."

"I don't understand," the harpy said.

"What do you mean?" he said. "I tried, my girl. But there were hostages at stake, and they would not be reasoned with. Nor bribed."

"No, I understand that," she said. "Why do you celebrate these warriors if you do not like war?"

"No, no, it's not about war," he said. "It's about who isn't killed, what isn't destroyed. I'm a knight. That armor… that armor is my duty. It's heavy, and protective. I needed help putting it on, even in my youth. It was forged by smiths in the manner of Los, blessed by the priestess of Our Mother In-cano, marked by Craethion and Enitharmon. My sword was given to me just as Urizen gave the world order and law. These are my traditions, my duty, my honor. I am nothing but a mor-tal man without it… but all those things, all those good things, made me a knight. My armor was steel, but I was armed by gods and men."

"Honor?" she asked.

"Yes," he said. "It was an honor. I am a man of privilege and power, land and title. I was no great lord, but I could run and ruin lives. If you *can* destroy, spare. If you *can* ruin, build. If you can trodden peasants beneath your boots, raise them up and speak to them with courtesy. Speak honestly. Keep your word. Never be cruel or spiteful. I was given rights and powers… and I had terrible strength, once… Oh, if you could see me at the tilt."

She did not know what he meant by a tilt.

"I had to respect the world that gifted me so. Protect the weak. Respect my subordinates. Honor my lords. Remember the fallen. Conduct myself with justice and mercy, even in bat-tle."

"Does the world work that way?" she asked.

She had always been told to win. Attack your prey, hurt them, blind them, and run before they can retaliate. Victory at any cost was paramount in battle. She had never heard of jus-tice in battle.

"It doesn't matter," he said. "The world should work that way. Even if the world doesn't, you should act that way. Even if you're alone in a den of thieves, you should act with chivalry and decency."

"You would die," said the harpy.

"Death before dishonor," he said. "Why live? How could you live?"

She had never found it particularly hard to live, except

when it hailed, but there was a twinge of something inside of her, something scratching at her heart. Why *did* she do what she did?

"Is there anything more that you need?" she asked.

"Oh," he said. "No, not now, thank you."

"Is there anything you'd like to talk about?" she asked.

"Hmmm... are you from Peresheyeka?" he said.

"Oh, the town?" she said, remembering the settlement below the cliffs of the isthmus, on the edge of the vast glades ruled from this keep. "Yes. The cliffs nearby."

"Didn't know anyone lived up there," he said.

"There aren't many of us," she said.

"What does your family do?" he asked.

She hesitated. "Hunt, mostly."

"Ah, interesting," he said. "If your family can spare venison, hare, gamebird… I'll pay you for it. Pay you well. I'm sick of chicken and fish and can no longer pursue the stag."

"Thank you," she said, not quite sure how to react, or what she would do with the payment. After a pause, she added, "Should I leave?"

"You don't have to," he said.

He rose up and made a painful walk to his wardrobe. He tapped his hand against the interior and counted two spaces over to his woolen cloak.

"Have you ever heard the tales of the Paladins of Magnus? Merovach and the Quinotaur Kings? The Werewolf Knight? The Bogatyrs of Dawn?"

"No, none of it," the harpy said.

"Would you like to?"

She listened to the old man recount the tales of the Paladins. Some of them, at least, as there were a dozen paladins with scores of legends around them. He left her on a cliffhanger, as the Knight Profumo lost his magic lance while fighting a rampaging hippogriff. He claimed to be too tired to continue, his memory clouded by fatigue, but there was something wily in his gaze, as if he planned on stopping there.

"I will kill him tomorrow," she told herself.

She departed the keep and flew swiftly back to the cliff of bones. She ripped into the rotten meat of a dead vodyanoy. Its taste resembled the frogs of the swamp, just as its face and limbs resembled a frog mixed with an old man. Like harpies, they were demi-elementals, a stable chimeric race of undine, frog, and men, just as the sirens were woman and bird fused by the sylphs.

Finding the grub-infested, slimy, meat distasteful, the harpy tore one of the bones from vodyanoy's leg. So advanced was the limb's purification that it slid out with ease. She cracked the bone with one twist of her talon and sucked out the marrow.

She looked into the eyeless, flaccid face of the week-dead frogman. She thought of the old man dead and rotting, and then frowned. Where would his stories go? She wondered if this old man had any stories that she would never get to hear. She wondered if there was some ugly little frog-girl who had been waiting a week to hear the end of one of his stories.

She stopped sucking out the marrow. For once in her life, she wasn't hungry. She tucked her head under her wing and began to retch. She wondered if the rain had made her sick, or if she had been poisoned by the vodvanoy, or if the knight had cursed her somehow. She stumbled over to the cliffside and vomited. She collapsed on her knees and passed out.

She awoke to screams and barks. Her sisters Ripper, Bone-Nest, and Eye-Robber had captured a lazavik and his dog and celebrated with playful torture. Lazaviky were little men-things that lived in the swamps below, rare and hard to dig out of their burrows. They had never managed to find one. Ripper was slowly ripping out its beard, and someone had torn out its eye. The harpy guessed Eye-Robber; it was sort of her signature torment.

Her younger sister Swiftwing was teaching her baby cousin Shriek-of-Woe how to attack on the fly. The dog howled as the snatchling ripped its ear clean off.

The harpy rose to her feet as Razor-toe and Piper flew in to join the torment. Her stomach churned again, and a sourness rose in her throat.

"Why do you look like that?" Bone-Nest asked as she ripped the lazavik's severed leg in half, one part for her nest of femurs, the other for her nest of fibulae. She would dig out another piece for her kneecap cairn later.

"Why did you come back with nothing, Night Scream?" Swiftwing added.

"Not hunting," added Ripper.

Night Scream spread her wings and slammed them back, darting forward. She closed her talons around the dog's head and neck, decapitating it. She came to a stop on the lazavik's head, crushing it. She screamed at her sisters.

Eye-Robber punched her in the face with a balled-up foot. Night Scream stumbled and struggled for balance, bleeding from the nose and pain addled. Ripper slashed her knees, opening a deep wound and sending her face-first against the rocks.

Eye-Robber wheeled around and punched Ripper. Harpy-sisters can freely beat or bite each other into submission, or for simple sororal torture, but it's an unspoken rule that you don't open deep wounds on the legs or damage wings. Then again, Ripper was a specialist in the field of ripping flesh open, and it may have been a thoughtless error.

Night Scream darted over the cliff and wheeled through the air towards the keep, conjuring a downdraft to deter the rest of the flock from following. They attempted to give chase but were forced back, with the exception of her cousin Rock Pusher, who continued to push her rock around, as was her wont.

Night Scream hunted along the edge of the swamp, where the deer come out to graze. She had studied the call of red stags, and let out the cry, a deep horn blow from the bottom of the throat. A two-headed doe wandered out of the tree line, mesmerized by the cry.

She dove, forcing all of her weight into the base of its bifurcated neck, snapping its spine. The previous injury caused her to scream and botch the left leg's strike. The harpy panicked as the second head continued to live due to her failure. She gasped and fluttered up and down, desperately kicking its left head to death without the momentum to make it quick and clean.

She clutched the dead deer by its spine and flew towards the keep with the assistance of harnessed winds.

She came to rest outside the keep's yard, where she decapitated the deer twice. She buried the heads and the entrails in the dirt and then drained some of the blood. *The humans were clean.* She waited for sundown when she saw a young woman in a cloak leave the keep. She dragged the deer carcass to the threshold shrine of Incano and knocked on the door. She flew up to the roof and lay flat against the slate tiles, turning her hair outward to appear completely black and gray. She listened as the domovoi dragged the carcass inside, hyphae sucking up the drippings as it moved. She cleaned herself with a blast of feather-shaking wind and slipped into the house with yesterday's route.

"Lord Volganin?" she said. "I brought in a doe for you. The domovoy is preparing it."

He laughed in disbelief.

"A cut, you mean?"

"I cut it several times," she said. "But it's everything but the head. Well, it had two heads. None now."

"You hauled an entire deer here?" he asked. "Alone?"

"Yes," she said. Then an idea dawned on her. "But it was a strain. I hurt my leg. Could you help me?"

That's why she came here, she told herself. The humans had medicines, and the knights of those tales could put their hands on people and heal them.

"How did you hurt yourself? Do you need a brace?" he asked. "I have one you could use, somewhere..."

"No, I cut myself, deep. On the knee."

He rose up fast enough to let out a strained wheeze, and tapped the door frame to a side room, and opened up a cabinet. Things jostled around. They sounded like a mix of Rock Pusher's rocks and Bone-Nest's bone nests when the winds picked up. He returned holding a bottle and a roll of bandages in her direction.

The harpy was utterly baffled at what to do at this point.

"Could you do it for me?"

"Oh," he said. "I don't think I should. You don't want an old blind man feeling around your legs."

"Please, do it," she said.

"Are you in that much pain?" he asked.

She raised her leg against the wardrobe, placing a toe against a hinge. He felt the leg raise in the air and set his hands out, scanning the air.

"Tell me when I'm over the injury," he said.

"There," she said.

"This is the back of your knee," he said. "How... Are you a ballerina?"

He gasped at the wound's depth. His finger moved a touch too low, and withdrew reflexively from the rough, scaled skin of her shin.

"Is this a scab? Scarring?" he asked. "Sorry, I shouldn't pry."

He unscrewed the bottle and poured it into her wound.

It was burning her! She knew it, the old man *had* poisoned

her, and was going to hurt her like everyone else. He had just been smarter, more subtle. The ceiling! The ceiling! She couldn't fly away or build up speed. Her leg was going to be seared right off by the magical murder water and he would reveal himself to be that wolf knight he mentioned and he would laugh and gobble her up—

She opened her eyes when the burning stopped. Her leg was still in one piece. The old man was dabbing some of the fluid away with the bandage and began to wrap the wound.

"Thank you," her voice quivered from the near outburst of tears. *The humans were clean.*

"Oh, that reminds me," he said. "What would your payment be? How does thirty grivenka sound?"

"Thank you," she said.

Fortunately, her voice sounded overwhelmed and appreciative, although she had no idea of how generous that was. "So, how did Profumo escape the hippogriff?"

He coughed, put on his storytelling voice, and told her that Sir Profumo didn't escape the beast. Hippogriffs are impossible creatures, the chimerae of chimerae, for the griffon preys upon the horse invariably. So, Profumo decided he could do the impossible as well, and rose up with a whip in hand. He leaped at the diving beast, pulling the whip through its beak like a bridle. Knight and monster tumbled through the air, with the beast flying through the boughs to scrape off the unwanted rider. It was to no avail, however, and soon the horse within the hippogriff broke, and Profumo had a second steed.

He next told the tale of Sir Osmet and Corabel, and the slow descent into villainy of his jealous lord and uncle Erobald, the tale of the winged knight Elfwine, the tale of Sadrubael the Argaman, and the birth of Merovach from the sea of eternity. Her favorite tale of the night was its climax, the story of the Wolf Knight, a werewolf who became a knight. It wasn't a popular story elsewhere, and its absurd elements embarrassed Sir Eol, like flowers with the faces of babes and a castle made of giant's tusks and teeth, and some of the romantic subplot was clearly a lazy rework of Osmet and Corabel, with a rose too obviously replaced with wolfsbane. But while the previous tales had fascinated her, she was enraptured by the tale of what should have been a man-eating monster that willingly bound himself in agonizing silvered armor and used his savage strength to both fight evil and build impossible castles.

The Wolf Knight's story didn't have a real ending. Most scholars believe him to be a tale dating back to the Hirti, the werewolf emperors of the Hirpic Empire, with the Matter of Magnus. He took the place of a knight called Sir Lupin, who had no tales associated with him and little known about him apart from a heraldic emblem of a silver wolf. Once his individual tale ends, he doesn't show up outside of a few lists of knights, and these were likely later additions by writers trying to smooth over his absence.

Eol delighted in the joy in her voice, her giggles, and her interested questions. He moved right into the tale of Sir Ancelin the Cursed, a knight with not much of a backstory or character but some interesting plots, and simply substituted his name and changed his Mantle of Might to the power of a wolf-lord. Hopefully, she wouldn't call him on only mentioning eleven knights rather than twelve.

Eol heard the girl go quiet when he finished recounting Sir Ancelin's final quest to break the curse – or rather, end the Wolf Knight's lycanthropy – with the blessing of a Sylph Queen's song.

He asked if she was tired. She was.

She flew off into the night, putting off killing the old man for another day. She did not return to the cliffs of galena. She slept on the edges of the swamp, where she felled the doe. The next day, she practiced stilling the air in her wake to move in perfect silence, easily killing a quartet of giant rabbits, eating one of them on a wide rock that made things taste salty.

She tried to find a way to pass her time, practicing the few tricks of air magic transmitted through her flock. She focused her efforts on the large lily pads in the swamp, coming up with rules and goals. She would have to spin a lily pad around without breaking the root, or navigate a detached pad from one shore to another without touching another plant. Other times, she would guide a flower with spiraling puffs of wind, losing if it fell to the ground. She graduated from brute force wingbeats to precise shifts in airflow, delicate channeling down a feather's hollow shaft.

She thought of the Wolf Knight sailing to the north to meet the beautiful Sylph Queen, with hair and skin and gown of winter white. It was a happy ending, after all. The Knight wouldn't have to burn in his silver armor or be afraid of hurting people. His strength was gone, however, that was sad. Maybe that's why he wasn't in the final stories.

She bit the serrated edge of her left wing's second remex. She thought of the breaking of the Knight's curse and ripped out her feather. She scratched at the rock, bracing through the pain of the quill dislodging. She repeated the stories to herself, waiting for the sun to set. She gutted the rabbits and flew to Halcyon Keep.

Tonight's stories were sadder. The knights finally met together, fulfilling their oaths to their king. They fought against a great alliance of evil and won. Many of them died, and Magnus and the Dragon Behind the Dark slew each other. But the young knight Merovaccinus slew his vile cousin, the Sea Serpent Rab, after three days of wrestling in the Deeps, and rebuilt the kingdom.

She wasn't sure why it made her sad. She never met any of these people, didn't know what they looked or sounded like. They were never part of her life, and even if they died of old age, it would have been over a millennium ago. They got to be remembered in stories that outright said they went to heaven to guard the Halls of the Holy, a good deal to the harpy.

But that heavy sadness did not leave her, and her thoughts drifted to her talons scratching the salty rock. She asked about writing. He found a pair of tablets in his bookshelf, wood framing wax. He handed one to her. She took it in her mouth and then dropped it on the floor. She ignored the stylus and scratched it with her toes.

He carefully scratched a letter of the alphabet into his tablet, named it, sounded it out for her, and rolled the wax flat after she copied it. She reached the twentieth letter of the alphabet before Sir Eol started to get dizzy and had to sleep.

It became a routine for her over the next few fortnights, hunting and practicing her spelling in mud and her spells in the air until evening, some light chores, storytime, then letters, and later, arithmetic. The Tsokiri language had many letters, many words with many letters, and a couple of letters that disappeared last century, but it was a fortunately phonetic language. He taught her how to spell her fake name, and his own, after she asked. She didn't care about the pseudonym, and continued to practice the name 'Halcyon Volganin,' ignorant of the name's feminine form.

The ancient legends soon blended with the tales of his life. He told of his father's martial training and his mother's witchcraft. He showed her an old swordsmanship manual and an even older grimoire, maintained by wards against fire, water, earth, and dust. She thought the exclusion of air was fortuitous, but it was impossible to ward against all four elements.

He spoke of strange places and titles and times. After three centuries of strongman Imperators binding the western provinces, southern principalities, and eastern territories to the Throne of Volgamozga, the Burning of the New Capital atomized the Tsokiri empire once again. Just under half of the

Volgamozgan boyars fell in the war against the Vankir and Dokhir, their families and holdings put to the torch. The court was lost.

The harpy knew none of this. She hadn't heard of the Cousins' War, called that both because the Kiric peoples consider themselves "cousins" and because of the five reigning monarchs involved, four were first cousins by blood, with the fifth by marriage. Eol was born in the last year of the war, eighty-two years ago. His father was a knight as well, his mother a lady nurse on those battlefields. Its wake was his life.

These once placid swamps gave rise to monstrous chimerae, spawned by the Commonwealth's horrible weaponry unleashed on the upstream Capital, pooling for decades. He fought monsters and bandits, rebuilt his people's home, drained the basin by tricking a chthonian into undermining it, and purified the swamp by capturing six silver swans from the Lake of Mirrors.

Sir Eol paused to clear his throat. His voice faulted, despite speaking of his triumphs and glory days. She knew that wasn't quite the whole of it. But she couldn't bring herself to ask about the empty rooms. She never did. She asked if he knew other witches, other than his father, hoping to draw out a hint of his wife. Instead, he gifted her a door lock.

Nobody used locks on doors anymore. Even from the beginning, every master thief learned the tricks of arcane lock-picking, manipulation of tumblers with wind or heat, aping a key with clay or ice, or simply moving the metal with earthwork. The printing press and pamphleteers taught every thug the tricks, once-occult lore squeezed between city gossip and pornographic etchings. These days, the wealthy use magic seals and commoners guard their doors with security barricades of *lignum vitae* or an ironwood. They are fire-hardened to steam out the workable water and reduce its potential to burn. Locks are now exclusively a training tool for apprentice mages.

"Would you like the grimoire?" he asked as she spun the lock on her toe.

She liked having a second toy, after her soapstone egg.

Her down stood up. The lock slammed into a still toe.

"What do you mean?" she asked.

"Would you like to keep it?"

"Those are important, aren't they? Sorcerers kill each other for them..."

"This was passed down from mother to daughter for seven generations," he said. "My mother had no daughters. I had two sons. They... you only came into my life so recently... but I think you would appreciate it more than any of my squabbling cousins. Pass it on to your daughter."

He gave her a heavy shoulder bag from his closet. She leaned in and kissed his hand, just like she saw in the pictures. That startled him, but his hand reached out and touched her hair, and then her cheek with quaking hands.

She left that night. She didn't tell herself she was going to kill the old man tomorrow. She hadn't returned to her flock in two weeks. That wasn't her family anymore. She wondered what kind of gift the old man would like. It was hard to think of something for him, especially when one cannot visit the shops and doesn't know of most things.

She spent the next morning looking through the spell-book, trying to decipher mysteries scratched in a cryptic short-hand that curled into exotic words and esoteric symbols. But maybe there was a medicine or a spell, something that could heal the old man's blindness.

A twinge of doubt crawled through her head. He wouldn't like her if he saw her. But she held her head high and told herself that if the old man could see his books, it was worth never seeing him again.

She began to puzzle out a cure from the medical recipes. Luckily, she knew words like 'eye' and 'sight' and 'eyesight,' and wondered for a while about non-eye-related sight but chalked it up to unknown magic. Blindness was a difficult issue, as vision was a matter of light, in the domain of fire, but the eye's vitreous humor fell under the domain of water. The polar elements, also including air and earth, could be synthesized as steam or dust, but a stable antithetical synthesis requires an insane level of arcane dexterity and awareness of yliaster, and refining those elements to their higher, attenuated chaoses. Such things required surgical magistery and blood sacrifice.

The harpy didn't even realize that there were chaoses or much beyond the use of wind to lift and push. There was apparently a whole ethereal "upper air" that she had missed out on, and some system of antitheticals and harmonies between elements that baffled her and made her feel stupid. The book also bore the bad news that, as an aerial-aqueous chimera, she would never be able to manipulate earth and fire. She had never tried it, but it was deeply upsetting to learn that hard fact from a book you just met.

She hopped through the swamp, looking for one of those frogs with cloudy eyes. After three hours of searching, she trudged out of the water in defeat. That was how it always was, the one day you want to find a frog with cloudy eyes, you can't. A week ago, she found about half a dozen of them. A week from now, she would probably find a few dozen more.

She cleaned herself in the upstream, smeared some lilac on her wings and armpits, slung her bag over her shoulder, and flew to the keep.

Katyusha did not leave the keep after sundown. The harpy waited for hours, but she didn't leave until nearly midnight, when she left with a few men in fine clothes.

She sneaked inside again through her usual route. Someone had moved furniture along the route, with doors shut and medicinal candles set alight. The armor was gone from its mounting. Eol lay in bed, looking weaker than ever.

"Is… that Romash… ka?" he asked slowly. His voice was weak and slurred. "Who… let you in?"

"I came in through the window," she said. "I thought something was wrong."

"It is," he said as though he had to push each word uphill.

She moved closer to Sir Eol. The left side of his face drooped, while the right side seemed hollow and stiff.

"Apo… apo… Stroke."

"Who were those men with Katyusha?" she asked.

"Vultures," he said.

She recoiled, head snapping back and forth, never having heard that metaphor before. Who could these vulture-men be? Are there male harpies somewhere in the world?

"Do you know them?" Night Scream asked.

"Cousins…and a royal collector," he said. "Come to carve up… the keep."

"Have they stolen anything?" she asked.

"No," he said. "They want this all…legal. Official… So other cousins can't… fight it. Kat's dragging her feet…but she's a peasant. Nothing she can do."

She could not hide from him any longer and brushed the edges of her wings over his right arm.

His right eye snapped open.

"What are–" he stopped to catch his breath. "Feathers? What?"

She rested her head against his chest.

"I… I can fly," she said. "I can find some kind of medicine for you. Tell me where to go."

"There's… no medicine… for this," he said. "This isn't a poison… or a… or a… what do you call it?"

"I can go on a quest," the harpy said.

"This is my body, dear…" he said. "I'm just old…"

"Please don't," the harpy said.

"Don't die?" he said. He made a sound that might have

been a laugh. "Only the monstrous don't… I outlived everyone, dear… I'm ready…"

"Not me," the harpy whispered.

"Take the trunk," he said.

Her head darted around for this trunk. A large, reinforced
box with a handle sat on the ground. She noticed that there
were books missing from the shelf.

"I had Kat… Kat, uh… it's yours… you would appreciate
it," he said. "They wouldn't… What… what are you? Feathers?"

"Please don't be scared," she said.

"I'm not," he said.

"I'm called Night Scream," she said. "I'm a harpy…"

"Oh," he said. "Oh… feathers… and that… that leg…"

"I'm sorry," she said. "I don't want to be… I want to be a
Volganin. I want to be a knight."

He laughed, clearer this time.

"Open… the trunk…"

She rose from his chest and stumbled over to the heavy
box, fumbling with its latches. She saw the fencing manual and
their storybook, money and a woman's clothes, his armor, and
sword.

"Sword," he said.

She wrapped her talons around the hilt and hopped over
to him, placing the sword on his chest. She turned the hilt towards his working hand.

She touched his hand with her talon. He let out a gasp as
he felt its power and sharpness, but she gently guided his hand
to the hilt.

"Kneel," he commanded.

She figured she should just flatten her leg against the
ground. Her knee couldn't support her body like a human
could.

"Yes sir," she said.

Sir Eol Volganin set the flat of his blade against her shoulder. She had seen this image and knew he would never hurt her, but her instinct to fly sent her legs trembling. She began to softly weep.

He lifted the sword up as far as possible.

"Rise," he commanded again.

She did, still shaking. After she moved clear, he brought his sword down, and rested it on the floor.

"Closer," he said.

She returned to his side. His hand fumbled for the back of her head. He pulled her close and weakly kissed her forehead.

"I love you," she said.

"I love you, too," he said. "They'll be back… they'll try to take that from you…"

"I don't want to leave you," she said.

"Go, be a knight…" he said. "Little bluebird of happiness, find your quest."

She grabbed the sword and raised it as high as her leg would allow. She spread her wings to keep her balance. She hopped to the trunk, replaced the sword, and fastened the latches.

The harpy gave the knight a final look and took the stairs to the attic. As nurses and agents of distant cousins entered through the front door, the last knight of Volganin Keep took off into the night.

Chapter 3: Essence and Extraction

Nicodemus Fade stirred an elixir into his morning coffee with a spoon of alicorn. The elixir was a cloying mixture of syrup of maidenhair, orange flower nectar, defrutum, a spirit of jenever, and cool, reduced until thick as treacle. The cool was Fade's original alteration to the recipe, a "crafted honey" of sugared ripe plums, ginger, and rice malt from Saro. It appeared to be more effective than the traditional mixture, although he did not have the time or resources to experimentally confirm it. He had been cycling through exotic tonics from the global markets of Harth-on-Lam and Vestingbrug, monitoring his internal flora, energized humors, and reserves of yliaster, the primordial matter of the cosmos that binds ideals and forms to Reality.

His primary hobby was 'trimming the fat,' seeing how much of a spell or formula he could cut without reducing its effect. Embellishment burdened much of arcane lore, caused by wizards stumbling upon a working and refusing to change the formula. Perhaps they were lazy, or feared failure, or were too in love with their own mystery. Or perhaps a familiar's love rarely survives the dissection. It was akin to words that retained letters which long ago fell mute; interesting to the etymologist, but pointlessly complicating.

Mr. Fade was an arcane philosopher, but hated mysticism, or, perhaps, mystification. As he focused his arts on the subject of the human body, nutrition, and life forces, he preferred to think of himself as simply an 'anatomist.' Practitioners of medicine became the avant-garde of thaumaturgy after the Modern Synthesis of Arcane Philosophy, a systematization of sorcery that arose with pan-global contact. Aquilan principles of ritual, alchemy, and humorous balance, Vulturnine vitalism, Favonian, and Zephyrian mana-winning, and skinwork synthesized into a new theory – arcana could be seen as a subset of medicine, or perhaps, the reverse.

The bodies of magicians were always noted in extremes – unnaturally wizened, or a prodigy; arrested growth or radically tall, reed-thin, muscled like a wrestling champion, or grotesquely fat; the blind, the deaf, the dumb, the silver-tongued or silver-eyed; the seventh sons of seventh sons; re-voltingly hideous or so beautiful one falls in love at first sight. Scions of ancient, storied bloodlines or those warped by con-tact with exotics. These were not just storytellers inflating their subjects to heroic oddities, but necessary to their nature as ar-canists, a product of cultivating the magistery within oneself. Once the New Arcanists accepted that great insight, all the old anecdotes snapped into place.

When one sees extremes, one must look to what balance is disrupted. Magicians must be a powerful vessel for essential yliaster and a precise conduit for the flow of elemental forces, purified, harmonious, disciplined, and, perhaps, poisoned. Those esoteric rites, body movements, and diets of mysterious spices, ground dog bone, and even human flesh are akin to the maintenance of a complex contraption.

Such complex corporal conditions are fragile things and, as most matters medical, unpredictable in effect. Child prodi-gies are tragic figures, often losing their talents and their will to live upon enduring the changes of puberty. This is one rea-son for the terrible mystique surrounding the eunuch. Great sorceresses have been known to lose all magical talent upon pregnancy, while the child-change to mundane women occa-sionally triggers acute magical power and odd appetites, as both mother and (potentially monstrous) child instinctively seek to strengthen their newfound might. It's one reason why witches and spinsters were so conflated; a young witch who passed through her fertile years unaltered is expected to be a force to be reckoned with.

Likewise, many mages, both women who admired the

mysteries and lunar majesty and men with a distaste for female
arcanists, griped and grumbled when the new arcanists
demonstrated that menstruation's effects on magic were
purely physiological and predictably cyclical. By the end of the
2310s, a majority of Aquilan schools and orders integrated the
sexes, and many dogmatic splinters and theoretical schisms
reconciled and consolidated by the middle of the 24th century.
The final systematization followed in the wake of the Maladon
Earthquake and Sea Wave of 2508, forty-two years ago.

It always comes down to the water, Fade noted, wishing that he
asked the vendor where these herbs had grown. His mentor
had told him that magic was most potent in places of mystery.
Deep below the earth, and in the Vorago, strange volumes
where abyss and deep sky meet.

He remembered the darkness, the whispers of the worms,
and the quickening of bones.

Fade snapped out of his trance as Elena came down to
work in her apron, caul, and kerchief, the brace still affixed to
her wrist. Two days ago, Fade noticed her diet of dandelion
and burdock mead, a folk remedy for the kidney damage that
followed scarlet fever. The disease also struck her left wrist
with arthritis from a young age. Fade prescribed and prepared
a maritime squill diuretic and a topical anti-inflammatory poul-
tice of clarified, white willow-infused olibanum. Her eyes met
his and she gave him a cautiously positive nod before she got
to work in the kitchen, frying up a leash of white rabbits that a
hunter had found in the woods, bearing antlers and wings.

This treatment was part of his barter for board, along
with a bag of palm sugar cakes, date jaggery, and carob.
Northernmost had its own mills for grinding sugar out of
beets, and even distilled it into rum in cottage industries, but
nobody gets excited by beets. The sweet, tropical flavors of
palm wine? Yes. The dark richness of carob biscuits? Yes.
Beets? Nobody waxes rhapsodic about the beet.

The Severnayans preferred barter to coin. Not right at the shorefront, sure, but around their inland community. It shocked Fade how little they trusted their own money. Global confidence in its currency was one of the Septentrine Empire's greatest strengths. By ingenious minting and arcane fiduciary rites binding each coin to the Crown of Wade, once could take a Coronet of the Empire anywhere in the world and it will be honored.

Alchemy made gold mundane. Empire made it God.

Mr. Fade started transferring his paper notes into his spellbook of vellum, using a portable tattoo machine, when he heard a familiar "Sir?" followed by a lilting "Oh."

Gustavus Augustus Lund sat down opposite of Fade. He was of classic Murmurish stock with some Undine ancestry, tall, broad, and blond, with a square jaw and gentle good looks. His nymph forebear showed through the sea-green tint to his notched ears and joints. He dressed like a rustic Murmurman, despite his middle-class, urban roots, in a mossy green tunic that matched his eyes and a formless, wide-brimmed cap that resembled a mushroom. Mr. Fade felt it was unbecoming of a physician.

Lund did the "Sir? Oh..." as a ritual greeting ever since he and Fade met in Vestingbrug. It was the common way people approached Mr. Fade. With his head down in his books and his prematurely graying auburn hair, his boyish face usually surprised people who came to ask him for, say, a meal order or to wake him from a public nap. It didn't help that, despite being in his twenty-seventh year, Fade's scrawny build made most people assume he was at least a decade younger.

He had his first patch of gray hair as he approached his twentieth year and looked like tarnished iron by the time he entered the Imperial Surgical College. It was a family trait, to the point that local legend around Botley Mot was that the graying gave rise to the surname Fade. The actual etymology was rather boring – the Fades were dyers and drapers that specialized in bleaching. They were a simple housecarl family – while no longer directly tied to a manored lord, killing him would cost much less blood money than the low-thane Lund.

Lund was drawn to the riddle of Fade. He enjoyed enigmatic people and legends and mourned the loss of magic's *mystery*. Of course, he knew he was part of the problem, wishing to systematize the creatures and chimera of the world, and to understand the nature of heredity and hybridization. But he found it to be a quest, something noble and ultimately futile.

And there were still countless mysteries left in the world. The tale of a ghost ship drew Lund's interest to Northernmost. Last summer, in the first week of Parchers, the Waylander frigate *Triumphant* intercepted the ailing pirate vessel *Nelumbo*, late of the Polar Seaports. The *Triumphant* was found adrift two leagues northwest of the armada's island fortress on Bastion, in the Hildebrand Islands. The crew had abandoned the ship. The sole survivor was found in Sigarkap, Alirune, trembling, and raving with spiritual torments, half his body paralyzed and his teeth falling out. Vegetable-lamb bladders in the looted cargo had burst, and a terrible curse erupted from the whirling mists. Most of the men were driven overboard. The survivor spoke of sea monsters in the water, and the moonlight maledictions of Dead Rahab – and all signs pointed towards Northernmost's eight decades of disease.

Fade spoke of coming to Northernmost with firm reluctance, but the curse was too important of a subject. Solving it would secure them lifelong fame and funding, as well as save countless lives. The Contortions of Northernmost were always said to be isolated in this port. An abrupt contagiousness could cause a global crisis, or the destruction of this city.

"What is today's plan?" Mr. Fade asked, marking his place in his grimoire with a pressed amaranth.

"I found a hereditary sample," Dr. Lund replied in Waylander.

"Where?" Fade asked. "Heading to the farms?"

Yesterday, Lund had shown interest in the hinterland farmers, who were of the most long-term and uniform True Tsokiri descent, far less diverse than the citizens of the port proper. They were known for lethargy and listlessness, so weak that they relied on their hobgoblins and trained hedgehogs for hard labor. They were a tragic lot, losing most of their traditional methods to a form of early-onset dementia, and several of them committed suicide each year. Much of the Severnayan self-image as hearty northern warrior stock is unfounded. The truth was, as usual, more prosaic. The peoples who dwelt in Severnaya prior to the Tsokiri migration rarely lived in tribes larger than a few hundred people. The Kiric settlers found little reason to take up arms against them, as their existence largely depended on fishing and seal-hunting. Rather than winter warriors, the early settler's true genius lay in innovative agricultural techniques of ash-sewing and wind-sheltering to thrive in such hardscrabble climes.

"No, found a better population," Dr. Lund said.

He pointed at Fade's coffee.

Fade glared at Lund. Nobody wants to hear that a hereditary scientist has chosen one's coffee for a sample population.

"What have you done?" hissed Fade with the voice of the grave.

"The Bookhangers," Lund said, referring to the Sarosaram of Northernmost. "They're not a cross-section of the people of Saro, but specifically a... uh... a sextet of alchemist clans in exile, a caste called *yangban*. They fled Saro during those invasions, a century back, think it was the Fujin, maybe the Guidonfolk."

"I see," Fade said. "Small population, chronic alchemical exposure."

"And a curse," Lund said. "They had rivals in the Court of

Willows. The Doctrine of Eternal Law and the Children of Heaven. Ritualists, blooded, and hexed, the same problem we have here. Maybe that's why they left Superna and bypassed all of Apheliota."

"Do you think it's real?" Fade asked.

"No evidence yet. Locals do. There were a few murders some decades back, but things calmed down. Eventually, their servants left them, and now a fifth of the town is part Saroman," Lund said. "That nurse, she's a diviner. A ritualist. We'll be going together to the Jooga. Want to come along?"

"Harpy," Fade said, playing with his signet ring.

Lund turned in his chair.

"She came in last night," Fade said as he continued tattooing his spell. "As a boarder."

"She's wearing a breastplate. Are harpies… militarized now?" Lund asked.

"I think this one is special," Fade said. "We might want to hire her for the academy trip."

The smell and sizzle of fried meats filled the air. Fade's coffee cup slid off the edge of the table, balancing on its rim as though affixed by a powerful magnet. He snapped his book close and yanked it towards his chest as a great stone bowl came down between the doctors, crackling with snaking slices of skewered venison, smoked with garlic oil and fern, garnished with cowberries and pine nuts. A hill of buttered and peppered potato chunks and mushrooms separated the venison from stroganina, salted slices of omul marinated in vinegar and stewed with onions, served with a pond of clotted cream.

Eight cups detached from the serving bowl like lifeboats dropping from a smoking ship, sliding across the table to rest in front of the diners.

Fade looked up at the server, a massive woman. She turned a chair around and sat down between the two men.

"Did you hear that a whale beached itself last night?" she said, her arching, smiling eyes bugging out. "Want to go see it before it blows up?"

"What?" Fade blurted.

"This is the nurse," Lund said. "Or what was the title?"

"Oh, *Ötmogan*, it means chef-shaman," she said. "Or sin-eater, if you have those."

The chef-shaman's skin had the stony violet tones of morning mountains. Her braided hair was a coffee brown, with direct light-catching elements of puce rather than the typical blond or coppers. Her hungry, searching, half-moon eyes were a rich purple, strengthened by make-up. Rather than the subtle shading of common fashion, her upper and lower eyelids were painted and lined with aubergine mauve in the pattern of gnomish women.

But she was no pygmy, standing taller than even Lund. She was large in general, with thick limbs, a plump belly, a prodigious chest, and a sense of ursine insulation over what would be a well-worked frame. Lacking the distinguished cheekbones of Tsokiri women, her puffy cheeks made an already round face a pleasant sphere of smiling joy.

Her clothing was both outlandish and antiquated, though conservatism is to be expected in religious vestments. Over a purple dress, she wore a pullover coat that resembled the oiled-sealskin and reindeer parkas of Severnayan and Pok-inutin peoples, albeit of a refined quality with bands of purple dye and unblemished white fur. An adorable pair of polar bear ears crowned her hood.

"So, I've never eaten sperm," she added.

"What?" Lund and Fade said simultaneously.

Lund's gasp jumped an octave and tripped on the hurdle while Fade's soft voice inexplicably echoed with a subterranean basso.

"We sometimes eat beluga from the Blue-Green Gök,"

she said with an oblivious smile.

"Right, the whale," Fade said, as Lund screamed on the inside.

He twitched his fingers and imagined the repelling force of magnets to break the binding on his coffee cup so he could lift it.

"Wait, you intend to eat a beached whale?" Fade asked.

"I have to," she said as she pulled ivory chopsticks from her apron. "I have to eat one of every species."

She handed out paired chopsticks and set a larger black serving set into the bowl.

Fade tried them out. He had used chopsticks before in the Caspar Street noodle shops, but this broad, heavier set curved with the grain of mammoth tusk, more of a crab claw than the usual wooden tweezers.

"What do you mean by that?" Lund asked.

"God ordered the world and all its forms," she said. "All beasts have spirits and aspects assigned by Heaven. If you eat all the forms, you grow closer to God. Simple."

"Maybe," Fade said. "You might want to talk to this one about that."

"Hmm?" she said with a mouth full of potato.

"I'm a naturalist," Lund said.

"You walk around naked?" she asked after a swallow.

"I specialize in the categorization of life and its essences," he said. "Atavism, metamorphology, trait acquisition, and chimerisation."

"Oh," she said distantly. "Right..."

"So, what you're doing, I think, is just another way of looking at what I'm doing," Lund said, "And your people have been doing it longer."

Fade admired how well Lund spun her befuddlement, before realizing that he had never got her name. His eyes scanned her apron for a name tag. When that pursuit came up fruitless, he thought of an old divination trick: take a piece of paper, fold it, dip its tip in ink, imagine someone's face, two parts fire, one part water, and open it up to see their surface name.

Lund and the Shaman both heard him tearing a strip from his notes.

"What was that?" she asked, before turning her head and spitting out, "Bird!"

Fade looked up, joining the rest of the main room's bird-woman-watching.

He wished to sketch the harpy's features, her sharp cheekbones, aquiline nose, and eyes like butter on cream, nothing but pupils from a distance. She wore her black hair in an oddly fashionable way, pinned up in the back, terminating in a bun, with spiraling whirls framing her face. It was notably more up-to-date than the backcombed heap of hair worn when local women wanted to dress up, which had fallen out of style in the salons of Aquilo some fifteen years ago.

"Hey, bird," said the shaman, switching to Tsokiri.

"That's not my name," said the harpy, and Mr. Fade found his in.

"Then give me your name," said the shaman.

"Kingfisher Volganin," said Kingfisher Volganin.

"That is a type of bird," said the shaman. She picked up a skewer of venison and shoved it into the harpy's face. "Are you hungry?"

The harpy's eyes drifted to the ground before she nodded her head in affirmation.

"Eat it," said the shaman. "I'm paying my board with cooking; it's not bad."

Kingfisher's head darted around, looking for the trick. Fade noted that she moved her entire head rather than scan with her eyes. That was definitely a woman's face, but with a bit too much bird going on behind the eyes.

The rest of the bar watched the harpy. Two old, twitching Kokunin whalers glanced over their shoulders, while a trio of salamanders hissed to each other, serpentine eyes locked on the harpy from the ironclad corner designated for their use. The overnight tender, a Murmurwoman with a graying braid pinned under her people's typical black peaked cap, peered out of the kitchen before ducking out of view, waiting for the harpy to leave before she went home.

"It's not a trick," said Lund.

The harpy bit into the meat and pulled it to the end of the skewer until its neighboring onion slice fell off. She glanced around at the three seated figures as she chewed and swallowed.

"That was good," she said.

"Do you want more? I'll make you a bowl," said the shaman.

"Yeah, sit down," said Lund.

"Thank you," said Volganin.

She pushed the chair to the side so she could rest her thighs on its seat.

"Can you eat mushrooms and cowberries?" asked the shaman.

"Yes. Just no onion or garlic," said Volganin, keeping to herself that her family had frequently eaten goblins.

"Aren't you going to ask who she is?" suggested Fade.

"I'm sorry, I was rude," said the harpy. "What is your name?"

"Mageirissa Kem-ucmok-yemecek Barvaci," said the shaman. "You can call me Mags. This is Mr. Fade, and Dr. Gustavus Augustus Lund."

"By the way, shouldn't it be Volganina?" Fade asked.

"I named myself after a knight named Volganin," she said.

"Right, but those surnames have a feminine form," he said.

"Oh," she said. "But I'm named after a man."

"Fair enough," Fade said with a shrug. His people didn't care.

Kingfisher scanned the trio with jerky, clockwork shifts of the head, and remembered the anatomical drawing and the old custodian's mention of a nurse that cooked meals at the infirmary. Her thumb slipped down and nervously scratched off an alula feather.

"You're doctors working to break the curse," Kingfisher said.

"Yes," said Lund.

"So… how can I help?" Kingfisher asked.

"What can you do?" Mageirissa asked.

"I can fly," the siren said.

"Sure," Fade said. He turned his hand to catch the drifting feather.

"Bird," said Mageirissa.

"I can do other things," Kingfisher said. "Need any sailing done?"

"Scouting," Mr. Fade said. "I wish to visit the Academy of the Northern Lights."

"I see," said Kingfisher, scratching at the root of another feather. "Isn't it haunted?"

"Possibly," Mr. Fade said. "The locals are terrified of it."

"Should be we digging around in the locals' haunted ground?" Mags asked. "Is it sacred?"

"I don't think it is forbidden in the religious way," Fade explained. "More like the 'plague area' way."

"Fade, that's a worse sell," said Lund in Waylander. He then returned to Tsokiri and added, "But don't worry. Ghosts are but the fossils of a person's essence, not the soul itself. There is no one left to offend."

Reminded of essences, Lund discretely downed a small vial of alcohol and seal fat he left to clarify and distill into its vital salts overnight, although he wished he had time to purify it further, according to the Principal of Magnification by Distillation. Then again, one does not transform into seals for their raw power. He quickly drowned out the flavor of the animal arcanum with sautéed onion. At least it tasted better than the distilled spirit of the greater greyhaunch satyr or the moose.

Kingfisher looked reticent to eat. Mags scraped the onion off the skewer against the side of the bowl and held it out for the harpy. She nodded in thanks and stripped off the meat.

"But yeah," Kingfisher started to say after swallowing. "I came here because, well, things that make humans sick don't always make harpies sick. So, a forbidden school seems perfect for me."

"You would make a good courier too," Lund said.

"Oh no," Kingfisher said. "The town guard shoots at me."

They ate quietly, mentioning hometowns, fathers' jobs, favorite dishes, travel routes, and prior ports. Kingfisher could barely relate to these topics, and her attention drifted. A small, closed cycling "economizer" engine capped the samovar, with two cylindrical bellows compressing and expanding in response to the rising hot air. Kingfisher knew little of machinery, but she had an instinctual understanding of the dynamics of air, and its functions clicked in her head.

That uncanny pressure of another's attention snapped her senses back to the table. Her eyes briefly met Fade's cold gray gaze, before he looked away towards the passing Elena. There was a general moment of awkwardness as the innkeeper's daughter stepped outside to quiet her father's quarrel with what sounded like an older woman.

The salamanders stood up, revealing a heat-nursed juvenile mewling against one's burning breast, a tar-slick reptile of charred flesh in a jacket of asbestos, shaped like the common amphibian that earned the *Acthnici* their vulgar name. One acthnicus had a head like a pit viper, with copper scales brimming with heat, two masculine arms, and a serpentine tail, the classical "ophidian" form. The other kept a bipedal humanoid form, with a woman's face, distinguished only by yellow eyes with crescent pupils, and patches of scales on her hairless body. It lacked breasts, preferring a set of folding vents to shelter the child. The fourth member of the family walked on four legs, and had absolutely no humanoid features, a brass alligator with a serpentine head.

Fade wondered what it must be like to parent yourself, in a sense. Salamanders were the odd-men-out of the elementals in nearly every respect. While the other tribes of the Sagani lead immortal lives in their element and possessed rather humanoid forms – the butterfly and bird wings of sylphs and the fish-tails of undines are a simple artistic shorthand for their element – the salamanders were a constantly shifting mix of humanoid and reptilian features. They were forever rejuvenating and reproducing in a cycle of self-consumption and wild mutation, a mess of immolation, shed skin, and ash. Salamanders destroy themselves in fire and toxins, splitting into small versions of their parent or parents, both in form and personality, but forever altered. Often it was simply a limb lost, though it was not uncommon for a salamander to break themselves up entirely into a batch of smoking eggs.

They were destructive beings. During the Saganarchy, the salamanders rarely made chimerae or took human slaves. Most simply dwelt in their blazing wastelands and jungle cities of burning brass. The modern understanding of the salamander has changed and complicated, though their true nature lacks the poetry of flame. They are chemical beings of reduction and oxidation – flame, acids, thermal reactions, fermentation, corrosion such as rust, and burgeoning fields such as electro-synthesis. Where once they had been a people removed from humanity, they have shifted towards the growing industrial core.

The salamander family touched the black iron duct as a great roar shook through it. A wave of intense heat rippled across the room, and the young newt celebrated with a rattle-like hiss.

Kingfisher stood up in alarm, sensitive to the magic permeating the air. This was more than a furnace springing to life. This was breath. Mags fanned herself with her hood, while Lund watched the salamanders.

It was then that Fade figured it out.

"What was that?" Kingfisher asked the innkeeper as he re-entered.

"Nothing, just an old problem customer," he said.

"No, the roar, the roar," the harpy sputtered.

"Oh, you Southerners don't know much about Samyy Severnyy, do you?" he said.

Unlike the true ancients of the gnomic, undine, and sylph races, a salamander kept growing and mutating as it aged, absorbing heat, toxins, yliaster, and the royal metals until it became an unruly monstrosity of fire, light, and darkness, regaining the true scale of its ancestors.

Fade mouthed the words as the innkeeper pronounced them. "The mayor of Northernmost is a dragon."

Chapter 4: Tremors

The four had decided to split their efforts, with Lund and Mageirissa heading to the doctor's appointment at the Jooga, while Fade and Kingfisher scouted at the Academy. The latter pair stood outside of Shura's Inn, people watching as they digested their heavy breakfast. The Kokunin man walked out of the door, bracing himself against its frame until his legs stopped shaking. A quake rolled through his squat body, twisting his heavy, slip-on gambeson, a traditional garment padded with sealskin and topped with a polar bear mantle.

The Kokunins hailed from the fishhook-shaped Krjuchók Island just off Northernmost, with a lifestyle revolving around fishing, seal hunting, logging, and, recently, the whaling industry. They were the most heavily afflicted population of Severnaya.

"That's this disease?" Kingfisher asked as the man walked out of earshot.

"Yes," Fade said. "The locals call it the Contortions. Though the Kokunins call it the Smothering Fog, as it dulls the memory, senses, and volition. There is a cold version, where the individual slips into catatonia or a coma and dies. There's also a hot version, where one goes mad and violent, quaking with pain."

"I think I saw a cat with it," Kingfisher said. "Cats get it?"

"Cats get it," Fade said. "Humans, elementals, chimerae, birds, seals... maybe even the whales."

"Birds?" she asked.

"Only locals develop symptoms," he said. "It has been going on for some eighty years now. Even after the quarantine was lifted, no outsiders developed it."

"What do you think caused it?" she said. "How can we help?"

"I don't know," said Mr. Fade. "Back home, we assumed

the Vankir fell to alchemical fireboats, like our Third Fleet used at Antaro Strait. It was a tremendously unexpected victory, and let the regulars and riverines turn south, and crush the main thrust of the Vankir. It was a miracle, and the Vankir would have been able to hold the city instead of burning it and fleeing. But now that I know there's a dragon involved..."

"Why didn't you know about the dragon mayor?" she asked.

"Why didn't you?" Fade countered. "You're from this country."

"I'm from a swamp," she said, then whispered, "Near Novoport."

"Ah," Fade said. "The rival."

"I don't understand that," she said. "They don't seem to like us. I mean, nobody likes me, but that wasn't a regional issue until now."

"Novoport was built by the Orlovs to hurt Northernmost," Fade said. "And be an olive branch to the Skeirons. Your Svyatopolk... the Third, I think? He refused to pay back foreign investors, after Skeiron and Vankiri's money and men built up the north."

"Why would they do that?" she asked. "Isn't it their city?"

"Look, this isn't my country, and I don't even keep up with Boreal politics," he said. "Caunias is a wide, mysterious backwater to Aquilo, especially Tsokir, and we don't particularly care. All eyes are on Achille right now. But I think this Mayor is your answer, again. The Orlovs are already on shaky ground. A dragon ruling one of their cities... it makes them look weak. Dangerous for a parliament, fatal for a strongman."

Kingfisher knew that name. The current House of Orlov is a fragile cadet branch descended from Grand Duke Henri of Zolotaya Ravnina, crowned Dmitri II after the death of his father and two elder brothers during the Burning of Volgamozga and the siege of Harmaneva. The Volganic Orlovs had only ruled the Homelands for eighty years before the Burning, desperate for a sense of stability after the destruction of the erstwhile Monomaxij dynasty, a succession crisis, countless pretenders with falsified blood, and three impostor kings with stolen faces. The Ravninan Orlovs that ascended after the Cousins' War took that desperation for continuity to paranoid ends. They abolished the traditional Kiric succession, which passed from brother to brother, and followed the Aquilan tradition of father to eldest son. Dmitri II appropriated his regnal name from the founder of the Orlovs and used the loss of records and lords to consolidate power and create cousins and allies as local lords.

Where once Volgamozga stood as a literal and figurative quagmire of squabbling houses, guilds, and tribes, Dmitri's Black City was a dry, charred fortress ruled by a tight network of cousin-lords. He sent his house's women to marry territorial rulers and sent for their daughters in turn. His successor, the Third Dmitri, established a school system, meant to drill the people of the Homelands in the new national culture and language. Within thirty years, more than half of the population could speak Tsokiri Proper for the first time since the nation's expansion to the East and South of Caunias.

But while the Orlovs stabilized the Kiric Heartlands, that brief interregnum allowed ethnic rulers to reestablish ancient hierarchies. Steppefolk elected new Horse-kings and Great Wolves, Ludjic Skeirons built a trade state along their river, like the Maritime Confederation of old. Ogres and Doghead troops swelled in numbers and rampaged across the middle-north. The Monomaxij Remnants carved out a duchy in the southern mountains in union with gnomish hive-keeps. And worst of all, a dragon set up an anarchic free city in Samyy Severnyy.

"That's why it's so odd here," Fade said.

"There are no serfs in Northernmost," said an old, creaky voice. "No lords either."

Fade and Volganin searched for the source of the voice in alarm, before glancing down at a gnome in a wide-brimmed capotain that hid his horns. He stood a bit over a meter tall, an ancient, craggy man with gray and brown skin striated like sedimentary stone and marked with ground sapphire – rather like a tattoo, such dwarvenmarks are precious metals or powdered gemstones set into the skin.

Fade wondered why a locally respected figure had only this one subtle mark. A wealthy gnome would be virtually composed of opals or jets or lined with veins of gold. His beard was a short, cropped wave of copper wire. His large ears were notched with age, but still resembled those of a bat or goat. Drooping eyelids disguised childishly large eyes, black irides that shone with silver and green in the subterranean darkness.

Under a heavy jacket, the gnome wore a leather vest studded with diamonds and sapphires over a mail shirt, with rigid braces attached to the limbs in a kind of supportive exoskeleton. His sash-belt held a motorized circular diamond saw, a common gnomish tool and weapon. He had shaped his iron-edged fingertips into precise, flat edges for delicate work, rather than the common, mole-like scoops.

Gnomes made great natural smiths and machinists, not just from their prowess at forging, but the ability to spin metal into wire finer than hair with a mere rub of the fingers. The Mountain Kings once ruled through this ease of arms, able to muster peasant and slave armies armed with mail, obsidian, and steel while those outside their rule had to contend with bronze.

"There's a dragon. A firedrake," Fade said.

"Who is our mayor," the gnome said. "The Mayor, or *Posadnik,* is a position elected by our *veche,* uh, our public assembly. It's a tradition, both of the Maritime Confederation and the Severnayan State."

"How long has he been your mayor?" Fade asked. "Since it burnt the fleet?"

"Since the season after the fleet," the gnome said. "The Mayor stood for election, and has won reelection every biannual term."

"Sure," Fade said. "That sounds like a square election. Hereditary governors, rotten boroughs, I've seen it all. Who runs against a dragon?"

"We've had other people stand," said the gnome. "But nobody can beat the dragon's tax rate. Three percent is good, especially on a port."

"It's about taxes?" Fade asked with a sneer.

His hand nervously came to rest on his quintet of horns, for gunpowder, sugar, dried blood, bone meal, and sea salt. The fingers twitched upward, to tap the cap of his silvered flask.

"Yes, and the free heat," said the gnome, smiling with rusty teeth, iron-hardened like a beaver's. "The ash for crops, the earlier Thaw, the steam and the fire for industry."

"Is that why you stay in a city everyone says is cursed and dying?" Fade asked. "Tax rates?"

"Everyone's dying. We just go out free," he said, a strange notion for such a long-lived race. "When the Mayor came, the lords were driven out, and the deeds went up in flame. As I said, there are no serfs or lords in Northernmost."

"Who were the lords of Northernmost?" asked Fade.

The gnome flared his nostrils. Gnomes have babyish noses, with a ring of muscles that can seal the nostril to keep out dirt, a trait shared with the amphibious undine. Fade learned long ago that flaring nostrils was a sign of distress and nervous contemplation rather than rage among the subterraneans.

"The House of Pridvornov," answered the gnome. "Storied yet impecunious. The remains of their estate lie east of the city. Why do you ask?"

"Nobody's more resentful than an ousted noble," said Fade.

"Odd name," said Kingfisher. "That name just means 'courtier.'"

"Oh, they weren't always called that," said the gnome. "They were Murmur nobles who intermarried with a family of Oyorpatskoye courtiers, from the Jasity Steppes west of Purga. So, their caste-title was just translated into Tsokiri, and it became a name."

"Oyorpat... the Amazons?" Kingfisher said. "They were the warrior women in the old stories."

"Well, sort of," said the gnome. "Bit of a misunderstanding. Human women around these parts are famously tall, and among those Steppe-folk, the height difference was negligible. Between the men and women, I mean. They say it comes from sylph heritage, but I don't know if that's true. They were pale enough, and used the antler bow and flail. Oh, but they all wore trousers and long braids. Their men shaved their faces. Those bearded Kiric warriors found female bodies among the enemy dead, and well, that's how you get legends. But those Pridvornova women, oof. Beware."

"What happened to them?" Fade asked. "The Pridvornovs, I mean. Killed?"

"No, there were never many of them," said the gnome. "They had a bad habit of disappearing. Bit of witchery in the family. Strange experiments. Odd mutations. There was just a posthumous bastard girl in the end, before the dragon."

"What manner of mutation? What were these people?" Fade said in the common gnomic tongue, Pharyean.

The gnome reacted in shock.

"I... I only ever knew the girl... the... well, she... that was a long time ago," he said.

Fade watched the gnome's feet as they went pigeon-toed and dug into the earth. Never look at their faces, Fade learned, watch their points of contact with the earth. Fade remembered the terror of gnomish thorn-wire and caltrops, disguised with a crust of earth. Always watch the ground. "I'm afraid humans don't live long."

"Yeah, it's a tragedy. Anyway, how long have you lived here?" Fade said curtly. "Were there signs of the Contortions before the dragon came?"

"Oh, uh," the gnome's eyes glanced off into the middle distance. "My grandmother came here with Lord Makelo... There were always stories of strange mutations in the North, but... it did get worse in the last century."

The largest island of Northernmost, the Royal Isle, was once called Makelonia, after the founder of the gnomish settlement on Capricorn Beach some two thousand years ago. Makelo was the last of the Telchines, a royal family of nine sorcerous seal-demons, likewise descended from the accursed titans. They terrified the heavens and the earth with baleful gazes that could shape flesh and metal and storms, their indestructible weapons, and venomous spines that could slay a god and render the land barren for centuries. For their power and malignancy, the gods slew eight of the Telchines. In turn, their venom crippled Los, Smith of the Seventh Sun, and killed Etheban, the old goddess of hope, a child of Orc.

"But which came first?" Fade said, his eyes narrowed. "Think."

"I don't know," said the gnome. "My memory is... foggy."

Fade glowered at him. The gnome raised his hand for a moment. People in the street stopped to watch.

"Answer me," Fade spat. "I know you're hiding something."

"I'm sorry," said the gnome, in Waylander. "I... I was never a master. We came here to escape those horrible hives."

"Me too," said Fade.

A woman in a riding coat, a demi-skirt, and coulattes peddled past on a hydraulic céléripede, with a frame of ivory culminating in a horse head with handlebar horns. The two-wheeler had been winterized, with wide, chained, pneumatic tires of kangaroo leather and a protective case over the drive train. She came to a stop.

"Good morning, Professor Loganev," she said in Merovene.

She had the look of someone from the northwest of the nation, around Pays de la Regol - red-haired, blue-eyed, and fair under a layer of white powder. Her skin and lips had a sensuous, dark blue undertone, and her pert nose had the sealing reflex characteristic of the undine-blooded mercantile class of the coasts. But it was her culture's morbid fashion sense that set her apart from a Septentrine, a beautiful web of funereal black lace, platinum chains, and a torso piece with ribs of carved ivory, wrapped in a grim grey palla, as though on her way to the crematorium. A jet teardrop marked the corner of her left eye.

"Good morning, Ms. Severin," the gnome replied. "You will be coming to the ceremony?"

"Yes," she said, letting her bag slide to her shoulder.

The shift revealed that she hid her ctenidium under the palla, indicating she was perhaps more of an undine than Fade initially believed – perhaps three-fourths ancestry, rather than some distant forefather, as with Lund.

"Mignard has prepared her speech. It's a shame that the sun doesn't go down at this time of year. Electrification is rather underwhelming in the light."

Fade eyed a glass-of-scars on the crossbar of her céléripede, a nasty weapon of the undines – a strong acid diluted with just enough water to manipulate into a liquid lash.

Severin looked up at Kingfisher, perching on the sign. She

walked her bike back and hunched her shoulders.

"Don't bother her," Fade said, intending to tell her not to worry about the harpy in a form of Merovene learned from books five years ago.

Severin eyed the harpy, raising a hand to shield her head. The bike slipped to her side as the other hand touched the stopper of the glass battle.

"I won't hurt you," said Kingfisher, in Tsokiri.

"Yes, she's quite benign," said Loganev.

"You're being looked for," said Severin. "You survived that bombing in the harbor."

"Who is looking for me?" asked Kingfisher. She dropped from the sign and hid behind Fade.

"Oh, it's a general notice," said the Merovene woman. "There's a bounty on you. Alive, of course. They probably want to torture you."

The harpy hid her face behind her wings.

"That's not your distinctive feature, madam," said the gnome. "But don't worry. We do not execute outsiders in our port. There's a forest on the Royal Island. Stay away from the docks, that's where the Imperator's soldiers and sailors are. Not many of them, and the portfolk don't like them, so they don't come far inland. They're a reminder that Chernograd's reaching north again."

"Why do you let them come into port?" asked Kingfisher.

"Trying to drive them away would be a pretext for war," said the gnome. "I'd like to think that we'd never turn you over to the Throne of the Fallen, but money is money and there's plenty of Southerners around."

"I won't do it," said Severin in Tsokiri. "See you later, professor."

She pedaled away, towards the Orange Café.

"I see," said Kingfisher. "I think I should leave the inn... I should find Kazamir of Staraya Stolitsa."

"You're looking for Sir Kazamir? Ah, he's in… uh, the House of Wisdom," said Loganev. "But don't worry, if anyone thinks of turning you in, Elena and the Boss will roast them…You should come to the ceremony tonight. We're holding it in the Mayor's Tower, at twenty bells. It's… dark enough to be dramatic."

"I will try," said Mr. Fade.

"I never got your name, lad," said Professor Loganev. "Saw you tattooing your book last night. Interesting tool."

"Call me Thrasamund Spiridionson," said Fade. "It's a gnomish tool, but I made it. You have no claim to it."

"I'm sorry," said Loganev. "Thrasa...Sir..."

"We all are," said Mr. Fade. "I'll come see your curiosities."

Mr. Fade walked along the Staretsy's Prospekt towards the Royal Isle. Kingfisher glided to his side and tucked up against him, hoping to shield herself from some prying eyes in his silhouette. She rather wished that she had joined the larger Lund and Mags.

Kingfisher noticed that the gnome walked behind them. She notified Fade with a small chirp.

"Why are you following me?" Fade snapped. The gnomes eyes went wide.

Kingfisher was taken aback by his voice. Fade always spoke in a quiet, modulated tone, as though forever trapped in a library that happened to be holding a wake. His anger didn't cause him to shout. It was more like how Kingfisher imagined the undead knights speaking in the Tale of Ormun of Sula, like two glaciers slowly grinding together in the abyssal caves of the Vorago, a hoarse whisper in the back of your skull.

"This is my place," Loganev said.

The gnome pointed at an alchemist's laboratory on the corner of the street, a short tower of solid stone, with windows that were not so much paned as fused with its surrounding granite like a greasy stain of transparency. Unlike many gnomish homes, it had a doorway, to allow access for other wights. Gnomes shape stone as men shape clay and passed through the soil as men move through the air. It had the typically Northernmost signage but was made of transmuted gold and three dozen varieties of gemstone. It read *The Engine of Creation* in Tsokiri, Waylander, Merovene, the Common Gnomic of Aquilo, and what Fade believed to be the Pharyean languages of the East and Notos. Gnomes are few in number and nearly immortal, so they have far fewer languages than mankind. As far as Fade could tell, there was only a single gnomic language family, and only one script.

"Maybe so," said Fade.

"Look, Thrasa... doctor-"

"Mister," corrected Fade. "Surgeons are styled *mister.*"

The gnome went silent and sunk into the pavement. Fade watched him disappear, crouched down, and felt the ground. When he appeared satisfied, he rose and walked to a store across the street.

The sign read *the Blue and Purple*, named after the dyes associated with the two major races of Hallazonia, the Domans, and the Argamen. Argamen enclaves could be found in virtually every port in the Winedark and Boreal Seas, but even in their Notan home countries, they never quite settled anywhere but the coastlines and riverbanks, allowing other tribes to fill out the hinterlands of their thalassocracy. They are natural settlers, to a fault; rather than permanently building a nation, their younger sons leave their Austerian ports, intermarry with natives, and fade away within two generations, leaving only the occasional conspicuous place name behind. They maintain a foreign presence by migrating to everywhere in an unbroken wave for over two millennia. The peoples of the Empire saw the Argamen as their southern counterpart and ancient forerunner, the maritime power of the Winedark rather than the Boreal Sea.

"What are your favorite colors?" Fade asked.

"Oh, I guess blue and red," Volganin said. "Why?"

Fade told Volganin to wait outside and entered the shop. He found it to be a confusing mess of a shop. By the signage and window dressing, he assumed it would be a drapery or clothier, and it was, after a fashion, but the proprietor had ambassadorial pretenses. He sold garments, ivory trinkets, date, carobs, harissa, Tammuzi wine, and, rather darkly, burning dolls, a toothless descendant of the ancient Argamanic rite of child immolation.

"Welcome to *the Blue and Purple*, friend! I am Mattan Baalimanzer b'Abdolonim b'Ashirdan, proprietor of this fair slice of distant Hallazon, with wares from across the Winedark!" proclaimed a jolly older man, portly, almond-eyed, and with grey twisting through tight black curls.

He wore a classically Argamanic garb that nobody in Argaman nations wore unless there was a festival on, baggy pants, and four types of wraps trimmed in gold. The cool blue undertones of undine heritage made the rest of his skin blaze a burnt orange in contrast.

"From where do you hail?"

"I'm from the island of Curtana, in the Septentrine Archipelago. Hard to miss due to all the volcanoes and glaciers," Fade mumbled as he wandered through the rack of fabrics.

He found a blue burnoose woven from barometz, the cottonwool of the vegetable lamb, or watersheep. The chimerical *yeduah* is the staple crop and foremost export of the Homelands, providing meat, horn, fabrics, and oracle bones, although they had to be carefully guarded against wolves and fed from troughs lest they devour all the grass around their umbilical stalk. Tedious, but less dangerous than the mandrake, the crop of the deaf, and their piebald beagles.

"I'll buy this," he said, holding up the lapis lazuli mountaineer's cloak with cherry trim.

"Oooh," said Mattan, as though winding up his act. "Ah, now I have quite a deal—"

"I'm not going to haggle," said Fade as he walked over and dropped the money on the store's front counter. "This is the listed price. I'm going to leave your store now."

Fade left the store and found the harpy pressing her ear against the window. What Fade found mundane fascinated Kingfisher. Knights were supposed to be above mercantile matters, but trade was an alien and lovely concept to the harpy, who had been raised in a world of raiding and snatching. The humans shared their love for shiny stones, but exchanged them in peace.

"Here," Fade said, wrapping the cloak around Kingfisher's shoulders. "Should reach to about your knees."

"Thank you," said Volganin. "How much was it?"

"It's a gift. Let's go to the Academy," said Fade.

"I don't understand," said Volganin.

"What do you mean?" said Fade. "It's across that bridge. You can see it, through the mist."

"You're mean, but you gave me a present," she said.

"I'm not mean," he said. "I'm efficient."

"The way you treated that old gnome," said Volganin, "That didn't feel efficient."

"Do you know how humanity first learned magic?" Fade asked.

"No," answered Volganin honestly.

"Elementals have a deprivation of their antithetical. Fire and water, earth, and air. Humans have no such limit, but no inherent strength but death and divination. Human magic is like a fine knife. Many uses, a great tool, but you have to be precise and keen. Elementals are a sledgehammer. Power, but specialized, almost crude."

"I'm a harpy, you're a sphinx," Volganin said. "I want straight answers."

"Hmm? No, that was my reason," Fade said. "And his reason."

"Is this envy?" Volganin said. "You have potential. You can innovate."

"No," Fade said. "That's not what this is about. It's simple. They can't do something. We can. We can be made to."

"Oh," said Volganin. "That... that must have been a long time ago. Mankind rebelled thousands of years ago."

During the Saganarchy, the gnomish and undine lords dammed the Winedark Sea between Aquilo, Argetes, and Notos, and carved deep rivers that still serve as the borders of the modern world. They ripped the salt from the seas, raised islands of silt, pumped waters from the Abyssal Vorago below the world, and made the north of Notos a fertile land. From their island castles, carved mountains, and subterranean holds, the elementals ruled over the humans that outnumbered them fifty to one.

It was not the pain of slavery that most enraged humanity, but the expectation of gratitude.

"My grudge isn't historical, Volganin," said Fade.

Kingfisher took a while to process his statement. She let out a slight gasp.

"Hence the poor disposition," Fade said. "Alright, I'd rather not broach this topic again."

"I won't," said Kingfisher. "Don't ask about me, either."

"In general?"

"Maybe," said Kingfisher. "I didn't think my position through. I don't want to talk about my family. Or childhood."

"Sure," said Fade. "So, can you turn invisible?"

"No," said Kingfisher. "Didn't know I could."

"It's hard, but something of a cornerstone of air work," Fade said.

"Why didn't anyone tell me?"

"I don't know," Fade said. "Probably some deprivation in

your mysterious childhood."

Kingfisher clenched her teeth, and wondered what secrets her flock had lost. If only her hag grandmother had not been senile. If only she had found the keep earlier. If only she had come across a benevolent sylph or a lost wizard. If only her ancestors came to her in dreams, furies rectifying the ignorance of their mortal descendants. If only she had been born a noblewoman.

If only, if only...

"You know how a mirage works, right?" Fade said. "Heat distorts the air, bends the light, makes an object appear to be in the wrong place. There are also *superior* mirages, caused by cold air inverting the light. If you look north, those great sheets of Hyperborean ice start to look higher than they really are, or even broken up into spikes, the so-called dancing towers. Sometimes, due to the global curvature, images can actually rise up from behind the horizon, even the Sun."

"How do I do that?" Kingfisher asked. "Bend the light?"

"It all depends on how you visualize your work," Fade said. "I have this, say, understanding of the arcane as lines of force interacting with humors, conditions, and tools. Like water passing through gates and pipes that need to be maintained and shaped. But you might view it differently."

"Well, when I work the air, I think of things in terms of my feathers and wings, and the inverse," she said. "The wing shaping the air instead of the other way around... this isn't something I ever thought about, sorry. It just came naturally."

"Yes, as one would expect," Fade said. "If I could be an elemental, I would want it to be air."

"Why? Flight?" she asked.

"Not just flight, but that is the king's share. It's the element with the unfair advantages."

"Like what?" she said. "I wish I'd known this."

"The greatest is their– your indirect manipulation of other

elements. Not as well as their native elementals, but still enough to make them paramount."

"Like… Oh, I know this, sailing," Kingfisher suggested.

"Right," Fade said. "The importance of wind to water-manipulation is obvious. Sail, the use of bubbles… a pure sylph can't drown due to the dissolved air that sustains fish."

"Oh, and fire," Kingfisher said. "I can snuff out flames."

"And raise hot or cooling winds," Fade said. "Air quenching steel at the forge. Or conjure up poisonous fumes. Though a great conflagration consuming the breathable air is one of the few things that can kill a sylph, I think."

"Is fire stronger than air?" she asked.

"No," Fade said. "Fire is the weakest. Any element can be heated or cooled on its own. Anyone can make poisons, acids, rust, and rot are niche and destructive, and… burning people is a bit much for me. Earth is better at the forge. Even illusion and light, usually the domain of fire work… well, I just told you how to make mirages and glamours with wind-craft. Fire magic's most unique capability is to quicken the emotions. Raising tempers, driving foes mad… and even then, a ritual could do that with enough time. And that's also invasive and cruel. Gunpowder, isolated cobalt, and hot air balloons make fire a touch more attractive, but if I was a salamander, I would resent my birth."

"What about earth?" she said. "The bane of air."

"Barely," said Fade. "Iron can bind a sylph's magic, but there's nothing more dangerous than an air elemental surrounded by sand, powders, or gravel. Do you carry anything like that? Abrasives, sand, caltrops? Flechettes? Humans once lived in fear of elf-shot, the unseen, rot-slathered arrows of the Aerials."

"I don't like the idea of poisoning people," she said.

"Why?" Fade said. "I understand why it's wrong, but why is it worse than any other weapon?"

"Poison is dishonorable," she said.

"But running someone through with a sword is all well and good?" Fade said.

"Depends on who you're running through," she explained. "But combat, at least, puts your life at risk. Poisoning someone's goblet is cowardly and poisoning an arrow that has already caused an injury is needlessly cruel."

"It's all needlessly cruel," he said. "Honor is an upper-class façade. Justifications. It won't get you anywhere, without a family."

"What do you mean?"

"Those honorable combats? They were between noblemen who upheld their status and fought to capture their peers for ransom," Fade explained. "All well and good, unless you were a peasant. *Villains, churls...* That's how the knightly classes view the people who feed them."

"That's family prestige," Kingfisher said. "Prestige will get you anywhere. But if you are actually honorable, you make the world a better place."

"Fine," Fade admitted. "But the leash on the dog is a restraint, not discipline."

"I don't know," said Volganin. "Maybe that's enough for a wild dog...Can we make a stop at the House of Wisdom? I'll keep it short."

Fade shrugged, and said he had the time.

Volganin led him one block north to the temple. It already loomed in the morning mist, a compound of blue walls and starry domes and towers that speared the sky. At the center of its courtyard stood a glass and stone reliquary rising from a basin of sea water. This allegedly housed a length of tar-smeared rope from the ship of the Sea-King Craethion, *Bonerig,* a vessel made from the spines of titans and the ribs of a sea-devil, with sails of dragon-wing leather. The rope itself was braided from the black hair of Dead Rahab, and slipped through a symbolic rowlock. Every harbor worth its salt housed such a reliquary, with a few pathetic ports holding a few hairs from his loyal dog Greimmair. The basin, however, was the key to local religious life. Ritual footwashing was a common way of breaking social and class boundaries, and even before Northernmost's egalitarian rebellion, kings and nobles were commonly expected to wash the feat of foreign sailors and their own serfs. Craethion was called the Clean-Footed King, usually depicted standing barefoot in moving water. It once made him resemble a half-mad and shipwrecked sailor, but modernity had turned him into a far-traveling unifier of the Thier's peoples and places.

Kingfisher wondered if anyone would dare wash her feet, before being alarmed by the presence of a large stone egg amid the offerings of wine, whiskey, and gin bottles. Somewhere along the line, throwing an ostrich egg into the sea became a prized offering to the Sea-King, something that horrified the harpy. Humans did not see eggs as valuable children, as they did puppies and kittens.

Fade knocked on the door of the House of Wisdom and was greeted by a young attendant.

"Yes, hello, is Sir Kazimir available?" Kingfisher asked. "I was wondering if he had anything that needed doing. Just volunteering to help the famous knight, and all. No need to pay me."

"Oh," said the attendant, a man in his early twenties with sandy hair. His sclera was robin's egg blue. "No, Kazimir should still be sleeping. But I haven't heard anything about help needed. Other than at the hospitals. There's always help needed there."

"Right," said Fade.

An old woman, hunched and wearing a heavy woolen mantle, walked into view, an amulet of black teeth and petrified claws hanging from her neck. Ancient ice clouded her aimless eyes. Such stigmas were a sign of the holy folk of the Fane, the shrouded eyes of Hedran the Prophetess, the wounded side of betrayed Urizen, and the silver *linea nigra* of Mother Incano duplicated onto the mortal form.

"Do we have visitors?" she asked. She briefly flexed her hand into a fist, exercising the inflamed fingers.

"Yes, some volunteers," said the attendant. "I told them the hospitals would be better served."

"I see, but I was hoping Kazimir had some adventurous work that needed to be done. Something to be sought, some beast to be fought," Volganin said. "That kind of thing."

"Oh dear," said the old woman. "No, I'm afraid the old knight no longer quests. The Contortions are a problem of study and gentle care, not swords and chivalry. If you wish for a fight, the farmers and militia contend with a mad woolly boar or shaggy unicorn every other fortnight or so."

"Wait a minute, you have claws," said the attendant.

"Right, it's fine, she means you no harm," said Fade.

"Let me touch your face, young amazon," said the old woman as she leaned in, left hand out. Her eyes never focused, her gaze drifting without concern for those present.

"Oh," said Volganin, "Sure. Are you… blind?"

"Now now," said the old woman. "I can see. But I never see the right time. Buildings, I can get around in, but people are always moving and changing. Let me know where you are now… you haven't shown up yet in my sight."

"Where you raised here?" Kingfisher asked.

The woman nodded.

That rare second sight and noble bearing made Kingfisher realize this was the Oracle of the North, a woman raised from youth in this temple, where prophecy and divination came naturally. Every high temple of the Fane worth its consecration had a titled oracle, but the North famously produced reliable prophets, back to the days when Hookmen foretold blizzards and early thaws. Kingfisher nodded, honored, and brushed her face against the old woman's hot palm.

"Now now," said the oracle. "Oh child, you have had a long, lonely journey here… Follow the horned woman."

"What?" Kingfisher said, echoed by Fade.

"That's all I can see," she said. "Follow the horned woman. Or pursue her. But beware. There's a woman with horns, all in shadow, lurking in the cold dark. Maybe a cave, maybe the lightless water. I cannot see a face. Her back is turned."

"I see, I'll keep a lookout for her," Kingfisher said, smiling nervously. "Thank you."

"Right," Fade said. "If Sir Kazimir needs assistance, send a message to Shura's Inn."

"Yes," said Kingfisher. "I'll be right over. Thank you, madam."

The oracle looked past Kingfisher, with a quizzical flicker of alarm. The attendant helped her back inside as she muttered something.

"Alright, we're going to go now," said Fade, leading Kingfisher back down the block.

The pair soon came to the bridge. It was covered like the bridges of Wayland, to shield the walkway from the snow, rain, and, back in Fade's homeland, the ashfalls of the Worldsmith. The cover was only pine-tarred wood rather than gnomic stone. On the left-hand side stood a covered shrine to Incano, the silver-haired mother goddess of birth, death, bridges, and thresholds. Inside hung a withered, silver hand, the only remnant of her original nature as a moon-crone of fate and the life cycle of women. She became a beautiful woman after her 'promotion' to the wife of Urizen ten centuries ago, though her hoary spinster's hand and elfin silver hair remained. On the left-hand side burned a matching shrine to Taqarth, her rough equivalent among the blazing gods of Hallazon.

"Have you ever seen the Bridge Cities of the Septentrine Archipelago?" Fade asked.

"No," Volganin said. "I've been to parts of the Boreal, but only the parts on Aquilo, in the east; the Swanlands, Palantoke, Blutgang… uh, Abalus."

"We don't control Abalus," he said. "That's Murmur."

"Oh," she said. "Your languages sound alike."

"Waylander, Alirunnic, Æglic, Murmurish, all closely related," he said. "I can read them, with some effort. So, as it was, we used to be fifteen great islands and three thousand minor islands. Bit of a mess. But though volcanic crafting, mud gardens, land raising, damming, and draining, we clumped them together into a clean thirty islands, all-black soil, and coastline. And between the islands and across the great rivers, like the murky Lam, we built massive basalt bridges, big enough for armies to march ten horses wide through them, and high enough for the tall ships to sail under. My family lived above our shop on Blueleaf Bridge for four generations."

"Wait, where is the River Blueleaf?" she said. "I thought you were from Harth-on-Lam?"

"Oh, no, it's not a river, it's a cold-weather cultivar of tobacco," Fade explained. "It was an, uh, exciting new product, back then, pressure-fermented blueleaf. I had an uncle who worked the screw jacks, pumping out the air. Knew a bit of windwork from his time in the navy."

The grey pair passed through the covered bridge, dark enough that Volganin saw the cervine silver shine of Fade's eyes. She decided not to ask about it. Instead, she asked if they had knights in Wayland.

"Sir is a title," he said. "To be earned or bought from one of the Royal Orders or granted by the assembled ministers of the Worldthing. We don't have many wisents in the islands, so the cavaliers are all gone."

He was glad for that. He had briefly worked with Aquilan bison drivers to earn some proper certifications, in the Vankir plains where the hussars rode. The beasts and drivers alike were riddled with phthisis.

The Academy of the Northern Lights came into view the instant they exited the cave, six towers in the mist, one slouching against its supporting walls, sunk into the earth. A pile of rubble remained behind, the legacy of the demolished seventh tower. Rather than fallen, it was smashed flat like the hammer of Exallon's wrath.

Fade paused to drink in the haunting majesty of the ruin, mystic blue shadows behind the mist.

"Is something wrong?" Kingfisher said.

She watched Fade open up his caped watchcoat and frock, revealing a dense network of pockets and belted harnesses holding flasks, two books, a heavy rod of dull metal, and several knives.

The Brandmen, the folk of Wayland, Tirving, Brut, and Brandtland, earned their name from their use of wavy fire swords. It was said that all true Brandmen carried such a weapon, and their women a red dagger. Volganin wondered what Fade's possession of only a small collection of scalpels, etching knives, and artavi meant.

She likewise noted the raised bumps on the ashen coat, quill follicles indicative of chrome-tanned terror bird leather. Its lapels were delicately folded and embroidered with white and blue in such a way to resemble eyes, indeed, she liked how the coat matched his ashen hair and eyes.

A deep snorting broke the chilling quiet, from the walruses on nearby Students' Beach. Fade opened his grimoire and flipped through its tattooed pages until he came across the section on invisibility. He tilted the book so the harpy could see the sigil and spell.

"I see those sigils in grimoires... I don't know how to

draw them with my talons," she asked. "Do you draw them on the ground? In ink? In blood? In the air?"

"You don't draw those sigils," Fade said. "Unless you're copying or enchanting something, but those are etched in blood and metal. They're diagrams of compulsion, for how one channels yliaster, the astral radiation that defines Nature. A pentagram maps the head and limbs. If it's inverted, you push the lines of force outward rather than channel towards the heart. A hexagram represents how you channel through the heart, for metabolic and binding effects. A seven-pointed star represents the skull, the paired point indicating the eyes. Octagrams are purely elemental, paired for negatives and positives, and the extraordinary meridians, and nonagons signify the major secretive glands. The overlayed lines, notches, strokes, what have you...well, there's a lot of coding in them, for order, strength, continuity, spinal alignment, and two score other factors involving the meridians. And old grimoires will have outright artifices, fakes, and traps to detect and curse plagiarists and thieves. So, you have to be quite careful with someone else's book."

"What about the spell? Or perhaps the incantation?" she asked. "Do you have to say it aloud? Because that could be a problem for an invisibility spell."

"See, that's an issue of great contention," Fade said. "The spell itself is basically a mental pattern or state. A spell to control water will have imagery involving salt and tides, the ocean blue. It's the spice of the channeling, what flavors the ingredients, and the cooking... I sound like that shaman now."

"Mags?"

"Yes," Fade said. "She compared her ritualism to cooking. Or made them the same, not sure."

"If it's just the images, why the ancient tongues and rhymes?"

"Well, they're not in older languages because old languages

are more powerful, that's nonsense, it's in an old language because it's an old spell, and people are afraid to change the wording. Rhythm and precise timing are important. They didn't have clocks in the day, for one thing. When you're inhaling and when your exhaling can make or break a working, particularly if you're dealing in fire, air, charms, regeneratives, or the void. And the rhyme simply makes it easy to remember."

"The rhythm is?" she said. "Oh, I guess if the channeling has to be precise, so does the timing. It's like a song and dance."

"You pretty much have it, yes," he said.

He smiled for the first time since Kingfisher had met him. He raised his left hand and asked her if he could touch her elbow.

She nodded, slightly weary.

"Alright, straighten your spine, tense up… make sure your neck is an iron rod… the spine is important… *Mind the beat, and hear the rhyme/Feel the spark, and keep the time,*" he said in Waylander, over-enunciating and exaggerating the beats.

A sharp tingle needled her on each downbeat, like static on the feathers during a storm.

"It's an old Boreal cantrip, a child's first spell. One of the first things you need to do when writing up a grimoire is your own system of stresses and time signatures. Or learn to write music. A good skald could make a man drop dead with one cutting, well-delivered rhyme. You need to mind that, alright, sound is a distortion of air."

Volganin nodded and tried to cushion her flight. Volganin fluttered up and clutched the edge of the Academy's outer wall, struggling as her attempt at silence only stilled the air and deepened the beating of her wings, like an instrument tuned down a few octaves. She raised herself so she was only visible from above the nose. The academy was a husk, a skeleton picked clean. A long building with a tree growing out of it marked the campus center, but this was no planned center-piece. The roof cracked outwards. Tiles had landed some thirty meters out. Volganin tried to figure out how that happened. A tree should have gradually pushed its way out of the roof rather than this brutal eruption. Perhaps a guided surge of wind and water punched through the rafters, but that would only explain the tiles, not the outward blast around the trunk.

"I don't see anyone, at the moment," she whispered. "Are you sure there's anything here worth finding after seventy-odd years?"

"I guarantee no treasure," he said. "But there are things here that I would value that a looter may not. If looting won't offend your sensibilities."

"Why would it?" she asked.

"Chivalry, and all," he said.

"Oh," she said.

She had never thought of scavenging as objectionable, perhaps too much of the vulture in her.

"Taking up a fallen friend's weapon to save people is no sin."

Fade spat out a puff of air that would have to pass for a chuckle. "As long as we're on the same page, dame."

Fade slid his arm out of the coat and rolled up his sleeve, thin, wavy knife in hand.

He held out his forearm, slammed it to his chest, and whispered to himself, "Memory, thought, the banner of the North, souls of the hanged and the slain fly forth."

Fade's forearm burst forth with the gory thrust of a gutting knife through a fish, a cloud of ill-formed flesh and black feathers snapping into a crow balanced on the edge of his blade. Kingfisher recoiled, briefly believing that the surgeon had cut out his own heart and chucked it into the air. He flicked the knife, sending the oily carrion crow off into the campus.

"Focus on the air around you," Fade said, covering his Kraken Sepia tattoo. "Feel the light passing through the air. Imagine it is like a crystal. See the edges and define them. Now twist that crystal-like the pilot's spar, letting the light bend, and then, slide it away."

"What direction away?" Volganin asked.

"In any one direction, just push the light away from you as a solid… unit," Fade said.

Kingfisher slid several feet backward, flickering slightly.

Fade brought out his wand, a rod of pure bismuth, the length of his forearm. Bismuth wasn't one of the sexy metals—your gold or silver, your platinum or orichalcum—but the White Mass was the heaviest known metal, and had the magical properties of lead, antimony, arsenic, and silver with little of the toxicity. Miners called it *tectum argenti*, the roof of silver, for its ores often cover and precipitate silver veins. It is also termed *stannum glaciale*, glacial tin, for its ability to manipulate ice and other stable structures. Bismuth could purify, poison, and pulverize. And it was much, much cheaper.

Magic is the capacity to exaggerate, extrapolate, and transfer properties. A surge of yliaster through the rod aped the reflective and purifying qualities of silver and the metaphysical weight of lead, stabilizing and intensifying the image.

"Something's wrong," Kingfisher said. "I can't see straight. I see bent."

"That's normal," Fade said. "The key to crypsis and miraging is learning to get the light to hit your eyes. Or cheating with another form of vision. I'm going to have to touch your face."

"Alright," she said.

Fade placed an index finger on each of her temples, running them up to the side of her eyes. She gasped as a sharp, hot twinge shot through her face. Fade then pulled back and heated his knife and raised it up.

"I can see it," she said. "It's strange, but I can see the heat. It's… weird."

"So, you won't be able to see fine detail, but you should be able to see things through walls," he said. "This kind of thermal sight is rather useful up here. Higher contrast than in the tropics… Ready to go?"

"Yes," she said. "I'll scout ahead."

"Well, behind the crow," he corrected.

She flew off, and circled the campus walls, slightly dim and displaced in space. Fade climbed the wall and came down on the typical pavement of schools of arcane philosophy, black bubbles of pitchblende in a matrix of volcanic ash concrete, and tar. Garden patches and trees dotted the campus, spliced and chimerized to produce copious and varied fruits. A warped binding hawthorn snaked through a patch of black fruit wolfberry, pollinated by rufous hummingbirds imported from Durendal. A vague citrus and berry scent covered the lingering odors of decay. Lines of platinum cut through this black yard of magestone, melted down alluvial sands dredged from the nearby White Meska.

"Keep an eye out for the Klaich," he said.

"Of course," she said. "Uh, what is it?"

"Imagine if someone tried to make a giraffe out of isopod and crayfish parts. They're silvery, with a long fleshy tail, covered in thick pink sweat. Almost like a stomach lining," Fade explained. "They tend to be covered in ulcers here."

"Are they chimerae?" Kingfisher asked.

"No," Fade said. "They were summoned here from Blazing Fuzon, the second planet. It's covered in dense, acidic clouds. They were going to be used to attack sylphs with their colorless fire magic and corrupt airs, but these wizards only managed to rope in gas miners rather than their Fuzonic counterparts. The poor wretches escaped, but wound up malnourished, dull, and short-necked."

"I'm surprised summoning magic was allowed here," she said. "Or even possible, with the ban."

"This came before," he said. "The ban must have come with the dragon, but you're right. Ports have always been afraid of the possibility of accurate arcane transportation. You can drag something somewhere, like this summoning, but it's one-way and dangerous, both to conjurer and the conjured. Engineers have, of late, developed evoker-culverines, cannons and handguns capable of conjuring a single bound beast, but those are costly affairs and each shot must be reworked. And transmission without the use of such gates and circular rites is likely impossible."

"Can you make a two-way gate?" she asked.

"Yes," he said. "But you need a terrible command of space and time. Take a golden gate and duplicate its properties on another gate."

"Which properties?" Volganin asked, taking flight.

"All of them," Fade said. "Even its position in space. Once the two doors are the same door, you move them apart. The key is to trick two doors into acting like one door. The cost would be enormous."

Volganin beat her wings for altitude, taking in a harpy's-eye view of the campus.

"There's a creature creeping down the yard towards you, across the sewage pipe," Volganin whispered in Fade's ear from a great distance. "It's small, though. Perhaps it's a weird cat?"

A shadowy flash captured Volganin's attention, but Fade turned to see that the initial curiosity was indeed a weird cat, in part. It was a mockery of a griffin, half-housecat, half-chicken, its wings in a twisted, painful molt, its legs trembling and bowed inwards. It stank of ammonia and wet soil, like a crowded coop. The characteristic head tilt of a contortion victim indicated it wasn't rabid.

His home could be traced by the musty smell of dried urine and animal feces. Fade slipped on his beak-like respirator and gloves and lifted the small beast. It hung limply in his hands, crooning weakly.

"It's a chimera," said Fade. "A common if cruel experiments in anatomy, a test to see if such a creature could survive and fly. The contortions have ruined the poor thing. I think I might take it for observation."

The creature escaped from some kind of kennel housed in the yard. Something had melted away its southern wall, from the outside. The nature of its stoneflow troubled Fade. Melted stone was a daily sight in the volcanic Home Isles, but rather than the slow, layered buildup of molten material, this wall sublimated like dry ice, with some remaining masonry whipped over the roof of the building and cooling into snaking lumps of foamy pumice, the drizzle of caramel over a cake.

He puzzled over the heat and complex yliaster pattern necessary to destroy a wall that quickly while not incinerating the rest of the port. It must have been a genius working of the higher chaos of fire, the *Astral*–the radiance of stars, or that of air, the *Aetherial*, the stellar material–to the point that, ever so briefly, a star existed upon the world. He wondered if the arcane accelerant was not incendiary, but temporal.

The eastern side of the kennel was basically gone, a mess of ash and metal coils. The western side housed the sad sight of mummified animals. Potentine macaques had starved to death in their cage, leaving behind the excess skin of their forced fattening, a substitute for the *Axungia hominis* and other body parts that must otherwise be human. There were several feline skeletons, domesticated male caracals, or lynxes, likely farmed for lyngurium. This organic amber of attraction drew in both metals and plant tissue and inverting qualities, sexes, and polarities. Finally, across the floor, he found the desiccated flesh of the Klaich, evidently consumed to summon the false star. Its crystalline support structures had partially transmuted to iron.

Fade tucked the mock-griffin under his arm and continued towards the hypostyle longhouse at the center of campus, admiring the statue of Hedran. Like all the major divinities, the Tranquil Goddess had many aspects and tales, but her patronage of study, mysteries, wisdom, trust, confidentiality, and the yliaster winds of the Hunter's Star made her worship common at universities and centers of arcane philosophy. What puzzled Fade was the damage to her idol. He at first thought it was simple, if powerful, vandalism, but a closer look showed that the stone had somehow suffered a leprous corruption, blackened veins running through her. Her nose had not been chipped away but sloughed off.

Fade quickened his pace and entered the hall. Volganin followed him from above, entering the building through the hole that the great oak tore through the roof.

Fade lit a torch with his off hand, but it fizzled out as he entered the central chamber of the building. He looked around the room, and found a fire-retardant spell built into the stonework. Kingfisher recognized some of them as well, from her grimoire, although the temporal wards were far too expensive and complex for her. Most libraries and archives are protected by anti-magics and apotropaics, from dangers as mundane as dust and the elements to the ceaseless march of time. It was also a fine place for arcanists to meet and eat without fear of coercion and treachery.

Volganin searched the corners of the room, trying to trace the limits of the suppression. Flying proved harder than it should have been, as her innate magic could not aid her muscles. Yet her ruffled feathers finally settled in the cool ambiance of this hall, no longer haunted by that uneasy sense of being watched by long-dead eyes. Paranoid shades no longer flickered at the corners of her vision, echoes burnt into reality by bursts of cosmic possibility. While a body blocking sunlight casts a shadow, the subtle radiance of the stars soaks through a body, infusing the yliaster with flavored lees and aural dregs. The death of so many great wizards in such a terrible surge of arcane might stained the land with occult terror.

The next section of the campus center appeared to be some kind of major lecture hall or audience chamber surrounded by administrative offices, independent from the towers. What remained of the roof sheltered statues of bull-horned Merovach, the Venom King Azimazda, the Witch Gvozdenzuba, local martyr of science Viktor Pridvornov, Ranko of Staraya Stolitsa, Urraca of Maladon, and the mathematicians Ritter, Auldburgh, Heap and Hatham. The latter four were paired up on one stand, serving as two sides of a bookshelf.

The one surviving book was printed one hundred and twenty-six years ago, a thick compilation of the major works of calculus and commentaries—Gregor Fortunatus Ritter's *On Integration and Differentiation*, Ethelred Auldburgh's *Motus Corporum and Analyticorum*, Shahahbarim Hatham's *hRakabal Mahamati*, and Rathwolf Heap's foundational treatise, *On Terminal Mathematics and the Tangents of Kappa Curves*. Fade was something of an admirer of Heap, not only for being the pioneer of calculus, but also because he too came from a family of Waylander linen drapers.

The calcification of calculus was the midwife of modern arcane philosophy. While ancient scholars worshiped sacred geometries and the like, it wasn't a particularly fruitful practice beyond knowing the basics of parallel and perpendicular lines of force, unbroken circles, and that spirals were powerful for some reason. Sacred geometry could describe random findings, but it took calculus to explain why. And once you get the *why*, you can move on to *what about*. It is now understood that moving yliaster through a spiral causes logarithmic growth in the charge's strength in the most efficient manner, like the power in a compressed spring. The current trend of empiric arcane philosophy is the search for optimal patterns, rates of change, and applications of mass, inertia, and total energy in a system.

"Math is magic?" Kingfisher asked, reading over Fade's shoulder.

"Magic is the echo of Civilization and the exaggeration of Nature," Fade said. "And if words are the language of Civilization, mathematics are the language of Nature."

She was so impressed by that line that Fade couldn't bring himself to admit that it was a Heap quote.

A massive slab blocked one of the doorways to a storage atrium, a slate with thousands of etched lines and runes that had once been filled with gold, silver, and copper. Someone had chiseled out most of the precious metal, damaging the text. Its front was covered in brown filth.

"What happened there?" Kingfisher asked.

She tapped her claw and something soft and cold flowed over her toe. She accidentally ripped open a pin-cushion-sized bag of pounce. The ground fishbone, usually used to soak up excess ink, was the rusty brown of dried blood. She wondered if it was the Sacred Sepia, the coveted kraken-ink, but her eyes soon found a trail leading to a bleached pile of wrist bones.

"Oh, is that…" Fade muttered.

He set down the chimera and ran to the slab. This section of the hall was not protected by the spells, judging by the damage.

"There are drag marks from the hall. Can't see where they end, though," Kingfisher said. "Was someone trying to steal it and then gave up at the door?"

"Thieves aren't particularly known for brilliance," Fade

said with the hint of a smile as he crouched down to examine the edge of the slab. He filed off the layer of filth to reveal the steel-black pitchblende below. The stone's octahedral crystals guided the etching across its surface, but the edge had a reptilian quality, its shiny black bubbles recalling the scales of a chameleon. Its arcane heat aided that vitality.

"Aren't we… sort of thieving?" Kingfisher asked, yanking his attention from the stone.

"No, my friend, we are performing material research," Fade said. He tapped on the stony surface with his wand, taking a sample of its properties for later analysis. He didn't see Kingfisher's eyes widen upon being called a friend. "So, this is a blood lure."

"Were people sacrificed on this?" Kingfisher said.

"Are you squeamish, Ms. Volganin?" asked Fade.

"No," she said, remembering the time she ate the six-days-rotten gallbladder of a river hippo as her sisters played 'scatter the shit' with its large intestine.

"It doesn't require a death," he explained. "Just blood. The more the better, though."

"Why blood?" she asked in a whisper, imagining some terrible rite upon that sacrificial altar "Why is it always blood magic?"

"Blood is potent," he said bluntly. "Rich in vital essences, lines of structural force and flows. It's pan-elemental, with antitheses locked in tension, water, and essential salts heated by metabolic fire, organic minerals binding vital air. And, most importantly, traces of magical heritage… and it's cheap. Nearly everything you can do with gold and your noble spices, you can do with a bucket of blood. These lures were something of a specialty of this school. The local people had a primitive version, standing stones that they would smear with blood and blubber, to make whales, squid, and seals beach. Easy hunting."

"What was this one for?" asked Kingfisher.

"This one… well, I think this is how we got our beloved mayor," he said. "Someone with a bit of salamander in them must have drawn in the Mayor during the invasion. Summoning by a tantalizing *feeling*. Put a bit of impulsive wanderlust in their heart. Maybe give the dragon a bit of a notion to drop by the port, see if there's a fleet to burn."

"Did they drag it towards this warded room to shut it down?" Kingfisher asked.

"Maybe," Fade said slowly, as he turned his free hand in an attempt to model the thieves' movement through the hall. "But I think the timing is wrong. Just a looting. Let's move away from the wards, towards the work area."

"Wait, would their diet affect this lure?" Kingfisher asked, nodding towards the table.

As Fade turned and took a step towards it, a candle distilled from the essence of glowbeetles and deep-sea fish sprung to life, illuminating the room with a cold blue. Kingfisher and Fade saw that a meal had been half-eaten in this hall, leaving bison bones, scattered silver dragées, traces of carob wrapped in goldleaf, and largely evaporated vials of frozen colloidal silver in their wake.

"Why are they eating those… shiny things?" Kingfisher asked.

"A diet rich in metals, and a bit of bloody meat," Fade explained. "It's a good magician's meal. That stain on the plate was probably liver."

"Oh, I like liver and bones and bits of metal sometimes," said Kingfisher. "Is that good for magic, too?"

"Yes," Fade said, tracing his finger across a gash in the wall, cut by a precise, optical discharge.

Its path was straight for three meters before terminating in a messy, jagged jumble of cuts as though the wand had been wrestled from a hand. Fade assumed it was a sign of deliberate violence. There was not only a disaster but combat between mages. Then the oddness of the harpy's comments snapped him to the present.

"Wait, do you eat the marrow or the entire bone?"

"You're only supposed to eat the marrow?" Kingfisher asked, perplexed.

"Well, that's all humans can eat," Fade asked. "And the metal?"

"Don't you eat little stones and metal beads?" she asked. "So you can grind things in your gizzard?"

"Humans don't have gizzards," he said.

"So that's why your food has to be cooked or boiled," she said.

She turned her head towards a glint of candlelight under a bookcase.

"So, your stomach is a universal solvent that breaks down bones and stones, but an onion will murder you," Fade said, shaking his head in disbelief. "What a mysterious universe…"

"So if humans don't eat metal…" she asked, her attention drifting towards the shiny thing in the shadows. "Why were these people eating metal?"

"Good question," Fade. "Metal was the theme of the feast. Aristocrats like to sprinkle goldleaf and a bit of silver, but this is too much. They were drinking it by the cup."

Kingfisher dragged a circlet of solid silver from under the bookcase, until it set into a groove between the tiles and began to roll. She gasped as the ring smashed through a growth of crystallized silver, shattering the dendrites into a ringing pile of needles.

"Far too much silver," she said.

She rolled it around on her talon, before flipping it into the air and catching it on her head.

"It's a crown, a circlet."

Fade made a circuit of the room and found a similar silver

ring embedded in the floor at the southwestern corner, in the jagged branches of Philosopher's Trees. There must have been dozens and dozens of them, before the looting.

"Ms. Volganin," said Fade, as he traced the indentation in the floor and recalled the local tradition of metal molded into carved wood. "I don't mean to alarm you, but I found an exact copy of that thing you put on your head, melted into the floor."

Kingfisher whipped her head around until the circlet sailed into the wall, ricocheting off a glowbeetle sconce and coming to a stop against a lectern. Fade winced at the clang, which drew his attention to a page presented on the lectern. What would have been a scroll in ages past was now a terse paper on a new arcane rite. A chalice and a dagger sat on the lectern's inner shelf.

Candlewax had built up in the chalice, melted, and pooled flat, in a way that indicated a rapid flash of heat rather than the slow, ropy drips of a properly lit candle. The ceremonial dagger's hilt was a polished human bone. Fade turned it in his hand, contemplating its use. Bone is a powerful material in airwork, its spongy pores housed stagnant air pockets, marrow is a powerful catalyst for regeneration, and nervous channels could conduct electricity.

Unfortunately, these parts tended to rot or collapse without a great deal of maintenance, making bone weaponry impracticable for anyone but a master of the aerial or healing arts.

"It's about the tension," Fade said.

He lifted the chalice and the dagger.

"Fire on water, earth, and air. Build up the opposite forces and let it collapse into an ordered chaos."

"Why?" Kingfisher asked.

She flew up to the hole in the roof and perched. "To perform this... destruction? Why demolish your own university?

Twist and kill your own kind? Maybe one monster, but this was… a joint effort."

"Yes, this wasn't some suicidal cult. This paper is about the magnification of metallic properties. It's rather ingenious. The basics are, well, basics, part of arcane theory for three thousand years. The First Principal of Properties. But this kind of magnification, it's remote and powerful, and fast," Fade looked at the streaks of melted stone on the wall. "Perhaps too rapid in the onset, all things considered."

Fade took out a small mirror and held it parallel to his left hand, tilted it until he found the right angle, and picked up a silver crown that rolled behind a bookcase with the reflected hand. He dropped it on the lectern and continued reading the paper.

"There are a couple of these silver crowns. Five from what I can see, here. One made its way onto that cabinet. And one's embedded into the wall here," Kingfisher said.

She shivered at some of the possible fates of the head that wore that crown.

"Could that have been the metal? There was metal in the food, but you don't put on a silver crown without that being the focus of the ritual, right?"

"Silver is the moon, silver is purity, silver is time and timelessness," Fade said, reciting properties by rote as he tapped his upper lip with an index finger. "It's used to break curses, extend life, and purge illness."

"Werewolf college?" Kingfisher joked.

Fade responded with a hum as he continued to read the paper.

"Wait, no, that was a joke. This can't possibly be… wait, secret hideaway of descendants of the Lupine Emperors? Some ancient program to rebuild the Hirpic Empire once Aquilo falls in disarray?"

"They were probably trying to cure the contortions," Fade

said. His slow, singular tapping accelerated to four-finger drumming on his chin.

"Right," said Kingfisher. "...and the spell interacted poorly with their werewolfery."

Fade looked up at Kingfisher with a puzzled look.

"What is it?" Kingfisher said.

"Nothing," Fade said. "I just thought you were flying around. A shadow..."

"No, I've been here," Kingfisher said.

They both glanced out of the hole upon hearing the crack of a musket.

Something moved in Kingfisher's peripheral vision. She hopped out of the hole and snapped her head around. In the middle of the courtyard stood an old woman in a heavy shawl. She held no rifle, arms hanging limp. She was no ghost, but still ghoulish in form. Kingfisher noted that the lady was slightly hunched, which was still decent posture considering that she had no head.

"Oh," Kingfisher gasped, as the head dove down, screaming from naked lungs.

As the entrails wrapped around Kingfisher's neck and torso, she screamed too.

Chapter 5: Exiles of the Willow Court

Dr. Lund quietly fixed the corners of his wind-whipped notebook, before pressing it tightly between Xantho's *Physiologus* and Anker's *Notes on Human Hereditary*. He waved as Mageirissa exited the constables' office.

"What did you have to report?" Lund asked.

"I saw some ogres and friends on the way to the port, on the road along the Meska," she said. "I wanted to check in and see if anyone corroborated the report. Something serious was happening. Ogre males are highly territorial, outside of famine-raids. They had troops of dogheads and giant hyenas from Translucomria. Maybe even a kaftar."

Lund had learned of similar activity. A party of Boazo-vazzi departed from their enclave in the port upon the sighting of multiple albino reindeer on the Hyperborean limit. Originally from Scrithipineland, on the far north of Borea, they hold reindeer in high regard, and hunted for a *stáinnak*, a sacred doe who takes up a "male" role, protecting the herd, charging into danger, and mounting other females. There had always been a mystical androgyny to reindeer and their arcane cousin, the pantheon, as both sexes grow antlers. The Boazo-vazzi had turned back upon a deadly encounter with a *Stalo* — an ogre.

"Why didn't you want me to come inside?" Dr. Lund asked, shaking off the morning chill.

"You look rich and foreign," she said. "Security might want to turn out your pockets, for evidence."

Lund had been conscious of his appearance and voice, dressing in a peasant's tunic and a simple floppy mushroom cap. He had even thought to exchange the bulk of his traveling money for beaver and moose pelts with regenerative enchantments and tattooed serial numbers, making them both practical, highly sought after, and difficult to resell if stolen.

He wondered what had placed him as a rich man, he had even minded his accent, making it sound neutral with some northern tendencies.

Murmurish is spoken by many in the Port, one in eight Severnayans would call themselves People of the Sea-Walls, and most natives have some none-too-distant ancestry. However, it is closer to the reedy, clipped dialects of the northerly Scrithipineland, like the singsong speech of Astragard, some twelve hundred miles and three centuries divided from the dialect of Ermenarich, on the inner seacoast to the south. Apart from the fresh blood of some sailors, the Port's dialect has not undergone the Heron Court's spelling reforms and national unification initiative.

Southern Murmurmen were unpopular, even among the Murmurish Severnayans. Even more so, in fact, as the hatred of cousins is always stronger than that between aliens. Two centuries ago, the Murmurmen invaded Northernmost in an attempt to secure the Polar Sea, Hans-Hagano-Land, and the land of the Timorats, relatives of the Tarnonnans of the Murmurish east coast. The war was unpopular among northern Murmurmen, who saw it as disruptive to Polar politics; the Southerners had always aligned themselves more with the Boreal Sea and Aquilo proper and were seen as blundering meddlers in a world they didn't quite understand. Murmur is, after all, a massive country, albeit dwarfed by the Homelands and the Septentrine Empire, there is a great divide between its southerners and northerners. The Tsokiri counter-offensive lost Talvenvasara and the Ducal Canal, and the war dragged on for a dozen years. The Tsokiri held the Polar Sea but lost southern access to the Boreal Sea for four decades, and that hold on the Polar Sea rested almost entirely on Northernmost playing ball with the Black City.

"Ah," Lund said. "Shall we head to the Jooga?"

She nodded and covered her hood with a headdress of

white fur, trimmed with a fringe of swallow tails made of black and gold threads. Her necklace of metatarsal bones jangled against the bright opal rings grasped by the twisted ends of her braids. Lund was rather struck by the newfound nobility of her bearing; she was no longer the jovial cook, but the scion of a line of mountain shamans. He struggled to find the proper protocol for this moment; was she, in fact, his social better?

"You are an *Ötmogan*," he said. "Is that a caste? Did you train for it?"

"It is my family's role in the tribe," she said. "We descend from miracle workers who duplicated bread from stone, flour from sand, and meat from moss."

"How long ago?" Lund asked.

"Twenty-two generation, perhaps? Seven centuries back, in the Long Hunger."

"Seven centuries?" Lund said. He hummed, trying to remember the history. "Murmur was devastated by a famously harsh winter in the 19th century. May have been the same."

"Nobody forgets a famine like that," she said. "One side of my heritage were the valley people, the other was a March, a... Perhaps you would call it an all-infantry army?"

"A horde?" Lund suggested. A burnt-orange butterfly landed on Mageirissa's shoulder.

"Yes," she said, with a nod. "They did not come as conquerors, as they had been in the past, when they could stand against Sylph raiders. The mammoths and unicorns of their ancestors died. These were scared people, in a desperate siege. The silos of molding grain emptied. They slaughtered the livestock, then the mounts and pets. The March ate the dead, and, in a great reversal, the valleyfolk ate marchers. Polar bears, dogs, hyenas, and nightwolves ate them both. And some say sylphs stalked into those rival camps, stealing the breath of the healthy and brave."

"How did they survive?" Lund asked. "Did spring finally come?"

"No," she said. "A marcher wandered into the valley's village and brokered a truce. The say that the Marchers had never parlayed before. He was small and lean for his people, and wise, very wise. Wherever he walked, snow melted and grain grew. Where he rested, fruited vines sprouted. Those he touched no longer felt the pains of hunger. He spread his miracle-working to others and brought about a great reconciliation. He was called Moga, though some people think that name came later. It means 'smart' or 'clever.'"

"Is Moga your god?" Lund asked. Another butterfly landed on his sleeve, and he looked around, wondering at its source.

"No, Moga is the prophet of Hunger."

"Hunger as concept? A god?" Lund asked.

"Both, perhaps. Or the very act of living. Hunger is primal. It is growth, consumption, and decomposition. The Great Devourer created life and set its cycles in motion. His consort, That Which Sleeps, is the ruler of rest. Eating is a sacrament, the essence of the Divine."

"Oh, so that's why you said your titled blended chef, chief, and shaman," he said.

"People may find it silly, but they will worship gods of war and sailing," she said. "There's nothing more essential to life than eating, drinking, and resting. We oversee the four houses of life, the hunter, the farmer, the shepherd, and the craftsman. Other priests will seal themselves away from the world, but we can't. There is nothing more sacred than dirt under the nail and flour on the apron."

"It makes sense," Lund noted. "My people worship the family of Urizen and Incano, and the house of Los, but gods of civilization are gods of civilization."

"I've heard a bit about them," she said. "Their mendicants

wander the Home Roads… but it is top-down. Mogan Aristology is more… bottom up."

"What do you mean?" Lund asked.

"So much focus on the cult of kings, royal ceremony…" Mageirissa lamented. "What's the point in meeting the religious needs of one man, one family? The spiritual world is no pyramid."

"The priests in the courts would beg to differ," Lund muttered. A kaleidoscope of orange butterflies hovered above the upturned roofs of a wide complex, some resting on gourds and pumpkins growing in their crenelations.

"Hmm…This must be the lodge of the Sarosaram," Mageirissa said.

They arrived at the Jooga, a single low, walled compound built into a stone mound with a common courtyard facing the Narrows. The walls themselves were shaped from still-living wood sealed in an insulating plaster and their own sap, decorated with wide, folded snakeskins. A single willow tree shadowed the center of the courtyard, sprouting from cutting brought with them from the royal gardens of their homeland. It was surrounded by a grove of treasury trees, dense canopies of grafted limbs rich with mulberries and lemons, and half a dozen other fruits. The compound crawled with shaggy liondogs called "exorcists" for their alleged ability to sniff out curses and dispel ghosts with their barks, and waterpigs. The waterpigs were barrel-bodied Zephyran rodents, larger than the dogs, who content themselves with fallen lemons and dozing in the heated ponds.

The Hwagasari loomed over the compound, its tail descending into a well and the rest of its steel-scaled body guarding the Narrows. Alchemists and blacksmiths forged such beasts to defend villages, as their skin sucked up swords and spearheads and their feet drank lead from the earth. The Hwagasari's sole weakness was fire, as its metal-melting touch, in turn, gave their flesh a low melting point. A nigh-invincible version, the *bulgasari,* was possible, but best left to symbolic paintings to ward off fires. The Hwagasari's vulnerability was the reason the bookhangers were allowed to construct the creature in the Mayor's city.

Lund found the bell system at the front gate, ringing the red one four times. Within a minute, Lund's contact, Baeg Byeol-i, arrived with her ailing grandfather in tow. The bookhangers wore colorful robes with a wide cummerbund that crossed from the empire line to around the navel. Rather than the fine silks that they would have worn in their home country, befitting their noble caste, these robes were spun from heavy pig-wool. The Baeg family in particular favored white with silver and black trim and had access to silks. Even the youngest generation was slow to adapt to the styles of 'the Northern Port,' and a local mangling of the Saroese name for the city gave this frail branch of the Willow Court the odd title of the "bookhangers."

The Elder Baeg was a small, hunched man with a drooping mustache and a tall, wide-brimmed hat of black, featureless felt. His fingers and folds were dyed a purple-gray, typical of alchemists who work in the silvers; his case was mild, likely due to his family's role as botanists. Some bookhangers are completely blue by old age, including the scleras. His granddaughter wore a short, rounded cap rimmed with fur, usually worn by old Tsokiri woodsmen. Her jet-black hair was worn in a thick braid that fell to her shoulder blades, loop up, and clipped to a butterfly of silver wire at the back of her head.

The pair smelled like citrus, as did the whole Jooga. They keep a glass-grove of the sylph-fruits, pale green frost papedas, and bitter oranges cultivated for their heartiness and ability to survive Northern winters. In one part, a humid hothouse, the bookhangers even manage to grow limes, sweet oranges, and shaddocks. The Sarosaram are known for distilling such fruits into vinegar, sour syrups, and perfumes. The latter is considered a tribute to the reclusive sylphs who rule the mountains of Saro. Modern medicine recently came to understand that sylphs need a great deal of citric acid in their diet, even using the heavy fluid and iodides as a natural barometer in their supernasal sinuses.

A court of pixies buzzed around the grove, the ascomata which replaced their abdomens leaving a trail of sparkling conidia through the air. This pixie dust was a mild hallucinogen in humans and caused further pixie infection in many insects. Rather strangely, a court could be multiple related individuals infecting different species, a menagerie of dragonflies, wasps, butterflies, moths, and beetles pledged to a queen who is almost always a bee. The bee is required to produce the mad honey, the poisonous, psychoactive product of a rhododendron harvest.

The pixie court had set up a trade with the bookhangers. The Saromen maintained the artificial tropical environment, while the court offered honey, dust, and a magical "pixie papyrus" like the paper of certain wasps.

Baeg Byeol-i consulted a small handbook and looked up at Lund.

"You, come in," she comanded in Tsokiri, and translating for her elder.

Rather than speaking in the tongue of Saro, she used a sign language with her deaf grandfather.

She then pointed at Mageirissa. "You, stay outside."

"Why?" Lund asked.

He looked at Mageirissa's frowning face, wondering if it was because her folk resembled the barbarian tribes to the north of Saro. They at least spoke distantly related languages. They crashed against the Wide Willow Wall, the Ten Thousand Hectares of thickets, palisades, and thornwire built by Saro Bannermen and the Hypouranids to keep out northern barbarians. Inviting one of those impure, horse-eating people into one's house is an invitation to disaster.

"The big woman has ogre physiognomy. Bad spiritual hygiene."

The nurse brushed her hair behind her high-set, ursine ear.

"Those marchers I was talking about? They might have been an ogre clan," said Mageirissa.

She snarled, revealing oversized canines, and looked down at her feet.

"And by 'might have been,' I mean, as a matter of indisputable historical record."

Lund bit his bottom lip. He couldn't let them turn away Mageirissa, but he needed their research and it was their home and hospitality. And she outright admitted to having ogre blood, so he couldn't lie their way in.

"She's a necessary part of this endeavor," said Lund. "Lady Barvaci is a shaman, a healer, and a respected leader of her tribe. Also an excellent chef."

"We abhor the eating of human flesh," said Baeg Byeol-i, with a sternness that clashed with her high-pitched voice. "In ancient days, we were hunted by ogres, salamanders, sylphs, and devils from the Inferno. We were driven from our home by sorcerers who ground the livers and hearts of children into sweet dew to prolong their wicked lives. For standing up to that abomination, we were cursed and cast out to die in foreign lands. All ogres and their kindred are damned by nature and heaven."

Lund's gaze darted between the Shaman and the alchemists, struggling to articulate a position that began with, 'Sure, eating human flesh is wrong, *but...*'

"It's fine," Mageirissa said, with a sweetness salted with passive-aggression. "I'll stay out here, in the cold."

"Thank you," said the younger Baeg. "Dr. Lund, come inside."

Lund stood still, visibly grinding his teeth.

Mageirissa stepped close to Lund's ear and whispered, "I know what you're thinking, and don't. This is a medical crisis, and you're a physician. My feelings don't matter here. Your feelings don't matter. You have a duty of care."

"I'll make it up to you," Lund said.

"It's fine," Mageirissa said shortly, while looking away. "I'm going to talk to the local fur trappers and coal burners, see if they saw any strange militant sorts over near the city limits. I'll meet you at the gate to the Academy in two hours."

Lund nodded at her, sourly mumbled in resignation, and entered the Jooga's gate. A dragonfly-pixie followed him and erected a glamor, appearing as a small woman with diaphanous wings.

Lund examined the bookhangers in the courtyard. Most of the workers were young, and all wore their iconic family colors, if only on a waist sash. The famed horse archers of the bannermen would have worn these colors on flags mounted on their armor, but the bookhanger's warriors had defected from the Jooga. They reformed as the Banner of the Northwest, making up much of the city watch. These noble families had restructured into something similar to guilds, with child apprentices plying the trade of their forefathers, with this training mostly involving menial labor around the compound. This is a society solely consisting of aristocrats; their lower classes realized that they were no longer legally bound to their masters in this foreign land and set out into the wild once their children overcame the language barriers. In a century and a half, there are small but salient Sarosaram populations in the Septentrine Empire, Skeiron, and Tizona, leveraging a great deal of power with their knowledge of ironclad "turtle ships." It was, after all, only the noble clans that carry the alleged curse; only they must be contained in Northernmost.

A curse is, in truth, no different than a disease or poison, apart from substance, a malady of will-worked yliaster rather than animalcule or toxin. They have symptoms, points of contact, and methods of transmission and prevention. Some curses are pandemic, such as the Great Insomnia of Henatin that devastated settlements from Demus to Parazonium from 1979 to 1981, or the Choking Fear that killed seventy-odd people in Jagiela two decades ago. These are indiscriminate and designed only to terrorize and kill, the only difference from a mundane plague is their preternatural effects, such as exterior bruising around the throat, and media of incubation and transmission, such as dreams or speech. However, there are perfectly mundane, nonmagical diseases with anomalous symptoms, such as the Dancing Plagues of three to four centuries ago, where populations would be struck by mad dancing, even to the point of collapse and death by exhaustion, aberrant somnambulism, or inexplicable crib death. There are, likely, curses that by all accounts have no outward distinction from mundane diseases, such as necrotic hexes.

Lund had Baeg Byeol-i lead them to their stores of medicine, where she translated the labels. The pixie flew down on the shelf and underlined the iatrochemical labels with her hands. Much of it was commonly used, such as ginseng, eye-of-newt, and other mustard extracts, lemon peels, mushrooms, cinnabar, dried Waylander banana peel, and willowbark. Some were more exotic and less effective, such as hyena bladder and powdered chicken hearts. The dried aconite root caught Lund's attention – wolf's-bane, northern sky, leopard's-bane, blue-dart, lycotonum, the queen of poisons, a toxin with no known antidote. He asked what purpose they could have for such a large stock of poison. The Baegs said it was used as a blood coagulant or analgesic.

Lund nodded and half-believed her, pending further investigation. The next substance was harder to translate, but they said it was paired with blue-dart powder as the King of Cures to its Queen of Banes.

It dawned on Lund, from its silvery appearance, that this was, or was supposed to be, a pantheriac, a universal antidote and antivenom crafted from seventy ingredients by Azimazda, confusingly also known as "the King of Poisons." Lund knew the story, a legend, perhaps, but with a legitimate historical basis. Born Ihnkandaat, Azimazda is considered to be one of the most intelligent monarchs in history, a master of lordship, warcraft, philosophy, and the sciences, with the capability to speak all twenty languages of his realm. He established the field of toxicology and was said to have built up an immunity to every known toxin by consuming minute doses over the years.

In his fifty-first year, he reportedly drowned in a naval battle against the Argetes in the Anasharc Sea. He returned eighteen fortnights later amid the chaos of his succession, a changed, strange man.

Ihnkandaat retook his throne and shed his old name, taking up the title of Azimazda, the Serpentine Wisdom, and married a foreign bride, said to be a salamander in womanly form.

The Pantheriac is one of the three crowning jewels of medicine, with the panacea and the panapotropaic– the latter of which is considered the universal disenchantment in maledictory medicine. Unfortunately, every crackpot, quack, and fraud in the world has their own formula. For the sake of three perfect cures, the world has been flooded with poisons and placebos.

Lund turned the vial in his hand preciously, as one would handle the most brittle and beautiful butterfly.

"This… this can't truly… have you used it? Does it work?" Lund asked, flabbergasted. "We lost the formula a millennia ago."

"I do not know for sure," said the younger Baeg. "But we

have never lost a clan member to the poison of vegetable or the bite of animal. Yet it does nothing for our curse or the contortions."

"What is the formula?" Lund asked.

"It involves a mixture of dried roots and orange peel, the lymph glands of dogs and pigs bitten by snake and spider, cinnabar, and spells of preservation, a trade secret," said the younger Baeg. She nodded towards a single-volume copy of Najiti's *Atharvanvalli* and *Rasashaastra*, and Hongwu's *House of Vermillion*. They were on a bookshelf exaggerated by still lives of books, a motif around the Jooga. The pixie flew into one of them and slid down to the frame, mistaking them for an actual shelf.

"Fascinating. So, it's an antiserum," said Lund as he rescued the pixie with an outstretched hand.

Quite ingenious, especially for people who traditionally handled snakes, haze-panthers, and basilisks, but clearly not the solution to the Contortions. Lund noticed that the antisera's box also contained a glass duct, tweezers, and a thin drill; in the east, surgeons are known to use cockatrice venom to repair bones, as the legendary "petrifying" in fact is rapid, crystalline ossification, something between true bone and a fossil.

The elder and younger Baeg struggled to open a large crate in the storeroom. Lund set down the antiserum and aided them. The crate housed the mummified body of a monster, the sight of which set the pixie fleeing from the room. The creature was twisted up, showing signs of death by arctic exposure. The bookhangers had probed and dissected it, removing most of its organs and cubes and strips of its musculature. Despite resembling a human in body plan, its clubbed feet ended in hooves, and the creature was covered in thick white hair. Porcine tusks overwhelmed its lower jaw, which must have prevented it from fully closing in life. Its hands at first seemed stunted, but closer inspection showed that the bookhangers, or an earlier handler, had severed its fingers. Its vulpine ears had been severed and placed in a silk bag. It must have stood around seven feet tall, if hunched.

The chest featured a trio of hard, circular scars. Lund speculated if they were horns, small arms, or even tentacles. It was impossible to tell, for every ouphe is a sea of possibilities. They all begin as roughly anthropoid, but drink up yliaster and corruptions, bursting into nightmarish metamorphoses. Most sylvestres are apish things with an aspect of fox, elk, and bear, but others become twisted birds of thunder and lightning, or writhing, cancerous nodes dwelling in hollow trees. Their painful, leeching reaction to magical remedies makes any kind of therapy impossible, as polymorphic channeling only accelerates the mutations, often leading to outright saltation into new chimerical species of airy species. Even divining the nature of the fetus can prove fatal to mother and child.

It was the first time Lund had ever seen a sylph in the flesh, as debased as it may be. Elementals fade into their material chaos upon death. This pitiful being had fallen so far it could not even return to its own people in death.

"This creature was a gumiho's child… a… you call them changelings," said Baeg Byeol-i. "The sylphs abandoned this child with a family in Kastorin, down the river. The Kastorinites didn't want the poor beast and left it in the woods. Two decades later, they shot this creature in a sheep field."

An ancient curse lies upon the sylphs. Their births are rare and take much from the mother's life; it is not safe to have more than one child in a century. Twins are usually fatal. The sylphide mother cannot even ease her burdens with magic, as the rapid pressure changes of their workings can cause premature birth, not much different than the "storm babies" of women. Worse, many births bring deformities, as two in three ouphes are miserable, mortal wisps of things, doomed to die as hairy wildmen. This is the reason the ouphe- the 'elf-child,' became synonymous with the hideous fool, though one would never say such things in the presence of the Lords of Air.

There is no greater humiliation for immortal creatures of air and beauty to birth fleeting, foul beasts. It is the greatest of curses, worked at the birth of civilization. Some say it is the work of the gods, punishing the sylphides for their capriciousness – many claim it was Incano, the Mother God, who cursed those who enslaved her human children. Others say it is the cost of their immortality, the great balancing act, or the punishment of Eternity, from whom Thieriel stole his children's great blessing in a daring raid beneath the polar ice. Some elf-foes chalk it up to incest, as they say that Thieriel was both father and mother of the sylphs, mating with his own beautiful reflection upon the Silver Moon. Others say it is the work of gnomish enemies, a virtual army of human wizards, or even the fallout of a spurned suitor or star-crossed lovers, one of those just-so tales explaining why the two races in question should stay apart.

"This creature is corrupt with curses," Baeg Byeol-i translated for her elder. "Every part of it filled with twisted skeins of yliaster. We have tried ways of purifying it with acids, salts, oils, spirits, and fires."

"Has anything worked?" Lund asked.

He looked over at their table and saw an organ bath, a glass instrument designed to isolate organs for chemical stimulation. To Lund's great surprise, there was an apothecary's vessel labeled in the language of Saro, with the technical marks for *Axungia silvani*. This was one of the rarest of pharmacological components, jealously restricted to kings in some nations – the fat of the light-elves, a dense brown mass filled with blood vessels, used in skin ointments and cures for blindness, deafness, bladder issues, ulcers, and cancers. The remains of an ouphe are so rare that wars have been fought over an intact body, the contest of mages and lords in search of the elixir of immortality. In ancient days, it was said that the mages of the Dawn Sea destroyed navies and entire nations with cyclones conjured up with brown candles of sylphic tallow.

"Somewhat. We have tried forms of metaphysical therapy on the corpse. The best was a…" she stopped to look at one of the labeled concoctions on the shelf. "A mix of phosphorous salts from bone ash and guano, powdered coke, and coal tar in spirits. After heating and distillation, it weakened the curse in the finger bones. But we haven't had the time or the techniques to clarify what is happening."

Lund asked for a sample bone. After a brief discussion among the Baegs, the request was granted.

"Thank you. I apologize for the forthrightness, but did the specimen come… intact?" Lund asked. After a confused silence, he added, "Its manhood, to be specific."

"Oh, no," she said.

"Pity."

"Why?"

He watched her eyes. The presence of the fruits outside, vital to a sylph's diet, and a corpse of a mutated ouphe sent his mind down a strange conspiratorial path, wondering if its death had been far more recent and close. But he found nothing suspicious in her question.

"I was wondering if the curse could have specifically targeted the seminal archaei," Lund said. Byeol-i furrowed her brow and he clarified, "The hereditary life force in the seed of animals. We could, at least, produce a homunculus from it. Or sylvanculus, as the circumstances may entail."

"Ah, unfortunately, no," she said. "It must have been eaten by a scavenger. Or someone wanted a trophy. Sylphs don't wear much clothing."

"Speaking of heredity… may I see the genealogies?" Lund asked.

The Baegs spoke among themselves and nodded yes. They led him deeper into their family lodge, to a small closet with a large book on a lectern. The yellowed folio, secured by chain and pages of book curses, contained a register of every marriage and birth within the clans, a way to prevent close-cousin incest and detail property rights. A separate section logged each death, state of the curse, if they were killed by the curse, and if they were blackened, which the younger Baeg explained as a term for complete alteration of the skin by silver nitrite. She pointed to the purple-blue stains on her grandfather's hands.

"Fascinating," said Lund.

He took out his reading crystal and scanned the page. After a brief moment of adjustment, the Saro-glyphs read as Murmurish.

The younger Baeg looked apprehensive as he read the family trees and cross-checked with the dates and manners of death. Each clan's generation was marked by a syllable taken from a poem, so each cousin was connected by a common sound pattern in their names across class names, with an intricate cycle of hereditary patterns. Lund puzzled over the dating system, but it was plain that these Saro-folk lived far longer than normal. The old man must have been twelve decades old. He traced the families' symptoms back to their home in the Willow Court.

Lund abruptly stopped, closed the book, and locked eyes with her.

"Who knows about this?" he quietly whispered.

"Please don't tell anyone," she pleaded.

"I won't," he said. "But this… the dates are too close. There's a small gap, but…"

"It wasn't us," she said, as she pulled out of the room, signaling that it was time for Lund to follow. "It was a coincidence."

"Coincidental curses," Lund said. "Massive, maddening, coincidental curses."

"It was the Dankhiri fleet," she said. The terse statement had an edge of intimidation, as if dictating his findings. She raised her chin and her shoulders tensed, puffing up like a parakeet. "They brought the spiritual pollution with them. Not us."

"Why not the dragon?" Lund asked.

The pair looked confused and then signed among themselves. Lund's attention shifted to the girl's unused hand, which rested on a ceramic container of pulverized sulfur, marked with Leviathan's cross. Lund wondered if she would burn the book, or him, if he pressed the issue.

"The dragon is a great benefactor," she said. "It would do no such thing."

"So it is," Lund said under his breath. He rubbed a ball of wool in his pocket.

He held out his hand, gently, releasing alchemical sendings. One messaged a butterfly with a scent, a basic transmutation of the finger's oils. The other was a simple working of air called the Shepherd's call, sending a twinge of static electricity dancing up a piece of distant wool. Good way to find a wayward sheep, get someone's attention, or detonate an alcohol bomb, as he learned during his time cataloging the bats of the Cane Sea. The Karhun tribe of Deep Cannaria weaponized the largest bats against foreign ships, burning sails at sea.

Mageirissa's could reply to the twinge or the insect. And if the younger Baeg tried to throw the brimstone, Lund could have it cling to her sleeves.

"*But even the finest physic becomes a poison, with the wrong dosage,*" said Fade, quoting King Azimazda's *Codex Salubrious*.

"Maybe so," Baeg Byeol-i admitted. "Please, doctor, keep this between us. We do not want to be targeted again."

"I promise," said Lund, touching his heart. "I'm sorry I

could not be of help, yet. But call on me if your clan need medical assistance. Quiet and complimentary."

"The rain can't wear away the boulder in one night," Byeol-i said. Her hand pulled away from the jar. She nodded. Her lower jaw quaked, though Lund could not tell whether it was the cold or apprehension.

"I will be leaving now. Thank you for your hospitality, well, towards me. I hope we can celebrate if this crisis is ever re-solved."

"Yes, thank you, until that time comes," she said, with a bow. Her elder followed with a slight delay.

"I know a great chef," he added as he departed to the gate. A butterfly landed on his knuckle, his messenger to Mageirissa. It flapped its wings in a desperate fervor.

Chapter 6: The Band of Bastards

Eumelia Salmacis watched the people of the port pass by her seat on a pickling barrel. A Ganish struggled with an odd pink sack, with the somewhat unique barred headdress and combination gray eyes and sallow skin of her people. It was rare to see them so far to the northwest. There are forty-three ethnic groups registered in the city with a population above a hundred people. There must be a hundred others with just a couple of representatives. And that's not even counting the invisible factions of political radicals and religious divergents. It was a nest of revolutionaries, a rogue state of discontented riffraff.

One of the charcoal-burners from the north of town walked down the avenue. His braided hemp necklace marked him as a *kochul*, a wandering Tsokiri people that nobody liked for some reason. They had an accent, walked around with blue ponies, and played long mountain horns like gnomes, none of which justified driving them from towns. Maybe it was out of anger and disappointment that those so-called "blue ponies" were actually a boring grey, like those blue dogs. He didn't even look different from other Tsokiri. Apart from the blackening layer of soot.

But, she thought, she had no right to criticize people for looking plain. Eumelia was an unremarkable-looking woman. Not thin, not fat, brown-haired and brown-eyed, shorter than these Severnayans but not short elsewhere. She had a bit of a thick jaw and a long face, but not conspicuous nor ugly. She was a mutt of the Boreal ports. Her grandparents were a Waylander privateer, a Murmurish courtesan, a Swanlander trawler, and a Timorat seamstress. But it made her a good scout in the cities. She didn't draw the eye.

She wore a heavy, dark blue watch coat from her husband's time in the Grand Riverine Navy of the Harn, two sizes too big. She loved that coat. It smelled like her Lieutenant, his hair cream, aftershave, and Favonian tobacco from Attalus. And his horses and camels, but she tried to ignore that.

Lieutenant Arild Salmacis approached her, followed by one of the young runners from the army gathering up north from the River Mutny, a native Severnayan named Chestimir. The mission was set to go. They only needed to gather their magicians and their dragonslayer.

"We just need Gultschakal's wolfman," Lt. Salmacis said.

He was an average-sized man, but years of marching and riding had given him strong legs. Eumelia particularly loved his calves, but couldn't get him to wear coulattes anymore, especially up here. He paused to cover his mouth, suppressing a rumbling burp.

"How are you holding up?" Eumelia asked.

"I'll be fine," her husband said.

He tried to hide it, but the Lieutenant's digestion troubled him greatly, and he had been using bilious calomel purgatives for his cramps and constipation. Luckily, Northernmost produced and exported cheap pills called *Thunderbolts*, a name that advertised their latrine-defiling potency.

"So yes, get the wolf doctor, and we're ready to gather in force at the tree."

"He's still in that bookhanger compound," Eumelia said. "The big girl went north towards the charcoal men."

"We grabbed her," Arild said. "What about the harpy?"

"We tailed her and Dr. Lund's compatriot to the Academy," Eumelia said. "The head-hag and the Pretender are over there. Not sure if we need them."

"Eh, it's another set of workers and a small bounty from the constables, if they were truly behind the blast," Arild said.

He rested against the neighborhood's *ilmakiur*, a traditional Rannikonian barometer of saltpeter and fossils set in clay. The stone darkened to forecast rain, and speckled with swelling salt in clear weather. It was currently an indecisive slate gray.

"And there's our man," Eumelia said, nodding towards the tall blond man in a mushroom cap leaving the Jooga.

"Did Pander have a plan for this?" Arild asked. "Does he expect us to wrestle a werewolf?"

"If he is a werewolf, he's a reluctant one," Eumelia said. "Lycanthropes used to run up here to hide and find a cure at the Academy. There are a hundred days without darkness, no full argent moon at night. So, he's probably not good at skin-changing on command."

Arild helped her to her feet. Lund was more concerned with the Pokinutiner-woman, and Arild and Eumelia reached him before he turned his head south from the Prospekt.

"Dr. Lund, come with us," Eumelia said.

"What's this about?" he asked.

"You're wanted as a fugitive from Murmur," said Arild. "So, you have a choice. Cooperate with us, help us on an important job, and we'll let you walk away. Otherwise, we throw you in a cage, smother you with an ether-soaked rag, and haul you in chains back to Krahold. Understand?"

"And before you think of running, we have your shaman," Eumelia said.

Lund could only blink and twitch his eyes in stunned silence.

"Hey, Dr. Lund," Eumelia said. "She's alive. It's just negotiations."

"Come along quietly," Arild said.

He revealed a pistol, concealed in his coat.

"We wouldn't want to make a scene. Silver is expensive."

Lund mumbled and nodded. He stumbled forward, found his footing, and allowed the pair to escort him north up Scheznik Avenue, cross Villa's Bones, the Log Station, and Chuhaister into the Severnayan Forest. It was there that the

Salmacis met with the Pretender's men and camelry. Karl-Dareiausch Faramarsi-Branderhof-Trebechavsky, the Pretender in the Den and Vice Arteshbod of the Verca, was a short, plump man with the paradoxical look of someone who was both a cosmopolitan and extremely inbred. His clothing looked expensive and slapdash, with a Skeironish military coat over a Merovene jacket and a Waylander shirt. He wore jeweler in the style of Arada, along with a traditional battle mask, pretensions of the eastern heritage dotted through his name. He held a kontos with a single-shot flintlock built into the head of the lance, a weapon used by the cataphracts and grivpanvar of the Aradic peoples. Rather than a horse, however, he rode a giant arctic camel.

He commanded some thirty men, dispersed through the forest on the backs of smaller arctic camels. The riders lead camels with swivel guns mounted between the humps, a troop of zamburaks. Three of them had guns trained on Kingfisher, Fade, and Mageirissa.

"So, do you know these people?" Mageirissa asked.

"No," Lund said, scanning the company for any familiar face or insignia. "No idea."

He shifted away from a cruel-eyed camel that had it out for him, swaying back and forth like a rearing cobra in a wool sock. The arctic variety had a nasty habit of headbutting and clotheslining unfamiliar pedestrians with their long necks and would vomit up the contents of their stomach. A desert dromedary's spit is a nasty surprise, but an arctic camel's wet torrent can lead to a particularly foul-smelling death by hypothermia.

Unlike the dromedary, which focused its stores in one large hump, these shaggy creatures sported an even layer of protective fat. They rather resembled bloated alpacas with comically long legs. The Pretender's camel stood some three meters tall, bred for bulk like a draft horse.

Mageirissa shook the butterfly off her hood and mumbled, "Got your butterfly, by the way."

"Sorry about all this," Lund said. He took off his floppy cap and softly wrung it.

"We are the Band of Bastards, and I am Karl-Dareiausch Faramarsi-Branderhof-Trebechavsky, Count of the Southern Canton of Den," announced the overdressed man with a broad, sweeping gesture. "I'm sorry about all this. It's a pitiful position you're in, but hopefully, we can put this initial unpleasantness behind us and come to each other's mutual aid."

"What do you want from us?" asked Kingfisher. "You attacked me. Where are these pleasantries coming from?"

The harpy's face pivoted towards an old woman. Lund turned to look at the hag, just in time to see the woman's head descend from the treetops and settle back onto the nest of scarves around her neck.

"Yes, yes, about that," said the Pretender. "Sometimes one needs a show of force before the negotiations can begin. A shot across the bow, a display of... positioning. That woman is one of our battalion's exotics, Old Dezdha. A witch from the Woods of Narvany."

"Detaching and remotely animating organs is an old but powerful technique," said Fade. "What kind of powers are you running with, Count?"

"Any we can get," said the Pretender. "It's why we wanted you and the harpy. It's like the old treasure-finding parties. Priests, witch-diggers, scouts, and diviners pouring over maps and tossing arrowheads. All rather adventurous, no?"

"Are you in charge of this company?" asked Lund.

"Oh, well, my business partner, Polybius Pander, and I are the financiers. We control the purse," said the Pretender. "But we leave the matters militant to Commander Fiala and his brave lieutenant here, and his wife, the glue that keeps our battalion running."

Arild and Eumelia did not care for the Pretender's mangled flattery, with the look of a couple who would rather be paid more than buttered up.

"Polybius Pander… that sounds like a Tirving name, Etesian," Fade said. "Who is really running this company?"

"We don't care about nations, just our client's interests," said Eumelia. "Pander has his deals, the count has his ambitions, and we just do what we're told."

"My birthright," corrected the Pretender. "Skeiron money paid for this port, but the Imperator did not honor his interests. My father and grandfather bought up the debts of Northernmost's investors, and I inherited ninety-five percent of the port. Once we pry off that dragon, I will reincorporate this town into a proper county in union with the Throne of the Fallen. I have the Tall Man's word."

"Good luck," said Fade, trying to puzzle out who this Tall Man could be. "Just beat the dragon and steady as she goes."

"Ah, you see, I have planned for that," said the Pretender. "This is why we're here, why we've seized you. We seek a dragonslayer, the Killer of the Lindorm of Deorland, the Slayer of Roteschuppen of Ruhren, the Eater of the Ethelinda of Widsith. The White Whirlwind."

"I know that name, from an old story," Kingfisher said, her voice drifting away into old memories of dockyard singers. "The *Kingavila*. What is it?"

"It's a demon, I've heard," said Eumelia. "A monster bound in chains, forced to do the bidding of saints. There's a Timorat tale of a creature called Konekarje Ebajalg, a mighty whirlwind bound in an oak tree in a grove desecrated by incestuous lovers. There's another story, of a woman driven to kill her daughter or a daughter who killed her mother… in any case, the dead woman became a vicious maiden of air, Ilmatutar or Virmalised or the Pale Mavka. The story is found far and wide. In Favonia, the Confederates of Yoaga called her

Dagwanoenyent, and the Oyandoni named her Kaniehtiio of the Winter Warband."

"I believe it's some kind of a weapon," said the Pretender. "A staff or poleaxe made of the bones of a sage. But it could be a creature. The prophecy was vague."

"It's a legendary hero," said the lieutenant. "Why else would it be sealed in a tree? You can just take a sword. Someone called Kingavila, the White Fox, a creature that dances with the dead and wears a crown of fingernails that makes the wearer invisible."

"Yes, I know," said the Pretender. "That is why I had a deed to the Severnayan hinterlands drawn up, just in case. If it is indeed a hero capable of destroying dragons, I want it appeased. Loyal."

"This is a deplorable plan," said Fade, as if delivering a diagnosis. The lieutenant glanced back with nervous agreement and blew a staccato series of cold puffs from his mouth.

"Well, that's not for you to decide," said the Pretender. He tried to sniff contemptuously, but the weather plugged his nose with molasses-thick mucus. After a piggish snort and throaty cough, he muttered, "Let's go, I'm already sick of this cold."

They gathered up their company and headed north, past the walls of raised earth and through the forest, until they met with a second party flying the battalion's colors. They were freezing, marching beyond the shadows of Blessed Danica's Mountains, whose leeward wind, the dry Danican, protected the port from some of the arctic's worst terrors and warmed the south of Hyperborea. Now they stood in the Frost King's Roar, a brutal katabatic wind that stripped the port's deeper hinterlands to the bone and buried the Severnayan interior in snow. The roar was the great weapon of the Hyperboreans, and the Severnayans knew to avoid its glacial wrath.

"Only outlanders would make this mistake," Lund noted.

He replaced his cap, and pulled it down over his ears.

Leading the mercenary band was a man in a blue cap. He had a somewhat dark complexion, with thick eyebrows and a thicker jaw. Behind them was a carnival of monsters best left unseen by the people of the port, men with the heads of dogs, a creature like a hyena in the shape of a man, and a dozen ogres, cruel creatures with stony skin standing three meters tall.

The troop of dogheads wore half-skirts over their trousers, covering their swollen rumps. Their snakeskin belts hung low with hooked knives, scavenged pistols, and rations of dried rats and smoked fish. Beetle-like pins decorated both their belts and vests of pink-dyed sheepskin. Most were young males, though they had a few female camp-followers with them, standing only about a meter and a half tall and covered in coiling blue cloth and lacquered crocodile leather, perfumed with fruit juice. The ogres were well-armed and armored, with plate and mail over their traditional snow leopard skins, their clubs worked iron rather than stone or wood. Metal reinforced their horns, spines, and tusks, and most still wore their post-hibernation coats.

"He's leading an army of trolls," muttered Lund to Fade, using the Boreal term for any other bipedal, at least somewhat intelligent wight capable of thaumaturgy, a humanoid that was not a human and not an elemental.

It was imprecise, but all he had for this nightmarish rabble. Fade did not respond, even with a nod, noting that some of the dogheads and ogres were tattooed with marks of gnomish slavers. Modern humanity was dangerous prey for the sagani, but men often turned a blind eye to elementals enslaving trolls. Most of the dogheads destroyed them with scarification, and the ogres had purged themselves of the spells.

"Ogres hold that they are Nature's curse-breakers," Mageirissa noted. "And it is true, at least in function. While curses are only broken by following their rules, it seems that it is Natural Law that an ogre can digest a curse. Perhaps that is why they were brought here."

"They're going to eat the people in the port?" Kingfisher whispered.

"Well, that would end the curse," Mageirissa said, hunching down to draw less attention.

Kingfisher locked eyes with the hyena-man. The creature ran its tongue across its blood-stained teeth. She didn't want to show weakness in front of the Kaftar, so she hissed.

The Kaftar let out a rumbling laugh as a wave of heat dried its dense hair. Fade was rather astonished by the creature. It looked like some bestial hulk, but wore a leatherbound grimoire on one hip, a book of gunner's field charts on the other, and the heavy apron of a tinker or smith. The creature had a linstock-spear strapped to its back, a pole with a pair of intertwined silver serpents coiling up into a galvanic fork capable of generating electrical fires, used to both light artillery breeches and shock or stab foes and retreating subordinates. This slavering hyena demon was an artillery officer.

Mageirissa approached the leader of the ogres, the tallest, fattest, and hairiest male of the bunch, dressed in fine black boots suited to wade through snow. A beehive hung from the ring of his spear, the chilled honey slowly dripping onto the censer below. Ogres have an exceptional sense of smell, so the captain clouded the air with expensive perfume and ostentatious incense. Mageirissa offered him a gift of food, a bundle of goat jerky originally intended for the Jooga. The towering captain raised his head, and called her a "sweet ogree," his jutting tusks adding a slight lisp. His sausage fingers wiped honey across the bridge of her nose. She nodded and thanked him, and his ursine ears twitched. Ogres, to their credit, value offerings, honesty, and oaths. Their scavenging, bullying, and gluttony are, in their eyes, a way of purifying the world of weakness and impurity and devouring the fetters of the dead. They desecrate corpses to draw the ambient evil of the world into the flesh, a faith of sin-eating. It's why they appreciate other carrion-eaters, like the kaftars and harpies.

"Count Faramarsi-Branderhof," Pander paused to catch his breath, "–Trebechavsky."

"Mr. Pander," said the Pretender.

"We will meet the commander's force at the tree line," Pander said, referring to the point at which trees stop growing and there's nothing but an arctic wasteland.

Polybius Pander was an Etesian aristocrat of Tirving, and wore the iconic Eurian conical cap, similar to the Freedman's pileus of the Merovene vanguard. The cap was essentially an affectation. The Etesians fled the fabled city of Meltemia during its sacking four thousand years ago, sailing out of the Winedark and settling in the Septentrine Archipelago, fighting its native giants to near-extinction. They are most prominent on Tirving, east of Wayland, and have so thoroughly mixed with the Brandmen, Wenians, Thulean-skeirons, and the other races of the Isles that they have no distinct traits but that cap. No language, no cuisine, no racial features. So damn it, they were going to wear that cap whenever possible.

"Do the Etesians have some esoteric claim to Northernmost?" Fade asked him. "Are you the other five percent of the Baron's claim?"

"Count," corrected the Pretender.

"Sure," said Fade, without breaking eye contact with the Etesian. "What's your place in this, Pander?"

"For the empire," said Pander, with a smile.

He took Fade by the shoulder and pulled him aside.

"Help me here, countryman, it's a patriotic duty. And it can be lucrative."

"What do you mean?" Fade asked, closing the distance with Pander.

"I'm an agent of the Imperial Vulturnine Combine," said Pander, showing a badge with a stylized Carnwennan flying fox. "And the Boreal Surveying and Prospecting Corps."

"Are we… invading?" Fade whispered. "Why here?"

"No, no, my boy," said Pander. "It's just a matter of the white metal trade. Tsokiri prospectors have found tin in their northeastern frontier. About fourteen fortnights back. Best to strike while the iron is hot, or the tin is still cold, whatever the case may be."

The Septentrine Empire was built on, of all things, tin. The ancient Argetese, Mitzan, Euric, and Argaman empires forged their empires in brass. While copper is a ubiquitous metal, tin is somewhat rare. The tin-hungry tyrants of the Winedark tracked the white metal's trade routes, terminating in the lands of the Wenian barbarians, in the Septentrine archipelago. Even today, ninety percent of the world's tin trade lies in the Septentrine Empire's hands. The rest lies on the western coast of Zephyria and in the island nations of Alunsina, Au'iowion, and Selatano, in the Farflung Sea off Vulturnus. The other great naval powers of the world have made claims and trade deals, but they're so remote from Aquilo that they're barely profitable. One lost ship can make a whole year's enterprise a catastrophic failure, and Septentrine privateers know where to strike.

"Tin? This is about tin?" Fade said. "Oh, you can't imagine how disappointing that is."

"Why?" Pander said. "It is a great business."

"I… I was expecting something a bit more epic than a land grab and mining sabotage," Fade said. "Give me a knight with a skeleton face. Or some kind of… murder wizard… This dragonslayer is something spectacular, right? Can we pretend it's about that?"

"I think you're missing an opportunity," whispered Pander.

"Don't tell the harpy. It would disappoint her," said Fade.

"She's a guileless romantic."

Fade caught back up to the company, and Pander followed.

"You're a mixed lot, aren't you?" Fade said to Eumelia, the least uptight human in the company, as she spoke to some of the camp followers in the wagon, complaining about the cold and the odd journey.

"Yes, your sigil is a knight on a yellow horse," said Kingfisher. "But you're not knightly."

"We were, once," she said. "We were founded as one of the Clean Free Companies in the Age of Plagues and Curses. By a group of bastard sons of nobles from Verka, the Den, and the Brass Duchy. They were the immune, the untouched by diseases, and with the great resistance of the nobility. They slew bandits and escorted plague doctors and census women. That was in, uh, 2109. The four-company battalion has changed quite a lot in its four-hundred and forty years, breaking and reforming and gathering men from across the rivers and wisent lanes of Aquilo. We are no longer bastard knights, but their descendants."

"Mercenaries," Kingfisher spat.

"Of course," said Eumelia. "It's good work. There is always a need for war and peacekeepers. The bison drovers need someone to fight off the lions and griffons during the transhumance. The Blue Lords always need their rivers defended and kings fear a conspiracy of their lords. But the locals are often inadequate or inconvenient, and there are too many monsters in the world to let the city watches go unmanned. Nobody has mustered a standing national army since the defenders of Timea petrified the Solar Dynast's Twenty Thousand. You've heard that story, the Gorgon's Lighthouse, harpy?"

"Yes," Kingfisher said. "The great hero Diomon tracked down the Abomination of Teolon, avoided her petrifying gaze with trickery, and slew her with the Sword of Blinding Light."

"Eh, three soldiers poisoned her water supply and cut off her head as she slept," corrected Eumelia, "But basically that. We barely fight, to be honest. We're largely a garrison force, getting fat on the coin of paranoids."

"We have an army," said Fade.

"You have navies," said Eumelia. "And glorified boarding parties in nice uniforms. No different than us, pressing people into service and fighting for plunder."

"Slaves," said Fade. "Impressment, blackbirding, coal-sacking. It's slavery. No wonder pirates plow the rivers and seas."

"Look kid, we're not going to brand you," said Eumelia. "You can walk away once we're done. Maybe a day, at most. Humans don't enslave humans. I'm not going to break the promise."

Fade knew humans practiced slavery. They simply used euphemisms like debtors, hereditary contractors, impressed labor, conscription, emergency compulsion, indentured servants, and the compacted. Or the alteration and chimeration of people until they are no longer legally human.

"And Lund?" Fade asked.

"He's different. He has a bounty on his head," said Eumelia. "That's an official matter, between him and his people."

"On what charge?" Fade asked, narrowing his eyes.

"He's a werewolf," said Eumelia. "At least, that's what the red paper said."

"He's no werewolf," said Fade with a chuckle. "Sailed with him during a full moon. I've seen him handle silver. His family's a bunch of bourgeois Murmurmen, not the get of Hirtus."

"There are wolfmen in the north," she said, "and as far south as Karmec. Wolfmen know to chart the passage of the Philosopher's Moon, and the Priestly Star Aschere. Does your friend keep an astrolabe on him, by chance?"

"Yes, but most arcane philosophers do," Fade said. "If they can afford it."

Kingfisher had seen these charts on Sir Eol Volganin's clock and on many ships. It was a mystifying sight, the intricate dance of brass hands sliding across latitudinal plates and wirework marking the constellations. The most elaborate astrolabes marked the most important celestial bodies with precious metals and jewels. The Philosopher's Moon was the gold to the True Moon's silver, its great dark seas hollow spaces filled with powerful mysteries that counteracted the Silver Mother's influence. Sailors feared it, for its passage could still the tides.

And just as the Sun keeps the physical world warm, Aschere keeps the spiritual world alive, and it's said that yliaster enters the realm from its scintillating radiance, ebbing and flowing as it twinkles with the True Light. The star fascinated the miracleworkers of old, who set it in the constellation of the World-Wolf or Houndshead and called it Alhabor and the Deer Hunter. Werewolves could draw power from it directly, and held the mysteries of the moon within them, the reason for their rule over the Hirpic Empire. The Wolf Emperors were not only terrifying savages on the field of battle, but dangerous sorcerers who commanded tides, dusts, moonlight, illusions, and scrying mirrors. Just as the moon reflected the Sun, the Imperial Lineage held sway over reflection, and could see a fleet sailing down the Turba from a reflecting pool in the palace of Luperco.

Werewolves are hunted not just because they are murderous brutes, but because of that far more dangerous trait, imperium. There are still wolf cults dedicated to placing a Child of the Moon on a throne, any throne, even as new republics rise across the world's stage.

Other ideologies fear not the might of the beast, but its odd egalitarianism. The Hirtus dynasty was not passed from father to son, but from an aristocrat biting a chosen inheritor. At times, family picked family, but such blood dynasties reeked of kingship and tyranny, and so frequently ended on the silvered spears of the lictor's argent.

And thus, noble families often fear werewolves as much as the shepherds. And so, Fade knew that if Lund was allowed to be taken to the courts of Murmur, he would be disposed of at their earliest convenience.

"Can you answer one more question?" asked Kingfisher.

"I have nothing else to do," said Eumelia, as she struggled with the snow.

"Who shot at you?" asked Kingfisher. "In the Academy, I mean. Someone shot at your… hag, and retreated, I think."

"I don't know who that could have been," Eumelia said. "Probably a frightened city watchman. The old bat scares me too, and I work with her."

The company marched for what seemed like an hour but was likely shorter. Kingfisher was the worst off, quaking and huddling against Mageirissa for warmth. Her legs were not designed for long marches, but snatching and lifting, and she was insulated against the cold burst of diving into water but not persistent trudging. She needed to fly to generate heat but knew the company wouldn't allow her to take off.

Fade took off his overcoat and set it over her shoulders. He picked up a fallen branch, ripped the water out of it with a desiccation spell, and set it alight.

"Trap the heat with a cushion of air," he instructed. "It's easy."

"I know," she said. "But it sucks in heat from everyone else. I- I- thank you, by the way."

"Don't be afraid to ask for help," Fade said. He reached over to pop up the collar to protect her neck, and to keep it out of his mind. He distracted himself with mental catalytic and reagent tables, but his thoughts drifted back to her. Maybe he could help her fly with levity of litharge, allowing the transfer of weight. Then again, decaying red lead was dangerous work.

They trudged on in cold misery until Lund gently touched Mageirissa and Fade's shoulders and pointed towards his left, behind a tree along a glacial eschar. Fade got Kingfisher's attention as well. She first noticed several small red deer eating lichens, and the long shadow of a man, but her eyes soon caught the shape of the massive elk-like creature casting it.

The beast was a Pantheon. Like their sylphic masters, these celestial elk were known by many names – kite, keresh, peryton, tharandus, and parandrus-- and were said to be blessed by all the gods. They were reindeer the size of moose or oxen, with the tail and ears of a fox, the eyes of a cat, the mouth of a wolf, a shaggy mantle around the shoulders, cloven hind feet, mannish forefeet, and the wings of an owl. Like mundane reindeer, both the stag and doe have antlers, but they appear to be silver and thornier, etched with glowing specks connected by thin lines. Each year, their antlers grow into a different constellation, mirrored. The wings grow during the winter and shed in warm climes or hot summers; polar pantheons keep their wings permanently.

This Pantheon changed the coloration and patterns of its fur and feathers to match the trees behind it. The unaltered pelt remained its naturally translucent, glassy white, dotted with silvery or lilac stars known as *"mullets."* Twinkling, starry phantasms danced between its antlers. Dangerously, a pantheon could hide in the night sky, a living constellation against the full dark.

"Watch yourself," whispered Lund. "They eat hearts and can shape the winds."

Indeed, they embody the winds and conjure storms, and only sylphs could ride them. Despite their solitary, predatory nature, they sometimes lead packs of mundane reindeer, red deer, or achlis, shepherds of the sylph's 'fairy cattle.' They also appear to have a bellowing tongue of their own and are said to be intelligent enough to have a demonic king or patron eidolon, Furfur.

"I don't like those blood red and blue marks under its antlers," Lund added. "That's either an intimidation display or a mating signal. Either way, that spells danger… I wish I had the chance to sketch it, though. Fascinating thing."

"It's quite beautiful," Kingfisher whispered back. Though she reconsidered when the creature turned its head. The long mouth unsettled her, as if someone had sliced open the cheeks of a reindeer.

"I wonder how it tastes," added Mageirissa. "Like a deer or like a predator? Have you ever eaten bear meat? Gamy, and pungent, even if they eat mostly nuts and berries. Somehow both greasy and coarse."

Lund turned towards the lieutenant and got his attention. He pointed at the beast, and the lieutenant quickly signaled for his men to ready their guns and spotting glasses. Pander had his ogres, under command of a huge, canny one named Fat Fasolt, ready their barbed pikes like spears against a charge. Fosolt beat his chest to rally his forces, and prepared to don his manticore hide. The dogheads scattered into the pines to skirmish among the branches.

The Pantheon retreated. At first, its withdrawal was met with relief, but the company watched in shock as the pantheon hopped up into the air and swooped down onto a polar bear menacing one of its shepherded achlis. The polar bear reared up, but the pantheon knew to keep out of range of its claws and kicked the bear between the eyes. The stunned bear collapsed backward, and the pantheon took the opportunity to gore the bear in the stomach before withdrawing and sidestepping. It cautiously hopped around, found an opening, and then gored again. As the bear weakened, the pantheon swooped down and ripped open the bear's throat with its teeth. It retreated again, and let the bear bleed to death, before extracting its heart with its oddly human hands.

The company hastily marched on in a tight formation, a phalanx of pike and shot ready to kill the merciless beast. The remover-hag chimed her bell and cackled, and the dogmen snapped and howled, warding off the pantheon with clashing spear and sickle.

Several minutes off, the sound of a baby crying echoed through the pines, sharp and shrill and terrible. Eumelia pushed ahead, plowing through the snow for the child. The lieutenant ran after her, telling her to watch out. He grabbed her, telling her that it was likely a trap. She calmed a bit.

"The lungs on that thing," said Karl-Dareiausch. He cringed and raised his scarf to muffle his ears.

Kingfisher scolded herself for her heartless ease with a scratch across her foot. The sound of a baby crying didn't distress her. It wasn't in her instincts. Harpies simply didn't cry like that. She flew up, her captor giving her some slack on her rope. She spotted it easily after focusing the sound to her ears, in a cradle of stones. She swooped towards it, then imagined the many ways that picking up a baby with her hideous talons could go, and instead let Mageirissa take it.

"Who left that here?" asked Fade, narrowing his eyes.

Mageirissa held the baby in her arms. Its eyes were fierce and cloudy, its mouth wide, its skin golden-brown. Its left leg was clubbed and kicked at the air.

The baby continued its shrill cry. It made Kingfisher nervous, and she began to quietly countersing.

Mags opened up her coat, looked at Eumelia, and tapped a hook under her apron that held up the breast panel of her dress. "Should I..."

"Oh god," Eumelia said, covering her mouth in horror. "Did we rip you away from a child?"

"No," said Mags, leaning in and then whispering, "Part of my, uh, role... A bit of magic, and I take herbs to, you know. Flow."

"Leave that thing be," ordered Fade in a harsh whisper.

"You're a wetnurse?" Eumelia asked.

"That, midwife, chef, healer, shaman," Mags said. "Woman of the world."

She turned the baby in her hands and looked at its strange, thin teeth. She nodded at Fade, grabbed the baby by the leg, and dashed it against the rocks. There was a chorus of screams and gasps, until Fade pointed at the remains; a wounded blackbird struggled on the stone, its long proboscis flickering through a shattered, tubular beak. Mags stomped at the creature's head, killing it.

"It's a groundborn," Fade explained as he kicked snow over the corpse. "Some say they're the souls of nameless stillborns, but they're just parasitic birds, shapeshifters."

Mags shivered, covered herself tightly, and turned away in disgust.

"What was that thing going to do?" Eumelia demanded, angry at no one in particular.

"What babies do," said Mags. "And what vampires do. Someone put it here, as a trap."

"Which means we're near something special," said Karl-Dareiausch.

"Boundless optimism," muttered Fade.

The company had turned slightly off course after the shock of the false child, only realizing that they had drifted towards the frozen sea when they noticed a heavy anchor chain looped into a harpoon crafted from a tree, a mighty frost giant tool for spearing and dragging up whales and lesser krakens, the only food that could sustain them in this climate.

Karl-Dareiausch cautiously scanned a map as they moved and called for the company to stop some fifteen minutes afterward in a frozen palsa mire. Freshly free from the deep snow, the camels stopped their prancing gait to cautiously prod the peat mounds for soft spots and running water. The high arctic sun painted the icy pools a pale tangerine spotted with pink algae. Kingfisher took in the famed Cinnabar Sky of the north, when the sun refuses to fully rise or set.

"It should be here," the Pretender proclaimed to the gathering company. "During last year's thaw, some foragers stumbled across a cavern here. It had been buried for ages, but the dragon's decades of melting and refreezing finally cracked it open. They only went a short way inside, scared off by sigils and what sounded like breathing. I think it's our remote."

Some white grousehares fluttered through the trees, birds with the heads and hindlegs of rabbits. The males had their summer antlers. Lund noted that several varieties of horned hares accompanied these wolpertingers on the ground level, usually a sign of magical experimentation. Rabbits breed quickly, so many a disused wizard or alchemist's laboratory spawned wild populations of grousehares, jackalope, rasselbocks, and the one-horned *mi'raj*.

That diversity worried Lund. A fresh lab will have a large and diverse population, usually of pairs and singletons that can't stabilize. They will collapse into one or two strains over time. This was a robust population with multitudinous variety in the subarctic, a clime unable to sustain such density. There must have been a powerful source of vital transmutation in the earth.

"Perhaps someone dreams of rabbits," Fade suggested to Lund. "We're seeing the *Ug*, the Faerie-Reverie."

"What's that?" Kingfisher asked.

"Nobody knows why we dream," Fade said. "Perhaps you are processing your thoughts, experiences, apprehensions. Sorting them into stories. Magical beings – the Sagani, your great monsters and sorcerers – bleed out the excess yliaster."

"Like when you have to get up at night because you drank too much," Kingfisher whispered.

"Yes, yes, not the comparison I would have made in mixed company, but true." Fade said. "Mixing the substance of Reality into the patterns of dreams... it breathes life into faeries and horrors, enchanted creatures and living nightmares. The lairs and mountains of salamanders and gnomes are oft warped into wonders; the realms of the mighty are dream-lands for this reason. And it's why even a witch of good intent may be driven out of town."

"It would also explain our visitor," Lund said.

A creature like a gibbon with the head and feet of a horned rabbit watched from a stripped tree around a standing stone. Its ears were long and its pelt black, unlike those of the arctic hares around it. The party tried to avoid its shining, golden eyes, and a few dogheads yelped at it. The púcai could shapeshift and speak upon reaching their hundredth year, and few are foolish enough to show their face to a mimic, particularly one as mischievous as the puck. These were faerie creatures of the magician's laboratory, like the rodent-men called the *far darrig*, with some remote islands entirely conquered by their space-warping warrens.

The tree itself was a deformed spruce, stripped and cold-bitten on the windward side. While perfectly natural, deliberately shaped *krummholz* trees are a common marker in the eldritches of the sylphs.

"I wonder if creatures develop towards bipedalism so they can better use magic," Lund said, tapping his lower lip with his index finger. "To hold catalysts and materials, to move and channel with arms and digits."

"What do you mean?" Chestimir replied. "Developed?"

"There are pressures in an environment, and aspects of creatures that make them more likely to reproduce," Lund said, scratching his lip. "Perhaps this Puca's ancestors were hares who stood upright to leap better through the trees, but soon found them better able to work magic, and the form accelerated down that path. Perhaps the gods do not give creatures mannish forms to be magical, but a mannish form allows one to be more magical."

"Strange," Chestimir said. "So, what of the harpy? The harpies? Aren't men just the children of the four high elementals?"

"Hybrids and chimerae do complicate the theory," Lund said. "But they don't disprove it. There may be some sort of transmission. Ancient Aradan cults in the Kermi still practice sky burial with harpies. Perhaps some humanity bloomed in the vultures."

Lund turned his head and licked his lips. He wiped a thick, dark hair from his mouth, and hid his hand in his coat. The cold and his imagination got the better of him, dredging up a brief, primordial change. His hand shrunk and shed its fur with a wisp of steam. He wondered if Chestimir noticed.

The Kaftar's conducted heat through the pingo and surrounding palsas, thawing the frozen peat to a workable softness. The company scoured the snow and boggy soil for a depression, hitting the ground with prods, pikes, and shovels. Kingfisher sang and waited for the hollowness to echo back to her, the way the old sea hags used to find caves hidden in the cliffs. The shifting reverberations signalled loose snow rather than the muffled groan of frozen earth. There were hollow places in the ground shorn up by worked stone, tubes that once held a post, and trestle carved from windthrown trees. A gearbox lay smashed to cogs and cranks and left to rust; the dynamo was gone. A windmill once crowned this cavern, the heart of sylph industry.

"It's here," she said, outlining the cavern's mouth with a whirl of her mitten.

Mageirissa sent down a small tremor to confirm and had

Lund hold her body as she projected her spirit into the earth. She said there was nothing living in there above worms and insects. The company excavated the hollow with shovels and the ogres' sharpened bowls, aided by the smothering furnace-heat of the kaftar's sorcery. Lund used a rotten-out log to create a pump, channeling the melt-off away from the cavern. The ogres and one of the larger men, Kaspar, cleared away the stones and branches that had settled in the narrow entrance once it was fully exposed and drained.

Kaspar's strength was terrible to behold. He had been a Cantonist, conscripted into the garrison schools of Tsokir as a child, to keep his father in line. He came from the Melkir who live in and around Gozhorod, a humble people who staged a brief tax uprising half a century ago against their Tsokiri cousins. For this, they were beaten down and forced to feed a fifth of their men to the imperial army. Everyone knew the rumors of the garrison schools, and the cruel officers and feral deserters they produced. Discipline not only involved corporal punishment, but corporal modification. His right eye was amber and feline, in the manner of the Tyger-blessed officers of the Skeironic Corps. Green, vascular cords flexed beneath Kaspar's pale skin as he crushed wooden beams and shattered frozen earth. He snarled like a great cat as he witnessed the frenzied decay in the darkness.

Beetles fought each other on the cave's mouth, devouring each other like victims of a long winter's famine.

"My spirit's touch will do that," Mags said sheepishly to Lund. "The hunger is its fuel, the price of ogre magic. I've used it to get sick patients to eat, colicky babes to nurse."

Kaspar loured at her and pulled out a stack of hardtack from his carrying case. Other men regarded Mageirissa with disgust or fear or averted their eyes. They kept far from her, just as they maintained a safe distance from Kingfisher, for on the western continents, witches projected from their flesh to torment sleepers and steal secrets.

Chestimir put on his Waylander-made respirator, lit a torch, shielded himself with a parvaise, and led a small detachment inside. Fade let out a harsh, steamy sigh when he saw Chestimir's bare forearm beneath the shield's straps; some Severnayan sawbones had spliced in a set of copper fire-tongs to replaced his radius and ulna and support a graft of swine-flesh.

Pander and the Pretender insisted that their four captives came in, along with the Kaftar. Eumelia and Arild remained outside.

Someone carved deep channels of sigils in the slick lime-stone walls, filling them in with gold and silver. Someone in the intervening centuries had chiseled off some of the precious metal, weakening the binding enchantment. The most outlandish symbol was the Drudenfuss or Elf-cross, the inverted pentagram that symbolized submission to the eldritches, the "kiss" of the elven foot.

"I think someone might have done our work for us," Fade said.

He clenched his jaw as the cave's acoustics twisted his quiet observation into a breathy hiss that lingered in the darkness. He scowled at the Elf-cross, as if the concentrated glare of his silvered eyes could scour that mark from the wall. He bristled at the arrogance of the Sagani, to poison the universal symbol of the star into a sign of oppression. He wondered what adamant shackles the world-spanning empires would forge from the few molten mysteries which remained. Rigid magical laws empower common humanity, bringing safety in regularity and Reason— but what would happen without the chimerical possibilities of dream-signs and open-ended enigmas?

"I must advise that you turn back," said Lund.

"There is no victory without risk," said the Pretender, but

there was a weak warble in his voice.

He moved deeper into the cavern, drawing a short sword.

Turning the bed, Chesti's torch illuminated a twisting tangle of roots. A dark crimson sap stained its gray bark with slick drips like the wax of a hanging candle. A net of fine silver chain ran through the roots, caked with resin, and engulfed by the growing tree, ebbing with arcane bindings and Aklo letters, the language of whorled stars used by the Eldest Race.

The Kaftar began a messy form of disenchantment, a fire fueled by ambient yliaster. Fire is often called a clumsy element, but a true master of pyrergy understands that it is a reaction rather than a form of matter, and it can be quite useful once one learns to alter its reactant and its output. One technique is to alter a fire to burn away silica, leaving only the molten metals of ore, or purifying air by burning aerial poisons and releasing clean oxygen. The problem is that such a working requires you to know the exact formula of the reaction, a depth of chemical knowledge beyond most people before the middle of the last century.

"Fade, help dispel the bonds," ordered Karl-Dareiausch, pointing out the sigils with his sword.

Fade glanced back at the Pretender with cold, dead eyes. A passing torch illuminated the pupils with a tigerish shine, startling the nobleman. Fade took out his notebook and calculated the longest second derivative of a fire spell he could manage, a nasty enchantment that would eat up yliaster and produce nothing but waste heat. He threw in some gunpowder as a catalyst and activated the spell with his bismuth rod.

"Ta-da," Fade said without joy.

Lund traced a train of chains burnt into the ground. They were brittle to the point that the clay alone gave them shape. They had been used as a consumptive, their binding properties and symbolic strength isolated and transferred to the roots. A few sharp, shallow scoops with his shovel uncovered a daisy chain of manacles and a bed of bent nails. The Pretender found a green-bronze rope chain so dense and flexible it resembled a serpent's spine. Sylphide witches used "viper-reins" to enslave animals as mounts, and such air-kissed copper would be animated with nerves of lightning and smeared with sedatives and poisons.

He turned to Fade upon hearing his breath quicken. Fade looked queasy and kept touching his knees, resisting the urge to bend down.

"I need to go," Fade mumbled.

"You'll stay until the bonds break," said Karl-Dareiausch.

Kingfisher's head fluttered like a clockwork toy as she glanced back and forth between Fade and the Pretender.

"Could he escort me outside? I'm not good with... underground," she said, slipping a few pinions free of Fade's greatcoat.

Chestimir looked at the pair. "Let them step outside, your Highborn. I will run out a message if you need them."

Karl-Dareiausch waved dismissively and told them to go.

"Thank you, my lord," Kingfisher said with a bow. She moved with face to the mouth of the cavern.

Outside, the men were shooing off a stray achlis, a type of elk with a long, soggy upper lip and long, rigid back legs that force them to sleep and sometimes walk standing up. Some sylphs have a taboo against eating animals that spend their lives walking on four legs, and breed these blundering brutes. The dogheads had climbed up to the top of the treeline to peer off into the arctic wastes, and perhaps spot a stray achlis ripe for the picking. As they scaled the branches, Kingfisher noticed that their half-skirts covered exposed, bright red buttocks, their trousers more like riding chaps. Despite the name, Dogheads were not canine, but a mannish relative of baboons.

"What happened to you?" Kingfisher asked Fade as he emerged from the cave.

"I felt a touch ill," said Fade. "Perhaps the atmosphere."

"What happened to you?" Kingfisher asked again. "Underground?"

"I don't want to talk about it," said Fade. "It was the binding spells and the darkness of the cave... I... it was upsetting."

"Understood," said Kingfisher with a nod.

"Thank you for pulling me out of there," said Fade. He bit his lower lip. He pulled a wad of dry tobacco from his pocket, and transferred its stimulating properties to the water of his canteen. He let Kingfisher drink first. She tried to hide it from him, but those wiry legs were not built for overland treks.

Lund emerged from the cavern, followed by the rest of the company.

"You burned out the binding spell," he said. "Whatever it was holding is loose."

The company moved northeast. Just as the trees began to thin and taiga became tundra, a hollow, windblown drone echoed, and the pines began to shake. Rather than a natural rustling that passed through the boughs in a rolling wave, this force targeted individual trees in a deliberate pattern.

It continued over a vast swath of the timberline, with sprays of settled frost and snow swirling up into the sky for hundreds of meters, like a spouting pod of whales. High pitched crackles rose from the patterned ground, and collapsed lithalsas, like fossilized faerie circles, rang with the noise of bells. A sound like an unseen brush sweeping across an endless canvas whispered and scratched beyond the pines. Sweep, sweep, sweeping everything away, painting nothing, defining nothing, pushing an amorphous whiteness around forever.

"If this goes foul, we're running," Fade whispered to Lund and Kingfisher. "I'd rather face a rifle line and the arctic than anything that can kill a dragon and needed that spell to trap it."

Chapter 7: Heavy Metal

It was not long after they left the cave that the sky-shattering shadow of a lonely tree loomed in the distance, rising from a stony hill blanketed in snow.

The binding hawthorn haunted those glacial erratics, a pale specter larger than any of its kind produced by nature. Its trunk yawned and wept, split wide as though struck by the ax blow of a giant. And yet it still lived.

Small white flowers overwhelmed the spiraling leaves and bloody berries, a gentle layer of pure snow covering a gruesome torment of thorns the size of crucifix nails. Blood trickled from the corpses of mice and voles impaled by gray shrikes, staining the pallid bark. These shrikes were one of many birds in the massive tree, song thrushes, circumpolar waxwings, cuckoos, and a merlin. There were too many birds in that tree. Too many of them albino, and all of them silent. The birds tore at the exposed wood, raw like soft red muscle. Death's-head hawkmoths drank from the dripping gore, crowding like beasts around the last lake in a drying land.

Blood.

Blood ran through that wood, not sap. The hollow within was distinctly amniotic. It was still warm and flowing, despite the chilling williwaw tumbling down the side of the Frost King, that glacial plateau visible on the horizon.

The lieutenant knelt down to retrieve something from the snow.

"This is a snaplock rifle," explained Arald, examining the frozen firearm. "Antique. Must be around two and a half centuries old."

Fade and Lund moved forward to inspect the unusual tissue, but stopped dead at the top of the hill, to overlook a scene of carnage.

This had been the site of a battle. No, a slaughter. This

must have been the bulk of the battalion, at least a hundred ri-flemen, four dozen cavalrymen, five score artillerymen, three score ogres, two hundred cynocephalic troopers, perhaps sixty camels, and some fifty women and children from the support train. Their bodies were covered in snow, fingers, and noses frostbitten, yet they could not have been dead for more than an hour with no snowfall in the meanwhile.

The lieutenant ran past Lund, paused, and shouted for his men to go to the ground at the crest of the hill, apart from a hand-picked group of ten riflemen and Eumelia. He turned to Lund and Fade and ordered them to follow his squadron and look for the wounded. Kingfisher and Mags followed.

Nobody stopped them.

The lieutenant was terrified by the fresh carnage, but a deeper, mystical horror filled him as he continued to spot snaplocks and signs of pike formations, sabot-loaded cul-verins primed to conjure griffins from their smoking clouds, and light cavalry dating back to the twenty-third century. Ei-ther the rest of the band fought an antiquated army, or this battlefield had substrata.

"Tell me if anyone finds a banner of this second force," Arald ordered.

Several of the dogheads uncovered soldiers in plate and shaggy-hoofed destriers, all frozen solid. One human scout cut off a frozen scrap of cloth with a coat-of-arms of some old Skeironic company, a blue goshawk on a field argent. The lieutenant was horrified by a line of burnt corpses, not a circu-lar bombard blast, but a spray of intense heat.

"It looks like dragon fire, but they wouldn't have frozen this quickly," the lieutenant said.

He glanced at Fade.

"Am I right?"

"Fire elementals can, oddly enough, freeze things faster than aquatics by drawing up the heat," Fade said. "It's one reason why dragons like to live on rivers."

However, all eyes soon turned to the battle's survivor.

A woman sat in the field of gore and ruination. An ogre's intestines lay wrapped up not half an arm's length away. A spine still attached to a hip bone drifted in a pool of mud and blood and viscera.

She was a beautiful white island in a sea of red tumult.

The woman was barely dressed, wearing little more than oxblood leather straps and belts connected by sliced vertebral rings. A rusted iron mask rested limply against her breast like a falling buffe and gorget, a grotesque creature with a grimacing muzzle with a tongue lolling between teeth biting a bridle. Circular frames had been welded to its eye sockets, resembling brutish spectacles. Only its antlers and wide, cupped ears indicated that it was supposed to be a stag rather than a snarling dog.

Or it's a pantheon, Lund considered.

Cones of yellow pollen and crushed joint-pine hung out of the muzzle's slits. Ephedra, a herb that sets the heart racing, kills the appetites and opens the throat and lungs.

The woman's head snapped up, and her diaphanous wrap fell from her bone headdress, adorned with the wings of a snowy owl, set to protect her ears.

She was taller than the average man, largely in the leg. Her skin was a bloodless ivory. Silver and iridescent starlight tinged her wild, white hair. A side-swept fringe covered her left eyebrow. A scrimshawed pinwheel spun around the base of a horsetail queue pulled through a vertebra.

Her soft, heart-shaped face tapered into a well-defined yet narrow jawline. Her large eyes slanted doubly, more snow leopard than any race of woman. Those crimson irides quaked, tracing silver-green streaks in the air like a flawed ruby tumbling past a torch.

It was then that one noticed her figure, all lean muscle, and feminine curves. The contrast of her gentle face and that powerful frame pushed her beauty towards the grotesque, exemplified by a swan neck widening into high and hefty shoulders. Her arms were a bit too long, her elbows set below the navel. She held her head at a tilt, cocked in something like languid curiosity. Combined with her headdress, she recalled a stag constantly prepared to lock antlers with a rival.

Everything about her was just left of wrong.

"Human albinos… they've blue eyes… not red," Mr. Fade whispered unevenly. "That… they don't shine like that either."

"Maybe it's an aberration," Mageirissa suggested, though the shaman's voice was faithless.

The headdress inspired unease in Lund until he noticed the absence of an arching band. Those bony bars were coated in soft, living velvet, rooted in her skull.

She had worried the velvet and quick of her antlers, scratching it until it was striated, and wrapped them in tight silver wire and chains adorned with teeth and rune-carved bone charms. The antlers failed to grow beyond a pair of upwardly tilting white rods, with only a single pair of prongs. Lund imagined that, despite the majesty of antlers, such growths would be horribly irritating to actually live with, shedding sheets of living velvet season after season.

"Are you… are you hurt?" said one of the soldiers, the boy Chestimir. "We have surgeons and a faith healer with us. In the Pokinutiner, er, traditions…"

She ignored him and rose to her feet. She wore a *naatsit*, a thong of reindeer leather normally worn indoors. Although covering little, they prevent sweat, that insidious killer, from gathering on the thighs. It was belted with a half-skirt of arctic fox tails sheathing stilettos. Like her curl-toed boots and other leathers, the *naatsit* was lacquered, dyed oxblood, and branded with arcane staves.

She tightened a pair of belts that snaked through the

cleaved skull of a pantheon, pulling it from a hole between her shoulder blades. Its antlers were pierced with holes, like a bone flute. This hollow resembled a gash in a rotten tree filled with a thousand secret evils.

Eumelia looked the nearly naked woman over, and, with a crooked smile, asked if she was cold. She chuckled nervously. The lieutenant muttered about how men dying of exposure will strip down to their underclothes before they go completely mad.

Gooseflesh raised on Fade's arms when he realized that the pale woman was decisively *not* cold. What would have been tantalizing in the bedroom was upsetting and wrong at this polar latitude. This was tropical wear, for comfort, nine-hundred and seventy kilometers from the pole. It was like seeing an orange slice in a bowl of gravy.

Lund, at this point, silently but vigorously gestured to his friend, miming the antlers.

"Where is your army's whorehouse?" asked the pale woman, softly, her eyes still focused on the nearby heap of offal and a mass of iron.

"Were you... a camp follower... for the other army?" Chesti sputtered. "We... our company has some girls in the baggage train, but... not a house."

"Oh, that's a pity," she said. "I want to cuckold your fathers after I'm done killing their sons."

She smiled.

The boy screamed.

That initial softness faded. She was sharp now. That tongue was sharp, befitting a skald. Her eyes were sharp, slit-like a great cat's. Her ears were sharper – dainty, vulpine things shadowed by her antlers, swiveling to catch the company's frightened whispers. And that smile revealed that her teeth were the sharpest of all. Hers was a predatory, cruel smile, both delightful and hateful, the shark upon the seal.

"I… I think that's who we're looking for," said the lieutenant. "I… I found the commander… part of him… She
wasn't a *survivor*. This other army wasn't an enemy. Predeces-
sors, more likely."

"We have to run," Lund said to Mags and Mr. Fade.
"Now."

This was a creature of many names: drude, sylvana, hulder,
light elf, sidereal, samodiva, vila, sylphide, *Voör*. One of the
White People of the Winds and Stars, the Hyperboreans, the
Lords of Air, the mightiest and rarest of the elementals, the
first children of the first son of Urizen, Rintra Thieriel. It was
once said that elves moved with an alien grace, which Lund
never understood until she darted forward. She was leaping,
bounding, and cutting through the air without a sound, even
as her horn, bullroarer, and skull drum smacked against her
hip. It was an elk's trampling sprint, it was the gale, it was an
arrow flight. Her pace was sevenfold that of a human, a terrible white blur. She was behind the group in a wink.

"I don't think running is an option," Fade said. He gestured at the dead soldiers, camels, and ogres all around.
"These fine gentlemen outnumbered our little sortie and were
better armed."

The pale sidereal's eyes shot Fade's way, those small irides
quivering uncannily. There were fangs in the smile, only fangs.

"Son of Man, why do you breathe my air?" asked the Sylphide.

"My… lady, please, we mean you no harm," Kingfisher
pleaded as she landed, balanced on a sword embedded in the
ground. "I… I wish to study the subtle arts of the Lords of
Air. Please, I can–"

"Subtle arts?" snorted the Sylphide.

She stepped onto another sword embedded in the earth,
whirling, dancing to the butt of an impaled linstock.

"I'll show thee subtle fucking arts, thou cock-footed cunt

of a chimera. I'll snap thy merrythought in my mouth and shit out a miracle."

The sortie got a good look at the elk skull on her back as she spun on the hilt. It appeared be chimerical at first glance, with two pairs of shaped antlers. One pair projected from behind eye sockets stuffed with feathers, like a curling display rack, with the second sweeping out on a horizontal plane, tangled up with bony wheels. The jawbone had also been cleaved, each mandible shaped into an ax whose iron-capped teeth bit into the frame of a stave-branded adarga.

A hundred hilts and a hundred handles, leagues of rope and barbed grappling chains, flocks of fletching, piles of cloth and defiled banners, and hints of ten score specimens of arcane wargear could be seen in that hollow in her back, as though she had been run through by legions.

And in its depths, catching the firelight as she turned, were the trophy skulls of those same legions.

"My lady… we've come to petition your aid," said the approaching Karl-Daeriausch, hands up.

The lieutenant glared at him, subtly gesturing with his nodding head to pull back. "What… what happened here? Was there a third party? This second army? The dragon? Did… you do this?"

"I'm not a lady!" she said. "My family were leather workers. Tanners, cordwainers, and cobblers. Fuck your soft-handed 'ladies.'"

"Please consider our offer–"

"No!" she barked.

"We will give you this land in exchange for your service," continued the Pretender. "You can *be* a lady. You can be your own queen if you want. Have Hyperborea. We will offer all of it to you. We just need your help against a dragon."

"I know I could be mine own queen," she said. "I have won crowns with ease, and thrown them away in boredom."

A ghastly whine rose on the wind. The air around her, once balmy, steamed with her rage and the sweat of battle.

"I know what is mine. Eternity does not need the sanction of mayflies."

Eumelia began, "We only–"

The lieutenant frantically tapped her shoulder.

"You want me to fight for you, in exchange for the right to live in my fatherland?" she said. "The nerve of these foul folk. The audacity of men."

"We only meant legally," Karl-Daeriausch said. "It's a deed."

The Sylphide rose up in a vastly inhuman bit of body language, arching her back, puffing up her chest, and holding her elbows out, hands positioned as if grasping a pair of vertical bars, as a prisoner in a cage. Fade noted the cord-like tendon that ran from the inner wrist to the elbow, and the tense rippling of dense muscle. Her lips peeled back to display that grimace. The reduction of her lips chilled the witnesses, as they were one of the few contrasting elements on a white-on-white face, leaving only the blood-red irides of her bulging eyes and the shadow-blackened plum of tongue and gums. The exposed skin of her chest and deeply defined abdomen came across as less of a sexual display than a threat, an apish oddity.

"It's… it's a legal document," Eumelia hastily explained, recoiling. She touched her face, dabbing at a nosebleed. The lieutenant tried to pull her back, but the boot-sucking snow had them pinned in.

"Does the hawk care how the mice divide her hunting ground?" asked the Sylphide. "I'll show you fucking deeds. Land isn't held by paper, but by blood and stone. You want me to fight? Fine. I'll be a one-woman war."

"Money! Money!" shouted the Pretender. "Thousands of grivenky."

"Where is it?" she said. "And why can't I just rip it off

your corpse?"

"It's worthless if you kill us," he said. "It's in a bank. Gold, sure, but it's liquid."

"I don't want your piss, mayfly!" she said.

"They mean you no harm," Mageirissa said. "We mean you no harm. But especially us, as we were abducted—"

"I don't care. *I* mean you harm," said the elf, the whine continuing to intensify as the lieutenant signaled for his troops to aim at her.

The doghead troop scurried around behind her, on the flanks. She hunched down again, on the balls of her feet, a cape of vertebrae-jacketed viper-reins unwinding from the hollow until the barbed hooks and ax-heads buried themselves in the hissing, melting snow.

"You're surrounded," said the lieutenant.

Dogheads and soldiers drew blades and readied rifles.

"By victims," said the Sylphide.

"You have two dozen muskets pointed at you," said the lieutenant.

His voice was strong but his eye twitched.

"Stand down or our guns will cut you down."

"Guns?" she said with a smirk and an odd shake of her hip-cape of foxtails.

"Firesticks that shoot bolts—"

"I know what a fucking gun is!" she interrupted. "They were named after me. Firearms *cutting* just sounds off."

"Ready!" the lieutenant said.

"How are you this stupid? I haven't eaten your brains yet!" she said.

She shivered with a teeth-clashing rage.

"Fire!" the lieutenant commanded, before the echoing crack.

"Wind!" the elf commanded, before a great roar.

Mad piping filled the air. The smoke blew back in the faces

of the gunline.

"Oh, they're little balls," she said as the smoke cleared, and she held a pair of bullets in her hand, rolling them against each other with her thumb. "A cone would be better, wouldn't it? Oh, when the sun takes weeks to rise and set, years can feel like days..."

She dropped the bullets to the ground and shook off the pain of the catch. The atmosphere grew tense and ripe with static that crackled and hissed from the barrels of guns and the points of swords. A coronal discharge flicked like violet candle flame from the tips of her antlers, fingernails, and hooked boots, like the corposant ghost fires seen on the masts of tall ships during a thunderstorm. Fade felt a rack of antlers with fully developed prongs would have strengthened the display, but after a certain point, one has to stop nitpicking the primordial warriors of the midnight sun.

"That hurts a lot more than arrows," she said, before blowing on her hand.

A diabolical chill shot through her.

"But time maketh fools of us all, I guess. Even the timeless. I'll teach you, sons and daughters of Man. Your ancestors feared me, and they were wiser than you. Ask of Cunigunde the Whirlwind when you meet them in Hell."

The strange whining paused, as she had been forcing air through those ribbed bone flutes, in a manner akin to special arrowheads designed to whistle in flight, either to signal or to terrify.

"Is that your powder carriage?" Cunigunde asked, thrusting her left antler stub towards one of the wagons in the train.

She flicked two fingers on the sinister hand, and a spark rooted in black soil. Two of the supply-women died outright, throttled by the blast and slashed by splintered wood. The eldest woman, the head-hag, was set alight, the shard of a beam penetrating her thigh.

"Sorry, answered mine own question."

The War-eager Whirlwind threw a gladius through the detached head of the hag as it made its escape and intoned a curse. It dropped and cracked against the ground like rotten fruit.

One of the dogheads worked up the nerve to approach with a drawn rapier and pistol as she bent down, but a silver flash from her eyes blunted the blade and caused his firearm to flash in the pan.

The elf picked up the blood-drinking spine and held it like a Dullahan's whip, studded with thunderstone arrowheads that crackled with heavenly static. The superior vertebrae grew into a leaf-shaped axe head. Blackened channels ran through this shaped tooth, the ancient rot of toxins and electrical burns. A narrow hip served as the two-hand guard, broken and re-healed and wound up with wires and winches like the machine head of a guitar. Judging by its strong neck and a tail of twelve bones, Lund believed it must have belonged to a pantheon, as their steel-hard bones are known to survive terrible impacts and falls while clashing in the sky for mates.

Polar in more ways than one, a slight, subtle twist of the grip and a nearly imperceptible fingering of flute holes shocked the whip erect. The Sylphide cocked an eyebrow flirtatiously and made a sound between a laugh and a howl. Not all of it came from her throat; the winds were her whispering chorus.

Kingfisher thought it was a sparth axe or a short bardiche, but its elegant curves sent the polearm diagrams of her knightly manual spinning up through her memory. It was perhaps a warscythe, a sovnya, a pollaxe, or a curved swordstaff. She had puzzled over those charts during long nights, trying to figure out why every slight variant in their heads deserved a new title, while so many blades were simply "swords."

The lieutenant ordered a rank-by-rank reloading as the

Pretender panicked and tried to fall back but found himself slowed to a crawl. The Sylphide's winds had surrounded the company with mounting snow.

She rapped the skull drum on her hip, and thunder roared through the clouded sky. The grey-blue expanse bled the green of the northern lights, as if wounded by the echoes.

"Do you hear the terror in the air? My victim's voices flocking like birds. An ill-wind roars south from Hyperborea. Scream your last words."

Untouched by the rifle shots that punctuated her poem, she was upon a squadron of men with a roar and a blast of thunder, smashing down like the club of a giant to break their formation. A more rigid shaft would have shattered under the force that shook through that alien weapon's vertebrae. She demonstrated its versatility, loosening it to entangle and melt through a spear immediately before snapping it rigid to parry one of the ogre's blows, releasing a blinding arc flash. It shook one's skull, the hammer of heaven's thunders and the axe of cutting lightning, the twin weapons of Craethion. She voided her left shoulder away from a counterattack and grasped the naked pair of fused vertebrae that once held the beast's shoulders, shifting to a polearm-grip to carve away the ogre's jaw with a bellow.

The ax-head briefly snagged in its hulking body, and his human and doghead allies used that loss of momentum to press in with spears. Even then, her cape of chained darts, hooks, and ax-heads kept them from a full-on charge, with one man losing a foot when a green chain tangled around his ankle and its flailing hatchet sunk deep. Those poisoned quills of antler, orichalcum, and lodestone spun on lines of static force, dancing madly with will-o-the-wisps.

Kingfisher realized that the weapon's flailing, hooked sections were meant to catch on its target, to grind, tear, and poison a massive gash of tissue with its bony drills. That's how you slay a giant or pull the wings and heads off a dragon. The bone weapon slipped from the ogre with a grinding of flesh and a spray of burning blood. In the wink of an eye, it went flexile and swept around the turning sylphide, a twelve-section-flail carving through two of the men and four spears with a smack of thunder.

The enormous wave of heat sent snow screaming and steaming as it passed over the ground, a thousand times worse than the boilers of the steamships Kingfisher had toiled above. One man screamed and collapsed as his breastplate spat a wet pop, the shock both rapidly cooking his flesh to burst and stopping his heart. She pressed down on the shield of his partner, biting through the pavise's rim like hardtack and availing herself of the weakness to punch it in twain. The shrapnel of burning wood and human bone ripped through the crowd like the shock of a cannonball upon the rank-and-file.

Not only was she fast enough to dodge and void attacks without parrying, implausible in human fencing, the Sylphide was literally leaving voids as she moved, ripping the air open. The holes gasped and sighed and collapsed with a bombard blast, vampiric vacuums drawing up and boiling blood that would have otherwise simply sprayed in spurts. Arteries burst like maroons as she struck, and a rusty frost fluttered through the air.

She whirled the sparking elf-ax overhead, carving out a sphere of control bathed in green-blue light, as fencing manuals teach zweihänder users to clear away pikemen. The now rigid twelve-part-flail sang and rang like the *atgeirs* of saga. The rippling, excited air crackled as the whining whirligigs between the vertebrae spun nigh-invisibly, turning with the expanding, electrified screws. Adamant wires as fine as spidersilk yet strong as hauling chains melted through flesh and bone, glistening with a morningdew of arcane diamond. The Sylphide, crowned with a sundog halo, controlled the electrical flow by directing it into leather dead-ends or along dancing green chains that hissed and poisoned like vipers.

Fade noted that a metal filling in the vertebrae clicked together when she sent a current through it, strengthened by polarized stimulation, but his best attempts to yank the metal around with earthwork died on contact with its overwhelming charge and its insulating jacket of bone. Students of science were only now understanding the relationship between electrical currents and magnetic forces in crude experiments with charged wire and compass. Something about that disturbed Fade, even more than the gore; a barbarous anachronism shouldn't have more advanced engineering than the greatest minds of the Septentrine Empire. It wasn't proper.

He reached down to pick up a leather driving whip, just in case he needed a weapon or a tourniquet.

Cunigunde's sylphblades, hooks, and axe-heads twirled on the edge of their viper-reins, air whistling through fluted grips and spinning on pinwheel guards. They could not move fast enough to hack, but were a nasty, nicking distraction striking like cobras, buying just enough time for her to work the air.

Her magic had a raw physicality to it, a weight. She wasn't channeling, with its fine incantations and arcane finesse, so much as bullying the air into shape. She ripped lightning from the sky like a knife slicing open an artery. She did not chant or intone, she screamed her will into the world, and the world obeyed.

With a startling crack of whip and thunder, lightning unrolled like a ghostly ribbon, fueled by the last breaths of the fallen. Those who once dared to face her stumbled back, while those within the sparking, blinding aurora burned or dropped quaking or dead. The sole survivor of that second wave fell to a dagger pulled from the folded cuff of her boot. She tossed it through his throat as she vaulted forward, flickering in and out of visibility. The red and white blur came to a stop with a head in hand, held by the hilt of her impaled dagger, dripping with arcane corruption. She catapulted the writhing skull at the ground, and the ghoulish grenade devoured vital penuma and spat out an unspeakable rancor. Its spirit-shaking scream blasted Fade and Chesti from their hiding place, a stray tooth lodging in Chesti's left arm. She grinned and whirled her grinding whip through the defenders, spears and shields deteriorating in one or two blows, falling weapons stolen and sheathed in their owners' hearts with the millennia-honed instincts of an eternal warrior.

Several dogheads simply burst open as she leaped past, like deep-sea fish yanked to the surface, and she snapped one woman's neck with an exposed intestine as she landed and rolled. Fade stayed on the ground, drawing up the might of earth and the flow of the waters beneath it. He gritted his teeth, trying to power through the vertigo and convulsing pressure that weighed on his chest. He was terrified of aerobullosis, arterial embolisms, the glassy bubbles in the eyes of animals subjected to air pumps, and, most frightening of all for a surgeon, the joint-hardening rheumatism in extremities. He had seen the cases of decompression sickness in the deep abysms of the mine shafts. The drillers doubled over in pain as their stomachs and veins knotted up. The caisson-builders twitched like hanged men as their spines seized and squirmed.

Fade set up a screen around his heart, a filter of natures that would only allow air fully dissolved in blood to pass. Anything that failed the screening would be broken up, reducing the size of any air bubbles. A gripping fist of muscle tension seized his chest, forced as he was to use his own blood as material and the firing nerves as a catalyst. He tried to purify the elements around him into their vital *Animae*. Earthen essential salt, the watery essence of lymph and plasma, the spiritual penuma of air, and the vibrancy of the mind, the psyche of fire. He channeled them through his rod of bismuth, refining them into abstract lines of force.

The only reprieve in the assault came when the wound-proof Whirlwind disengaged from the mercenary band, weapon circling like a probing quarterstaff. She turned invisible and leaped some thirty yards to attack a warren of white rabbits, ripping one from the ground by the ears and swinging it with enough force to decapitate it. She collapsed the burrow with several furious stomps while screaming for them to be quiet as a few stray shots whizzed around her. After breaking into the warren, her punch gathered up a cloud of noxious, bluish gas to flood and scour the tunnels.

"They scream, they scream like the daughters of woman!" she howled, her sweet, soft voice worn husky and hoarse under the torrential strain of vulgar ferocity.

The air hissed, serpentine, as she poisoned the earth with that dull, heavy cloud. Lund, from his hiding place behind an overturned wagon, was astonished that she spent twenty seconds killing rabbits, slightly longer than her entire attack on the company.

The lieutenant shouted for Eumelia to run to the wagon and for his men to scatter and snipe at will. A bunched formation was pointless. A tight, volley could be anticipated, countered. He hoped for a random and lucky shot while she was distracted. It was a distant hope, but there was at least *some* hope.

Kingfisher wheeled in the air, searching for an opening, fighting the cold and the intense pressure for every inch of altitude. Her ears had popped, and she could feel her bones shaking and her stomach sloshing with that monster's screams. The Sylphide was a nightmare of rapid pressure changes and brutal, clashing drafts. Kingfisher was a stream trying to reverse the currents of the ocean, a breeze against the Whirlwind.

Mageirissa held one wounded soldier's intestines in with an alcohol-soaked rag. There was a poison in him, some thick black sludge that smelled like death and reified corruption. She recited a rite of healing over his gasping and pleading, tapping into the vast sea of humanity. She dragged the soldier backward in the life cycle of man, from death to a painful rebirth.

Push push push, I will deliver you once more.

She could hear them, the chorus of healers, her lineage of shamans all chanting in unison across the arrowflight of time. It was easier here, in the North, where time's flow can be fought. Alcohol burnt away, effervescent spirits empowering the body's natural healing. And so, the wound closed, the intestines slipping back from her medical probe, winding up and reverting with nothing but a rapidly fading scab. That vile black toxin seeped and pooled outside of his gut. It reverted and reformed into strips of mangled human flesh.

"Yeah, no," the Whirlwind said, before smashing the soldier's head off in a bony blur, leaving only the back of the skull and an ear attached to flesh.

Mageirissa struck the ground, her face blistering under the spray of boiling blood and flash-heated brain. A streak of metal, a long knife, or a short sword, cartwheeled through the air, just a few hairs' breadth from her cheek.

"Shaman's magic," noted the Whirlwind, as she caught the blade and returned it. "I have tasted the food of God, which calls itself Man. What divinity can you muster?"

Mageirissa covered her mouth and heaved, forcing herself to swallow to keep the vomit down.

"Are you a midwife?" asked the Sylphide, deadly serious, as she shoved the dead soldier's musket into the hollow on her back.

She pointed at the left breast pocket of Mageirissa's apron, which held a tincture of fennel and fenugreek and a sprig of milk thistle.

"What?" Mageirissa said, nearly choking. "Yes? What?"

"Ah," said the Whirlwind, dodging a bullet. "Stay out of the way."

She waved her hand. Mageirissa let out a gasp as shards of white bone and thorny black vines erupted from the body at her lap, wrapping around her stomach and legs and staking deep into the earth. A hot wetness ran down her leg.

The Whirlwind darted past the shaman, towards the dispersing body of troops, so quickly that the dog-green sheen from the back of her eye trailed through the air, reflecting firelight. Two walls of white mist sprayed up as she plowed through thigh-high snow, a combination of physical force and a sleeve of blazing hot air wrapped around her leather boots.

Only one ogre mustered up the courage to act. Fat Fasolt bellowed and charged through the snow like a moose, overcoming the pain of the blade caught in his thigh. The eerily manlike face of the manticore covered his own, and the hide's lingering magic empowered its wearer while eating away its flesh and sanity. The Whirlwind bugled like a rutting elk and met him with a roll of thunder and a flash of blinding white lightning, a raging beast of monstrous appetites and hideous strength against a poor ogre who did not stand a chance. The coruscating Sylphide spun in the air, with no guard or armor but blinding speed. Fasolt howled as his intestines stained the ground through his fingers. His thigh muscle hung loose in a red slab, carved clean when the Whirlwind returned her blade to its boot-scabbard. His thick fingers bloated and burst open like an overheated sausage in the thunderstorm heat, the bones sloughing out as he desperately shoveled up his spilled innards.

The Whirlwind snorted and snarled to clear the blood from her nose and suck it down her throat, reversed the rotation of the adamant saws, and jerked into the sky. The elf-ax disentangled itself in a burst of gore, the rupture of a giant cyst. The Sylphide's scythe scooped through Fasolt's open belly, dislodging a clump of lard the size of a human torso. She did a bit of quick firework after shifting the air pressure, metabolizing the grease into a sticky, bubbling fire easily spread on the wind.

Her asp-keen eyes flickered and flashed like a smithy's flame, dulling the mass of approaching blades and bayonets. She spun forward, sliding her fingers into the gap between the scythe's two points of connection, whipping the hip bone guard into another soldier's neck with enough force to crush his windpipe. Vaulting off his body and assisted by a conjured updraft, she kicked a cynocephalid's muzzle flat after catching his sword between the flail's vertebrae. She crushed another's kneecap in a cartilage-snapping bounce, letting sail a volley of needles poisoned with Decadence and aeolian daggers of whirling ice. The smell of the flesh cooked and charred by her superheated legs nauseated the crowd as the hooks and green chains peeled meat from bone. The spine and tusk-tipped chains flailed and sparked freely like the jerks and snaps of a dying snake, scaring off one lunging doghead. The other combatants choked on the wisps of blue-green miasma rising from the sweat and blood sublimating off her skin.

She pulled up a fallen sword with her off-hand and slammed it through the breastplate of the company's sergeant as he fumbled for his pistol, too distracted by wind-carved cuts splattered by the broiling grease fire. The blade bent and broke under the force, scrambling the man's left lung. A ghostly gasp escaped the shattered cage of his chest. His arm shot up almost comically as steel erupted from his armpit. His ally took advantage of her exposed back and lunged with a fixed bayonet, an attack that would have pierced her through the heart if it hadn't deflected off the raging whirlwind enveloping her, and if one of the chained darts hadn't stabbed into his arm.

The flanges bound to the elf-ax's posterior processes aligned into a cutting edge with a magnetic click and a crackle. She landed on the ball of her left foot and took his head with a ripping, backward slash while kicking through the skull of the recoiling doghead. The shockwave painted a crimson comet across the blowing snow. She executed a reverse split, caught the blade with the hook of her boot, and slammed the sword through the shoulder of the final member of the squad, less than four seconds after Fasolt's fatal charge. She retrieved the scythe-head, dragging out the foe's heart.

Her horsetail's pinwheel spun wildly, and she laughed. Blood stained the Sylphide's grin and most of her skin, her red eyes shining with a silver lunacy. She dragged one fallen but still living doghead's dogface into the grease fire, grinding it until its skin peeled off.

Mageirissa matched the warty texture of the ogre's reddish skin to the Sylphide's bumpy, whorled leathers, if you factored in the tanning and dyeing, and the branded staves and sacred pentagrams. The straps seethed, breathing through the pores. She wondered if ogres were, in some primal age, hybrids of man, bear, and petty titans bred for meat and skin by the Airy Lords. Stupid, bulky, omnivorous, easily felled by arrows. An ogre *would* eat anything. The elf *could*.

The thought filled her with religious terror, the awe of the doomed. What did the mouse see in the emerald eyes of the cat triumphant? What of the antelope and the lion, the deer and the bear, the sow, and her butcher? This was fate, she knew. She was nothing rarer than the wedding of ogre and man. An even finer food for the Lords of Air. Never before had she felt so fat and slow and weak. Mags worried that her mongrel body would disgust the cruel yet perfect immortal. She would be tortured, she feared. She would be flayed and tanned and worn and eaten.

You hear those old descriptions of the Hyperboreans, elf songs that spoke of mysterious warriors as white as snow and as subtle as pure ice. They had the strength of a dozen men, the speed of cyclonic winds, and the arcane might of a demigod. They laughed and sang while they fought, and it sounded so joyous in the songs.

But you're not supposed to sing while you slay. Battle is a nightmare incarnate in hacked-up flesh and confused panic and young men screaming in agony. Kingfisher had heard tin-pot philosophers say that war was man's natural state, but never bought it. She did not fear the sky, fish did not fear the sea, and salamanders did not fear the flame, but men fear war. Men break in battle and long for hearth and wife.

This beast did not fear war.

"Please, please stop!" shouted Eumelia, on the verge of tears. "Please! Anything!"

From her seated state of imprisonment, Mageirissa stopped gathering up a heavy carriage chain, hoping to twist it against her own binding, when a sharp twinge of pain jumped through her palm. A taste like walnut butter filled her mouth, and hairs in her braids coiled up from the static. She looked up at Eumelia, and wiped away a combination of tears, blood, and the pus of bursting blisters. Fade, who had been concentrating with his bismuth rod pointed at the sky, gawked at the woman.

The Whirlwind had punched through one of the shorter soldiers, right below the ribcage. She held him up as though his spine were a bow, and slammed him to the ground, lightning striking with each hit and each joyous, war-mad scream, until Eumelia's blubbering pleas gave her pause.

"Why does the warmonger weep?" asked the Whirlwind, her voice quite soft and gentle, yet magnified on the churning wind as though in an amphitheater.

She pulled her hand from her latest victim, taking his heart and part of the spine with it, folding him in half.

"Do you not hear it? The heartbeats? The rush of blood under the skin? The sanguine call to war?"

Wearing the stolen vertebra around her inner three fingers, she crushed the heart in her hand. She snapped her head to the side, reflexively dodging a musket ball.

"My hand fits so perfectly around the heart… it's almost perverse to keep them apart," she said.

She took a bite of the heart, drunk in the yliaster and the aerial potency of the blood, and dropped the rest to the ground. Another flex of fingers shattered the vertebrae

"Whatever you want, we don't want a fight!" Eumelia sobbed.

"But I want a fight," said Cunigunde the Swan-White, almost taken aback by the tears and slightly gagging on tough, raw heart meat.

She combed her billowing hair down with the unbloodied fingers of her right hand, as the static had caused it to wildly puff up.

"And then I want silence."

"Please, we'll give you everything we've got," Eumelia said, falling to her knees in submission. "Take the baggage cart, the company chest, anything. I won't fight you… please…"

"You can't," said the light-elf, some of the fresher drops of spackled blood running into her mouth and unblinking eyes. "You *can't* fight me."

"I can't, you win," Eumelia said. "You win. Please, just let us go."

Cunigunde waved her hand dismissively and turned away in contempt, the cruel pride of a war god's wife. Eumelia's eyes nearly popped out of her head, wet and pink. There came a roaring out-rush and a scream from collapsing lungs, punctuated by the stomach-churning snap of Eumelia's jaw. The air collapsed with a pop and the greasy hiss of boiling fluids, and, finally, a razor-sharp silence. The lieutenant shouted and fired his pistol at the Sylphide as his wife dropped dead. A great gale blew snow into the air, churning and blurring land, sky, and sylph into a white whirlwind that tore the heat from everything around it. She was gone, invisible. And despite a wind so forceful that the ice scratched at the skin, a universal silence ruled, as though the air had frozen over like water. The cold enveloped everyone, killing all other sensations, an ice pack on a wound. It was maddening, numbing, and cold on a metaphysical level. One's brain began to scream to fill the void.

The bodies of the Sylphide's victims burst open with a thornbush of antlers, growing from a skin of pale pink velvet that weaponized the hearts and bones and rapidly rotting meat of her fallen foes. The prongs twisted off as they grew, spiraling up into the raging air, slick with the toxic rot of human Decadence.

Lund found himself frozen. He was no warrior, not a violent man. He had grown up on stories of the 'elves,' who once ruled the north of Murmur and Alirune and still, they say, dwelt in those forbidden, foreboding forests from whence no traveler returned. While that unmatched strength and speed sounds heroic, seeing it was monstrous beyond words. Madly, he laughed at himself when something clicked in his head, a little scientific connection. His botany professor had specialized in soil chemistry, and discovered that lighting strikes precipitated the growth of mushrooms and other fungi. Elves were traditionally associated with rings of toadstools. He never understood why until he watched her dancing and striking the earth with thunderbolts. He tasted blood on his cracked lips, and saw the Hidden-Folk dancing mad, a galloping drumbeat of blood and thunder.

But the Whirlwind was no longer dancing. The wind calmed and the detail of the world slowly returned. Lund could hear again. He could see and feel. He could hear himself laughing maniacally, nearly screaming. The Sylphide was no more than an arm's length from Lund, her face and curving neck covered in frost, blood, and pink meat, the lieutenant's crushed skull pressed against her breast. It took Lund a moment to process that she was eating the man's head.

The weapon had locked into the lieutenant's spine, its hooks and whirls ripping the lungs from his cleaved rib cage. A pair of bloody wings stained the snow, the shadow of the blood eagle.

Lund sunk deep inside of himself, into the primordial darkness. Something ancient and mighty struggled within him, turning and churning. Something tremendous and triumphant rose beneath him, a shadow under the ice. Lund felt his heart quicken.

"Hey, are you going to fucking stand there?" said the Whirlwind, stopping to lock eyes on Lund.

"What?" Lund said weakly.

The Whirlwind kicked him in the stomach. Not with the force that she had earlier used to disembowel a soldier, but with an annoyed prodding. The teeth that cleated her soles bit into him with a stunning shock.

"Come on, fight back, Son of Man. You're not a lump of shit yet."

She wiped the lieutenant's brain from her face and tilted her head. The corpse fell from her embrace, coming apart in segments as she disengaged the vertebral weapon. Blood pooling in her navel radiated over her chiseled abdomen as though traced by an unseen hand, forming a snowflake stave of terror.

She lapped at her lips. "Salty. What is your heart doing? I know I'm gorgeous and terrifying but–"

Lund warped and twisted. His skin split and burnt away, crackling and curling into ash as the earth beneath his feet rushed up into his changing form. Lund watched himself fall apart, further and further away with every heartbeat.

"Are you cooking yourself for me?" she asked. She simply watched it happen, happy that one of the humans was finally doing something interesting. "How sweet."

The Sylphide's smug smile dropped away when she heard the beating of metal into the earth. She snapped her head to face the source, through the smoke of the Murmurman. With her blurry, light-washed vision, she thought it might have been a tent peg, but that didn't make sense. She blinked hard. Sometimes, even if she cocked her head in the usual position, her eyes began to quake and smudge the world. She swiveled her ears towards the ground and cycled air into her nostrils and across her tongue, tasting ozone and the electrification of sanguine copper.

The thin man etched some pattern through the frozen soil. Earthwork worried her. She had no way to register gnome-spells until the stones struck her, and the pulse had broken the Saint Chainer's stolen spell and her traps hidden in the snow, so anything could be lurking down there. But luckily, earth magic was rather earthbound, so she had a field advantage. She jumped, expecting to reach tree-top height. But her stomach lurched as she came to a stop mere inches from the ground.

The dead man's cold fingers groped at her thigh. And a massive hand was at her side. She tried to figure out what this new thing was, this black smudge against the white canvas. This creature was not a black bear. It had huge, mannish hands. It was not a pink-brown ogre, who stood taller, nor one of the wiry satyrs. And it was larger than the true men or their more robust whistler cousins. She could handle ape-men. She'd fought ape-men. She'd eaten ape-men. But this was more of a man-ape. It was a huge ogre-ape with leathery, black flesh. Perhaps some chimera, perhaps some exotic creature from the remote south.

"What are you?" she asked as she blocked the creature's off-hand punch, a blow with an ogre's strength.

She wanted to twist it off, but only managed to snap two fingers. They grappled and rolled and the air grew cold. She had the oppressive strength of the winds but it had leverage, weight, size, and reach. The beast was smart enough to take her by the wrist with fingers on the guard, preventing her from swinging or accurately directing her charges.

The Whirlwind pumped volts into the muscles of the creature and sent an impulse up the wiry nerves of her weapon. The toroid coils in the vertebrae discharged, burning the ape, and stunning its meaty arms. She channeled the high voltage into a web of silver wires that formed a cocoon around the molten salt in a dragon-throat bag. The excess charge climbed the silver filaments woven through the dorsal rack of antlers, white sparks dancing up to the stars. She managed to stun and burn the hand on her wrist, but the impulse only sent the dead man at her hip into strange, groping convulsions. The corpse nearly pulled down her *naatsit*, leaving a long strip of soggy skin where he caught himself on the hard silver conductor tattooed into the magic staves.

Another hand ripped one of the foxtails from her corpse pants. It was the pale corsac she caught in Dzomdzen in 794, not one of those arctic foxes she could snatch up by the brace on a lazy afternoon. In frustration, she sent a surge of power through the silver ink. The lieutenant's dead nerves reflexively recoiled, and she kicked off his gnawed head. She twisted in mid-air as six more dead hands grabbed her. She roared in frustration, let the spiked tail fall limp, and whipped the chain-dart around to clear space. The churning sky matched her rage, and hail came down like grapeshot.

Beneath the canopy of a rifleman's parvais, the thin man whispered. Lines of animating force pulsed through the earth into the corpses, weaving phantom ligaments through rotting meat. She burnt away the blood painted across her skin and tried to damage the flow of spirit, a process of air, but the complexity of this animating thaumaturgy confounded any easy counteraction. Aquatic cycles of bodily fluids, terran structures of flesh and essential salts and vital minerals, empyreal influence over metabolism, and organic acids.

So, she tried to perform her favorite form of counter-magic, throwing a hatchet through a wizard's head. But before she could reach the jawbone ax attached to the skull on her back, she was rudely interrupted by a trio of bayonets, a pair of chains, and a diving harpy. She yelped as four dead men, three living men, one silverback gorilla, and two grinding chains dragged her down, slashing, piercing, and tearing. She reached for a dagger and slashed at the dead and the living with a flurry of blades, but both her limbs were soon pinned by bone and sagging flesh.

"We were going to crown you," said Karl-Daeriausch, under a canopy of three men with raised shields and pistols. "Now we will cremate you."

The Whirlwind shrieked.

The cushion of balmy, breathy air that surrounded her chilled and stilled. The stone-hard hail ceased its meteoric fall. Her eyes locked on the young soldier who had been brave and foolish enough to run her dead center through the chest. She kicked off one of Lund's arms, sending the great gorilla form collapsing in a spurt of blood. Two pistols discharged, fruit-lessly, and the shield-bearers dashed forward to make a wall. With a backhand through a shield, the Whirlwind sent Mageirissa reeling and bleeding from the mouth, the shaman's earthwork bonds breaking away from Cunigunde's ankles. Before Mageirissa hit the ground, the Sylphide's fist smashed through the skull of the Pretender.

Karl-Daeriausch retreated oddly, walking backward, half-aware, a stumbling, hissing, one-eyed wretch with half of a head. Karl-Daeriausch repeated a flat, primal 'ah' with each footstep before he collapsed in the snow.

The Whirlwind pulled Chesti's bayonet from her breast. It loudly scraped against strangely solid ribs. There was something between the gaps, a spongier bone that came out in small chunks, as if she reinforced herself with misplaced antler.

She glanced at Chesti and smiled strangely. Electricity surged through the chains at her back, sending them snapping and whipping like the arms of a speared octopus.

"Just die," Chesti said, both to the Sylphide and the Pretender. "Just die."

"She's dead, she's finally dead," Kaspar blurted out as he stabbed her in the stomach and pulled her down.

"I'm alive, I'm alive like an animal eating," she said, kicking against the chains and coughing up a pink mist that blended with a furious, humid wind that returned in force.

Flaps of skin hung from her, exposing the staves branded on the underside. The velvet of her antlers had sloughed off in the wind and the stress, exposing the blood-raw bone.

"...I'm still biting. Still dancing, Still crowned."

"Fuck your crown," Kaspar said.

He grabbed her by the jaw and ran his knife across her throat. She did not make the gasping hiss of someone dying. There was an outpouring of air, a backdraft so forceful that Kaspar's wrist broke. The Whirlwind disappeared. Chestimir was quite certain that she pushed herself off his bayonet. Two of the undead burst apart, with the head of Eumelia flying a dozen meters away. Fade stumbled at the severance of his animating lines of force, the finger-breaking jerk of one's human-sized marionettes snapping off their strings. He caught his breath, and marveled at the elf's endurance, her hyperaerobic blood redder than an arterial sample fresh from the lungs.

Kaspar turned to follow the ghostly thrust. His head atomized under the blow of bone and thunder, the spray of bodily fluids evaporating with a crackling report. With a series of clinks and snaps, the spinal weapon went rigid and drank its bloody prize.

Cunigunde the Whirlwind became visible again, hunched and soaked in crimson.

"My blood is my imperium.
Tooth and tendon, my tool.
My antlers are my velvet crown.
By skin and bone alone I rule."

A sultry wind blew up around her, carrying off blood, viscera, and mud, devoured like dying sparks. Fresh, brown bone filled the nicks and dents in her weapon. She lifted the crossed leather straps around her neck. What the air touched, the air healed. In a moment, she was pristine, uncut, unscarred, unharmed.

"The undine thrives in water, the gnome in the earth. The salamander is reborn in the flame," said Cunigunde, a voice as terrible as the eagle diving. "Now consider the terror of air and aether."

She screamed again, a nauseating Pantheon cry. It was the bellowing stag, and keening banshee, and the howl of the Wolf Behind the World. The light around her danced and her visage shattered, mirrored, and refracted as though the air crystallized into a sunstone. Columns of lightning struck the earth, snow and stone exploding. A salt lick in her hand disintegrated, and the air behind her soured into a heavy, green-yellow poison. Vomit climbed up her foes' throats. A rattle echoed in their skull. A chill chattered teeth to the point that Fade feared he would spit out powder. Capillaries popped, and soon the Whirlwind's red eyes had company.

Kingfisher sang, and the wind calmed.

"Are you sure?" Cunigunde said.

The pinwheel at the base of her ponytail slowed its rapid

whirl and the dirty lime cloud dissipated. Her foxy ears curled up and swiveled away to muffle the sirensong.

"You're even trying at this point? Your last, best hope is to give me food poisoning, carrion-eater."

"I'm not afraid of you," said Kingfisher, terrified.

"I can hear that chicken-heart pounding," said the Sylphide. "Smell that reek of rot in your gullet as you whimper."

"I am Kingfisher Volganin, a knight of the Homelands."

The Whirlwind laughed, rattling the teeth beading her silver chains. "Wait, this got interesting. Are there harpy knights now? You know we bred you for parts, right? Fine, hollow bones. Aphrodisiac song. Magic feathers. Good meat."

"It doesn't matter what I was bred for," said Kingfisher. "I'm a knight now, ordained in an ancient line of *kiryy bogatyri*, from the Paladins of Magnus and the Knights of the Northern Order."

"Aw," Cunigunde said. "You're adorable. Hey, here's to girls from the backwater climbing the ladder. How about this? You give me a good duel, and I'll let your friends go."

"What is this?" Kingfisher asked. "Some show of honor after all this slaughter?"

"Fight with honor? No, no, I'm a raider. I strike, grab, and run. If you want honor, find a shovel and a battlefield. This is just a bit of sport, for a laugh," she said. "Death is a tragic failure. We did not invent a warrior code, to give your sacrificed young men meaning. Your civilization is decadent. Evil."

"Fine," said Kingfisher. "I'll agree to your game."

"Kingfisher, fly," said Mageirissa, seated on the ground and trying to revive Chestimir, the last possible survivor of the company, besides Pander and his Kaftar, wherever they may be.

She cradled Lund's head in her lap as the man regressed from his metamorphic spell.

"You might be able to escape. Tell the port, please... It's

not worth dying for."

"Have some faith in your friend, shaman," said the Whirlwind. "Do you not have hope for deliverance in the shadow of thy champion? You sound like an unsupportive friend."

She let out a rapid-fire, "ho-ho-ho," the puffy laugh of someone who is usually walking around nearly naked in freezing temperatures.

Mags looked around, squinted her eyes in a mix of disbelief and outrage, and said, "Faith? Hope? Friendship? After this?"

"You can lead a temple in worship, but can you send men crying for their gods? Can you cause women to bury their children in their breasts and weep for deliverance? There is no god behind the stone, only on the open field, in the mortal terror of the naked heart," said the Whirlwind. "Who were you, that did not know the fear of battle?"

The Whirlwind raised her hand and held her spinal ax up in the other by the gap in its head. The shaft shrunk, the whirligigs closing up and descending, and the vertebrae hunching together and lining up their black blades. A skeletal chest emerged from the hole in her back. A dozen kinds of weapons from three dozen lands stabbed into a floral chaos of hellebore, blades, and barrels disappearing into a space beyond space. Her weapon snapped into the welcoming ribs and aligned with her own spine, before the storage chest retreated into the hollow. The weapon's pelvic guard hooked into the belt of her quiver and hip-cape, while the topmost vertebrae locked into the elk-skull, the blunt side of the bardiche sinking into her neck. One could hear a series of hisses, snaps, and whirs as the weapon drank from batteries and tubes of foul poison.

In the same fluid motion, one hand pulled the innermost pair of antlers from the elk skull, while the other unhitched the wide pair with strange wheels curled in its prongs. With a forceful punch, another snap of magnets, and a whine of wire, the antlers had assembled into a bow, kept ready on her shoulder. An other pair remained in her left hand, hook swords intricately shaped from antler, pruned like ornate topiaries.

Now that she was quite a bit less frantic in her motion, Fade realized that the strange opening in her back was actually a stable bit of ether-manipulation magic, a Hulder's hollow. The sylphs are known for such spacial tricks, hiding entire campsites in folded tarps, thousands of arrows in a single quiver, stuffing gale-force winds into bags, and housing villages in an empty tree. She likewise kept a pair of quivers, one for arrows, the other for a set of strange, bony rods, in 'loops' on her boots. He wondered what else she could be hiding in those small pouches.

The spinal weapon made a final whir, and the hollow sealed up beneath it.

"Humanity is decadent," the Whirlwind said. "But you may prove noble."

She tightened the goofy scold's bridle to her face. She chewed the tubing inside, and sucked the ephedra pollen into her nostrils, quickening her breathing.

"Stops magic," she mumbled, her words all slurred and thick from the bridle. "And my rage is literally bridled now, so that's fun."

She turned her cylindrical thumb ring so its prong turned outward, and let the string of her recurved, compound bow rest against her leather bracer.

The bow was strung with adamant wire, threaded around eccentric, vertebral cams with antler-prong axles. This harplike pulley system was typical of the sylphbow, adding a terrible amount of force to the draw weight. She nocked a helix-etched javelin tipped with a two-part prong held in a vertebral grommet. It was a toggling harpoon, like those used to hunt whales and walruses.

"Shall we dance, daughter of the sea breeze?" asked the Whirlwind, as she aimed at Kingfisher's breast and trailed up and to her left.

Mags covered her mouth in fear, feeling chapped lips and cheeks split by the harsh, ever-changing atmosphere. Lund shook, with only the barest, dreamy flicker of consciousness. Mags frantically wiped away the yolk-like residue of the transformation, trying to keep the dangerous dampness at bay.

Kingfisher nodded, and, instead of flying up into the path of the harpoon, dove straight down into the snow and released a strong and aimless blast. The harpoon, lacking fletching, was directed by a rush of air through the helical rifling. The harpoon sailed overhead, and she fluttered into the settling white cloud, darting towards the trees, barely off the ground and into the tree line. The harpoon penetrated a tree, the spinning prong shredding the bark and wood, opening a wound for the growing prong to fill.

Cunigunde let out a sharp laugh that rattled the bridle. She darted towards the trees, gliding over the snow, screaming, the antlers on her back rippling with a flickering luna-moth aurora that broiled the air like phoenix wings. Holding her bow in one hand and a hooked sword in the other, she swung into the boughs of a barren larch tree, disappearing into the swirls of disrupted snow.

Kingfisher tried the mirage trick Fade had spoken of, bending light around her by shifting air like a lens. It was messy, amateurish work, but she only needed to scramble the already simple, chaotic image of pine needles and snow.

Cunigunde, however, did not rely on sight. Her vision was poor in the light, as her eyes lacked pigment and shook wildly. She preferred the darkness, relying on the moonsilver in the back of her eye to drink-up starlight and foxfire. She hooked herself upside-down to a tree branch, swiveled her ears, and coned up the air, increasing its pressure to intensify the speed and volume of sound.

Fade collapsed next to one of the company's cannons. He compressed the snow beneath it into a circle of ice and carved it loose with the 'cutting' properties of a scalpel, allowing it to rotate. He stole the calipers and calculators from a fallen artilleryman, blasted the man's brains off of the ball with some watery Purification, and unscrewed the cap of his silvered flask. He pressed his philosopher's ring on one pole of the sphere, and held the antipode in his other palm, charging it.

He struggled for a solution and landed on equalization. Wind and lightning were both caused by a disparity between regions, either in pressure or charge. Magnetism is a new and experimental field, a difficult blend of electrified atmosphere and energized earth, a complex and poorly understood manipulation of polarities and fields. He opened his pouch of materials, rummaging for his sewing kit and a lodestone, isolated its magnetic properties, and duplicated them in the ball by stitching a heated wire into it with a metallic needle. He charged the sphere of annealed iron, creating a potential path of least resistance. With his off-hand, he fueled his enchantment with the secret of the gnomes, the stone oil.

He found the linstock-spear and lit the canon's breach and the delayed effect with a petty timing cantrip. He placed a trigger on his thumb and ring finger, and backed away. He trudged towards Lund and Mags, muscles burning, and ankles straining like the cables of a bridge on the verge of collapse. He stumbled and impaled the linstock-spear into the tundra. The air filter around his heart stole his stamina. Fade went into a blind sprint, falling near Mageirissa. She caught him with a mama-bear hug. Fade's trembling hand touched Lund's neck, confirming the pulse.

Cunigunde had put away her bow after one shot, realizing that an arrow may not be the best weapon to use against a fellow-creature of elementary air. She remembered, one time, facing a wise gryphon with enough intellect and power to use its feathers as a way to disrupt archers, transferring the properties of its down to the fletching of the arrows in a bit of sympathetic magic, causing them to fall in low arcs. She decided to pull out one of the muskets she looted, supposing that a bullet would be impossible for the harpy to manipulate.

Before her centuries of imprisonment by the Saint Chainer, she had used firelances, hand cannons, Gregalean ribaldis, and Nandakan cetbangs. She remembered the fateful siege in Castle Runting, Wayland, when her employers brought out a great bolt thrower charged with a warhead of black powder, partially of her design, brought from her journeys in Near Hypourania. They had named it after her, the *Lady Gun*, for it howled and tore through men with a terrible speed and inhuman ferocity.

She held in her hand the child of that device, the child of her mind. Something like pride flickered in her smile. She loaded it with black powder, and the ball, as she had seen the men do. She liked the weight of the rifle and its bayonet, recalling the weight of her singing *atgeir*. She pressed her hand on its muzzle, compressing it with the pressure of a vacuum rather than the awkward, masturbatory ramrod technique of the soldiers.

A bad taste filled her mouth, and she wondered how long she had been out of Time. The men did not resemble the Skeironic Landsknechte she had run within her last days; they wore jackets, tightly woven overcoats, and strange, bland pants. Their Waylander and Skeironic was hard to understand, though the shouted Tsokiri was almost the same. And of course, the strange guns.

She actually found the gun rather lacking. The major improvement had been a small beaked hammer connected to a trigger mechanism that allowed for ignition, rather than having to directly ignite the powder through a touch hole. She thought the need to load through the muzzle impractical, especially with the messy powder. She considered how to improve it, jacketing the powder and bullet, and allowing loading through the base of the ignition mechanism.

But that would be for a different time. She steadied the gun with one hand and waited for the sound of movement.

Kingfisher concentrated on the neighboring tree and shook it vigorously. She used it as an opportunity to dart to another tree, closer to where the Sylphide had disappeared. She listened for the whistle of a projectile moving through the air. She dove out of the way of an ancient sica dagger. It was nearly too narrow to see, but its flimsy edge warbled, far louder than the rigid edge of a stronger, heavier knife.

Cunigunde pulled the trigger, and the gun hung fire. She realized that the powder had failed to ignite, and did it herself, agitating the metal with a touch of plasma, a trick she had learned from a salamander handgunner in Soyayer. She screamed in frustration as the gun exploded in her face and the harpy's wicked claws tore into the meat of her shoulder.

She twirled in the air, twisting like a cat until she landed on her feet. She hopped out towards the open snow, brushing the black crust of back-blast from her face. She screamed with an outrush of air as the harpy clawed at her neck and shoulder. She blindly struck with the gun's barrel with her free arm, batting the harpy to the tundra, breaking her wing. Blind with rage, she picked up the harpy by the neck and tossed her some four meters away. It would have killed her if she hit permafrost rather than a bank of snow.

Cunigunde loosened the bridle and slammed the gun under *Wirbel*'s vertebrae, pushing it into the otherworldly armory.

What a disappointment, she thought. *Does a mother's love mean nothing?*

She leaped into the air, stomping on the harpy's wing to

make sure it couldn't fly. She pulled back and placed a handful of snow on her face, using it to flush the powder from her wound. With the metal and salt gone, her wound started to heal on contact with air. She screamed again, bellowing like a bull moose, scarring the tundra with lightning.

She looked up at the necromancer, the skinchanger, and the shaman. In the distance, one of the cannons had moved, and turned to face her. The wizard did something with his blurry hand. She simply hopped out of the way as the cannon fired and tilted her head in smug amazement that the children of Man still defied her.

An enveloping, inducting charge tugged at every part of her body. Her bones rattled and her skin tingled with potential. The makeshift electrophore sailed past her, and lightning erupted between her positive fields and the ball's negatively charged mass.

"Ah," Cunigunde said, understanding the necromancer's gambit. "Nice."

The equalization of regions bound her to the iron core with a leash of lightning, dragging her backward on a trail of excited air until she slammed through a tree trunk. She stayed on the ground for a few seconds, catching her breath. She pulled a large splinter out of her back and smacked her hand into the ground in a frustrated tantrum when she realized she would be pulling splinters out of her hollow for days.

The bullets, though, were a cause for worry. Swords, darts, and arrowheads were easy to pull out, but a musket ball could stay in the flesh, burning away, retarding regeneration, and binding her to a solid form. Just like the ensorcelled chains in the blighted hawthorn.

She had a brief moment of clarity. She had fought for twenty-two centuries and spilled blood on thirty thousand battlefields from Balming in the Septentrine Archipelago to Yasuka in the Holy Shinatobe Empire. How many people had she killed? It must have been in the millions by now, perhaps ten. This group of six hundred was above average for a battlefield. No shame in letting these kids go, to tell that ice-fishing hamlet of the return of Cunigunde the Whirlwind.

She lifted her body up with exhausted arms. The trees had sapped her, both her hawthorn prison and the fir she splintered. The first regiment had tried to enslave her with chains. And now this...cannon trick. The impact of the iron still stung like alcohol on a wound. She stood on her hands, waiting for her spinal column to heal before somersaulting to her feet.

She walked towards the humans and the harpy with an apish, arm-swinging swagger. Even at a stroll, she caught up to the small party, slowed by the snow and the weight of their unconscious.

Kingfisher had briefly blacked out from the pain of a broken wing, but she sighted the Sylphide walking on top of the snow, barely visible but for a carmine glove thrusting for a helical brown horn etched with runes, bouncing from a swaying hip. A deep, sonorous blowing echoed through the clearing, rousing Lund and Chesti to wakefulness.

"How was the Legion of the Gray Forest lost? Who traces the spiral on the window in frost? Who makes widow and city lament that they sinned? The answer to all is I, Cunigunde the Whirlwind."

The elfin warrior sat cross-legged, on the snow, playful swinging the weapon's chain dart so it blurred into a buzzing silver circle. She cocked her head, and her braid settled on her shoulder as the pinwheel at its root slowed to a deliberate turn.

"So…" the Whirlwind said. "Why are you getting out of here alive?"

"I don't understand…" mumbled Chesti as he held close the flap of skin on his side. "There was this… whole prophecy. You…"

"Right, I made that up," said Cunigunde.

She smiled and squinted, with an eerie glow around her eyes, as though she trapped the starlight in her glassy lashes.

"As a contingency. Such plots are easy, for the sons of Men are easily seduced by promises of power and voluptuous asses."

"It was written–" Chesti stuttered out through wind-bloodied lips.

"Another good thing about humans is that you die young and forget things. Bully bully, all you have to do is whisper in a mad woman's ear and thirty generations later, someone is will-ing to seek out the legendary Whirlwind for aid. You don't taste too bad either. Never got my answer, by the by."

"Please just kill me," Kingfisher said. "Let them go."

"That was if you gave me a good fight," said the Whirl-wind. "Killing you would be pointless, because you're worth-less. You're no knight. You're pathetic, and the only monster you'll ever have a chance of killing is yourself."

She smiled as Kingfisher broke down into a sobbing fit. She reached into her back and pulled out a heavy red sack of silver rings and gold coins minted in the city-states of the Ar-getes. It sunk into the snow in front of Fade.

"My murders are paid and you are unworthy slaves," she said.

She closed her eyes as the ghosts of the battlefield clung to her.

"Leave me."

"What year is it?" Fade asked.

"What?" Cunigunde said.

"Do you know what year it is?" Fade said.

"The bloody eagle is such a rare bird in these climes, but we might see another one soon," said the Whirlwind. "Its cry sounds so close to a man's–"

"What year is it? What nations stand in this age?" Fade

asked.

"Fuck you," Cunigunde said, and stepped forward. "Slavery may suit you."

"Where are your people?" Fade asked. "Where's your family? Where could they have gone?"

"Alright, fuck this," Cunigunde said. She shifted her grip and the broken hip slurped up the chain with a clash of bone and adamant. "I'll find a calendar and a map, you little prick. You think I need your wisdom? I'll defeat the world without wearing pants. You think you can get under my skin? I'll flay you and wear your face while I fuck you father."

"Fine," said Fade. "Do it. I can't stop you. You're strong and scary, we understand. You're a mass-murdering bully. Great way to spend eternity. So, either kill us or let us get back to work, we have people to help."

"Have you ever done that?" Kingfisher weakly asked. "Helped someone?"

"Anyway, point taken, but I have to piss," said Cunigunde. "Have fun freezing to death. If any of you make it back to Man, remind them why they feared me."

Lighting erupted from the Whirlwind, and shook hands with the excited cloud above. She rose on the thunderbolt through a chorus of owls and terns and vanished before she met the sky.

Chapter 8: New Order for the Ages

Kingfisher, Mr. Fade, Dr. Lund, and Mageirissa stood on the fringe of a crowd gathered on the ground floor of the Mayoral Tower. At first, they considered skipping Loganev's Exposition, but there was free food, liquor, and the heat of a hearth.

They had trudged through the wilderness, fought off a wolf, and cleaned and dried themselves off in the cave of chains. The transformations exhausted Lund and burnt away body fat, leaving behind a dangerous layer of greasy, chilling sweat that had to be wiped away. Still, Lund insisted on attending to his duties first, and filled the deep wound in Chestimir's side with a melted stick of isinglass. The gelatinous paste of cod swim-bladders adhered to his flesh, and Lund worked it into human musculature. Mageirissa made a meal of some of the company's rations. She set a fire and prepared a salt pot of popcorn and toasted hominy. Once they started popping and cracking, she melted a cube of butter and reindeer fat over it. Fade prepared eight ash cakes over some wood char. They stored away much of the weaponry that they had looted. Fade took a saber and everyone but Kingfisher took a warlock rifle, a pistol, a cartridge, and a powder horn for their own protection. They wrapped a dozen other rifles and other materiel in a canvas bag and hid it under rocks.

Fade took the Pretender and the lieutenant's short swords and destroyed them with his hammer and an anvil of hot stone, bending them into a circle mimicking the Ouroboros of Rebirth and burying them as part of the funeral customs of Brandman. It distracted him from Kingfisher's angry scratching and hissing and Lund comforting a blubbering Mags. He thought of his grandfather's bones in the fire of the forge, the old man's spirit worked into the iron. The Brandmen are the people of the sword, and that was their famous funerary rite, the working of bones into the holy steel. Fade knew the modern truth of the act, the working of carbon and iron, but he couldn't help feeling the power of ancestral swords and the tales of ancient houses. There was something morbidly beautiful about your mortal bones strengthening the steel of your descendants. He looked up at Kingfisher as she worried at her toes. Perhaps that was why she loved those foolish stories. She had no tales to root her in this society.

After finishing some preparations, they set off for town, which was much closer than the ordeal suggested; they had only traveled five kilometers. It was the tension and the heavy snow that slowed them. Traveling in a line through the wagon trails sped things up considerably.

Fade and Mageirissa took turns carrying Kingfisher. Her legs stung with elf-shot, the talons involuntarily seizing shut at times. She had lost half a dozen primary flight feathers, and the radius and ulna of her left wing may have been fractured. She had fallen silent, and at times whimpered at the mere thought that she would never fly again.

Lund walked with a worrisome sway, but held his head high and reassured Kingfisher that her wings could be healed. He brought up the topic of imping, the repair and replacement of feathers with simple glue. If such simple crafts could allow an injured hunting falcon to fly again, magic and surgery could work wonders on a harpy. He asked her if she had ever seen the hercinia, a bird whose clear feathers are filled with luminescent sprites, so they glow sky blue in the night and leave trails through the dark forests of Aquilo. She shook her head, and Fade suggested that they check the port markets for their plumage, a popular commodity in the milliner's trade.

At the edge of town, Chestimir departed from the group. He had been quiet and terrified the whole time and was eager to report what had happened. There was no sign of Pander or his Hyenaman, with even Chesti unsure of where and when they had left the main body of the Bastards.

The five's first destination was the constabulary after reporting on their abduction and the release of the Whirlwind, handled by Mageirissa and Lund while Fade put a cast and splint on Kingfisher's wing. Rather than full coverage, he perforated it so it could heal on contact with air.

The next stop was the steam rooms of the Banya, before returning to their rooms to get dressed. Fade drew up a map to the clearing, so a party could retrieve and cremate the dead. Mags put salves and make-up on everyone, reducing and covering up bruises, cleaned up chapped lips, and lining puffy eyes. She scrubbed the cold-chapped skin from her cinereous cheeks, staining them a raw pink. They dressed up Kingfisher in a heavy hood, a wrap, a shawl, one of Mags' long dresses, and Lund's large slippers, disguising her as a doddering old lady.

They arrived at the Mayoral Tower about an hour late, quietly forming a precise, rapidly advancing raiding party that overtook and plundered the snack table in seconds, using the larger Lund and Mags as screening units as the smaller, more maneuverable Fade and Kingfisher seized Meat Bread Hill and Baklava Point under the watchful eyes of a vicious Olarian pocketdog. Facing little resistance, the assault on Buffet Table Two was a decisive victory for the forces of starving postgrads and their harpy ally.

The feasting victors stood around an alcove containing the Ashes of the Old World, a flowery name for an urn. After the dragon came and the nobles were driven out, the Severnayans raided the archives and burnt all the tax records, lordly deeds, royal charters, and other documents. This wasn't a mad riot, as it was portrayed in the foreign press, but a prudent, targeted attack on external, national power structures. They avoided birth and death certificates, shipping manifests, lower-class property filings, and documents of businesses owned by local artisans. Like a human, they left the remains of their feudal history in an urn filled with saltwater, though most of the locals have a story of their granddad pissing in it.

The tower was dense with the city's people and a couple of visiting dignitaries from Merovy. The Pilgrims of the Furnace, lizard people with heaters on their backs with lines running to their hearts, attended to the needs of the banqueters, servants of the dragon. Some of the salamanders even wore grills for skewered meat.

The rest of the crowd fanned themselves and held jackets on arms, and the attendants opened a few windows, but Volganin, Fade, Lund, and Mageirissa relished the heat. The Hyperborean cold had rooted deep in their bones, and this was paradise. With an open buffet.

Lund approached one of the officials of the Mayor's office, a salamander in fine black leathers with a humanoid form with skin like black magma cracking with veins of orange fire. He stood by the athanor, an alchemical oven housing a perpetual, purified flame. A hearth-shrine was suspended above it, dedicated to the crippled sun god Los, Orc Sunhair with his flaming sword, and Fuzon, the son of Incano and Urizen who presided over flame, heat, summer, fevers, dragons, and ardor, among other things. While a minor god elsewhere, Fuzon was popular in the frozen north, and devotees had carved his servant spirits, the Kindlers, from Lentoran amber and dragon's-blood resins and set them in a basin of white ash. The soothing heat of this shrine sent a shaking twinge up his arm. He and Fade proposed that the legendary 'stabbing pains' of elf-shot could be explained as the nerve damage of electrical arcs, conflated with their poisoned arrows, and the "elf-blast" with barotrauma. They hoped their hands were not permanently afflicted.

"My name is Gustavus Augustus Lund. I have a note from a fellow doctor," he said. "I've cosigned it. It's the location of several hundred bodies to the north and a warning about an entity named Cunigunde the Whirlwind, an ancient sylphide criminal. Incredibly dangerous, both in might and sorcery, a skald of old."

"How so?" asked the salamander.

"She tore through a mercenary company like lightning. And with lightning. I'm rather at one of those crossroads where literal and figurative start to blur..." Lund said, realizing he was losing the thread. "I don't want to cause a panic or disrupt this meeting, but this should be considered a top priority. Warn the Mayor. I have no reason to believe she intends to attack the tower immediately, but it's a distinct possibility."

Lund found the salamander's reptilian eyes and alien expressions a cipher.

It simply said, "Of course" and moved to the spiraling staircase leading up to the top of the tower.

Lund was worried, too, about his friend's interest in returning for cadavers. Bodies do not rot up this far North and must be burnt.

Mageirissa paused her feeding of Kingfisher to watch a male gnome ascend the steps of a small platform placed in front of the tower's new dynamo, attached to a flywheel over the dragon's athanor. He wore a hickory brown capotain and matching justacorps, trimmed with an umber and stone-red sash. He had run a dye through his hair, to give it a consistent, dignified grey rather than the earlier patchiness, and snipped his wiry beard into a point. He had capped his short horns in polished brass and clipped them to his hat with fine chains, highlighting that he had shaped them to spiral tightly like an Tammuzi oryx. These horns were meant to fit under the conical caps of an academic, rather than curving like a goat or spread in a bovine fashion, meant for the helmets of miner and warrior gnomes.

"Welcome to this little exposition," he said. "I am Lem

Loganev, some of you must have seen my alchemist's shop around town. And I'm happy to present Northernmost's first fully electrified block. The whole city should be lit up come winter. Can we get the windows?"

At that, several salamanders with hooks undid the bound curtains, blacking out the windows. Loganev flipped a switch, and a network of glass tubes illuminated as a current excited their filaments. A helical array of amalgam mirrors bounced the golden light up the tower. Mags put the serving spoon in her mouth and clapped at the technical marvel. The lighting startled the harpy and Fade softly touched her shoulder. Fade nodded, trying to respect the town's progress, but he wasn't impressed by the display. Harth-on-Lam and most of the Septentrine Empire's major cities had been electrified for Fade's entire life, and Achille for forty years.

The audience applauded politely.

"Thank you," said Loganev solemnly.

Overwhelmed by the attention, the old gnome closed his eyelids, so only the pupils peeked through. He vaguely resembled a mole startled by the light of noon.

"This was the culmination of my life's great work. And this community has been here to support me, believing in me. But I'm also an engineer, so I would like to turn over the public speaking to someone more qualified. Thank you."

"Lem!" shouted the Innkeeper.

He applauded loudly. His daughter looked embarrassed at first, but then joined him. Some whistled, and a handful of Hookmen ululated and trilled.

"Thank you," said Loganev again. "Let me introduce Olympienne Mignard, of the Merovene Summit."

Loganev stepped aside as a woman took center stage on the dais. She wore trousers tucked into high riding boots and a militant, high-collared jacket over a cavalry cuirass with a set of hip-mounted cooling ducts. A narrow rapier and a brace of pistols hung from a crossed belt studded with bullets and small powder horns.

Kingfisher recognized the arcane sigils on the rapier's hilt. This was a sympathetic blade, a kind-sounding name for a terrible class of weapon. Exceedingly rare, they use thaumaturgic principles of sympathetic properties to devastating effect, their steel passing through steel with the ease of water. They were typically small, only affordable in the size of daggers and nails.

A rapier, even a thin one, must have cost a fortune, looted from the treasury of a king. Such a weapon also required a terrible amount of magical power and finesse. In a duel, you would have to both channel through the weapon and instantly suppress the property to parry, as your opponent's weapon would easily pass through your own. The woman was either a master fencer and channeler or an arrogant fool.

Kingfisher idly wondered if the Whirlwind's bone weapon was also sympathetic.

Mignard had the Argamani look of someone from southern Merovy, likely the Carme, swarthy, with black, slightly curly hair and large, almond eyes. She had a quiet intensity, a piercing gaze, and a tight-lipped look, rather harsh apart from a weak, slightly recessed chin.

Her paradoxically graceful and awkward movement set her apart from common humanity. She trod lightly, feline like the sylph, but with a jerky quality, half-ballerina, half-marionette. There was a deliberate quality to each step, without the natural movements of voluntary motion. It reminded Fade of when you read about breathing and find yourself a bit too aware of your own involuntary respiratory cycle and have to command yourself to breathe until your attention wanders enough for instinct to seize the reigns again.

"Good evening, citizens of the free world," said Mignard. "We have witnessed the first steps towards the modern age.

The harnessing of heavenly fire, the mastery of elementary powers. Your city and my nation are united in a new order, an age of reason, progress, and civility, and age of equality and liberty. Nature is no longer brutal savagery, a great mystery to be feared, but tamed and tempered with mortal understanding and worldly design. We are in command of our future, free from the wills of lords, kings, divines, and ancients. Northernmost is the eternal friend of Achille, an ally of Merovy and the Age of Reason. Thank you for your warm welcome in this cold clime, citizens of Samyy Severnyy, and enjoy a life liberated from the dark."

A heavy, older man clapped and cheered for her, catching the eye with both his size and fine Merovene attire, purple frilled with gold and trimmed with funerary lace. His fine silk and barometz jacket held medals showing his leadership of the Asterean Order of the Solidago, the Theurgical Committee of Merovy, and the Achillene Commune's Academy of Arcane Philosophy. Light purple flowers wreathed these tokens, lilac, and lavender, popping against silver-gilt embroidery. Upon finishing his slow travel through the crowd to Fade's side, Lund leaned in and asked if that was Perdurabo Legrand. Fade nodded and said he was almost certain, as he fit the uncommon profile.

Legrand finished clapping and retrieved his drink of Bard's Blood from his assistant. He was in his sixties but looked over a decade younger due to imbibing of alchemical elixirs, with wiry silver curls and a skin tone darker than Mignard's. His background was uncertain, and likely exoticized to play up the wizard's mysticism, but he was said to have a Windwarder mother, from the Guabanches Islands or Deep Cannaria, and a father with Giaran and Hirpic Austerian ancestry.

Fade meandered towards the mage, hoping to talk with the master. He brushed through the gathered throngs, dodging finery and dessert plates and pointy clothing. He stumbled over something out of view that he assumed was a child, a pet, or a hobgoblin, but could not find it to apologize. Fade managed to squeeze into the orbit of Legrand.

"Good evening. I am Nicodemus Fade, a surgeon volunteering in town... Oh, that's fleabane," Fade said, noting the shape of Legrand's light purple flowers.

"Yes, yes," Legrand said. "Everyone in this town is chronically itchy."

"I've noticed," Fade said. "But it's a sign of the Contortions rather than an infestation. I've seen it even after delousing in hospitals. Their skin crawls, an internal, neurotic effect."

"Astute observation," said Legrand. "Oh, this plague is worrying. I've been eating food and drink from our vessel the entire time. But those little fish cakes are quite tempting."

"Well, you can't be too cautious, but I wouldn't worry," said Fade. "Anyway, I've been an avid reader of your work for years. Your political and arcane work. *The Foundations of Liberty*, *Polemic Chansons, the Lives of the People, the Romantic Review*."

"Ah, and what about *The Book of Roses*?" said Legrand with a coy and conspiratorial smile. "I've had so many young men admit to reading it before they should have. Less for the esoteric erotic alchemy, more for the illustrations."

"Well yes, they weren't bad," said Fade. "But I'm more interested in the expedition to Mitza, under Aurélien Galbasi."

"Oh yes," said Legrand. "Quite swampy. The ancient Mitzan dynasties had several techniques to preserve their documents. Bronze plates, heat-carved stone, lacquered dried wood, clay tablets… the Khamsin invaders of the Seventh Era preserved paper in fine, clear resin. Ingenious, but the eight millennia turned it to precious glass."

"What did you find in the river tombs?"

"Oh, General Galbasi had a contingent of savants, myself among them. Scholars with the Merovene Expeditions. The greatest discovery was the *Athnarian Book of Kings,* a catalog of cartouches also recorded in Old Eastern Khamsinite and Ancient Tammuzi. It took us a year, but we broke the code. *The Book of Reeds, the Compendium of Theologies,* and *the Register of Antiquities.* Primordial ceremonial magics, my boy. The history of magic is no longer occult."

"When will your colleagues publish a translation?" asked Fade.

"I'm afraid it's a bit of a hush-hush affair," said Legrand. "We can't have the Republic's greatest finds fall into the hands of its enemies."

"That's a damn shame," Fade said. "What about the progress of arcane philosophy? Mortal knowledge?"

"Well, one day," Legrand said. "But we are under threat from all sides. And I'm afraid you are a citizen of an enemy empire, Mr. Fade, if I am correctly judging your name."

"What are nations to men of learning?" Fade said.

"In better days, boy, in better days," said Legrand, wistfully. "If you come to the City of Catacombs, we will have a place for you. Though you may not be allowed to go home, for some time."

Fade did not like the sound of that.

"Those ancient tombs," Fade began. "What did they say about the Great Mystery of Life?"

The pinnacle of arcane philosophies are the Great Mysteries, work thought to be beyond human achievement. Some of the mysteries, such as abiogenesis and psychogenesis, violate the rule that nothing can come from nothing. These mysteries are often considered low-priority, as spirit and matter can be manipulated from pre-existing materials - one can, through strange labors, work a rabbit out of a pond slime, and work a mannish mind from the rabbit's brain.

Some have peculiar mechanical restrictions, such as the Grand Aegis, the perfect defense, as every such measure must by necessity have a countermeasure, or Divine Charisma, the ability to permanently persuade people without direct domination or charming. Others are matters of scale, such as Absolute Atomism, as mages have failed to manipulate anything at that size. Time manipulation is not uncommon, but Antiparadoxical time travel must logically be impossible.

Finally, there are the three great mysteries of life, True Resurrection, Perfect Immortality, and Apotheosis. Some think these are actually the same mystery, a sort of mastery of personal being. It may be a matter of volume – reanimation of dead tissue is possible, an extension of life is common, and human flesh is just as malleable as anything else. Any form of ascension, however, is limited by that same principle. You can mold a chunk of clay in countless ways, but not every way at once. There is no such thing as truly limitless potential.

Legrand smiled and said, "It was all just deliberate bog mummies, of course, wrapped in crocodile leather and lead cases. If they knew of immortality and return, by all rights they would still rule. I suppose we should leave longevity to the sagani."

Fade's gray eyes went dull.

"They knew less than us, in most ways," said Legrand. "The idea that magic was stronger among the ancients is conservative mythmaking. But they had the naked roots in their hands, rather than our vast cornucopia of modern fruits."

"I see," said Fade. "Has there been anything… of interest?"

"Their world, and thus magic, was no different than ours," said Legrand. "Thaumaturgy is the art of isolating, exaggerating, and mimicking properties. Contagion and transference. Firework is easy, for you can make fire with the clash of flint or the decay of phosphorous. Water is everywhere. As is death. Killing is trivial. But where in the world is a drop of resurrection? In the shedding of salamanders? No, it is metamorphosis, no greater than a butterfly's. In the tombs of slumbering kings? Royalist legends. Who has found the nest of the phoenix? Who has felt the second kiss of Incano? You have a keen mind, boy, and ambition, that's clear. Don't waste your life on abstractions."

Fade mumbled out a "thank you for your time," in Merovene, bowed slightly, and stumbled into the crowd, and the magnetic foreign sage turned his attention to some interested ladies. Fade leaned against the wall, where Kingfisher shivered as Mags fed her a meat pie.

"Hey, your stupid knight dreams aren't stupid," said Fade.

Kingfisher's head darted to face Fade. She then raised her head to swallow, and quietly said thanks. She continued to look at her covered feet for some time, before walking outside. The rest followed.

Chapter 9: Between Dark Stems the Forest Glows

Baeg Byeol-i attended to her duties in the communal glass gardens of the Jooga. One greenhouse grew taro, carrots, ginseng, and similar crops. The other plot, the Baeg's specialty, housed exotic plants. The tree of the dreamer's lotus, giant's blood moly, olieribos, the aglaophotis peony, the key, rooted raskovnik, and the mandragora, pruned by her deaf grandmother. Blue and black lotus grew in a small pond, the twin crops of vital enlightenment and deadly delusion.

A third cultivated pond sustained the barnacle trees, as its crop of geese proved too tenacious and destructive for any other plant to tolerate.

Last year, Byeol-i had earned her mastery by harvesting the fern flower, said to only bloom on the eve of the summer solstice, and only visible to lovers and rodents. However, the fern flowers are protected by evil spirits and malicious ghosts, which plot to devour the luck of those who seek the fern. She conducted an experiment, using an exorcist dog and a pair of mated waterpigs, who covered much more ground than the hedgehogs and were immune to supernatural malice. It proved wildly successful, and she managed to find eighteen of the mystical flowers, distilling them into potions of luck and animal communion.

It was similar to how the raskovnik, called the 'herb of thieves' or 'hinge-breaker,' is only distinguishable from the four-leaf clover to hedgehogs, serpents, and tortoises. Her great grandfather circumvented this rule by forging scores of bright rings held together by locks. He attached them to snakes- where they fell, the herb of unlocking grew, marked by a trail of screws. It made his name and stabilized the position of a family faltering in an uncertain time and alien clime.

As the summer solstice approaches, the Bookhangers planned to put her method to the test, with teams of water-pigs and dogs. It filled her with great apprehension when she could remember.

She heard footsteps on the rooftop and picked a citron. She climbed a ladder, undid the hatch of the glass tile, and handed the fruit to Goldentooth, one of the jooga's Godokkaebi. This species of hobgoblin was exceedingly tall, the size of an adult woman, and their muscular arms, which hung to their ankles, enhanced their formidable skill with bows and polearms. Their faces were red and leathery, with yellow fangs, and their shaggy hyphae a green so dark it verged on black. The godokkaebi bowed his head in thanks.

Once she finished watering and pruning, Byeol-i consulted her schedule. After recalling her next task, she opened the top of her stovepipe shako, slipped the handbook within, and clasped it shut with a button disguised by a cockatrice plum. The tall hat of the Harnep Fusiliers housed several such note-books and pressed ginko leaves grown in an eastern plot, an old remedy for memory issues.

Byeol-i descended into the caverns of steam with a basket of scrap metal, bones, food waste, moss, and fragrant wood. She overturned the offering into the altar pyre. A salamander rose from a steaming aqueduct, a pythonic form with four crocodilian arms. It rolled over the offerings, consuming them like smokeless wildfire through a dry brush.

The salamander coiled around her at a distance of a meter, encircling her thrice, in an uncomfortably warm embrace.

"Gangcheori-nari," she said. "Have I done something wrong?"

"Dear Byeol-i, do you remember what's coming?" the sala-mander said.

"No, I'm sorry," she said. "I can keep hundreds of herbs and extracts in my head, but my life is just scraps."

"Ah, such a shame," Gangcheori said. "Do memories blur together? Or do they never form in the first place?"

"It's a fog," she said. "I can remember people's names. But what I know of my life is more from what people have told me happened. I don't actually recall it."

"I see," Gangcheori said, coiling itself up further, and diminishing its heat to a gentle ambiance. "Sometimes, it feels that way to me. As if my history is a text, and my eyes can only focus on a few lines at a time. I have been in your clan's service for a thousand years, when I was but a newt in the billows of the Sagong's smithy."

"It's your millennial birthday," she said.

"You've figured it out," said Gangcheori. "Now, you know the legends of the *imugi*. For centuries, I've forged a cintamani within me. Draconite and draco-elixir. The flaming pearl of Parash Pathar."

Part of Gangcheori's head became transparent, like a flickering flame. Dancing with yellow and orange, a nascent Philosopher's stone formed like a pearl around a crude base of red sulfur. Yet its light was colder and duller than it should be, and adulterated with liquid silver. Any elemental or human could transform into a dragon-like being after a millennium of life, bloodshed, and arcane working upon a philosopher's stone, with a handful of 'tunnelwurms' arising from a dwarf king's mountainous horde of gems, and stranger daemon kings springing from the world's most puissant alchemists. However, only a thousand-year-old salamander can resume the true, fire-breathing, winged form of their ancestors, naturally developing a pearl of transmutation in their living hearths. They are, after all, living athanors. Byeol-i marveled at the pearl's luster, and thought of the stories of a new city in the Dawn Sea built upon an accursed island in a rotten swamp, purged of its poison by three cintamani. Could Gangcheori do the same for Northernmost?

"For fifty generations, I have been your banner's faithful ally," said Gangcheori. "And yet you fail to honor my service. Paltry offerings. Adulterated metals. Where is my chimerical hepar? Gold and silver? Ash of myrrh and saffron crocus?"

"I'm sorry we have failed in our pact," she said. "But we are confined to this compound, and the port's reach is shrinking year by year. If you wish, there is a convention of the family heads at the beginning of the next fortnight. Is there anything I can offer you? My portion of the fern flower harvest?"

"This one is diligent and devoted," said Gangcheori. "I don't blame you. You've done your duties and fed me well. You, alone in the last three generations, have fed me exotics rich in yliaster. You remind me of your great-great-grandmother, Lady Sohui. She shot down a griffon for me. If only the Eun family had made me an ichneumon."

The Eun family bred chimerae, particularly hatching cockatrice from the eggs of hermaphrodite roosters incubated by poisonous toads; their signature breed of *kyeryong* were prized for their beauty. Gangcheori had commissioned an ichneumon, a rare mongoose fed on a diet of picked asp, vipers drowned in sacred wine, honey-fermented crocodile meat, and spider crabs marinated in chili powder and gold dust. A mature ichneumon was immune to venom, fire, and water magics. They shield themselves in transmuted mud, track down a dragon, and swim through its golden hoard, waiting to ambush and kill the dragon by burrowing into its heart and stealing its pearl. Unfortunately, they are incredibly expensive to produce, particularly in this climate, and all three ichneumons died of the contortions.

The siren sightings worried Gangcheori, as the harpies of Notos were known to eat mongooses and could easily overcome the ichenumon and its poisonous flesh. It wondered if the Mayor anticipated his plot to seize their pearl and planned a counterstrike. The old imugi wondered if the Eun family could instead breed and train an enhydros, a hairy serpent known for erupting from the gullets of crocodiles, hippopotamuses, and any other creature foolish enough to swallow it.

Byeol-i held still for a moment, and said, "I remember something. A foreign doctor came here earlier, interested in our genealogies. And curses."

"Did you tell him about me?" Gangcheori asked.

"I don't think so," she said. "I know that the foreigners suspect that the Mayor is behind the Contortions. Telling them of an aspiring dragon could put you in danger. All of us."

"Ah, aspiring, am I?" said Gangcheori.

"Ascendant," she said.

"I will be a dragon. It is merely a matter of time. But you can expedite it," Gangcheori said. "There is a man named Pander, funding an expedition north to find a dragonkiller, the Seonpung Gunhigunda. If this is not folly, we must aid him. I want the cintamani of the Mayor."

"Won't that endanger all of Northernmost?" she asked.

"We will have a dragon, and the Hwagasari. Indeed, I will transmutate it into a bulgasari… when I have risen. And then who can oppose us?"

Apprehension clawed at her chest when she thought of waking the Hwagasari. She softly asked, "Who would we sacrifice?"

The last time someone activated the steel protector, the priest dropped dead, bleeding from his pores. Consultation with their ghost left the other speakers puzzled, as the ghost had no answer for what occurred. He was simply ripped apart from the inside. The autopsy confirmed it, the man wounded as though some force pulled wires through his body.

"I believe it was a fluke that can be remedied. No such thing occurred in the days of old, in the sack of Sangcheon," Gangcheori said. "I told Pander of the foreign doctor. We may need his cooperation and the support of the Septentrine Empire. Bring him and his minions before me. He has a kaftar with him, a wight with a talent for fire. I will give you a contingency, a touch of assurance."

"I just need to bring Pander here?" she said.

"Yes," Gangcheori said. "Now, let your mind drift. I need you to meditate on emptiness."

Byeol-i wondered if this was wise, but the old imugi had never stirred her clan wrong. The salamander's tail marked her forehead with a summoner's rubric of red ochre. She closed her eyes and focused on the darkness. Soon came a starscape, and visions of cold fire.

"I have filled your mind with a pattern, protected by a tongue of my flame," the salamander said. "It will protect you from the firework of the Kaftar."

"This is strange," Byeol-i said. "I can see flashes in my eye, like when you close your eyes for too long and sparks race across the lids."

"It is a memory of an elemental from a world around Arax, the chief star in the constellation of Lamprotita the Dancer, the zodiac of Middlekindle. Now that it's in your head, the Kaftar cannot harm you due to the exotic fires, nor can I meddle with you further. Think of it as a sign of trust."

"I trust you," said Byeol-i. "How, when will it get out? The elemental?"

"As I said, it's a mere memory, a shard," said the Salamander. "As soon as it passes from your mind, you will lose the protection."

"Then I'm the worst person you could have chosen," she said.

"No, no, you're the best. For the shard cannot root in your mind. You're a perfect fit for this engrammatic magic. So, I need you to remember. I need you to bring me Pander."

Chapter 10: Gun

Gog the gunsmith began his nightly routine of closing up shop and activating the powder trap before descending to the cellar and the seaside caves. The shop, a blast-proof bunker of concrete, had once been a processing building for a nearby nitrary. The tall tower rose from the cliff face of Alchemist Isle, grown out of it like coral by gnomecraft. Northernmost produces quite a bit of "cold nitre." Saltpeter is usually collected in salty fields because it rapidly dissolves in water, but it can be found frozen in the gypsum-rich tundra soil, and the nitrary was built around caves teeming with the guano of arctic fox-bats, transplanted, flightless Cannarian nightcrawlers, and the excrement of seabirds and humans. It's foul-smelling work, but some of the workers like the constant heat of the boilers.

Gog Unsang had grown up in that heat, working with his father. It was rough and disgusting, but it meant freedom from the nobility of the Willow Court, their blue-stained skinned and ancient law which protected no one but the masters.

He heard the delicate snap of a wire, and the twang of it slapping into a stony wall. He spun around, reached for his pistol, and, in his panic, realized that he grabbed a display piece.

A figure in a white cloak patterned with mossy green-brown stood before him. Despite the bend in its legs, readied to pounce, it was taller than Gog, and a strange wide structure held its hood in an inhuman, horned shape. Antlers curled from its back, holding a firearm like a gun rack. One hand held a knife, while the other tensed up like a snake ready to strike, whiter than its cloak.

It was, however, the hint of fox tails that frightened him most, the telltale signs of the demon women of legend. Her hand was already on the barrel of his pistol, pushing it towards the ceiling and twisting it from his wrist until it was in her grip. She hooked it to a prong on her back and pulled down its neighboring musket.

The Sylphide ripped off the musket barrel and peered down it, shifting towards the light of the foxfire plates.

"That's the barrel," said the gunsmith, nervously, hoping to buy time from the ancient evil. "You pour the powder down it and ram the bullet down inside."

"Yeah, why is it smooth?" she said.

She turned into the light, twisting the barrel like a kaleidoscope. He noticed that she wore two other weapons on her back, a long, thin sword, and a curving woldo encased in a spine. Gog tried to figure out why and how they vanished into her back.

"Oh, you mean rifling," he said. "We do have rifles, if that's what you mean."

"Why are they not all rifled?" she said, her dialect oddly archaic. "That would be more accurate. Like putting spin on an arrow."

"Why, yes," he said. "It is, but the problem is that rifles are harder to clean. It causes the weapon to foul. So, they're mostly for hunting and sharpshooting, not for a formation of infantrymen."

"Use windwork to clean it and clear the smoke," she said, her finger already tracing out hypothetical Voörish runes into the barrel, encoding the spell. "Bore a small flute hole at the top, I could clear it like it was nothing."

"Well, yes, but not all soldiers can use air magic," said the gunsmith.

"I don't care about them," she said. "Wait, why are you pouring the powder into the barrel? Just package the powder at the base of the bullet."

"You bite the paper cartridge and pour the course powder into the barrel, then drop the musket ball in. The finer powder, the primer, is the ignition factor, placed in this part, the pan."

"Yeah, and that's dumb," she said. "Make the bullet a cone with a bit of rifling and build in the powder primer. Make it smokeless with spirit of hartshorn. You don't need the pan, hammer the bullet directly."

"How?" he said.

"We have a trick where I'm from. Sulfur, charcoal, and moonsalt. You use it to make smokers and noise grenades. Gas bombs and the like."

"Moonsalt?"

"*Terenzingr.* Salt-of-silver," she said. "It is sensitive. Volatile. A drop of water, a violent fall, or a bit of static… Oh, it's so much fun. Pour lunar caustic and spirit of niter into alcohol. The burning mirror."

"Fulminating silver?" he said. "Are you talking about silver fulminate? *Argentum Fulminans?*"

"Sure," she said. "Sounds right. We don't have the same focus on metallic alchemy as your folk. But we have quite a bit of knowledge of gases and the like… did you know that the stars are made of air, excited into a blazing chaos? They are more like stable lightning than eternal fire."

Her fingers traced the constellations on a calendar hanging from the wall. The Aquilan calendar is divided into twenty-six named fortnights, each aligned with an astrological mansion and a chief star. She eyed a strange red date. Every fifty years, a Jubilee Day is inserted between Yearsgrave and Freshtides to re-reckon the calendar. Astronomers noticed a slight drift between the mansions and their proper days, and added another Reckoning Day between Sowcorn and Firstflowers, to be celebrated every 682 years. 2550 was thus "the Long Year."

She briefly paused to figure out her new age. It was easy enough, as she was born in 5.

"The salamanders can work the sun's grand heat, but the cool, distant stars belong to the Fair Folk," she said. "That's why so few of us remain; the great bulk of us have gone sailing across the stars."

"Oh," he said, clearly not sure how to process that, or if she was even telling the truth.

He watched her hand struggle with her hold on the rifle's trigger. Her palm was longer than a woman's, as were her fingers.

She wandered over to his anvil, grabbed one of his bullets with tongs, and heated it with crude convection. She struck it until it deformed into a more oblong point.

A strange glee flashed across her garnet eyes like a meteor burning through a stormy evening sky. Her tongue lolled out at a thumb's length, like a salt-lapping elk. Gog felt a strange revulsion as he realized her lips were naturally the color of venous blood, and that tongue the red-purple of plum syrup, Carmetic grapes, and Hallazoni dyes.

"So, we'll prepare that, bundle it at the end of a bullet-like this, flute the rifle like so, and have the barrel slide forward on a rail, or move on a hinge so you can reload over the elbow rather than pointing it right in your stupid face… and… what is this wood bit called?"

"The stock," he said. His eyes wandered down her squatting form and the parted skirt of foxtails and he added, "Well, uh, that's the butt."

She stood up and asked if it could be made from horn or antler.

"Ivory is expensive to import, not sure if I could get it here," he said.

"But it can be done," she said, not quite a question.

He nodded in affirmation. She reached into her *nábrókarstafur*-branded *naatsit* and pulled out three gold coins as a preliminary payment. "Bully bully bully… I have some staves planned. Bit of cleaning and cooling, a bit of luck, a touch of stealth, a ward against weather and rust, bit of the good old unerring mark, the archery classic… and silence."

"You think you can silence a rifle?" he said.

She smiled. "I can silence anything."

Chapter 11: Eating My Wings to Make Me Tame.

Kingfisher, alone in her room, slowly picked at her wounds, torturing herself to pass the time. Her head snapped up at the sound of a gentle knock on the door, her voice quavering when she told the visitor to come in. Fade identified himself, and she repeated the assent. The young surgeon entered with books under his arm.

"You don't lock your door?" he asked.

"I can't work the bars and latches," she said.

"I see," he said.

She nodded with her head towards the empty half of the bed. She slept in a ball, resting her head against a stack of pillows within a nest of swirled blankets. Fade gently kicked his bookbag into the room, sat down on the bare mattress, and opened the topmost book across his lap.

"Thank you," he said.

"Thank you for joining me," she said.

He reached over and fixed the bandage on her wing and told her he would redress it later. Her tail feathers compressed and slipped behind Fade's back as she scooted closer. She had lost some of her blue-grey plumage in the fight, revealing a serpentine tail beneath it. She tried to hide the bare scales under the comforter, but feared that the weeping preen glands would leave it crusted with a waterproof wax. At least it would ward off the mites.

He returned to his tome.

"What are you reading?" she asked.

"It's an old medical text," he said. "Written in High Hirpic, with Middle Skeironic commentary. One of the only decent texts in the town archives."

"What's to be found in outdated medical texts?" she asked.

"Isn't newer better?"

"It's certainly easier to read," he said. "But I thought of elf-shot and folkloric magic. I wonder if this town's curse is actually a forgotten poison, from the old elemental lords. Like, the *alpdruck*, or elf-nightmares, or the association between sylphine touch, epilepsy, and nerve damage. Or this is a passage on *Gedwaesnes* and *dweorging*, a dementia caused by, and effecting, dwarfs. Respectively. It sounds rather like the Contortions."

There was the rather polite notion that the elementals could carry diseases they were immune to, spreading them to humans unawares, rather than through deliberate malice.

"It also affects them?" Kingfisher asked. "Could it be a sylphic curse, instead? Are we sure that those Hyperboreans haven't been poisoning the portfolk?"

"Perhaps," said Fade.

He flipped roughly fifty pages. The scent of musty dust accompanied the faint trill of aged vellum parting for the first time in decades.

"Sylphs were known to use weapons of the atmosphere, poisoned gases, miasmas that cause disease. They launched them in grenades and great censers."

"What's a gas?" she asked.

"Oh, it's a form of matter, the chaos of the air."

"How's it different from air?"

"Oh, the air is actually not one substance, but made up of discrete elements."

"I thought air was the element. How can an element be made up of other elements?"

"We were incorrect in certain assumptions," he said. "For example, we used to think that acids were a contamination of aqueous essence, but it's also a product of aerial and terrestrial elements, while having properties of decay like fire. Fire, as I said, is more of a reaction than an actual element. And the air that we breathe is largely inert, the type of gas vital to human and harpy life is only one of several gasses in the atmosphere."

"What about the elementals then?" she asked.

"Perhaps we should call them the Sagani, again," he said. "Human arcane philosophy was shaped by their worldview for too long. Just because the nymphs and silens believed that they were commanding elements, doesn't necessarily make their magic truly elemental. Perhaps they simply have a mastery over their bodies, aquatic, etherial, and earthly. The Salamanders have control over strong chemical reactions, while gnomes are beings of clay. The *Pharyes* can even shape themselves into other forms, like fish, small mammals, and tunnel-dragons."

"I see," lied Kingfisher. She was surprised to hear a human use the name that the gnomes used among themselves. "I wonder if harpies are air elemental like sylphs, but a stinkier gas. Like swamp air."

"Possibly," said Fade, flipping back to the section on gnomish diseases. He noticed a cooling dullness in her yellow eyes and added, "You don't smell bad, if you're worried."

"I try. Why did you want to see me?" she asked.

"I just wanted to see a… a friend, I guess. And Mags is visiting Lund," he said.

"Does she not like you?" Kingfisher asked, with an abrupt tilt of the head.

"No, they just needed to be alone."

"Why?"

Fade gestured at the wall, and then Kingfisher's ear. She heard movement on a bed, wrestling and a slippery slapping sound. She mouthed 'oh' and asked if they had known each other for a long time.

"No," Fade said. "Sometimes tragedies, or absolute terror for your life, will bring people together."

"Do they want to have children?" she asked.

"No," Fade said. "They simply want the pleasure. And the contact."

This perplexed her. Sexuality was a thing of horror and cruelty, the birth of some new chimerical evil to the world. It must have been different for true women, but still, there was the danger of childbirth.

"So, are they getting married now?" she asked.

"Probably not," said Fade.

"But you're supposed to get married first," she said. "It is the blessing of Incano and Urizen."

"Jubal and Rahab have a stronger hold on young people," Fade said. "And the longings of Craethion. Have you not seen the prostitutes in port?"

"Aren't they bad, though?" she asked. She had seen many conduct novels, like *Virtue Rewarded* and *Chastity & Vice*, and prostitution was the penultimate state of failure for a dissolute life, especially if gin and ether came into play. Then again, other novels seemed fascinated with hierodules, the temple prostitutes of old. Humans were confusing.

"No," he said. "Unfortunate, probably, but most people are simply trying to survive...don't worry about Mags, she had her own ways and customs, and training in women's matters. And Lund is a religious dissenter. There are interpretations of Jubal's path permitting the free 'alchemical union' outside of the confine of marriage. The worldly hierogamy is said to 'recreate the Rebis,' but it's convenient for a tall, wealthy young gentleman."

He tried to read her face as she quietly bobbled her head. Her cheeks and eyes were sunken, as if by starvation and exertion, and the cold winds chapped her skin raw. She tucked her wings close to her body, as a woman would retreat into her cape, and scratched the flakes from her nose.

He returned to the text, mouthing out the archaic words,

trying to connect them to his mother tongue's historical forms, but it was from an age of solitary, idiosyncratic works rather that the modern age of mass publication, medical conventions, and standardization. He soon noticed the harpy looking over his shoulder.

"You're really smart," she said.

"Thank you," he said.

"Animalcule," she said. "Is that a tiny animal?"

"Well, yes," he said. "One so small that it can't be seen by the naked eye. Using microscopes, we've learned that they're all around us, and in us. Some are elementals, sprites. There are small plants, too, algae, the likes of which live in the hollows of sylph and undine hair, which is why those races often have green hair in summer and the tropics. And yeast, the earliest known variety."

"Do they make people sick?" she asked.

"We think they may," he said. "The mechanism of contagion is still controversial. Some hold that chemical imbalances in the body cause illness. Others, the introduction of more alien substances to the body such as poisons, malicious geniuses, miasmas, or possibly invasive animalcules through water and food. I believe it's a mixture of all these factors."

"So, the old stories are wrong," she said.

"Many of them, I suppose. What prompted that?"

"The gnomes are supposed to have an ancient treaty with the small animals. They protect them, do not eat them, and are not harmed by them in return," she said. "If that were true, then those animalcules shouldn't harm them."

"Yes," he said. "That would follow… Maybe you're right. Maybe it's not an animalcule. And an imbalance systemic enough to infect a town over generations is unlikely without severe inbreeding, which one wouldn't find in a port. Especially as it also affects the Saromen."

"So, it is a magical curse?" she said, almost excitedly. "Who bestowed it? The Mayor?"

"Maybe," he said. "Perhaps its very presence is a miasm, of sorts. They exhale poison, after all… Perhaps the coalburners up on the periphery should be studied, to see if their exposure to similar exhaust exacerbates their symptoms."

"Should we go there tomorrow?" she asked. "Or return to the Academy?"

He shook his head and said they should stay in tomorrow. To recuperate and compare notes with Lund and Mags.

He added, "You need to keep a low profile, and let that wing mend."

She looked through the book of herbal lore and remedies, Bogdan the Brilliant's *Florae Aquilonum*, looking for flowers called 'Elena' and 'Mageirissa.' She barely understood what was said. She bit down on the remnant quill of a broken covert, focusing on the pain as it slowly ripped free, distracting her from the far more terrible state of social stupidity. An oily taste flooded her mouth, and she told herself that Fade must be lying; she smelled revolting.

"That's Old Vankiri," Fade said.

She felt like a better reader, but even more stupid than before.

"I hope it is someone," she whispered.

"What do you mean?" Fade asked.

"Someone is responsible," she said.

She examined her bandage again.

"For a curse. I… That monster, the Whirlwind… I hope there's some witch out there, that we could fight and kill, and this would all end."

"That would be nice and simple," he said.

"I wish I could help you," she said. "But I couldn't even beat the monster. What good am I here?"

Her talons dug into the mattress and scraped against the bedframe. Fade reached down and slid his fingers around her claws and pulled them up so she wouldn't do any regrettable property damage. He felt the signs of her self-mutilation but kept quiet. He could think of nothing above condescending platitudes and impropriety. Her claw curled around his hand, gentle yet cold and hard. Her head fell against his shoulder, and they were asleep within half an hour, her wounds knitting from the lingering magic of his touch.

Chapter 12: The Ogress

Mageirissa dried herself after the steam bath, dressed, and went downstairs to join the early kitchen rounds. She prepared three dozen bison pies, tea biscuits, and a stock of carob bread. She helped the inn's hobgoblin, Perchinka, decant a barrel of mead. Unlike the large domovoi of most Tsokiri households, Perchinka was a small boggle from the Swanlands. The hob was highly intelligent, almost like a human child, but it lacked the strength of its heartier northeastern cousins. Its spores were refined, and capable of brewing spirits with the same potency as alewife's yeast, if Mageirissa remembered her cobalogy lessons and the draughts of the various species.

She could identify most of the Aquilan goblin species by sight and spirit. The sooty-elves, boggles, boggarts, brownies, blue burches, billy blinds, bauchans, goodfellows, lubber fiends, urisks, greenmoss, winter whitecaps, the vile redcaps, and lie-by-the-fires. Perchinka appeared to be a robin round-cap, his broad head and light brown flesh recalling a bread roll. Perchinka had to be kept from the stores of cream and milk, as those same spores caused the milk to curdle and spoil into a revolting "goblin-cheese" only good for feeding the mush-room men.

Elena advised one of the customers on his toothache, caused by indulgence in the sweets, rum, and tropical fruits of the Cane Sea before spending two fortnights on a boat. She advised him to seek out the Hypouranid dentists in the profes-sional district, who specialized in amalgamation.

"They would be paid in silver coins. Pure silver," she warned, "As they would be melting one down and binding it to your teeth."

Mageirissa left the kitchen to the watchful eye of its oven's grass snake and advised the sailor to wash his mouth with salt and oil of thyme; vanilla or garlic could also do, in a pinch. Elena thanked her for the help, in her quiet, sad way, and the shaman bowed and traveled to the herbalist in Mason's Ward, two blocks west, and bought samples and extracts of hypericum wort, valerian, and vervain.

She encountered a team of black-jacketed sailors hauling heaps of echeneis in wheelbarrows. She smiled and tried to strike up a conversation and perhaps make a purchase. The echeneis are small fish that cling to hulls and slow them with natural drag and magic hindrance, and their oil is used in lust potions, ligament spells, and to slow fluxes in the womb and delay what would otherwise be premature births. The men brushed her off, with one demanding that she leave a public market. She sat down on a bench and pretended to nap. Her spirit departed from her body, strung up in astral threads spooling from her spine. She peeked at the men as they extracted the oil in a warehouse and began to mix it with barrels of what looked like sealing tar. Rather than a mere fish-gutter, the leader of the operation appeared to be a cunning man, and the hooded figure's gaze shot up from his distillery and locked eyes with her astral form. Mageirissa retreated to her flesh, and moved on to the far side of the market. She bought a block of wax and an envelope of wicks from the chandler and returned to the inn as fast as she could.

One of Mageirissa's clients came to her not long after. She was a Timorat woman approaching her forties, who had finally had a child after two decades of struggle. The Contortions had ravaged her body, shaking and quaking so severely that she bound her child to her trunk in a rigid sleeve. Her husband was the owner of the largest lumber company in town, so she had a relative degree of wealth and security. But with such status, the family had a need for an inheritor; and due to the common nature of frontier work, his closest relatives were in a country on the other shore of the Polar Sea. She was at least capable of carrying the child to term during the deep freeze with purified provisions, household servants, tranquilizing incense, and other pricey precautions against natal monstrosities.

The woman sought out hirelings to nurse her child, for fear of the Contortions's enigmatic spread, but female itinerant workers grew rarer and rarer, and usually brought the risks of the prostitute's lifestyle. Mageirissa went to her room to nurse the child, drinking another cup of fenugreek tea and her daily extraction of fennel and milk thistle. Mags brought the child to her teat gently, as he already had a pair of canine teeth, inwardly curved and so long that the poor thing struggled to close its mouth. His ears were likewise pointed and fringed, somewhat elfin and undinic, yet swollen like an old boxer's. Two cord-like muscles ran from under his ears down to the center of his clavicles.

She had seen worse, those sooterkin born from women poisoned by smoke and smithy, vermin-children that gave rise to beast-folk if they managed to survive. But still, he was tragic; she hoped that his royal violet eyes stayed with him into his adult years, not lost like the baby blues. She wondered how the Contortions could have accelerated such a chimerical birth, and what disease or foreign influence could cause such a radical transmutation.

She applied an ointment to his arm, a thin cut where his mother scratched him during a spasm. The thought overwhelmed Mageirissa, nearly to the point of tears. She tried to calm herself and the child with a song her mother had taught her, on the names and calls of the birds.

With her off-hand, she dipped wicks into her small cauldron of melted wax, ground herbs, iron shavings, and oils. Valerian warded off "the envy of the elves," that is, their curses and divination. Hypericum irritated their senses. And vervain—red verbenna, the *hiera botane*, the herb aristereon—was not only for healing but, when prepared in a ferrous circle and suffused with iron, prevented elementals from changing into their chaos. Hence its other names, irongrass or medical ironwort. Lund returned later, with wind-chimes and bells, which could detect and banish sylphs and salamanders. Not only sleighbells and small finger-cups, but a mighty iron handbell best used by a town crier. Unfortunately, neither could find the ingredients for a garland of marsh marigold and primrose, nor a staff of rowan or mountain ash. Lund sealed the windows tight. Sylphs could easily disperse incense unless the air was allowed to grow smoky and stagnant in an almost sealed room. They cannot be overcome in an open field.

She and Lund spoke of nutritional theory, and how the vital energy of life flowed from the Sun, into the plants and slimes of the sea. Yliaster leaks into the world from the Deer Hunter, and soaks into the world's base elements, rising through plants and concentrating into the intelligent wights of the world. That vital solar energy is lost with each new consumer, but yliaster intensifies further up the chain. It is why monsters must prey upon man and chimerical kine, and mannish flora like goblins and mandrakes. It's the only efficient way to get yliaster, despite the dangers of hunting a social, tool-using enemy. The doctor soon departed for work, thoughts of strange animals turning in his head.

At the end of the hour, Mags descended to the main room of the inn to return the child to his mother. Mags smelled a familiar bouquet of scents. Pine, mulled wine, moss, mead, and master-of-the-woods, befouled with the odor of butcher's blood and wet leather. Her heart pounded and her throat tensed. She was a cornered animal in a crowded in. At the bar sat a woman in a gossamer dress, with her spine jutting out of a black gash that closed as she turned to face Mageirissa.

"What was the name of that man who led the gunners?" asked Cunigunde the Whirlwind.

"What?" Mags gasped. She let out a strange sobbing croak that surprised even herself.

"Kind of haggard-looking but with a bit of strength to him, lead the gun line? Answered to that idiot?" the Sylphide asked.

Mags paused for a moment, trying to remember. "Arild Salmacis... But everyone but his wife called him Lieutenant... That was the woman whose head you blew up."

"Yes, she was worthless-" Cunigunde said.

"Eumelia," Mags interrupted. "Her name was Eumelia."

"She wasn't your wife, calm down... I thought him a fool. But when the wind rose, he fought valiantly, under incompetent seniors," she said.

"You ate him."

"And the hunter eats the stag. But what adorns the halls where men gather, and the banners that lead them to battle?" said Cunigunde. She turned away from Mags and raised her tankard, and spoke:

> "Arild, groom of Eumelia,
> scented by powder and horses,
> Arild, the strong-legged son
> Of slow rivers and cold courses,
> Master of a band of steel bows,
> Commander of the unseen shot,
> A heart that feeds the battle crows
> And the foe he bravely fought.
> The warrior who stood his ground
> And aimed with point-blank volley,
> Heir of Salmacis hall, fell,
> For the rich fool's folly."

Several drinkers raised their glasses and tankards to toast, but none of them knew the subject of her poem, and few understood her dialect. She dug into her backless dress and unhooked a silver chain jeweled with rubies and emeralds and handed it to Elena.

"This should pay for a dozen rounds, and much of everyone's wine-debts," Cunigunde said. "I ripped it from a queen's dark neck."

Elena froze in shock, until her back quaked with a jerking shiver.

"Is my wealth not honored here?" said Cunigunde, barely above a whisper, as she placed the jewelry in her hand.

"No, it's just…" Elena mumbled, pausing to peer into the shining ruby, and the matching glare of the sylphide standing before her. She did not see the Whirlwind enter her family's establishment. "Um, I don't know how much it's worth."

"Then is my word not honored here?" asked Cunigunde.

Elena shook her head and muttered, "It is, it is, I'm sorry, it's just...overwhelming. I've never seen anything like this."

"It's fine dear," Cunigunde said. "I am overwhelming. I will have a hippocras and a small bowl of milk."

Mags' rising eyebrows pleaded with Elena to just take it and go. The barmaid got the point, put the necklace in the coffer, and turned to pour the drinks with the help of a waiter.

"The dead are dead but remember them. Don't regret, but remember," said Cunigunde. "Sing in the joy of living. Sing in the joy of killing… Though I should work more on its meter."

"What do you want of me?" Mageirissa asked.

"Nothing at the moment. I came here to gift the community after my battle. And to talk," she said. "Never fight someone twice, if you can. When you crawl bloodied from the same pit, covered in the common gore of battle, you are reborn as twins. And no one's sins are so heavy as to deserve the Whirlwind's second coming."

"What made you into this?" Mageirissa dared to ask.

"This?" Cunigunde asked as she brought the cup of hippocras to her mouth, just high enough to almost cover a wry smile. "What do you mean by 'this?'"

"A monster," Mageirissa said.

"I mean, I'm an ancient folk legend who stalks the wilderness at night and eats people's bones," Cunigunde said. "And I reject society while holding up a dark mirror to its ills, but...Maybe if you don't have anything nice to say, you shouldn't say it."

The Sylphide leaned towards Mageirissa and the babe in her arms. Her bloody irides contracted as the serpentine slits waxed into lunar crescents shining with morning light and a playful cruelty.

There was a nervous pause, before Cunigunde laughed and kissed the child on the head. The Sylphide decided to play the human's game. She knew in her heart that she had never once broken the taboos of her tribe, station, and the star signs of her birth: She had never killed or robbed a charcoal burner, a leatherworker, a cobbler, nor a nursemaid. She had never told her water-name, the one given by her mother, to an outlander. She never had one in the first place, but the world only new her by her breath-names and blood-titles, those she had earned by raiding. She gave rich gifts to others after victories and on her midwinter birthday. She had never eaten the meat of a creature that solely walks on all fours, and never tortured a seal or walrus or Rival Bear. She had never silenced a bird mid-song, and never ask questions of the snow owls. She had honored the shed antlers of the reindeer and her folk, and never buried her shed teeth pointy side up. She had never behaved submissively to a lesser being without eventual, and fatal, rebellion, nor had she tolerated an inferior to rebel. She had never let a mortal slave die of old age, nor thirst or hunger. She had never lain with the same human lover twice in a row. She had never put out a fire with water. She sang songs to the most valorous of fallen foes, ate the hearts of victimized kings, and offered concubinage to their wives. She had never stared at the Sun, nor broken a promise or contract sworn on the stars or her mother's name.

The only sin she had committed was killing a member of her own tribe, but only in the cruelest interpretation of what transpired.

But Cunigunde knew that humans were horrified by her mores, just as they were decadent and disgusting in her eyes.

"No, I get it," she said. "I was always a monster, sweetheart. I was born a twin, a rare and usually fatal event for a sylphide. My mother didn't beat the odds. She passed into the Blue Winds of Heaven, reborn somewhere, I imagine. Never been able to find her. Maybe she didn't want to find us. My father took it out on me. My sister had her look. But I was always a hard, cruel, angry bitch."

"How so?" Mags asked.

"People said that I just looked mean," said Cunigunde. She opened up a rawhide parfleche containing a red ball of pulverized jerky, lichens, dried crowberry, and saxifrage clumped together in bloody seal fat. "My family were tanners, saddlemakers, and cordwainers. Our ice huts reeked of the boiled skin and offal. I was born into blood, piss, and shit. We were lowly people, at the edge of the village, protected with palisades of spears because it attracted the bears and wolves. Skinning things, the raw meat, cutting the throats of beasts...it made my sister squeamish, but it never bothered me."

"I was trained in handling meat and delivering babies," Mageirissa said. "I understand."

"Yeah," Cunigunde said. "I figured. I would help you out there, but sylphide milk will kill a human child. I think for the same reason polar bear liver will kill a man, a toxin in the fats... So, one day, this tribe of men... there was some political arrangement. I don't know. They left their chief's son with us. With my family, since we handled the animals. One day, we went down to the river, he and my sister and me. To club seals. Something came over me, and I pushed him into the water."

"Why?" Mageirissa asked.

"No real reason," Cunigunde said. She shrugged. "I had never seen a human die. Never seen anything drown. You look like us, but you're weaker. And uglier. And he had yet to develop the muscle of a man grown. It was easy. My sister tried to fight me off of him, but she knew she'd have to truly hurt me to stop. Couldn't do it."

She went quiet and looked at the hippocras.

"You turn purple, and bloat," she whispered. Then she smiled, and added, "Imagine what you'd look like. A chimera of pig and grape."

Mageirissa clenched her teeth.

"I bet you'd taste lovely, though," Cunigunde said, before popping the pemmican ball into her mouth. Mageirissa closed her eyes and turned away. The Sylphide touched her with in- humanly taut and warm fingers. Mags recoiled from its oddity and recalled handling arctic foxes and hares. A Hyperborean's body must be all muscle and brown fat as dense and bloody as blubber, a living, twitching furnace.

"Now, priestess," said Cunigunde as she finished chewing. "Worms. Wolves. Vultures. Everyone is eaten by something. Why not be part of something greater than yourself? Isn't that the point of religion?"

"Shut up," Mageirissa spat.

"I've said nothing false," Cunigunde defended. "We're just beasts, after all. You have strong faith in something higher, right? Yet you pissed yourself, just a little, when I killed that man in your lap. I could smell it, up until his bowels loosened his greasy rations. Life and death are foul things. And I smell the blond man on you. In your rolls and crevices."

"Shut up shut up shut up," Mageirissa hissed.

"I'm merely jesting. I won't kill you, not as long as you nurse. Look," Cunigunde said, "I understand your carnal needs. What makes life worthy?"

"Family, faith, life, living…" Mageirissa said. "The little joys. Things you rob from people."

"Yes," Cunigunde said. "My family sent me to die in that camp of men. Or worse."

"You killed their son," Mageirissa said. "I think they traded you away to stop a war."

"Yes, yes," said the Sylphide. "But why avoid a war? Some poor sense of justice? Oh, but two nights into my imprisonment, a blizzard hit. I was liberated by the winds. That cold cut the men down, and I help, white against the white. The wind and the snow had teeth. I only killed the chieftain and his wife as they slept, and two of his guards as the snows bogged them down… but none of the tribe survived the blizzards, and the bears. The tale grew that I slaughtered them all, returning home with their blood on my mouth, meat in my tunic. My tribe feared me. I was a creature of death, the spirit of the pantheon and the polar bear. So, I was shunned, and turned out."

"Good," Mageirissa said. "You should have hanged."

"We are wind-gifted. You can't kill us that way," she said. "But as I said, we return to life, eventually… as long as the winds blow across Thier. So, we have no need for religion. For faith… We *know*. So, I seek the small pleasures in life."

She looked out over the bar, and softly recited:

> *"Where are your beautiful youths,*
> *and tall men with ax-trained arms,*
> *Where are your fairest daughters,*
> *So I may carry the finest to bed?"*

The corner of her mouth turned up.

"These people are old and ugly, withered and diseased," she said. "Perhaps I should fuck your blond or the thin gray boy. At least they have youth."

"Don't," Mageirissa pleaded.

"I could take him from you," Cunigunde said. "What man

would prefer you to me?"

Mageirissa's lips quivered, and a tear ran down her cheek. Cunigunde whipped it away with her thumb and popped it in her mouth.

"Sorry, my little salt-lick," said the Sylphide. "I won't take him. As long as you know that I could. What you did with him, though, that's what makes life worthy. Faith, politics, philosophy. It's all worthless shit to justify what you did up there. I've fought in a thousand pointless wars. And you know why?"

"Money? Killing?" Mageirissa said. "You enjoy murder and pain?"

"It's for the thrill," Cunigunde said. "The purity of the fight. I've led men. Maybe a million now, over the centuries. Not always great heroes. Almost never, really. Just men, hedge-witches, other nobody mercenaries. When you're out on the field, leading a squadron or cavalry or fold or rank-and-file… whatever your folk or age calls your warband… you're alive. Your life has meaning, because you're with your… your unit. Your brothers. Outside of war, they're just men. Fleeting, forgotten things. But in battle, I would die for them. It's some meaningless skirmish for some inbred king's glory, before he dies popping a blood vessel while shitting. Or some company wants a gold mine some savage tribe thinks is sacred. Or just some lie. But after the battle, sitting around, trying to forget the dead, singing and drinking and grabbing one of your mates - an ugly, smelly bastard with calloused hands… letting him love you, *deeply* love you, licking the tears off his face as he calls you the most beautiful being in the universe, the pure gratitude on his lips as you push him down your belly… What is more glorious?"

Mageirissa said nothing.

"You would be surprised," Cunigunde whispered. "It's always the ones with a missing finger or two, who know how to touch you… I'm glad I could share it, the pleasures of the survivor."

"How many of your men did you send to die?" Mageirissa said.

"Bully bully, fewer than the gods," Cunigunde said. "How many men have called out to them on the field of war? And yet I alone offered them salvation and beauty."

She thought of her men in her last campaign, when she served as the *Feldweibelin* of a Forlorn Hope charging into the Rannikonian bastion at Kohdevalo. Her daring band had cut through the foe's defenses behind her whirling wall of snow and beneath the Blood Banner of the vanguard. She lost two men out of three dozen, in an attack that command had believed damned. Oh, the mortified look on the paymaster's face when he had to deliver on that promised doubled wage was delicious.

"And how many more have you murdered?" accused the shaman, snapping Cunigunde back to reality.

"If the gods did not will it, they should not have put me in their path," Cunigunde said, green-tinged silver flickering through her pupil. "Nor should they have made you out of meat."

The elf reached out to jiggle Mageirissa's belly. The priestess recoiled and slapped her hand away.

Cunigunde laughed, and her plum-colored tongue curled out of her mouth, briefly touching her nostril.

"Hey, it was… Mags, I heard," Cunigunde said. She finished her drink. "None of this matters. But that's not a sad thing. Do whatever you want. Know who you are, what brings you joy, and what makes you angry. Feel icy rage. Feel blazing joy. If you want something, take it. If you hate something, destroy it. Never doubt yourself. Never feel regret… Never stop turning. If you're bored, if things are stagnant, or dusty… kick it up. Be the whirlwind of change."

"I don't need your advice," Mags said.

"I think you'd make a great mother," Cunigunde said as she slid her hand into the hollow on her back and conjured something forth. "And a wonderful wife. Keep up with the blond. He's a doctor, and a skinchanger. Good catch. And your life is short."

She handed Mageirissa a pouch containing condoms made from intestines. Of animals, Mags hoped, but a dark doubt crept into her thoughts, one of the elfin's sickening pranks.

"Immortality was wasted on you," Mags spat. But she didn't give the pouch back.

"Immortality needs a bit of violence. Keeps it exciting," said Cunigunde. "Now, I'm going to go find the fairest face in town and sit on it."

She slipped her hand into the hollow of her back, turned to Elena, and handed her a string of green jewels and several gemstones. "A jadeite necklace of the Hypouranids' Elder Capital, pink diamonds from the crown jewels of the Surarine Dynasty, and red beryl of Favonia's Dead Cougar Mountains."

She nodded her head and left the tavern, vanishing into thin air before she doubled back across the window.

"What was that thing?" Elena asked.

"Cunigunde the Whirlwind," Mags explained. "A sylphide warlord."

"That was Kingavila?" Elena said.

She held the necklace high, wondering who had died for this prize.

Chapter 13: Among the Dead

Fade and Lund rented camels and a timberjack's sledge to return to the site of the massacre, following a trail of scavenging birds and beasts. Among the yellowpines and censer cedars, their mounts were driven to feed on the pixie-cups and freckle pelt lichens growing in the shaded loam. Fade and Lund dismounted and pulled out a pair of paperboard tubes stuffed with powder poppers. Lund dyed his powder with mauve extracted from the cones of a climatic hemlock, while Fade kept his flour and phosphates a pale gray. The men stood back to back, marched twelve crunchy paces through the snow, turned, and fired.

As the powder cleared, Lund looked down at the blast mark on his tunic.

"You went for the kill," Lund said. He scooped up a handful of snow to pad off the powder.

"I think you killed that pine tree, if it balms the pride," Fade said.

"A gentleman fires into the air," Lund said, with mock offense.

"So does a dead man," Fade said.

They soon caught the rare sight of a rosmare, the legged walrus, which Fade briefly confused with the rosemarine, the skinny walrus of the Cane Sea. Lund asked that they stop to study it, with Lund sketching its face and carefully approaching to estimate the length of its tusks. The irascible creature calmed as Lund extended a hand. It lowered its head in submission.

The rosmare showed signs of penetrating wounds to the dorsal ridge. The doctors speculated that this was due to male competition, but the curved downward thrust made them wonder if it was inflicted by a true walrus, or perhaps a frost giant's tusk. There are several types of giants, as that term can refer to any large being, and such "freak" giants can occur among members of any species. True Giants, however, were roughly three dozen varieties of bipedal pachyderms, woolly frost giants of the northern reaches, Winedarkers with a shortened, tapiric trunk, and Notic creatures horned liked the rhinoceros. Most were wading creatures like the hippopotamus, using rivers and lakes to support their cumbersome bulk. Then there were ettin, the overgrown lords of the ogres, a malformed race of mountain men filled with the powers of elemental earth. Finally, legends spoke of the titans, who resembled humans but for their stature, broad feet, and horns.

As the tranquilized creature nodded off and fell asleep, Lund harvested a single hair from its back, and returned to Fade's company.

"That calm," Fade said. "How do you stay so...relaxed?"

"You never struck me as a particularly excitable lad," Lund said. "Rather dispassionate."

"Cold," Fade said. "People say I'm cold."

"Blame it on the weather," Lund said.

"It's that serenity," Fade said. "How do you...achieve that?"

"The best cure for your worries is an expanded perspective," Lund said. "I used to be an anxious boy, always fretting about the future. My university fellows taught be the liberation of drinking like a fish, and that leporine energy sublimated into an anserine haste. A young squire wanders around the animal kingdom, looking for his lord."

"His lord," Fade mumbled.

"I don't wish to presume, but I think you buried your worries. Hardened into the grim, gray professional. I see it often among men of medicine. And those of the mortuary, and the battlefield," Lund said. "Some try to survive through humor, but there is always a morbid tint."

"Death," Fade said. "I have seen that great finality, and

that which remains. And returns. That expanded my perspectives, Lund. But I don't know peace."

"I can see that," Lund said. He wondered if he should tell the surgeon to blink more. "I'm a few years older than you. And I know the appeal of becoming a cold, hard man. Or climbing into a bottle. Or to rage, to burn away the wild energy of manhood. Anything to dull the pain. But death is only an end, not a comfort. Focus on vitality. Your vitality. Living, loving. Life. The pleasures of the beast."

Fade's lip curled, and he mumbled, "We had one of those lads in the Bridge, too familiar with the sheep."

"Hold your tongue, we're gentlemen, Fade," Lund said. He tried and failed to hold back a smile.
"Once you've seen all that nature has available... Every animal has a unique set of experiences. A world of senses, scale, and lifestyles. The idyllic sleep of the well-fed bear. The nose of a bloodhound. The rampaging joy of the dolphin. The transcendent beauty of an albatross's flight."

"So I'll fly, then," Fade said, as he climbed back into the saddle with an embarrassing boost from his taller friend.

"Perhaps you should try," Lund said. He grunted as he mounted his camel. "Oh, the knees of a large man in his third decade... Human life is short. A gentleman's life is ordered and fettered. So learn something from the kingdom of the animals. Go into the woods. Eat something exotic. Love as much as you can."

Fade grabbed the reins and started moving, before adding, "That rather had the air of parting words."

"Yes, it did," Lund said. He was quiet for a few moments, before adding, "No, that's you being grim again."

"No, I mean it had real weight," Fade said. "Finality. Now what can we talk about? We're only halfway there."

So they remained quiet, but the initial awkward silence became something placid, as both men appreciated the crisp breeze and the brilliant desolation of the arctic.

The pair soon reached their cavern storehouse and retrieved the plundered rifles and weapons. The journey proved much shorter than during their impressment, and they enjoyed the camel ride. But their smiles fell when they came to the site of the massacre. Smoke rose over the hill.

"That powder carriage is still burning?" Lund asked. But no, a cautious ascent answered the idle question.

The Kaftar ignited a bonfire. The beastman was there, devouring the body of a half-warmed draught-camel, the head and neck still frozen. The creature did not care. Around him, a quartet of goblins shrieked and skittered, dipping their caps in the congealing blood, letting it soak deep into their gills.

"Redcaps," Fade said, the apt name for the most vicious and mad of goblinkind, empowered by blood magic and an unmatched cruelty. Goblins don't kill for food, but to grow on the bloody decay. Hobgoblins can content themselves on the offal of slaughtered animals and rotting crops, but their vile cousins want the flesh of men, dogs, and horses for their strength and the thaumaturgic potency of death. Many mannish, canine, and equine monsters haunting swamps and bogs are mere goblins growing in stolen frames.

The younger red caps had woven their hyphae into the hair of some of the dead, knotting up the braid of one of the women and the beards of some gunners.

Fade bit his lower lip in embarrassment as Lund helped him from the saddle. Lund was an experienced horseman, with training in northern camelry. His great-grandfather was a cavalier on the wisent drives. His father rode elks as an officer in Murmur's unique Royal Alcery Corps and kept a livery of hauling horses. And, of course, he had that uncanny affinity.

They attempted to sneak closer, rifles readied, but paused when the massive hyena-man raised his head to sniff the air. His body was a strange mixture of savagery and artisanal talent. Blood stained his face, while a blacksmith's apron covered his broad chest. He had set the fire to work the metal scavenged from the company, binding the power of blood into the iron. He yelped in a language of nasal guffaws and scanned the hillside. A mesmerizing calm overtook Fade upon simply seeing the red of his eyes. He dreaded what would happen if they made eye contact.

Two hobgoblins rose in similar alarm. Fade recognized them as Dunters, a breed from the Septentrine Archipelago. His suspicions were almost immediately confirmed when a voice asked what was the matter in Waylander.

"What is it?" Pander grumbled as he rose from his seat on a ruined baggage carriage, wrapped in layers and scarves and a fur cap upon his saggy felt cap.

Lund pushed down on Fade's shoulder, keeping him out of sight from the camp as he crested the hill. Fade aimed his warlock rifle and muttered a countermagic ward, hoping that Lund knew what he was doing. The salted silver ball of the warlock rifle would break through his target's enchantments, but the hyena man would still have his teeth and claws.

The Kaftar let out a gasping yelp and hunched down, ready to surge through the snow which melted at his touch and smith's-kiln breath. The moment that unnerved Fade, however, was when the beast-man gingerly set down his artillerist's ephemeris. Such handbooks chart the trajectories of celestial objects and collect nomograms for calculating the flight-paths of cannonballs, reagent ratios, and transmutation rates. This technical tangle of astrology, alchemy, and artillery would be utterly wasteful on a battlefield populated by mortal men, but against a dragon or rampaging sylph...

He knew, Fade thought. His jaw clenched, half in anger, half to keep his teeth from chattering.

"Mr. Pander," Lund said. "Why have you returned?"

"To salvage the wreckage," said the Etesian.

"I can tell by the retinue of scavengers," said Lund. "A poor court for a noble, but what else would have you?"

"They may not be to your taste," said Pander, "but you may be more palatable to theirs. I have come to make something of my investment in this company."

"You knew they were going to die," Lund said.

"Not necessarily," Pander said. "I hoped that band of bastards would succeed. But one should always have a contingency."

"Feeding them to the jackals was a poor plan, Tin Man," Lund said.

"The nations grind up their fallen fighters for fertilizer," he said. "And I doubt two medical researchers would leave this field of corpses without a few useful cadavers."

"Right. The bodysnatcher is a despised profession, but he is more humane than the vivisectionist." Lund asked. He folded his arms. "Where is the profit in this?"

"Foreign blood," Pander said as he quietly moved the clockwork wheels on the cover of his almanac and flashed the tidal diagrams under the front cover. "It feels foolish, to believe that the different races of man and sagani have their own magics. Even traditional crafts should converge onto some truth. And blood is blood, in its constituents. And yet, some acts need foreign blood."

"Why?" asked Lund.

"Have you studied your mareographs and bathymeters, the tide tables, and the plots of the moons?" Pander asked in turn. "Yliaster flows down from the Deer Hunter, refracted by the Philosopher's Moon like light through a prism, just as sunlight shines off the Argent. And just as sunlight heats the globe and the moons churn the tides, yliaster flows over Thier unevenly, spicing the winds and currents. This port was surrounded by a ward after the dragon came, to keep out other great powers who would seek to dethrone it. But such spells have prices and stipulations. If you wish to ban outsiders from your lands, you can't go around letting foreign blood spill across your domain."

"You're planning an invasion," said Lund, not quite a question.

"Well, not a naval action," Pander said as he closed his almanac and rummaged in his pocket. "I'm not here to start a war. I'm a mere surveyor. I'm here for the lie of the land."

The Kaftar tuned back to his bonfire, where the coppery smell of burning blood and cooking organ meat rose on a pillar of smoke that carried away the magic of the ban. Lund noted that someone had stirred the viscera with a linstock, breaking up the livers of horses and humans. The doctor assumed this grotesque haruspicy was the work of Pander, as surveyors are trained in rites of divination, both modern and barbaric.

"Why does the Septentrine Empire want to end the Ban?" Lund asked.

"We don't," said Pander as he straightened his Etesian cap and stepped into the blood-speckled snow with a pained groan. He ate a chalky pill of locally-manufactured blue mass, a treatment for several ailments, from birthing contractions to phthisis to parasites to piles to venereal disease. "And my work here is almost done."

"You're just leaving after this?" Lund said.

"Yes," Pander said. "Why would I stay here, in this accursed glacier of rotten fish?"

Fade rose to his feet in a rage, gray eyes glaring down the sight of a rifle.

"And how are you getting out of here?" Fade asked.

"It's a port, boy," Pander said. "Plenty of options. Or are you going to murder me? Perhaps torture me? Is that your plan? When the Kaftar is worrying your throat and the redcaps pull off your nails, will my death be a comfort?"

"Who hired you?" Lund asked. "If you're leaving the nation anyway."

"Sorry, professional courtesy," he said. "But your bounty from Gultschakal was an independent contract, and no longer applicable. You are no werewolf, after all, no threat to the kings and kine."

Pander smiled, and handed Lund a bottle heavy with colloidal silver, the common solution to a nobleman's lycanthropy, as opposed to the wolfbane poisoning and fire reserved for the peasantry.

"A parting gift, to make up for your trouble," Pander said. "I can't allow myself to leave without asking... Who taught you to change your skin into some great ape?"

Fade turned his head towards his friend, as he also wanted to know the source of this metamorphic talent.

"I sailed the seas in my medical training and learned the art of animal spirits. From the wolf priests of Aquilo, seal-folk of the Pagrean coast, the Leopard Societies of the Rammou Bight, windyellers of the Cane Sea Karhun, medicine men of Hespera and Dysis, water witches of Scirocco and Garbino, the mana-molders of Tsotranesia and the Hitamo hide-changers of Subsolaria," said Lund.

"Then where are your hides? Where is your wolf-skin belt? Your swan-feather cloak?" asked Pander.

"You know of the theory of base metals, the elements, and the atom, that matter which cannot be divided further?" said Lund. "There are such elements of the animals and plants of the world. Easier to transport than a wardrobe of hides."

"Animalcules?" said Pander. "You've filled yourself with germ plasma? Are you... drinking it?"

"How about I describe the process to you in a letter?" Lund said. "I'll be here for a while. Send for me at the hospital, I'll reply."

A twitch snapped up the left side of Pander's mouth, as if

he wanted to snarl but the cold stabbed his nerves.

"Oh, I hope the Contortions aren't getting to you," Lund said. "Perhaps you should get going."

Pander whistled. The Kaftar and the goblins finished up their bonfire and grabbed their bags and boxes. They marched past Fade and Lund, with the hyena-man snapping his jaws with a flash of furnace heat, a petty parting shot. The doctors said nothing and watched Pander's party trudge south. Fade and Lund passed around their bottle of Hesperan banana aguardiente and chuckled nervously. Their smiles quickly collapsed as they trudged through the mid-shin snow. The cold prevented the horrible smell of rotten meat and postmortem feces, but the corpse fire filled the air with a scent like roasted pork, burnt hair, and the unctuous, sickening sweetness of boiling bodily humors.

They worked under a pallor of mournful quiet. They picked up intact human corpses, weapons, other supplies, and the fulgurites left behind by the Whirlwind for the sledge. They threw beasts, body parts, the headless, and the eviscerated onto the bonfires, with Lund muttering prayers to Mother Incano and Father Urizen. When their work was done, they rolled the remaining cartridges of gunpowder onto the flame.

"So, those animal essences," Fade began to ask as he found the silver crown that he had looted from the Academy on one of the bodies. The Company had confiscated it from him early on.

"Oh... Yes?" Lund said, distracted by a meter-long fulgurite. It branched like arteries, colored vermilion and sulfurous yellow by the region's glaciofluvial sediments. "It was no bluff."

"Right," Fade said. "But is it... the hereditary matter? Egg and seed?"

"Oh, no no no," Lund said. "Yes, I will eat fish, bird, and

reptile eggs, but I only need the animalcules, the atoms of life. I keep those acidic patterns in my own. It's more efficient than a skin cloak, like I said."

"I see," Fade said. "Still, rather unseemly."

Lund laughed in mock outrage and said, "Oh, and what of your homunculi?"

That morning, Fade had bartered a pint of heavy cream for chicken eggs and yeast with the inn's hobgoblin. Alone and secure, he thought of the plates and poems from *the Book of Roses* which titillated him in his youth. He thought of Kingfisher's face and neck. Mageirissa's breasts, each the size of his head. The coy, shadowed eyes and mouth of Severin. The Whirlwind's long, muscular legs and the narrow *naatsit* which barely covered her. The warm body of the slave girl, Pleyone of Eurus, who he once nursed in the caverns of the Lord of Dust.

The Whirlwind returned, as flashes of sharp teeth, red eyes, and vulpine ears. He thought of Kingfisher again, this time her gray-blue feathers, and the strange feeling of her talons wrapped in his fingers, and the perfume she slathered onto her flower-crowned hair. He gasped, shuddered, wiped himself clean with an alcohol-soaked cloth, and sucked up the final ingredient into a copper pipette. He covered his face and cringed at his work, as he injected the vital concoction into the egg's yolk with a surgical needle. He wondered why it was the monstrosity of those women that excited him most.

Harpy eggs, noted both Xantho's *Physiologus* and Ancalima's *Metamorphica*, made excellent incubators for homunculi, but he could never bring himself to broach the topic to Kingfisher. Even this silent fantasy-filled him with shame, to the point that he sneaked past his two female companions as he departed for the northern limits.

"Don't be afraid to embrace those animal urges," Lund said with a smile. "Live a little, young Resurrectionist."

"Was it all about living? All about new perspectives?" Fade asked.

"No," Lund said. "It was about dying."

"Beg your pardon?" Fade said, his cheeks billowing in the cold.

"In my twenty-first year, I was overcome by megrims," Lund said. "My eyes exploded with flares, like a meteor shower in my skull. The Constellations of Hedran. So I turned to drink. Spirits, sometimes with a dash of ether or tincture of opium. Anything to dull the pain. But my deplorable diet and the agonizing flares ruined my magic."

"Right," Fade said. "An arcanist is half-demigod, half-diabetic."

"So a quarter god, then," Lund said.

"Alright, let's not be pedantic," Fade whispered. "What happened?"

"After one hard night, my right eye lost vision," Lund said. "I went to an optical diviner. It was neither the liquor nor the stress of the medical student which inflamed the nerves. I had a growth behind the brow, size of a Two-Throne coin."

"Urizen's Wound," Fade gasped. "Cranial cancer? What...Are you..."

"I'm alive," Lund said. "I depleted my coffers, traveling across Thier's western seas. Both seeking adventure and a cure. I saw the beauty and terrors of Nature, and the follies of Man. Paid my way through the Cane Sea in service to a hard-headed captain. He was fond of whiskey and whips until his men mutinied and stranded him on a cay. Like I said before, I studied the arts of shapeshifting among those varied peoples, gathered together by misfortune and the sins of empire. I combined it with the ways of the cancer-kings of the Solar Dynasty, who etched their crawling capitol onto the shell of a divine crab. The conquerors and their court were karcists, letting the sunlight and yliaster proliferate through their bodies and exoskeletons, their black magic strengthened by their malignancy. Maybe this synthesis was Nature's blessing. Or a stroke of genius. Or an accident. But all that knowledge collapsed into a spark of inspiration. And now I command my body, control my life. A man must master himself, yet always test the limits of life."

"The cancer's gone, though, right?" Fade asked.

"We've come to a mutual understanding," Lund said as he tied down the heavy canvas covering the sled.

They brought the corpses to an abandoned coalburner's hut on Alchemist's Island they had secured legally and warded against animals and intruders. A member of the city watch stopped them, unnerved by the corpses. Lund showed them their papers from the hospital and the lichman's writ issued by the House of Wisdom.

The watchman shook his head and said that Fade was wanted for questioning by the constabulary. His public argument with Lem Loganev had several credible witnesses, and he was one of the last people to speak with the gnome before his death.

Chapter 14: Thro' Dreaming Towns I Go

Kingfisher sneaked out of the Inn two hours after noon, when there were fewer people in the inn and the street. She ate the dumplings Mags had brought to her and glided to the earth from the second-story window. She made her way to the House of Wisdom, garbed in a thick kerchief, a shawl, and a dress long enough to drag in the slush. She wished the town had a proper night this time of year.

She wondered if she should dip her face in the wall-mounted basin used for ablution. Humans were obsessed with cleanliness. Harpies preened themselves and each other, but humans boiled and burnt their food, washed their hands before entering buildings, had an almost fetishistic attachment to fire and water, and beat the impurities out of hot metal. They cared about kinship, and honored their ancestral dead with fires and bread, even as they burnt incense to scatter the lingering traces of other family's ghosts. It all came down to the fear of corruption, of death in an inhuman form and monstrous births.

It came down to not being like her.

The attendant greeted her again, and she asked if she could help. The Oracle approached through the adytum arch, some aberration of time stamping the glint in her eye into the darkness like an invisible candelabra.

"I knew you would return," she said. "Come inside, Sir Kazimir is up and about."

"Can I see him?" asked Kingfisher, her voice shaking.

"We were preparing this season's Rite of the Rainbow Fish," she said.

"Oh," mumbled the harpy. "Sorry."

"Would you care to join us?" clarified the Oracle. "You're in a foul mood. Though the waking dreams will take up your entire day."

"Thank you," Kingfisher looked around, and considered her schedule.

She had nothing to do, but she wondered if she should somehow inform the others. But what could she do? She was an idiot, who could not help with their medical pursuits. She was poor and could not fund them. She even failed as a warrior against their captors and the horned woman. Perhaps religion could bring her some insight, any scrap of hope.

She fumbled for her pouch, set a rhombic grivenka on the ground, and pushed in towards the donors' coffer. The attendant bent down to grab the silver coin, to spare his elders the joint pain and the harpy the embarrassment. He ran his finger over the mint mark of Kladenots, on the junction of the Prilivat and the Blue Meska, the rivers which service Novoport. They shared a look that Kingfisher couldn't quite understand, so she quietly thanked him.

The Oracle led her to the Chamber of the Eternal Waters, the centerpiece of the house, a pool lit by candelabras of eulachons impaled on tridents. Northernmost and its hinterlands are heated by volcanic hot springs which feed underground streams which never freeze. The Chamber circled the largest and purest of the Severnayan springs, an aquarium of green glass. The most well-stocked species were the goldine, salema porgy, and the dusky spinefish of the eastern Winedark. Unlike the Holy Family and Solar Lords of the temple's nave, this chamber was dedicated to the darker, chaotic gods - Craethion, Hedran, the Archrebel Orc, and Dead Rahab. Many of the world's faith have one god of treachery or chaos, or a single force of evil. The Aquilans find their rogues gallery of bumbling divinities a far more fitting explanation for the nature of the cosmos.

Kingfisher saw statues and symbols of Craethion in every port, his place of power. He was the god of flow, moving water, storms, sailors and maritime trade, travelers, bloodshed, drunkenness, madness, birds, tears, volcanoes, literacy, the transmigration of souls, and two dozen other aspects. This statue, however, frightened her. It stood nearly three meters, and looked like fatherly Urizen but grizzled, unhinged, and smeared with blood. His hair was painted the red and orange of the setting sun, the raw vermilion of Northernmost. It made sense, as he was born from ichor and the salt of the sea, mixed when Orc wounded Urizen in the First Betrayal. Urizen could not be harmed or defied by anything in the ordered spheres orbiting Urthona, the Brilliant Home of Los, so the Sunhaired Rebel tricked his father into attracting a stone from between the stars. When the meteorite crashed into Thier's Bitter Sea, Orc dredged it up and forged it into a treacherous spearhead. Or perhaps a dagger or a sword. Kingfisher noticed that the humans couldn't settle on that detail, but it was always shaped like the iconic weapon of their tribe's most hated enemy, who were always descended from Orc and a diseased whore.

Kingfisher, however, favored Orc's second child with Rahab - Setebos, the Bastard Crown'd. They were the protector of castaways, bastards, the deformed, discarded, and barbaric, offering respite from a brutal life. Setebos lives on a beached white whale on the far side of the Philosopher's Moon, and Kingfisher had often dreamed of flying there.

The Bastard's mother, however, was the focus of the ritual's attention. Rahab was the goddess of the Argent Moon, tides, falsehood, seduction, vengeance, victims, filth, curses, manure, sea monsters, birth defects, scavengers, poverty, destitution, and error. She was also a goddess of beauty, persuasion, agricultural fertility, fishing, sowing and reaping, the overcoming of weakness, strategy, the destruction of enemies, political wit, wells, and the depths of the sea. Rahab's statue was laid sideways and used as a serving table, as her priesthood are sin-eaters. During spring and summer, she is Dead Rahab, and her idols are buried and her statues toppled. During the harvest season and winter, she is set upright, and crowned with stalks as the Corn Queen.

The strange blend of fish, filth, and fertility lies in her most common rite, the burial of seeds with the guts and bones of fish. While vital, she is the most sinister of the gods, as she comes from "outside" the core families of the pantheon, with no canonical origin. There are tales of her being crafted out of driftwood or ambergris by Craethion or rescued from the belly of a whale or shark or springing out of part of a colossal ketos slain by Orc, Urizen, or Hedran, but none of them are of great provenance or widely accepted. It is suspected that she is an emanation of Eternity, the Great Leviathan the founders of the other families fled into Time to escape.

A serving plate marked with the scars and seas of the Philosopher's Moon rested on Dead Rahab's shoulder. Slices of raw dreamfish lay with the early bounty of Sowcorn, sliced and pickled beets, lettuce, and spinach. The recently thawed fish had been prepared with vinegar and citrus juice to kill parasites, and then basted in a spicy red sauce of peppers and pulped sea bream head. A piping samovar and a tray of nutmeg tea biscuits accompanied the rite.

Northernmost revived the tradition in the last decade. During the early days of the Contortions, a folk belief arose that the dreamfish were the cause, perhaps contamination or a curse for sacrilege, the wrath of the irascible Craethion or the sinister Rahab. Others wondered if they were victims of a worm-host's reproduction – the Vorago is home to diabolic trilobites that bore into the tongue, trading powerful alien incantations for human blood, vital sulfur, and hosts, including those less willing than the treacherous pact-maker. These vile sea-lice are harvested from dreamfish catches in the port, and ground up to make spells of translation and understanding, so mass contamination could easily happen. These theories made sense at first, as headaches, hallucinations, violent dreams, and delirium plagued its victims, but stopping the rite did nothing to slow the disease's progression.

Seven humans in dark blue robes sat around the spring, pairs of eyes following Kingfisher as her talons sharply scraped the mosaic tiles. She turned to look at a fair old man seated next to a large, dark man, who eyed her with interest. Her head snapped forward, and she looked down at her feet.

"Dear girl, don't be embarrassed," said the large man, who almost floated to his feet with an unnatural grace. He walked towards the Rahabite altar, and insisted on serving up the dreamfish to her, despite the presence of a female attendant. He raised the bident to her mouth.

"Thank you," she said, and swallowed the fish in one bite, and then awkwardly napped up the kelp wrap.

"My pleasure," he said. He placed the bident in a soapy basin. "I remembered your feeding needs from the Mayoral Tower. You were with that young, gray-haired doctor, no?"

She nodded.

"Perdurabo Legrand," he said, tapping his breast. She told him her name, and he invited her to sit next to him.

"I never figured you as a man of faith, Legrand," said the old man. "Surprised your female companion hasn't skewered you for coming here."

"I'm not," he answered. "But I'm fascinated by the anthropology of it. And the fantastic experience. I've eaten the Tsotranesian Chief of Ghosts, and the dreamfish of my mother's Guabanches. Her people dress Incano in a local wrap instead of the Robe of Clouds, and blend her with the native Ocean Mother, and the Kothema Storm goddess Nkyinkyim. Incano Palliolata guides the visions there. Rahab is a sea serpent."

"A curious corruption," said the old man.

"Corruption? Perhaps," said Legrand. "But gods change when people meet. Incano was once a crone goddess from Suscitar, hence the silver hair and the withered hand."

"The gods can change?" Kingfisher asked.

"The nature of gods are subject to interpretation, *the* Interpretation. And new understandings," said the old man.

"The gods *are* the interpretation," Legrand whispered to Kingfisher. "But let's play nice with our host."

"Those women you were with, could they not come?" Kingfisher asked.

"Oh, for all my jabs, I cannot match Mignard's hostility to the Fane...and Severin is one for more sensual pleasures," Legrand said. "We will be departing soon. The dreamfish's ordeal begins after two hours and can last for three days. Maybe two days for me, as I'm quite rotund."

He patted his stomach.

"Good way to spend the trip back to Achilles," he said. "You should last two days, maybe fewer."

"But I only weight two and a half pudi," she said.

"Oh no, sorry, I wasn't calling you fat," he said. "A siren such as yourself should have a finer digestion. It shan't linger in the system."

She *had* eaten some vile rubbish in her time, she thought.

"I hope you two don't think of this as something to dabble in for fun," said the old man. "This isn't a salon filled with opium smoke and dilettantes. This is an ordeal, a dream-quest. And it can be quite frightening, just as it can be enlightening."

"I understand," Kingfisher said. "I have seen true horrors. I can face an imagined fear."

"Good, a brave face," said the old man, "May you keep your wits about you."

He rose up to wash his hands in the ablution basin. He muttered a prayer and clutched a medallion with a heraldic device of a snow leopard. Human noble families often made pacts with eidolons, passing down the empowering patron spirit in exchange for ritual service. Kingfisher wondered if that is why the old man had bright gray-beige eyes and salt and pepper hair, matching his heraldry.

"Are you Sir Kazimir of Staraya Stolitsa?" Kingfisher asked cautiously.

"Yes," he said. He smiled sadly. "A fantastical quest is the last errand these old bones will allow."

"I… I… I don't think I've found my first quest," said Kingfisher. "The knights in the old stories always fall into the adventures. Or serve a king or queen with many interesting problems."

Sir Kazimir chuckled and said, "I know the frustration. I traveled far and wide, even into Idyrea and Superna in the far east, and to the Voörish ruins of Hyperborea. I gathered two dozen so-called panaceas, none of which worked. I won the dagger of dispel, which could bleed out one's curses. The caladrius I captured in the Skysaw Mountains dropped dead without flying away. I even found a silver-beaked swan from the lakes of the moon. And its touch could not cure this miserable writhing."

Kingfisher's blood ran cold. If he had failed in those quests, there was still the hope that she could complete the journey and bring honor to his efforts and comfort to his suffering. But what then, when the cup of healing is just a cup, when the magic ring is just a band of gold? Kingfisher wondered if it was better for the questor to die on the journey than to find a wasteland at his destination.

Kingfisher found the chamber almost empty, but for Legrand, Sir Kazimir, and the Oracle of the North, the rest of the participants retreating from the harpy. Legrand, too, grabbed his jacket, gave a polite bow to the harpy and the knight, and walked towards the door. Kingfisher stood up, and felt her stomach turn and her head spin, as though she toiled on a boat in her own belly, sloshing on an acidic sea.

"Oh my, it's setting in fast, isn't it?" asked someone, she thought Legrand, but his voice rolled in like a storm.

Kingfisher looked towards the statue of Hedran, in her aspect of sacred virginity. Hedran Virginia's black cape came to life, creeping over her marble body and sparking with new stars. The sacred darkness rolled over Kingfisher.

Her mouth dried up, and someone was touching her. The small and wet hand may have been the Oracle's, though the Knight's strength had diminished in his old age. She turned her head and saw Sir Eol. His mouth moved, but nothing came out.

He lay in bed, an island of illumination in the darkness. The earth rose up beneath his deathbed, or Kingfisher descended into the world. She came to the body of a woman laying on her side, wrapped in dry husks and long wet hair. A purple dullness rimmed her slate eyes, and her skin was bloodless and a buff-white between statuary marble and cod flesh.

The size of her startled Kingfisher. She must have been four meters tall, and the upper end of her shoulder met the harpy's navel.

"Bastardess of Sea and Sky," whispered Dead Rahab, a death rattle of a rasp. "Why not fly to the far side of the moon? My child will crown you in laurels, in a kingdom without bodies or faces. Only knowing, only closeness, only oneness."

Rahab's silvery eyes drifted up like a dying fish, before an iris rolled into the blackness. The Argent Moon spun through the night, and Kingfisher turned to follow the melting and dripping sphere into a sunset sea of blood. She gasped as her shoulders shed weight and tripped onto fresh legs with five small toes.

She looked back to see a common kingfisher, fully avian in form. Volganin looked down at her bruised arm, where the

Whirlwind had broken the bone. The purple sunk into the skin, and the pain subsided in waves of warmth. She looked back as the small bird flew away.

"No, wait!" she shouted, her throat painfully dry.

The mosaic tiles beneath her glittered and glistened, the scales of the Rainbow Fish who taught Craethion the mysteries of the dreamfish. Someone grabbed her by the arm, but she pulled away from the weak grip and was through the narthex window.

Legrand looked up at her, and she used him to get her bearings as a white sky blurred into a white earth. He said something, but the wind whispered sweet nothings in her ear. He chortled and shook his head, and walked up Scheznik Avenue, past Kiril the Blessed Infirmary, and the Driftwood Theatre. He approached the Quill, an old bar that serviced the playwrights, actors, and audiences, and the kingfisher bird followed him. There was nobody else in the world but the wizard and giant crabs in blues and greens and pinks so bright that they hurt her eyes and made her cough with their cigars. The crustaceans reached out for the marine snow drifting from the carcass of Dead Rahab, one of the cosmic whale-falls which suffuse the world with divine detritus and scraps of new creation. Volganin lost her command of the sky and tried to reach for her kingfisher on the windowsill, but her fresh human arms cut through the air and stung in the snow.

She wondered if this was the curse of Dead Rahab. The grim goddess made so many bastards and chimerae that unmaking one would be a trivial miracle.

Perhaps it is her blessing, Volganin mused. Perhaps she was finally free from herself. Volganin's birdness sat at the window and her femininity lay on the ground. The bronzed cuirass rattled on her now narrow back, but the dress was no longer awkward. If she stood up, and simply walked away, would she be a woman for the rest of her life?

She thought of Fade, and his subtle smile as they walked through the Academy. His worried glances as he carried her from the site of the massacre. Would he like her womanly legs?

Leave the bird at the window, she thought. *Leave Night Scream behind.*

She remembered her sisters, and her stomach churned once more. Most were bird-bodied maidens, but one had been born with a vulture's head and clawed arms, and she had a half-brother who was a high-jumping horse with a feathered mane. Both had been abandoned when they migrated to a new cliff, after the forest fire. She wondered what happened to them.

She wondered who her father was.

The cuirass grew heavier and heavier, a crushing knighthood, a smothering falsehood. The cold sucked at her feartherless limbs. Volganin considered staying here, and fading away.

Her sister, Eye-Robber, as the seventh daughter of a seventh daughter, had the divine gift of foresight. One evening, that bedraggled prophet looked up from her eviscerated deer and casually informed Night Scream that she would die surrounded by tar and warm water.

Falling asleep here would defy her fate, at least. There was something heroic in that, she told herself.

Legrand pulled her out of the snow.

"Are you in pain, Dame Kingfisher?" he asked.

"I'm just Volganin," she said. "The kingfisher is at that window. Can you see it, with your eyes of wizardry?"

"Oh, that window?" he said with a chuckle. "Haha, that uncommon appetite is not so uncommon in my circle. Let me help you inside."

"No, I'm a harpy, they'll kill me," she said with a sob. "They'll feed me to the Cane Sea Coconut Crabs."

"No, no, it's fine, don't cry," he said. He pulled a strand of black hair from his pocket and muttered a spell. Kingfisher watched as the hair sprung to life like a worm on a hook and buried itself in her scalp.

"You're under a glamour," he said. "People will see you as someone else. Just don't let them touch your wings or linger too long in speech. Let's just take a seat, drink some coffee, and wait for my companion to join us."

"You're so nice!" she said and started to cry and pressed her face into his chest. "What is this jacket made out of?!"

"Broadcloth and silk," he said.

She bleated, noting the goat pin on his lapel. The mountain goat was the political symbol of the Summit, climbing up three ascending peaks in front of a setting black sun. It was an ambiguous icon, as goats were also a cultural symbol of Aquilan gnomes and a symbol of the stubbornness of non-monarchal conservative traditions. The Summit, however, favored the mountain goat in particular, due to its sure footing and ability to climb to precarious heights.

"Baa," she said.

"Now please, lower your voice, and come with me," he said.

He pressed his index finger to his lips.

He led her past women and young men painted with brilliant colors, rouge like fresh blood alight with the orange of the setting sun, the Vermilion Brides of the Narrows protected by Ol' Sea King Craythur. There was a song about them, sung on the Ducal Canal. She tried to sing it but realized that she was simply repeating "the Vermillion Brides of the Narrows" in Murmurish, and something about warm touches and cold waters.

Legrand hummed and held a biscuit near her face. She ate it and went quiet.

"Do you frequently… accompany prostitutes?" he asked.

"You're quite dedicated to this knightly persona. Though they were rarely as chaste as they are in songs."

"No," she said. "No. But I don't know… but sometimes, I wanted men to want me. And not fear me."

"Ah," he said. "I understand. Dress yourself in finery and glory. Look at me, a fat boy from a carob plantation across the sea. But I found ways to make myself attractive. Be the unique one. Be the exotic. Be the heroine. And if all else fails, learn a glamour or two."

The bar was filled with people whose face was nothing but make-up piled up like paint. Three clowns sat next to her, drinking bloody mud, and reciting lines from *the Death of Hauheinsa of the Reirono*. An ancient sailor trembled with blood-ied hands, and poured out a whiskey libation to Craethion, the rainbow fish swimming in the bottle. A copper bust of local legend, Dryope, the Pig-Faced Woman of Alchemist's Isle, blinked and snorted. The harpy looked up at the mirror be-hind the bar, which rippled and flowed as the maid poured cider into a seven-toed cat. Volganin did not see herself re-flected on the silvery drips, only Olympienne Mignard. She looked up at Legrand and swayed in her seat. Pain crept up her knees, and she hopped up to her feet, catching the atten-tion of some clowns. She moved upstairs, looking for her kingfisher on the second story. There were rolling racks filled with costumes that rippled and reached for her with boneless arms. She turned to her side to avoid this groping squid of linen, wool, and velvet, and came to another mirror, full-length for fittings. Two women gasped and moaned in the door to her left, the climactic intensity snatching her attention.

A watery glimmer caught her eye, and a gloved hand reached through the rippling mirror and Olympienne's mutat-ing face. A shadow the color of the deep sea loomed over Volganin. She recoiled, and her shoulder struck the door. The sound of rustling covers followed her yelp. She tried to run away but her legs were jelly and bent the wrong way. By the time she stood straight, a hook parting its eye jingled through a small crack in the door.

"Oly?" said the red-haired nymph.

Blue and purple watermarks ran down her collar bones and across her hips and webbed feet, mixed with fresh bruises on her neck. Volganin needed a moment to recognize Justine Severin without her elaborate clothing, and the sharp kiss on the cheek alarmed her to the point that her head stayed cocked, matching the posture of the woman in the bed.

"Who is this?" said the Whirlwind, in a similar state of dishabille.

She sat up, almost curling into a pouncing position, her hand reaching for something concealed in the gap between mattress and bedframe.

Volganin's mouth fell open, paralyzed with fear. The sylphide grabbed a cup of hypocras from the flat top of the heater, and lapped like a lioness at the oasis, without breaking eye contact with her prey.

"Olympienne. She and Perry are my long-term companions. The wizard, the fencer, and the banker," she said. Her gaze returned to the disguised Volganin. "Care to join us?"

Volganin stammered and stumbled towards the window. She struggled to open it, and eventually kicked up her foot to undo the latch.

"It's already cold," Severin protested.

The Whirlwind sniffed the air. The muscles in her left arm tensed up. Severin yelped as Volganin flew out the window and the creaking floorboards signaled Legrand's return.

Volganin passed through the little kingfisher, her arms sprouting back into wings. A compulsive wanderlust seized her, and it grew stronger as she rose, like a fish struggling against a hook. She glided over the Narrows, which felt not so narrow at the moment. Her arms strained as she passed over the small Prince's Isle to the eastern beach of the Royal Island. She beat her wings until her back muscles felt like they would tear, struggling against the cold dead air above an evergreen forest that reclaimed the Old Ward. She rose high enough to discover a vast clearing, and found a palace, an old imperial residence. By the standards of palaces, it was rather modest, but its stony facades were a beacon of splendor by the spartan architecture of this wooden city. She wheeled around and spiraled to a landing on a balcony made for a troubadour's serenades.

The doors were already open to her.

"Hello?" she said as she stepped inside. "Don't be afraid, I mean you no harm."

"You have come to aid me?" said a puissant voice.

Her wording was somewhat archaic, and an uncustomary blend of the Severnayan and the posh Capital accent, which voiced its fricatives at the back of the throat. The voice itself wasn't particularly deep, but it echoed with a gentle authority.

"I didn't come to help, but I can help," Volganin said. "What do you need?"

"Oh, you're in a dining room… leave it, and turn to your right. There is a gallery room. Quite obvious." said the voice.

"Rahab?" Volganin quietly asked, more to herself than anyone. But she wasn't sure how well the gods could hear. She waited for an answer, only to be startled by the reedy, mocking laugh of a Parasitic Jaeger. She readied a talon on each foot and advanced in a skipping manner.

The gallery replaced her apprehension with awe. Statues rose from floor to ceiling, kings and imperators and the founding governor of the city. At the center of the room spread tableaux of the hero Exallon beating the Luverian Petrinodon to death with a petrified mare's leg, and the Quinotaur of Merovy splashing from a sapphire sea. Perhaps the spirit of the estate spoke to her. Nobles draw upon their lands for political and magical power, and they in turn gain an intellect of their own.

Man-sized frames hung between plundered bookshelves, concealed by heavy canvas covers. Kingfisher pulled down the largest of them, revealing a group portrait. Three gnomes stood at the bottom third of the frames. One of them was Lem Loganev, looking not much younger. To the left side stood a slightly larger gnome with a beard and oil shale skin, ears framed by ram's horns. Between them stood a young gnomide in peasant's clothing, dyed a noble black. Her hair and eyes were also black, a stark contrast with her white face.

At the center was a tall man with some possible sylph heritage—there was a beautiful androgyny to his ageless face, and his hair was silver and his eyes emerald green. To the right was a man in a mariner's jacket. He had a plain, square face covered in stubble, and dark brown hair shaved short. His shoulders were broad and his limbs thick and strong. He looked like a farmer or longshoreman. Volganin had seen thousands of similar men across the Boreal Sea's ports, though his eyes were the color of pale tea. The legend to the side of the portrait labeled him Erazm Aleksandrovich Makarov. The elfish man was one Isztarion Lesnik. The stout male gnome took the human name, Theobard Helmich, while the gnomide was Gerana Nikneveny.

Volganin's attention turned to the woman on the left, tall and beautiful. She wore a dress of three blues, something from the early twenty-fifth century, perhaps, worth more than Volganin's life. She would have been a classical Boreal blonde, but the ice blue of her eyes was matched by tigerish streaks that highlighted her already strong cheekbones and jawline. Such lines also reached out from her scalp and highlighted her slightly webbed ears. Volganin had never seen this style of make-up before. Her long hair was braided to the left and folded over itself into a crown, impaled on a headdress of short horns, three to each side.

"Closer," said the voice again, from Volganin's left.

The harpy's head snapped to face the covered portrait and pulled off its wisent-hide cover without a second thought.

The woman was there again. But rather than a mere fine dress, she was covered in a mantle of Hyperborean unicorn wool and held an armillary sphere and a silver scepter. A thirty-pearled tiara covered that horned headdress, dotted with morion gems that shined like a spider's eyes. An Oyorpatskoye curved sword sat in her lap, and the scrimshawed tips of mammoth tusks radiated from behind her, the back of the Imperatrix Consort's throne.

This was Ludmilla Miluvna Orlova, mother of the current imperator.

"You have my gratitude," said the voice in the back of the harpy's head.

A sense of overwhelming majesty forced Kingfisher into a bow. This was a monarch out of legend, for heroes to serve.

Kingfisher could not bring herself to look up. She wished she had brought Eol's sword, to salute her overlord. The light pouring through the rose windows took on a golden quality that glorified the orange scales of her legs. Her tail shined like a peacock's feathers, or the passing of a firebird.

"How may I serve you, my queen?" Kingfisher asked. Her stomach churned, and she was on the verge of tears once again. Her throat dried up and tensed like a fist. "Your grace? Your majesty?"

"You have done more than enough, my child," she said. She laughed warmly. "My style is Her Imperial and Royal Majesty, but I am a mere queen mother. A dowager. Your clear respect is more than enough, my child. So uncommon in Northernmost."

Kingfisher wondered what she looked like now. She looked no older than the middle of her second decade in that painting, but she must have been much older. The numbers turned in her head. Her fashion and the ages of the current and former imperators, and the age this palace was abandoned…

She must have been at least a century old. Humans almost never lived that long, Kingfisher thought, and she wondered how to broach the question. She nervously clawed at the frame's leather cover, dragging it flat across the floor. It left behind a trail of Sepia. Her heart skipped a beat when she noticed the branded binding staves and considered the horns.

When she looked up, the painted throne was empty.

Chapter 15: Gunpowder and Ivory

Baeg Byeol-i poured a cup of coffee for Mr. Pander in the steamy baths of the Jooga. She watched Pander's face for any signs of weakness and hesitation, but she was no expert in negotiations. She had put on her lightest silk dress and pulled back the sleeves to reveal her shoulders. A decorative lattice of clovers and lotus concealed a dried raskovnik tucked into a belt patterned with pink flowers. But she had never played the role of the seductress, and her toes curled in embarrassment.

"So, how long were you waiting on the docks?" Pander asked, savoring the heat after his subarctic trek.

"We had shifts," she said. "It was mostly our goblins on watch. I came out when Goldentooth spotted you coming down from the timberline."

"It's flattering to be wanted," he said. "Though dangerous to be so well known, in my line of work."

"Perhaps you should lose the stylish hat," she said.

She gestured towards her shako and his Etesian cap, both hanging from hooks at the door.

"Oh, I try to have some pride in my people," he said. "We're both enclaves, in exile. Though ours has been much longer."

"Meltemia," she said. "The gods fought there, four millennia ago."

"Maybe," he said. "Heroes, definitely. Armies from across the continents. The splendor of it must have been chilling, especially in those less well-traveled days. And the horror. The blood darkened the seas, they say. The rivers frothed with the fury of the mage-winds. A battlefield of five million people, they said. Imagine. Even today that is mind-boggling."

"That's a fifth of the population of Saro," she said.

"'What the ill-fated Etesians have lost for the glory of our heroes,'" he said, quoting an ancient lay. "Do you dream of your homeland? The old courts carved into the mountains of Superna? The bannermen rising past walls of sculpted trees? I've been to Saro. Beautiful land."

"I try not to think about it," she said. "We would probably be killed as soon as we were identified. This courtyard is enough for me."

Pander's finger traced the outline of a compass rose etched into the floor. In the Hypouranias, and neighboring nations like the Golden Kingdom, Saro, and the Dawn Sea Empire, the will-workers divided their magical world not into four elements, but the Four Cardinalities. They bound vermilion and fire to the south, water and blackness to the south, white metal and yellow earth to the west, and blue and the winds to the east. These were realities of Apeliotean and Supernal geomancy, just as true as the stoichiology of Aquilo and Caunias. Pander wondered, after all his travels, if culture was the fountainhead of magic, or the clouding mire. Pander also pondered if the Bookhangers carved the eastern sea-drake turning its neck aside and hiding its face for a reason — the other cardinal beasts, a phoenix, a turtle, and a tiger, held their heads high. The turtle looked downright smug.

"You have carved out a little chunk of Saro here," Pander said. "Those...dok- er, dokkaebi goblins. They're armed with Daybreaker rifles. The Golden Kingdom's pattern."

"Yes. They were the best muskets in the world," she said. Her eyes drifted to an animated gunpowder flask in the shape of a pond turtle. Another of Gangcheori's traps.

"Two centuries ago," he said. "They've fallen behind."

"I know," she said. "But it's not up to me. I'm young, and a gardener. And it's all we know. We're drilled in those old guns. Even I have to take one apart and put it back together."

"Right," he said. He touched the handle of his pistol, tucked into a holster on a wide belt. "But the times are changing. Faster and faster. Those who are left behind are not forgotten, but enslaved. So, how can I help your kind rise above the times?"

"Your dragonslayer," she said. "What came of it?"

"It got out of hand," he said. "It's a lost cause. We've pivoted towards a more direct approach."

The kaftar came into view through the doorway, summoned by the mention of dragonslaying. The beast's sinister grin sent a chill up Byeol-i's spine despite the heat. The mnemonic daemon in her head squirmed against the confines of her mind.

"So," she said. She read the notes she had written for herself. "What... what of our deal?"

"Where is your master?" Pander said. He beckoned the kaftar closer with a curled finger. "You did not broker the agreement."

"My master has chosen not to reveal himself to you," she said. "Your failure to secure your weapon has left your position wanting. By honor, you should propose your recompense. Dr. Lund, Mr. Fade, and the *Inmyeonjo* survive, further endangering us if they choose to question these events."

"We'll arrange for a payment for your efforts. I have a line of credit from the Combine," Pander said, the corner of his mouth rising in annoyance. "Your city barely has a bank, but a payment can be secured quickly enough. And quietly."

He opened a booklet, wrote something on a lined strip of paper, sealed it with a stamp, and handed the torn note to Byeol-i. He rose up and joined the Kaftar at the door.

Credit, she thought. *A type of riches that an imugi could not use, a mathematical hoard.*

"Since your master has chosen not to reveal himself, we shall be leaving," he said. "Thank you for the coffee. Everything else was unpleasant."

Byeol-i rose up and threw a handful of herbs into the brazier and muttered a charm. Pander watched her intently and clutched at a horn of elephant ivory. He tightened the cap.

"What is in that horn?" she said.

"In the south, elephants and true giants are the enemy of dragons, for their ivory can keep a firedrake from changing shape or breathing fire," he said. "In their true form, an elephant would have to somehow gore a dragon for it to matter, a difficult task. But if you catch the drake in their guise, say, a beautiful young woman, you need mere pinches of powdered ivory."

"Beautiful young woman, you say?" Byeol-i said.

"Some security," said Pander. "You should return to normal by morning, based on the dosage in the coffee."

"How did you know?" she said, playing their game, while still baffled by his assumption.

"My readings of the stars and bones foretold your secret. There are two dragons in Northernmost," said Pander.

"What?" she whispered, despite herself.

Did Gangcheori already count as a true dragon? If so, had all this plotting been wasteful, risking the Mayor's wrath for nothing? Her face reddened in rage.

"Don't play the fool," said Pander. "You are this vague, unseen master. A dragon plotting against a rival. Of course, you are a dangerous liability... and you are stripped of your power to change."

The Kaftar lunged forward, and, in one fluid motion, pushed her head into the steamy water of the baths. It tried to cast a binding spell and some manner of firework on the water, hoping to boil her. The effect failed, and the entity incubating in her mind thrust from her consciousness, attacking the kaftar.

The kaftar laughed in shrill distress. Its magic was impotent against her. But she was a small woman, while the kaftar was a two-meter-tall beast with the arms of a smith and the claws of a predator.

But Byeol-i was not abandoned. Gangcheori emerged from the water, solidifying from the steam and charcoal smoke. They struck at the hyena-man's neck, mouth brimming with choking cinders and venom. A second bite broke the beastman's neck, and Byeol-i flailed in the water as it blackened and smoked with its fiendish blood.

Pander drew his pistol with the intent of bartering his life for Byeol-i's, only for the firearm to fall apart in his hand. That was Byeol-i's work -the herb of opening. Thieves used them to undo hinges with the magic of their screwing roots; she unscrewed the Tirvinger's pistol. Mainspring, sidenails, and breechplugs clanged across the tiles.

Pander's surprise barely had time to register before the great imugi's white-hot fangs penetrated his skull.

Chapter 16: Bars and Chains

Mageirissa purchased two malformed specimens and an expensive, full-analog mandrake from Mr. Kains, a timid man born without eardrums, whose farm swarmed with piebald beagles. He lived on the eastern limit in the old octroi house, where the farmers are quiet, sleepy, weak-muscled, and plagued by dreams of "a green lion in the corn." Kains carefully pruned and shaped the high-grade root to closely resemble the human form, down to wire-dented mouths and crafted genitalia. The potting suffused the soil with human essence, from waste to bones and hair from the crematoria and battlefields.

Mageirissa let the most malformed mandrake, nothing but a root, drink up her milk from a cup, breathing a subtle life into its limbs. She poisoned it with arsenic, a powder altered to glow with the essence of foxfire. She ground its corpse with a mortar and animated pestle, mixed the grindings with purified water, and fed it to the next wave—simple mandragora roots, indistinguishable from roots, which had never grown into a humanoid form. She would return to it after they died and dried enough to pulverize and feed to the well-formed Mandragora.

She decided to stretch her legs and go downstairs, only to find the bar packed and mourning the death of Lem Loganev. An electrified lantern was set upon the bar in a sealed dish of acid, one of the engineer's legacies. His habitual stool was left empty, and Elena and her father poured rounds for a toast to a dozen old humans, half a dozen gnomes, and a couple of undines and salamanders.

This was commented upon by the old bartender, saying that Lem, "Didn't care who you were—men, *pharyes*, *kuliltu*, *acthnici*, *voör*, or any chimera in between. He wanted to make your life better. And may he make the world better in his next life."

The old man looked towards the window, clenched his jaw, and quit the room. The crowd drank a toast and cycled around to poured libations in a stone bowl. Two gnomes solemnly bowed to the crowd and announced his funerary arrangements, and revealed his Pharyean name, Lenrokar. The death rites of gnomes are grim, chthonic affairs of carved poems and memorial idols, not the lively funeral games of men.

Mageirissa tried to make herself as small as possible and slowly slithered through the cracks in the crowd. She caught the end of an argument of hisses, growls, and batlike shrieks between Elena's father and an old gnomide as she stepped outside. The gnomide, obscured by a heavy black cloak, vanished in a puff of dust when the bartender looked towards Mags.

Before Mageirissa could ask the reason for the confrontation, the innkeeper stormed back inside.

She decided to stay outside and watch the foot traffic on the Staretsy's Prospekt. The sign of Shura's inn had a functional Eternal Flame, a carved and shining red stone, feeding on stored light and the dragon's ambiance. Across the street stood the Elders' Manor, the Watch's Constabulary, and the Clocktower. A man with a garish sash stepped outside of the manor, with the badge of a 17th-Rank Fellow of the Order of Enlightened Elders. Typical of established gentlemen, a long strop of leather hung from his belt, branded with all of the other social lodges, hunting and shooting clubs, cults, and mutual aid societies to which he paid his dues. He began to smoke and watched as Captain Rhee of the Watch escorted Nicodemus Fade to a holding cell in the Constabulary, with Lund following. He would report what he saw to the Harbor-Master later.

Mageirissa stopped leaning against the inn's stone wall and whistled to Lund, and the doctor beckoned her over. Rhee was annoyed and gestured for her to keep some distance as the constable opened the door and escorted the prisoner inside. Fade said nothing and kept his head down. His face was cold and blank.

To resist the magic of the elementals, the Constabulary was a squat fortress of fire-hardened wood and enchanted ceramic stuffed with ground glass, ash, and salt. The heavy door's frame depicted the Nine Universal Downfalls - Rage, Vanity, Vainglory, Treachery, Avarice, Impurity, Impiety, Obduracy, and Negligence – as wretched people with animal heads.

Inside, the watchmen separated him from Lund and Mageirissa, and Rhee informed them that it would be better for Fade's case if they said nothing until they could be interrogated separately. An officer took a measuring tape to Fade and had him step on a floor scale, noting him as 172 centimeters tall, and weighing 63 kilograms. He was brought to the door of a microsolarium, a greenhouse-like glass box, and his hands dipped in an inky shellac. He pressed his hands against a piece of rice paper, which Rhee fed into a slot. Fade was then allowed to wash his hands in a gentle acid. The microsolarium held a fecund, snub bananas tree grafted with plantains and shaped into a boxy frame. A dense, cloudy spiderweb hung between the twisted boughs, surging with cognitive activity. The glassy, colonial spiders spun these neurons and fed this brain with ground banana and salt. They stripped off the remains of the shellac. Once they finished devouring the crushed beetles and storing the pattern in their collective web of memory, they expelled the paper for retrieval. The red stains were archived in the constabulary, though the cognitive spiders were able to cross-reference handprints and detect repeat offenders on their own, weaving warnings to officers. Every year or so, a clutch "missionary" spiders were shipped from this colony to others throughout the Polar and Boreal Seas, to spread information on fugitives.

As Fade was placed in the holding cell, Chesti emerged from the office in the City Watch's uniform, a blue watchcoat and bullet-resistant jerkin padded with layers of chimerized silk.

"What did Fade do?" he asked. He walked over to the entrance and closed the door, blown open in the night winds.

Lund and Mageirissa wondered if they should speak, and Rhee explained that he was wanted for questioning in the Loganev murder. Chesti raised his inflamed left hand, the tense muscles a sign of stitches and cramping.

"Elf-shot?" Lund half-asked, half-diagnosed.

Chesti nodded and said, "Captain, I think I know who killed our gnome."

"Hmm? Who? Mr. Fade was seen speaking to the gnome in a threatening manner not long ago," Rhee said. He scratched around the rim of a silver coin used to seal a hole in his skull, exposed bone growing through the bores. "It was odd that he would be killed as soon as the outlanders start in after the Thaw."

Lund recalled the animation of those fallen soldiers, and wondered if he should broach the subject of judicial necromancy. In exceptional cases, a justice of the crown, or local equivalent, and an oracle can approve of retribution by revenant. Unfortunately, the Gray Process relies on surviving sensory traces in the victim, so the body has to be recovered, intact, with only days or hours to spare. Any killer foolish or hasty enough to leave behind such a corpse will be easy to catch by mundane means. The Rite of Second-Walking had only been promulgated once in Murmur since his father's childhood, and only because the snow of a mountain ravine preserved the cadaver without freezing the tissues. Lund had not seen the remains of the gnome, but he doubted that such a shell could even be resurrected; the elemental essence had already migrated to its next life. Was it worth exposing Fade's ungentlemanly interests?

"Fade's a good lad. I have an outlander who just arrived. Cunigunde the Whirlwind," said Chesti.

"Right, the report on your band," Rhee said.

"I filed that," Lund said.

"Yes," he said. "That's why I signed up with the watch. Only survivor. You needed someone who could recognize her if she showed up."

"I don't mean to be rude, but a note saying, 'albino sylphide in red leathers wielding a spine' could have sufficed," Lund said. "Not exactly one of the ten-a-copper dockyard thieves."

Rhee had a moment of recognition, and went to the bookshelf, and found a tome bound in cracked leather. He flipped through Ardaschir Goschtasber's *Combat Manual of the Heartlander Armouries* until he arrived at a reproduced woodcarving from the print houses of Gezern, dated to 2256 After the Founding of the Wolf. It was of a smiling woman in a vented breastplate, puffy, striped clothing, and thigh-high boots. Two antlers grew in the shadow of a large, floppy hat decorated with pantheon feathers. She wielded a flamberge which blazed with snaking lines of heat and appeared to be slashing at the viewer as two skeletons danced beside her.

"I don't remember those dancing skeletons," said a soft voice.

Mageirissa yelped and Chesti bolted from the room to the cells. Lund turned towards the voice, swinging. After a moment of silence, Cunigunde became visible.

"It's a symbol of death," said Fade, his cell now exposed to the main room by the sucking wind.

"But I'm already on the page," she said.

"How did you..." Rhee started.

"Think of all those stories of magical creatures and demons and gods," she said. "What is the one thing you aren't supposed to say aloud?"

"You're not some storybook monster," he said, without confidence. "You're just a sylph."

"It's not nature, it's presentation. Every good tale has a monster at the end of it. Sometimes it's a beast, sometimes it's a man, sometimes it's an idea with sharp edges," she said.

She walked past Rhee to flip through the book.

"People like to hear the ones where the heroes win, but there are so many where the monster triumphs. Horsemen of the Osibar steppe speak of an unseen griffon that tears through their legions in the night, harrying them for days until only one rider survives. The lowlanders of Ruhren speak of an enchantress in the mountain, haunting those black woods and killing with word and bone. In the darkest decade of each century, in those days of famine and a cold that eats at fingers and toes and nose, a Northman hero goes out to face a vicious white spectre, a tall naked horror with antlers and fang and the north wind in a horn. They never come back. You know what all those stories have in common? I was the monster at the end."

She vanished, and reappeared behind Rhee, with a hand around his neck.

"So," she said, "will I be the monster at the end of your story?"

"I don't deal with monsters," he said. "Just criminals. Petty thieves. Violent drunks. Squabbling families. Boring events. Not stories."

"Hmm… my breasts are out in this one," she said, pointing at a smaller plate. "I didn't say he could do that. Who carved this?"

"He's been dead for centuries," Rhee said.

"Maybe he has descendants to terrorize," she said. "But I do look cute. So what am I accused of?"

"The poisoning of Lem Loganev," Rhee said.

"Who?" she asked. She let him go and stepped away, the fresh skulls impaled on her antler's prongs and hooks rattling.

"Don't be coy," Rhee said.

"How was he poisoned?" she asked. Her eyes began to shake, so she tilted her head so her ear touched her left shoulder. "Sword? Arrow?"

"That's what I want to know," Rhee said. "How'd you do it?"

"Was he a mercenary? An ogre? A cynocephalic?" she asked.

"No, none of those," said Rhee. "Gnome."

"I haven't killed a gnome," she said. "Well, not for three hundred sheddings. Antlers, I mean. And look, I'll poison hook and head, but I'm not one for food and drink. Where's the challenge in that? I'm innocent."

"Where were you, an hour after noon?" Rhee asked.

"I was with a lover," Cunigunde said.

"Do you have any witnesses?" Rhee asked.

"No, I came to the room invisible, and she left town an hour ago," Cunigunde said, playing with the tip of her helical horsetail. "But I was with her from noon to diner."

"Oh… a woman," Rhee noted. "Uh, wait, who?"

"Justine Severin," she said.

"Oh, uh… wow," Rhee said. "Do you have evidence for this?"

"No, I washed my hands and face," she said. "But I'm innocent. You calling me a liar, mayfly?"

Chesti peaked out from behind the door and said, "And what of the Band?"

"Oh, I killed them," she said. "But that wasn't a crime."

"It was a mass murder," Chesti spat.

"Get over it," she said.

"You admit to this charge?" Rhee said.

"It happened in Hyperborea. A mercenary slaver army invaded my territory. They wouldn't leave when I told them to. And…" she raised her arm and leaned to reveal her armpit, "it regenerated, but I came to, wounded. Pierced by some sort of duct leading to a tap. They were stealing my blood and fat. Like syrup. So, these *slaver sorcerer vampires–*"

"We did no such thing," Chesti insisted.

"Bully, bully, look who's upset about false witness now," chided Cunigunde. "So, these slaver sorcerer vampires… going to add pederasts here… were trying to deprive the world of my breasts, possibly to enhance their frankly unremarkable womenfolk."

She pointed at Mageirissa and added, "Probably why they press-ganged this cow."

"Hey," Mageirissa and Lund both objected.

"You're a wet nurse, you sell your milk for money," the Whirlwind said. "But see? It was self-defense."

"You're a cannibal!" Chesti shouted.

"I would never eat a sylph," she said. She thrust her right hand into the air, pointing at the sky. Thunder shook the building. "I demand a trial by combat!"

"Trial by combat has been abolished for centuries," Rhee said.

"How about a duel?" she said.

"No," Rhee said. "But you will be allowed to hire an advocate, using public funds."

"Humans are consistently the lamest race," Cunigunde said. She scrunched up her nose and sneered at the Urizenist chain and horseshoe mounted on the wall. "Alright, how about this, you read the ancient covenants between the Lords of Hyperborea and your ancestors. See what they say about leading armies of dogheads, ogres, and slaves onto our land."

"What is this about slaves?" Rhee asked Chesti.

"Yes, your boy's boys clapped up the harpy and these doctors and dragged them up to visit me," Cunigunde said, her voice dripping with a feigned innocence. "They wanted to en-slave me too, to fight against that dragon. And probably worse, I saw how they looked at me. So really, I'm the victim in this situation. Give me compensation."

Rhee paused to compose himself, glared at Chestimir, and asked, "You were plotting to take down the Mayor?"

"I was just a local hireling," said Chestimir. "Up the White Meska, from Kastorin."

"Lock him up!" said Cunigunde.

"You're a fucking monster," Chesti said.

The Whirlwind's hand snapped at his jacket so quickly that its topmost button shattered. She pulled him towards his face and hissed, "When I get out of here, I'm going to fuck your father so hard he'll stop loving you."

"What does that even mean? I hope you hang," Chesti said, stumbling back from her loosened grip.

"You'll be my last meal," she said.

"Hold on," Rhee said. "They thought you could take down a dragon? Alone?"

"Dragons are just oversized mayflies," she said with a shrug.

Rhee looked at the chamber containing the cells, and asked, mostly to himself, "So how are we going to hold you?"

"Ah," Cunigunde said. "I will turn myself in willingly. Un-til my innocence of the murder of... Len? Len was it?"

"Lem Loganev," Lund said.

"Aren't you Lem?" she said, squinting and thrusting her neck forward.

"Lund," he corrected.

"That's confusing," she said. "Right, I'll allow you to hold me in a cell. Would a guilty *vör* allow that?"

She raised her hand into a fist and projected her index and little fingers upward and outward like antlers, the famed voör-ish sign. The hollow in her back snapped open, and a quartet of gossamer petals erupted from her back with a hair-raising burst of static and sparking dust.

She took off the left-hand glove and its associated brace and mounted arbelos, the crescent blades used by cobblers and leatherworkers. She tossed it into the hollow. The petals folded like dragonfly wings, collapsed into a line against her spine, and sealed the phantom space. She was disarmed, for what little good that meant.

One of the officers began measuring her. She said she was one *Gezerner klafter* tall, and just shy of eleven stone, which the officer clarified as 1.8m and 69kg.

"What's your game?" Chesti asked.

She smiled, and asked, "Where's that harpy?"

"We haven't seen her since last night," Mageirissa said. "Fade was with her."

"So…" Rhee said. "She was spotted flying away after the harbor blast. The militia shot at her... And your lot took her up north, Chesti? Is she our killer?"

"No, no, she's no murderer," clarified Cunigunde. "She's an uptight, idiot moralist. She wants to be a storybook knight, on a quest. So, I want her as my advocate."

Kingfisher explored the old palace for some time, looking for any inhabitants, carefully calling out for them when the house creaked. She checked the hearth, where humans often keep the ashes of the sundered patriarchs and matriarchs. The most honored elders of prestigious human families, those with many grandchildren, great-grandchildren and cadet branches, volunteer for a rite of sundering that removes them from the wheel of reincarnation. They are said to oversee their family for generations, but only as long as their urns are honored and their names are remembered by their descendants. These wraiths are something more coherent and wise than the faded echoes of most ghosts, and abandoning the Sundered of one's clan is a terrible sin to humanity. Yes, there had been many urns here, and they had all been removed in a hurry and without care, the gold leaving deep scrapes and dings in the floor. The family had either fled in the night, or sent workmen to retrieve the urns, smuggling them to the Blackened Capital.

Her stomach churned with the dreamfish, and she longed for a drink, finding a bucket of fresh water in the kitchen. She eyed the room suspiciously, lowered her head, and sucked up the water. She sloshed it over her tongue, detecting a dull, earthy hint of leaves without the particular tang of green vegetation. Dead leaves were an unusual thing to collect in a bucket, unless one was using them as a catalyst for air-work.

Her head shot up when the soft footfalls of someone coming down the hall alerted her to the palace's last custodian. She retreated to the nearby window at the end of the hall and raised its latch.

A lanky man in a light robe, still youthful and beautiful, raised a willow wand at Kingfisher. She recognized the face of Iszt Lesnik from the portrait and said his name.

"Yes," he said. "If you have come here to plunder and devour, be warned that I have driven off bands of looters before and have a mastery of aeolian magic."

"Are you a sylph?" she asked. "Is this your home?"

"My great-great-grandmother was one of the rangers of the limit and was seduced by a light-elf hunter. He visited her down the years, until she passed, helping her map out this region," he said. "My family has lived in this port since its founding by the crown. We helped design this palace. When the royals stopped coming here, it became mine by right of investment. Why have you come here?"

"I was drawn here," she said. "Compelled by a voice in a dream."

"Whose voice?" he asked. "What have you done?"

"It was a woman's voice," she said. "I think the queen mother."

"Ludmilla," he said. "What did she tell you to do?"

"I went into the gallery…" she started, before he ran out of the room, shouting about the wards falling. She fluttered through the door and asked what he meant.

"You idiot!" he roared, and a bolt of force crackled down the wand and electrified the air around Kingfisher.

Kingfisher sputtered and tried to explain, but Lesnik held his arm out, completely still. He did not breathe or blink. She took this as a sign to leave and launched herself out of the window and into the still-bright night sky.

She rose high in the sky to avoid detection and the sniper's aim. She followed the winds southeast towards the docks, where an ironclad with unknown markings and heavy hauling chains attempted to dredge the wreck of the *Imperitor Dragomir*. On the shore, a team of men in naval peacoats rolled three dozen barrels of pitch from a square topsail schooner out of Talvenvasara, with a second unit loading them onto a telega and four-horse covered wagon. A certain alcoholic distillation of wood tar was recently found to protect against the dreaded turu worm, a Teredo clam known to bore through wood and render piers and hulls into brittle sieves. It wasn't completely effective, but it was far cheaper than the copper-sheathed hulls of the Septentrine Navy and the Merovene Argosy. But she couldn't understand why these seamen would transport them north, rather than keep them at the shipyard. As she listened in, one of the workers mentioned something about 'new orders from the Tall Man,' which caught her interest.

The harpy landed on a whalery in the Monosovskiy Yards on Seal Skinner Head, where men rendered a ziphius, an oily beast with the body of fish, the head of an owl, and tailfins like a giant's scimitar. Something she thought was a live whale lurched beneath the waves, and she wondered if one had escaped the butchery. Legrand, Mignard, Severin, and their crew walked out onto the dock and took a ramp to the whale. Its top opened, and they climbed down inside of some kind of fully-aquatic vehicle, the likes of which Volganin had never seen before. After a quarter of an hour, the crew completed the loading and preparation, and departed out into the Polar Sea, with barely a ripple left in their wake. The nearby sailors shared her astonishment.

Terror ran up her back, as she recalled her time as a spotter. Even with her avian eyes, she would almost certainly never detect such a thing. What human sailor would have a chance?

She wondered if she had hallucinated the sharkship, shivered, and departed, swinging back to the Eternal Flame. At the window, after listening for certain activities, she found Mageirissa feeding a distressingly humanoid mandrake a wet mash. She monitored its roots with the help of Lund, copper wires, and a liquid battery.

"Dame Kingfisher," said Lund, after rising from the experiment and opening the window. "Fade is held at the Constabulary. You've missed the visitation hours, but he's, well, safe at least. It's all a big misunderstanding. But you should go there. On the morrow, I mean. I'll go with you."

Kingfisher scraped the window ledge with her toes. Lund helped her inside.

"What are you doing to that mandrake?" she asked, before turning her attention to Perchinka the Hobgoblin, playing in a bag of rotting produce.

"Testing how poisons travel up the food chain," Mageirissa said. "It was a hunch. And not… good."

She handed a letter to Perchinka, who crawled outside.

"Your research notes for Mr. Fade?" Kingfisher asked. "I

could deliver it faster."

"The guards are looking for you. And wouldn't want us around, in case we try to pull him out," Mags said. She handed a second letter to the harpy. "And this is for you, but… Forget it."

Kingfisher let the folded note fall to the ground, opened it up and began to read.

"This is a court request…" she said as she read. She glanced up as Mags reached out to fix her friend's wind-ravaged hair. "For my legal aid in favor of… Cunigunde out of Arvenial by Aras, called the Whirlwind, who has pleaded innocent of the murder of Lem Loganev."

Kingfisher wanted the sylphide pushed back into the tree. But then she caught the time of the death and realized that she saw Cunigunde's alibi. Among other things.

"I'll do it," Kingfisher said, after a quiet minute of contemplation.

"Why?" Lund said.

"I know she's innocent," Kingfisher said. "Of this charge; I must clarify that. When it comes to law and justice, we can never let an innocent suffer a false conviction. Never. Not once, not even if they've truly committed a thousand other crimes. Once you start bending the rules, you go crooked. Once you get sloppy, you hurt someone. Never, ever compromise your principles."

"Are you sure?" Lund asked.

"No exceptions," said Kingfisher. "Even to bring down a demon."

Northernmost rarely had a need for large-scale incarceration after the collapse of its aging population, and the City

Watch's jail mostly served as a drunk tank. The Contortions made people irritable and delirious, but the victims were usually too weak, tired, and aching to do anything too severe. Before this bloody week, the execution of short-seller marked the last legal circus. He was hanged on the main pier, for those who deliberately under-prepare a ship's store with rubbish are charged with the murder of all sailors aboard the vessel.

Cunigunde and Fade were held alone in single cells, facing each other.

They served Fade bread, diced pickled radish, and beet soup. Cunigunde, ground chicken livers fried with onions. However, it was not all gruel, and she was surprised to see them serve Golden Apples, the chimerical honey citrus grown in the hot spring's caves of Hyperborea, one of the secrets of the sylphs. She was both disappointed and relieved when Fade explained that it was actually a similar fruit called a satsuma, which grew on a tree rather than in the earth. The humans had not penetrated and plundered her homeland. But that old comfort fruit was not known here, either, becoming a thing of myth and quests for immortality.

The mixture of citrus and earthy scents forced Fade back to his youth, when his mother made sandy brown dyes from boiled walnuts and beeswing or argol from the vineyards. The sour, nutty taste would sit at the back of the tongue and taint the bread. He remembered his mother's arms, darkened by the dye, and his father beating down the linens. He remembered granny Luscinia's lemon pies, and how she taught him to mend wounds and the secrets of herbs. He turned to his work, and pondered Mags and Lund's research on trophic accumulation, smuggled in by the hobgoblin, and made notes on the nature of arsenic chemistry and its affinity for lead, and pondered volcanic ash, realgar deposits, and groundwater contamination. He wrote up a survey request for the port's magma tubules and subterranean water, and tried to find insights within his reading material, Sulfatelluris' *Fire and Earth* and Urraca of Maladon's *Geurgy, and the Matter of an Unkind Planet.*

He occasionally looked over at Cunigunde, trying not to let his nervousness cross his face. He could never show weakness to her. Her weapons had been taken from her, at least the superficial ones. She still had mastery of the hollow, which could not be taken from her. The only crack in his façade was a pained groan as she shed her boots, revealing that parts of her outfit were hooked into her body with silver piercings.

Her jailers placed iron bands on her hands, meant for chain gangs, in the superstitious belief that "cold iron" prevented the light-elves from doing mischief. She played along with it, as it was best if the others never learned the truth. The *al-voör* were the People of the Stars, and the cold iron they feared lay in exhausted stellar cores, one of the few things which could truly kill them on contact. The most ancient souls of her people became stars, and those cores held the power of death magic over the sylphs, just as skulls were used in death hexes against men. She could leave at any time, simply turning into an aerial form and crossing through the bars.

But she had promised not to leave, swearing that she was innocent, and would not work the air unless specifically allowed. When Chesti asked why they should trust her, she barked that her word as a sylph was paramount.

"What are words, after all, but the most mundane working of the air?"

Her God was the Occult Lord, the secret mover of all things, the flap of the wing that stirs the tempest. When the Darkness Eternal swept across the heavens to swallow her ancestral stars, the Occult saved them, igniting the day to hide them in the light. When the blinded Beast spat out its blazing prey, the ancestors fled to the depths of the sky for safety, their white light cooling into dust and scattered clouds. The

Hidden God pushed his enemy to the edge of the world, sliced it into Behemoth and Leviathan, and bound the beasts between the Vorago and the Inferno, between water and land, between magma and ice. The Leviathan's sense of place was hidden from even itself, and the Behemoth was stripped of its sense of time, and so Eternity and Everlasting Creation were separated from the Moving Winds of Time and Fortune. God went to the ancestral stars and gathered the dust and the clouds lost in their exodus. He crushed the dust in His hands, and sucked in the clouds, and descended to Thier. He breathed the clouds into the world's dead air, causing them to stir with spirit and twist into the First Sylph, Thieriel, Lord of the World. The Occult opened His hand and dropped the compressed dust onto the dead earth, which quickened and birthed the first titans. God instruct Thieriel to love and protect the hidden things – the air and the light, the invisible passions and forces of the world, the perplexing taboos and riddles of life – and Thieriel's Get would forever be hidden from Time and Change.

So spreading a little falsehood among the humans would be a good deed.

When alone in their cells, Fade asked, "So, what was that? What ploy is this? Or some sign of honor?"

"What kind of honor?" she asked, snacking on the flowers and candied roots of Elecampane.

"However your people define it, I suppose," he said with a shrug.

"Battlefield honor is something humans use to justify throwing away the lives of their young men. Social honor? I only care that you fear me. Personal honor? Perhaps."

"It's a matter of personal honor," he said. "I just want to know where you stand."

"I would say pride," she mused, a wistful slowness in her voice. "Let me share the sober wisdom of the berserker. I have lived a life of terror, cruelty, and naked butchery. I capture, conquer, and consume, for no higher purpose. I have reveled in merciless savagery for centuries, finding nothing to love in Man or the Heavens. I believe in a world of war and treachery, twisted wishes, and starving dogs. And nothing in my red days has ever contradicted the wasteland of my convictions. But one must give your words power. If I say I will do something, you need to know that I could or would do it."

"I understand," Fade said with a nod. "I also know that need for respect. For pride. The dignity in being feared. And the fear that this life has no point."

"Oh, my life has meaning," she said, punctuated with a snort. "Whatever I want it to be. That's what's great about life. I am no pessimist. The Subtle and Supreme God made me perfect. I'm here to have fun, do whatever I want to whomever I want, and be whatever I want."

"I'm afraid I don't have the time for that," Fade said.

"I understand," she said, with a dissonant motherly tone. "I don't care, but I understand. Do what you need to do, mayfly."

She paced across her cage, watching Fade.

The Anatomist tried to view her in the most clinical way possible, repressing both his fear and his physical attraction to her. He focused on the odd feet. He had read before that sylphs had the feet of deer or, somehow, birds. Cunigunde had rough white pads on the sole of her feet, which stretched up to the toenail, and on the bump at the base of the tibia; these would have been black on a non-albino, perhaps, though her electrical manipulation had blackened her feet and fingertips, an effect that faded throughout the day. The standard sylphic stance, on the ball of the short feet, must have inspired that deer-like impression. He sketched the anatomy on his scrap paper.

Cunigunde began her routines. A soft buzz ran up the elf-ax embedded in her hollow, stimulating her spinal meridians, which Fade speculated to be some kind of electrophysiological therapy akin to acupressure, perhaps drawn to those silver piercings in her boots and pectoral straps. If true, it would have constantly kept her yliaster channels open, dissolving the alchemical dross of transmutation and flushing out the fatigue residuum built up in the channels. A similar hiss accompanied the beginning of her duel with Kingfisher.

"So, you're the only light-elf I've seen in person," Fade asked, largely to break the silence. "Are you physically typical? Or is this level of fitness an aberration?"

"I'm on the stronger side, but not strange. Humans always say that elves are androgynous, but for some reason, you think that just means our males are pretty and long-haired," she explained, almost annoyed with the question. "Sylphides are tall, muscular, and long-armed. What do you think a race of tree-climbing archers looks like?"

Cunigunde spent three hours on calisthenics, running, squatting, jumping in place, and pulling herself up against the bed and the bars. She found herself overheating, panting loudly, and struggling to clean up. The jailers had left her with two pitchers of water, one for drinking, one for sanitation. The jailers had a stove in their secured corner, but it was too late to request hot water for a wash. A rolling tray under the bunk housed the chamber pot, a sponge and bowl, a bar of lye soap, the slop jar for the wastewater, and a small box of random pieces of newspapers, pamphlets, obsolete calendars, worn-out novel pages, half an almanac, and a corn cob. She had used pessoi, ceramic shards and bits of broken pottery carved with curses and the names of foes, and the tersorium sponge. But there was something about the notion of these humans giving her their trash that set her off.

Cunigunde breathed a long, pained sigh. Opened the hollow on her back and thought of her collection of moss and fine leaves. She pulled out the chamber pot, pulled her tunic over her knees, and let her *naatsit* work its way to the floor.

Fade looked up from his charcoal doodling and registered some slight shock at the sight.

"Hey, I need to be alone here," said Cunigunde. "Tie that blanket around your neck and hang yourself until dead."

"I'm not going to kill myself so you can have privacy," Fade said.

"Why not?!" she snapped. "What kind of gentleman are you?"

"Turn invisible!" he spat, before theatrically shielding his face with the raised cover of his book.

"I said I wouldn't," she hissed through gritted teeth.

"Just be quiet, talking will only make it worse," Fade dramatically covered his eyes with his hands and turned completely away from her.

"Wait, no, watch me. Make eye contact with me as I shit. I'm asserting dominance," she said. "Like a tiger."

"Do tigers do that?"

"I don't know, ask Lund the animalologist," she said. She grunted and struggled for several minutes, eventually covering her face in embarrassment.

"Are you… unwell?" Fade asked. He lowered his hands, his arms aching.

"Are you sure you don't want to kill yourself?" she said. "If you want a wank before you go, I promise to cover it up. I'll even show some tit."

"Are you constipated?" he asked with a laugh. "I never thought of elfines shitting, but I guess you don't, after all."

"Oh, you're lucky we don't share a cell," she said, cocking her head and shaking it as though trying to gore with her antlers.

She picked up the corn cob and tossed it at Fade. He ducked, and it bounced around his cell before coming to a stop against his window.

"Shove that up your ass and pretend it's me," Cunigunde growled and grunted.

"Wow, very androgynous," Fade noted, before ducking out of the way of a metal scoop, which buried itself in the brick behind him. "When you can't kill your way out of a situation, you're just hot air, eh?"

"I have crushed the skulls of a thousand weaklings like you with my mighty thews. And even mightier hews! I bet you don't even know what thews and hews are!" she yelled.

She raked her nails up her thighs with such forceful rage that the electrically-blackened skin on her hands faded to white and then pink as hot, healing blood surged to the surface.

"They're tendons and ax-blows," Fade said. He smiled at her pathetic anger, the lonesome pride of a warlord screaming atop a mountain of corpses with no way down. "At least you're immortal. Since you're going to be there for a year or two."

"You only rent mercenaries, you know?" she said, between pained panting. Half a dozen swords erupted from her back as she strained. "They're finally putting up a good fight. *Mmmmn-ngh*, we should get Chesti in here, pay his respects."

"Tomorrow, ask the watchmen if they'll give you some of that blue mass that they make up here," he said. "It's for this sort of relief... the locals have a high meat, fish, fat diet. Not much roughage."

"Me too," she said. "Well, I don't eat fish. Or wisent. Or deer."

"It's nothing that spends its life on four legs," he noted, recalling a scrap of elflore.

"We can eat bears, birds, achlis, seals, whales, macropods, monopods, and the children of Man," she said.

"So why not fish?" he asked. "Fish should be an important part of a diet in this clime."

"That's not a spiritual taboo. Too much fish drives us mad," she said.

"Is it the dreamfish?" he asked. "Another curse?"

"No, over time. Centuries," she said. "Like the madness of dark-elves in their mines… It's also why we don't eat seal organs… so what makes the blue mass blue?"

Fade went quiet, before mumbling. "The *Triumph*, the alchemists, the fish, the metal amplifying spell, the cinnabar and vermilion…"

"Cinnabar would make it red," said Cunigunde. Her eyes went wide and her mouth shrank. "Oh. *Oh*."

"There's no curse," said Fade. "It's mercury."

Chapter 17: Quicksilver

Kingfisher flew to the stone house of Lem Loganev, practicing her invisibility. She found it only worked when she did not move, and it blinded her. But revealing one part of her face allowed her to observe over the lip of a roof. The watch had found the house ransacked, Loganev's work files ripped from the bureaus and scattered. They had gathered them up and were attempting to sort them and translate them from Pharyean for clues and contacts. They had taken everything as evidence, or perhaps plunder. The watchmen seemed quite interested in the engineer's samples of precious metals, distilled to purified powders – the gnomes held that the macrocosm was not built from overarching divine dictates from on high, but from the interactions of relatively few microscopic principles and mindless laws. She hoped all of that fine work would not simply vanish into those overcoat pockets.

For the first time since the murder's discovery, the crime scene went unwatched by the constables. They were off interrogating members of the candlefish industry and the chandler's guild, as they had an obvious economic motive for killing the proponent of electrification.

Kingfisher, however, had a dual suspicion: Mageirissa had told of the Innkeeper confronting a suspicious old gnomide for the second time, and a gnome would actually hide his most precious—or damning—work in stone. The watch had either not thought of it, or was unwilling to tear up the house just yet

Kingfisher took a handful of dried oak leaves, lichens, and pine needles, and mashed them into an aerated powder to the point that it resembled a ball of fine spice. She turned it invisible and tossed it into the house. A guided downdraft caused the ball to explode outward in a layer across the floor.

She read her grimoire, repeating the spells in her head for hours, and fantasized about the tale of Sir Borko and the

Basilisk of Beregreki, who used a leaking flour bag to hunt a beast that would kill him on eye contact. At three hours after midnight, she heard the characteristic sucking sound of her trap activating. She shot to the ground, hoping to catch the thief in the act.

She had hoped that the fiend would come in above ground, invisibly. The invisible powder would cling to them and reveal her target with a counteraction of air and earth, along with their path through the building. But she knew that a smart gnome would move through the earth itself, and burrow away with whatever treasure Loganev stored there. In this case, her powder would mark the pathway out of the building, displaced by the tremors.

When she made the trail visible, it led almost all the way to the old Imperial Navy Yard, the wharf from whence that odd dredging vessel appeared to operate. Kingfisher expected to lose the trail when the gnome burrowed under a building, but the perpetrator followed the road, above ground.

Kingfisher remembered that eerie breeze that brushed past her after she exited the *Imperator Dragomir*. It seemed trivial at the time, considering the disaster that followed, but that phantom breeze moved perpendicular to the prevailing wind.

It was an invisible creature.

A sylph would have flown rather than wait for the ramp. An allied undine could have done more to help the sinking vessel, while an enemy would not have resorted to flame nor waited for port. If an undine wanted their ship destroyed, they would have vanished at sea. A salamander could have easily caused the blast, but Kingfisher would have sensed the heat in passing, especially in contrast with the circumpolar weather. Another chimera, daemon, oddity, or curiosity from another Sun or star would have surely been noted by the crew and require extraordinary accommodations. Her unseen suspect was almost certainly a human, a gnome, or something nearly indistinguishable.

The current evidence pointed to a gnome.

A cat with two tails watched Kingfisher from the opposite rooftop, its prison-warden acerbity driving her to fly toward the wider trail.

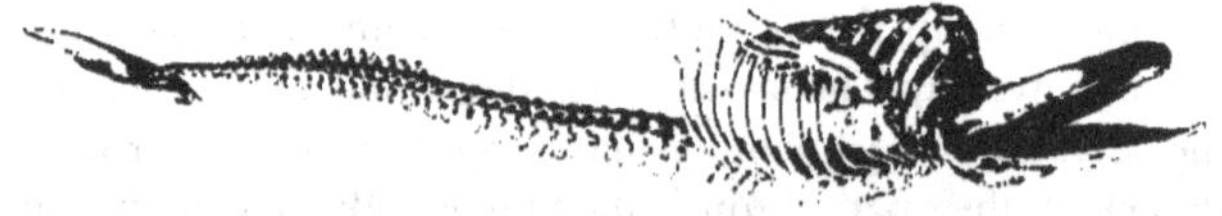

The next morning, a shivering Fade asked for another blanket and requested that one of the watchmen summon Lund and Mageirissa. They had, after all, asked him to translate Loganev's documents. They denied him the blanket and regarded the summons with skepticism until he said that he may have uncovered the root of the Contortions. They also agreed to buy a pitcher of carob coffee and senna to solve Cunigunde's issues. She amended her prior agreement to say that she wouldn't use magic to escape, but perhaps to conceal certain bodily functions.

Cunigunde unhooked herself from her makeshift nest, an upper bunk, some chains, and her harnesses. She rolled up her blanket into a thin cigar and tossed it into Fade's cell like a floppy javelin. When he thanked her, she told him to kill himself, but she could tell her heart wasn't in it.

As his fingers poured over the bumps, ridges, and triangular pyramids of the Pharyean script, a tactile alphabet developed for use in pitch black depths, the Whirlwind asked him to read aloud. He did but explained that it was simply technical documents and engineering notes, barely complete. Like many such notebooks, half of it was lost with its author's passing. She sucked air through her teeth and asked him if he had anything better to read. He said it was simply Loganev's work and his tomes of arcane philosophy. She said the current work would be fine, anything to pass the time.

He asked if she could read. She explained that she was literate, in the main Aquilan, Cainian, Argetese, Apeliotese, and Voorish scripts, but her albinism made the actual act a strain. In the centuries past, when literacy was rarer, she had put this knowledge to good use against dishonest paymasters and to help compose skaldic verse, but she preferred to have others read to her.

A cold rain tinkled against the stones, causing a seven-toed cat outside to wail and run for cover. Fade closed the book to protect against the damp drafts and asked if his fellow prisoner ever had pets.

"Are you offering?" she asked with a smile, before slipping on a worn birrus.

"I probably don't live long enough," he said.

"That's the problem, isn't it?" she said. "I've been around a few familiar foxes and elk, but they're gone in a few sheddings. In the southern eldritches, the sylphs sail between islands on small boards with javelin-launching bow sails. They form strong bonds with pods of whales and a breed of giant tortoises who live for centuries. Some voör would even paint and etch their shells with messages to the local men, and the tortoises became known as messengers of the winds and the hidden folk with the folding boats."

"Imagine a poor tortoise trying to keep up with you," Fade said.

"No need to imagine, my poor mayfly," she said. Her slight smile collapsed and she asked, "Is there a reason that your hair is so gray?"

"It's a family trait," he said. "My dad and granny Luscinia were gray at twenty, my uncles and grandfather by thirty."

"But do you age quickly? Relative to other humans, I mean," she asked.

"Are you concerned?" Fade asked in return.

"No," she said. Her eyes began to shake, and she turned

away into the darkness.

When the cell inspector came in, Fade asked for several magnifying lenses of different sizes, and reading material for Cunigunde – Goschtasber's *Combat Manual.*

Around noon, the police acted on the summons. Fade, Lund, and Mageirissa decided that the best way to treat the hydrargyria was to develop a binding agent for the mercury. Lund and Mageirissa traveled to their workspace at the abandoned charcoal burner's mound, for its ventilation and access to a furnace. The basis of the reactant would be the spirit of amber, an acidic metabolic intermediate obtained by distillation. Lund struck a deal for blocks of the fabled hive-amber of Lentora, resin-rich with fossils of the region's notorious scalding ants. Fade was happy to find a practical use for this ancient folk medicine.

The shaman and the doctors recruited a research team from the infirmary and hospices. The staff spent two days attempting yliaster-rich aqueous solutions with sulfuric acid and primary alcohol oxidation reactions. They tested the acid of Valeria root, laurets of laurel oil and milk, the myristates of nutmeg, and spermaceti and ambergris purchased from the Guild of Whalers. The latter was inspired by a cryptic reference to the "alchemical wedding of grey and electrum ambers in mage's alcohol" as a cure for lead poisoning, found in Goderic of Gezern's translation of *Codex Salubrious,* attributed to the arch-poisoner King Azimazda. Fade requested a remote library search of *The Book of Samskara,* an Ishvarist religious text on the practice of detoxifying metals for ritual working.

The strange variation in the symptoms was not due to some general malediction in the town, but different forms of hydrargyria. Gastral poisoning from the diet of fish, childhood acrodynia, vascular mercularism from water, and erethism in industrial workers.

Kingfisher put herself to use as a courier, flying between

Fade's cell, the charcoal mound, the library, markets, and the Jooga, with a special dispensation from Captain Rhee. Fade operated remotely with his homunculus, projecting into the nerves of the centimeter-tall man to perform micro-surgery on living human organs. Cunigunde even managed to help out, using aerugy to create vacuums and high-pressure distillations.

Mageirissa and Lund commissioned a specialized alembic from the local glassblower, a rhö-imago with a transparent sandbox shop on Mirror-Makers' Lane. The crystal house grew next to the mundane office of the town's ophthalmologist and a row of mirror manufactories, their businesses bound by joint shares in a mine. The rhö came to Thier fifteen centuries ago from the fourth planet around the star Durada. The creature appeared to be an orange and mauve isopod made from starfish, with limbs the length of a man's legs, covered in what could only be called a work apron. While few in number, they monopolize the glass trade, as their dry world had seas of fine sand, as far as the eye could see, hardened by lightning storms. The two Thierans marveled at the notion, as the undines had irrigated the great drylands before the history of humanity, and they knew only the sand of beaches. Lund paid the alien artisan with fulgurite and examined the creature's glass thaumaturgy closely, as it spun molten sand with a sextet of wands held in six of its ten legs, which each branched into ten fingers around a multipurpose orifice. It used the principles of water-working with sand, a completely unorthodox working by Thieran standards.

Lund, Kingfisher, and Mageirissa spent the third day humiliating and sickening themselves with guano-handling on the seaside cliffs, to produce nitrates and phosphate of lime. Lund eventually broke up into a swarm of dung beetles and bats, though the strain of so many creatures caused him to black out for a few hours. On the night of the fourth day, they de-

tected a strong odor somewhere between garlic and onion rising from their working vials, the telltale sign of *mercurio captans*
compounds, the mercaptans which bind with mercury.

Lund and Mageirissa came to Fade's cell with the synthesized agent.

"We've hit something of a snag," Lund whispered. "Your
anatomical specialty would be required for testing on the ac-
quired subjects. We can't do anything with an inert circulatory
system."

Fade nodded at the string of jargon and euphemisms.
They looked over at the watchmen who circulated through the
Constabulary, wary of the arcanists in their midst and the dan-
ger of a prison break. The charwoman, an oddly burly old
Sarowoman, came in, and slipped a change of bedding and re-
freshed commode to the prisoners.

Cunigunde pressed up against the bars, watching this new
face for signs of danger and weakness. The charwoman refused to be intimidated.

"You're showing quite a bit of décolletage there, troll-
wife," said the charwoman. "And whatever you call the…
lower thirds."

"When you're from the north pole, nothing looks better
than a bit of southern hemisphere," said Cunigunde.

"You should cover-up," she said. "Dangerous to dress like
that in a jail."

"Would you cover up a work of fine art? Kill yourself for
even suggesting that," said Cunigunde. The charwoman thrust
her broom through the bars until Rhee came in and pulled her
away, clearing the room of officers and staff. Cunigunde
slipped the piece of fallen straw into her top, letting her clavi-
cle piercing pin it down.

"Thank you for the privacy," Fade said to the Whirlwind.
He then turned back to the doctors. "Even if the Contortions
are slow, we're running out of time. I don't want the subjects

to become useless. A fine balance between rot and freezing."

"Won't freezing preserve them?" Mags asked.

"The organic structure could be preserved, but reanimated organs have a radically different metabolism from living tissue," he said. "I entered this field of inquiry to help poisoned miners and transplant organs – and the danger lies in the subtle changes and unseen toxins."

"Me," said Cunigunde.

"Beg your pardon?" said Lund.

"What do you mean?" asked Fade.

"I've traveled around the world and was trapped in a tree, but I still must have some bit of mercury poisoning from living here. Maybe a century in total. That should be enough," she said. "And besides, even your medical malpractice can't kill me. I'm dead hard."

"Don't tempt us," Lund whispered.

"Ooh, ominous," Cunigunde said with a laugh.

"We will need to biopsy the test subject," said Fade, deliberately ignoring the back-and-forth. "Or autopsy, in our… prior method."

"Right, which is why I'm great and better than any human," Cunigunde said. "I have antlers. The quick has been growing out in this cell. Tons of blood vessels, freshly growing bone. And if something goes wrong, you can break off the antler. I shed them every year. Also, your medicine is a mineral. You can easily work that through my body if I go slightly aerial since Sylphs and earth magic barely interact."

"She's right," said Mageirissa with a smile. It then soured into a frown and her eyes narrowed. "What are you getting out of this?"

"Glory," she said. "I am the Whirlwind. Savior of the north. Crowned by nature, ennobled by science. What more could I ask for? And what more could you ask of me?"

"Goddamn it," growled Mageirissa, her balled fists quaking. "I hate you so much. But fine. You're right."

"You are forgiven for doubting my boundless benevolence," said Cunigunde. "To err is human, to be astonishing and beautiful and terrifyingly strong is me."

She began removing her piercings, beginning with the trio of silver arrowheads and bone cornicelli pinned to the helix of each ear.

"I do wonder how transferable it may be. Across the races, I mean," Fade warned. "This form of mercury has a great affinity for the lungs and body fat. In a human, it slips into the nervous tissue quite easily, particularly the brain. Sylph lungs are stronger, with more aeration of the blood. And they never lose their infantile brown fat, storing it through the muscle tissue, filled with webs of blood vessels and adaptive basal tissue. It's why they can be skinny and hairless yet adapted to the poles, even without air magic."

"We were blessed by God," Cunigunde said with a smug smile.

"Or you're just oily," Fade said. "You're basically herring. Or candlefish."

He pointed at a eulachon mounted in the cell, still dried and wicked, smelling up the place.

His tired eyes twitched and he added, "At least the cell's dark. When does midnight sun end, by the way?"

"It runs from the start of Softrains to the last week of Parchers," Lund said.

Fade let out a long sigh.

"How about gurry sharks?" Cunigunde suggested.

"Those sharks that live forever and taste like stagnant piss?" Mageirissa said. "Sure."

"So," Cunigunde said. "When I was in that tree, do you think I was... tested? For this quicksilver disease?"

"Perhaps," said Mageirissa. "Or it could have been a vampire."

Cunigunde's eyes narrowed in disgust at the thought, humans hexing themselves and leaching their lungs to ape their elfin betters, turning into mists and immortal corpses.

"Or you were tapped to make brown candles," Lund said.

The Whirlwind smiled without mirth, like a chimpanzee's threat display. "I was in there for two and a half centuries. How much did those bastards get? What kind of storms have been conjured? What serpents have been struck by my red lightning? How many ships have been dragged to Craythur's Keep?"

"Why the outrage at the carnage?" Mageirissa said.

"I didn't get to see it! And I didn't get credit! Some Tsokiri sorcerer siphoned my strength! Some weak-kneed Waylander wizard got rich off of my ass fat!" shouted the Whirlwind. "No offense, Fade."

"None taken," Fade said.

"Let's do it," she said. "Give me the medicine. And put my name in the grimoire."

"It's going to be a paper," Lund said.

"No! People wipe their ass with those!" she shouted.

"Medical paper," he said. "As in a medical journal."

"Won't the research get lost if it's just one piece of paper in a daily book?" Cunigunde asked. "How many scholars are writing? And aren't journals private?"

"Oh, we use a printing press," Lund said. "You can make many books in a day. As for the rate of publication… actually, wait, why are they called journals? They're usually quarterly."

"Fuck it, I'm bored! Put your magic science needle in my head!" the Whirlwind shouted.

"Well, there are serious ethical concerns," Lund said. "We need you to consent to the experiment, in writing."

"Fuck writing, fuck ethics, fuck consent," she said. "Never needed any of them. Needle me!"

"It's a series of pills. Metallic salts silvered in vark filigree," explained Lund. "You'll swallow it."

"Ah," Cunigunde said. "Then I want the big woman to put it in my mouth. With her bare hands."

"Why?" yelped Mageirissa.

"A sick power game," said the Sylphide. She locked her vibrating eyes with Mageirissa. "I feel like you don't *get* me."

The Shaman responded by lighting a Mugwort cigar. Cunigunde began to cough, and Mageirissa popped the pills in the Whirlwind's mouth during a sharp inhalation and closed her narrow jaw with both hands. As the cigar rolled on the ground, Cunigunde found herself forced to swallow. The berserker issued a vulnerable whimper and wiped her pink-shot eyes.

"Alright, you got me," the Whirlwind said in weepy wheeze. "Good one. I will blind your great-granddaughter."

"I'll put you back in a tree," Mageirissa said.

Cunigunde reclined on her bunk and cocked her head up, ears swiveling. Lund hummed in spite of himself, noting that her arctic-adapted ears had less surface area than most adult humans, without lobes and fewer interior folds. The story-book light-elves had always had larger ears. This finding came from his studious efforts to neither look at the sylphide beneath the shoulders nor make eye contact. Her quivering eyes scanned the room, what Lund identified as a combination of nystagmus and a search for a petty reason to escalate the situation.

"So, we wait for two hours and then work the compound to your velvet rather than letting it pass into the black bile," Fade said. "Then we take a biopsy."

"You two should leave," Cunigunde said to Lund and Mageirissa. Her ears curled and swiveled. "The watchmen are getting itchy. Listening at the door..."

Mageirissa walked up to the door and knocked on it. She turned the handle after a grunt muscled its way through the wood, and found a watchman with a cup in his hand and a ringing in his ear.

"Sorry," she said. "We'll be on our way. There will be a need for supervision in two or three hours, and Mr. Fade will need to perform a surgical procedure on the Whirlwind."

Dr. Lund followed her through the door and handed Rhee a canvas package containing a scalpel, forceps, probes, a curette, a drop of the mercaptans, and an empty sample vial.

"He will need these. I assume you would like to have several eyes on him, and he will have been let out of his cell. The procedure should last no more than fifteen minutes," he said.

"Alright," Rhee said. He set down his meal, a bowl of turu and white fish chowder with fermented carrots. "If either of them pulls any tricks, you will be held responsible."

"Fine," Lund said.

He and Mageirissa left, crossing the street to *The Eternal Flame*.

Cunigunde listened to the conversation until someone closed the door. She immediately glanced at Fade and smiled.

"He bends and curves and holds the nerves. She binds the leaves. The scholar preserves. It fills the veins with toxic reserves. It grants to my foe the fate it deserves," she said.

"A riddle?" Fade said. The voör told rhyming riddles as a cultural rite, sacred speech probing for the unanswerable. They revered one deity, a nameless, sourceless figure of infinite mystery. The Occult God did not impose order upon the world as Urizen did, with chains of Law and Reason, but metered Nature and made history rhyme. "Can you repeat that?"

She did, and he answered, "Oh, a spine. What prompted that?"

"Thinking about body parts. So…" she said. "It's not just the mineral. It's the dead tissue around it."

"How did you figure that?" Fade asked.

"You would have had the half-ogress do it if you wanted

the salts," she said. "But you're a corpse-worker."

"I'm an arcane anatomist," he said. "And physiologist."

"Sylphs can perform a limited form of reanimation," Cunigunde said. "You fill the lungs with a charged breath. You can get a fresh body moving. But you can't control the body, and the brain is still damaged by the fatal cessation of blood. Long ago, we killed the process of rot with poison gases, raising armies of toxic green men – but the Children of Orc had no memory of their lives, only the drive to raid and rage and sink into faerie-reverie. Undines can get the blood moving, but that's it. The pharyes fill bones with iron and copper wire to make skeletal soldiers for their war against the Devils and their fossils of ancient beasts. Kalimac the Conjurer and Mylokoth the Malicious both raised legions of bony warriors and terrible lizards… but what you did was beyond that."

"It was nothing special," he said. "There is a reason we burn our dead."

"Humans are ephemeral, those Dearest to Death," she said, playing with a braid woven from horsehair by spinning it on its brass ring, denoting the rank of auxiliary commander in the Hirpic Cohorts. "Your skulls are potent tools for death magic. Both murderous hexes and necromancy."

"I remember your grenade," he said.

"Your ghosts are potent, your revenants dangerous. So many great tyrants and killers have consulted a senate of skulls, chattering out strange wisdom. The Dead Kings of Skyleumata, the Damned of the Dawn Sea, Baalhemon the Baleful, Sarmana the Spider–I have fought many necromancers and skeleton-slavers of the races of men. But how did you manage to animate several fresh dead men against me, without the use of their ghosts?"

"You're smarter than you look," he said and reclined on his bunk.

"Yes, I look clever, but I'm actually a monumental genius,"

she said. "This is what you mean. Unless you're dumber than you look."

"That's what I mean," Fade said. He started reading.

"No, hey, don't turn away from me. How did you learn that?" Cunigunde said. "Wait… Blood, breath, bone… What of nerves? This poison is a nervous issue. Is that how you knew what to do?"

"My mentor dealt with a metal poisoning among his...workforce," Fade said. "He handled bones, plating them with metals. We discovered an element we dubbed heavy zinc, an impurity in calamine, with properties similar to mercury. It was useful but quite toxic. We found that it and lead were extracted from the soil by willow trees, that friend of alchemists."

"That explains your medicine," she said, head tilting so her sinister antler touched her shoulder. "Not the soulless resurrection. And frankly, this use of lead reminds me of Mylokoth. You don't want to remind me of Mylokoth."

"I presume one doesn't earn the title 'the Malicious' through kindness. But no, It's the same principle as controlling a homunculus," Fade said. "I use a bit of metal in the body's nerves to bind it to my brain. It's easy enough, once you understand the principle. In fact, I think I saw another innovation earlier. With that Mignard woman."

"What about her?" Cunigunde said.

"She's controlling her own body, since her spine is severed," Fade said. "Somebody stabbed her in the back, and the blade broke off. That's why she walks so strangely."

"What would happen if you revived someone with airy spirits, and then had them control their body with this technique?" she said. "Would that be a true resurrection?"

"Maybe," Fade said. "But the complexity of it would be tremendous."

"I can imagine," she said.

She paused as Fade switched his shirt under his blanket. She had never seen him bare-chested, though he was not otherwise overly modest, and one late night urination revealed he was one of those peculiar skinny lads who was hauling a hog home.

"I have seen men enslaved by the undine's curse, stripped of automatic breath. Having to consciously command every other organ as well would drive one mad," Cunigunde said.

"And it would have to be done at the moment of natural death," Fade said. "The body decays rapidly, especially the brain. And you would still have to handle any trauma or issue that led to death. Death by heart attack would still have you revived with a failed heart… And if you're reactivating motor nerves, you would have to figure out a way to stop the agonics from blinding you with pain. I've experimented with motiles, those sprites old wizards used to animate things, but I could never keep them from growing yliaster veins through my tools."

"Might let you rip out the heart and replace it," she said. "I'd be good at that. I once swapped a prince's heart with that of his draconic brother."

"Why?" Fade asked.

"It let me be the power behind the throne for a while, until I discarded that kingdom. And it was funny," Cunigunde said. Fade was clearly unhappy with the explanation, but decided to move on.

A watchman they had not seen before entered the cell block.

"We would need years of advancement in inhibitor drugs and sedatives," Fade whispered. "Mandrake tonics, cannabis incense, and opium euphorics are not enough. You need the brain working for them to work."

Cunigunde glanced at the watchman.

"So, are you going to let Fade out to perform the

surgery?" she said. "And if Nico here slips, I'm going to do a bit of magic. Just a warning."

The Watchman nodded, pulled out the sealing ring, and opened the cell. He then tossed a rolled-up cloth into Cunigunde's cell. She reached down and lifted it up.

"A blindfold?" she said.

The watchman nodded.

"Whatever you're into, kid," she said. She leaned towards the cell's bars, sticking her sinister antler out of the cell, and put on the blindfold.

"I need my tools," Fade said. "Lund should have left them with Captain Rhee."

The watchman left and returned with the pouch. Cunigunde roared in frustration, the sound echoing around the dense cell. Her ears twitched and shifted away from the surgical site.

"I'm going to draw the metal to your antler," Fade said.

He focused and divined the mercaptans in her tissue with his own sample. He guided the collected mass from the renal artery to the superior mesenteric artery up to the aorta, into the carotid artery, and finally up into the capillaries of the scalp, the pedicle, and the burr.

The watchman returned and walked with a new imbalance in his step, his right leg heavier than it was on the way out. He handed Fade the packet. The surgeon unbuttoned it and tapped the end of the sylphide's antler.

"I shall begin the cutting," Fade announced.

"Wait a moment," Cunigunde said.

She reached out and grabbed the watchmen as he raised his handgun and slammed him into the bars with enough force to fold his neck backward. The watchman let out an inhuman screech as it died.

Fade shouted "No!" and hopped back with the scalpel in hand.

He prepared for a counterattack, until the watchman shrunk in Cunigunde's hand, becoming a two-tailed calico cat with six toes on each paw. The beast popped and collapsed in on itself as its air pockets collapsed. She tossed its corpse and her blindfold into the corner of her cell.

"Continue," she said.

"A shapeshifter?" he said.

"It shifted shape, so it seems so," she said. "It's not un-common. Sagani shapeshift. Your friend Lund is a shapeshifter. The wolf-emperors were shapeshifters. Hundred-year-old animals can shapeshift."

"Right, but aren't you concerned?" he said.

"Not now," she said, looking at the corpse. "You know how many times I've had shapeshifters sent after me? Maybe once a year. Before the Saint Chainer and the tree. Now cut me."

She jutted her antler out again. Fade stroked the velvet, slightly combing away the fine hairs. He told her he was going to take the sample and performed the easiest surgery of his career. Blood poured out of the densely vascular tissue and landed on her face. She licked her teeth, playing with the half-risen replacement for a lower carnassial lost in the fight. He peeled the velvet away with the forceps and placed it in his vial.

She reached out her hands. He handed her the vial, and she created a vacuum in the glass before corking it, keeping it from growing. He placed it in the container.

When he looked up, her hand was still reaching out at him.

"What's wrong?" he said.

"You're so fucking stupid," she said.

"What have you done?" he asked, looking for signs of her plot.

"Nothing," she said. "Don't make this weird."

He stepped back towards his cell. She raised her head and

wiped the blood from her cheek. She tapped the crossbar again.

"The cells are sealed with different rings," Fade said. "I can't let you out."

"I can leave whenever I want," she said. "And I can kill you whenever I want. So come here and touch my hand."

Fade glared at her and wondered how to ground himself when she tried to electrify him. He reached out and brushed her hand. She grabbed him by the wrist, and then slid down his hand. He awkwardly shook it.

"Do you have sisters and brothers?" she asked.

"Only child," he said. "Mother and father are still alive. Have a lot of aunts and uncles. Family of drapers and tailors. Nothing special."

"Twin sister," she said. "You were right. I don't know where she is."

"Sorry," he said. "But you lot don't die easily. So, there's a good chance."

"Don't," she said. "Don't do that."

"It's not pity," he said. "It's empathy."

"I don't know what that is," she said.

"I know," he said.

The door handle turned. He ran back to his cell, while the Whirlwind silenced the room. He nodded in thanks and slammed the cell door shut. Cunigunde let out a pained hiss as the apotropaic witch-wards inscribed in the ceiling caused a backlash.

"Oh, so they only deactivated *yours*," Cunigunde said, glaring at Fade, who answered with a raised hand.

"We couldn't find the package that Dr. Lund left," said the night watchman.

He inspected the cells with a raised hooligan lantern.

"Another jailer oversaw the operation," Fade said, handing the case to the watchman, with the exception of the sample vials. The Watchman shrugged it off and left for the night.

Cunigunde kicked the corpse of the cat into Fade's cell.

"Reanimate it, necrologian," she said. "And have it drop the sealer into the front room. I want to see it."

"Capital idea," he said.

He picked up the corpse and burnt away the tails to reanimate the rest of it. The corpse twitched back to life and let out a piercing shriek.

Cunigunde hopped in place and clapped.

"Nice, you've made an abomination!" she said.

He held up his free hand and mapped the movement of its legs to his fingers. He bound the head to his middle finger, the jaws closing as he curled its joints, snatching up the ring. Cunigunde wondered about the nutty, sour scent rising from the work, until she realized that he had covered up the necromantic damage to his fingernails with a black varnish of alder char and iron-gall, just as she covered her electrical strikes with carmine polish. Fade set the cat down, puppeteered it towards the partially opened door, and slipped outside. He set the body against the captain's desk, let the ring drop, and piloted the corpse to the front door, where he let it return to death.

"Fascinating," Cunigunde said. Then she added, "Bare feet on a cold tile. I am quintessential and vile. Choleric, sanguine, and bile. I push on through the pit and end in the pile. After a struggle, I end with a smile."

"Humor?" Fade suggested. "The humors?"

"No, blow out your light," she said. "I need to take a huge shit."

Chapter 18: Time and Tide

Volganin flew southeast past the old estate of the House of Pridvornov, to a glassy lake on the White Meska. The snow cranes were migrating north as summer approached, reversing their annual path across Caunias, over the Alaria Sea, to the mountain lakes of Apeliotes and the deltas of northern Carbas. Tsokiri, Nandakans, and Hypouranids marveled at these hearty birds. Some specimens flew over 4,500 kilometers, pierced by the missiles of far-flung hunters. These crane arrows became a fetishistic weapon empowered by blood, wind, and water.

Volganin came down on the shore of the lake, where a muck-encrusted, black-scaled frogman sat on a floating log, fishing with his long limbs. He kicked a furred trout and tried to spear the stunned fish with his forearms. The vodyanoi croaked in outrage as the cranes flapped towards him and stole the fruits of his labor. He noticed Kingfisher and wrung the water out of his algae-dyed hair. A sad frustration darkened his eyes, which smoldered like coals on a fire.

Kingfisher nodded at him and rose into the sky with a song that charged the air with a magnetic pull. The flock of cranes had a moment of strange contemplation as their migratory instincts awoke once more. She swooped across the pond, snapped up a trout in her talons, and dropped it on the vodyanoi's lap. She pumped her wings and circled into the sky towards Northernmost, the snow cranes in tow.

After nearly an hour of flight, she reached the edge of the bay. She scanned the ground for the dragging marks of the dredging efforts and spotted her primary target, an otter. She had watched this furry foe for hours as it swam alongside the iron-clad dredging boat, one time climbing its heavy chains for a better view of the operation. This uncanny otter did not leave spraint everywhere, the dung often burnt at sea to ward off storms. It watched. It observed. It gestured with its paws and head. That thing did not behave like an otter. Perhaps it was a witch's familiar, or some yliaster-soaked wise-beast, or even the eidolon Otter wandering in the flesh... but she had another theory to test.

Kingfisher spearheaded the attack at the edge of the Imperial Naval Yard's primary dock. The otter panicked as the cranes immediately dove at it, smelling the magic of their ancient enemy. The otter glanced at a normal cat on the dock. It did not respond, so the otter shrieked at an auk on a rock, which followed her into the water. Kingfisher went invisible for the few seconds she could maintain the working and raked her talons into the otter. Her nails shrunk into clay, not flesh, and the writhing of the beast forced her to shift between her legs, groping at whatever new blob of metamorphosing earth elemental she could manage. The cranes continued to follow, pecking at the otter, until an albatross swooped up to counterattack, staining the white cranes with spots of blood. The tenacious cranes continued their attack, and the gnome could do nothing at this range; their diet of hellebore root inured them to magical madness and the poisons of dwarfs.

Kingfisher had mapped this route in her head, looking for wooden roofs rather than metal-clad or tiled houses. She zigzagged as the men on the boats shot at her. They missed, and Kingfisher swooped behind the clocktower, ready to toss her target into the tar-slathered fishing net she had prepared. However, the albatross was on her, tearing at her feathers. She kicked back at it, but the otter-mass took that opportunity to work one of the soldier's bullets into the bottom of Kingfisher's left foot. The harpy screamed and reflexively raked at the gnomish captive. She shifted her feet again and dove towards the net. She howled at the bullet broke her foot's scales and lodged against the tendons and bones. The otter reached up with a childlike hand, and a snaking wire scratched scales off of Kingfisher's talons as the albatross bit her right biceps. She dropped the otter towards the net and hoped it closed under its weight. She turned around and swiped at the albatross, only to meet the eyes of a primordial beast with leathery wings, something between a bat and the flying lizards of Zephyra. It pecked at her. She caught its beak in her mouth and slowed her descent with an abrupt turn and a one-wing flap. The creature clearly did not expect her to bite back, and an all too intelligent fear caused its eyes to dart down to the fallen gnome, and up to Kingfisher. She grabbed the creature by its own talons and tucked up her wings, forcing it to bear the effort of staying aloft.

The struggling pair hit the roof. The shock rippled through Kingfisher, but she knew how to save her neck. The creature didn't, as a wet, bony snap testified. She tucked her wings tighter and rolled to the side as the creature shapeshifted again. She pushed it over the edge of the building. Kicking an enemy when it was down stung her honor, but one can usually only kill a shapeshifter in its original form if you lack its bane or Three-Goddess Silver. The simply have too much control over their own bodies.

The mimic returned to a smaller version of its inherent form, a malevolent great auk. Kingfisher heard of such creatures living in the chilly lakes of the north, the Boobries, vicious hunters of magical birds and fish. Even after burning away mass to heal, it stood taller than her, about the size of a man at the shoulder, with another meter of neck ending in an obsidian hauling hook of a beak. Kingfisher found its presence amusing—boobries are the archenemy of otters and calves but will not attack gnomes.

The creature bellowed like a bull and began to shift into a quadrupedal form. Kingfisher ignored it, and grabbed the edges of the net, just as the amorphous gnome began to pull away from the pitch.

She rose into the sky and swung the net in a circle to disorient her target. She performed a bit of sloppy water magic, forcing the water in the gnome in the opposite direction of the swing. She wasn't talented with precise hydrurgy, but "stomach-churning" is one of the easiest and most effective forms of combat magic, and every little bit helps.

She hung the net on the streetlamp near the Constabulary, opened the front door with her foot, and fluttered inside. The three officers inside shouted, and one grabbed a musket off the wall and pointed it at her.

"Stop, stop, stop!" Kingfisher announced like a royal courier riding to a gallows. "I've found Loganev's killer. It was a gnome!"

"Who?" said one of the watchmen, an officer of uncertain rank.

Kingfisher looked down the barrel of the musket.

"Please put that down," she said.

"You're the harpy spotted during the destruction of the ship, aren't you?" asked the officer.

"How did you do it, monster?" spat the musketeer, reaching for his powder and paper cartridges with a crocodilian hand.

"I did nothing," she said. "I was in the crow's nest for most of the trip, and on the docks during the blast. I went back to save who I could."

"Who did you save?" asked the officer.

"A sailor," she said. "He was unconscious. I never learned his name."

"You better find out," said the musketeer.

"Quickly, quickly, before it cuts its way out!" she said, hopping backward to point out the net.

The confused watchmen pushed her out of the way and pulled down the net with the musket's bayonet and released a tarry otter onto the ground.

"Pull it off the ground before it burrows!" she said.

The quietest of the men wrangled the otter and carried it inside.

"Return to your native form, villain," Kingfisher commanded. "We know what you've done."

The otter looked over at a burlap bag and attempted to scrape the tar off its fur with its roughness. It recoiled and fled when it tilted over and spilled its snow, revealing the dead cat packed inside.

"What happened?" Volganin asked.

"We found a dead cat here, in the morning," said the officer. "Packed it in snow in case it was important. Maybe a threat."

The otter hid under a chair.

"So, you brutalized this otter," said the musketeer.

"How do you get a shapeshifter to revert?" she said. "Do any of you have silver in stock?"

"We had silver bullets," said the officer. "Aquilans used to imprison werewolves and werehyenas in cells across the Bay. In Timorat territory. Midnight sun drowns out the yliaster of the other stars. It suppresses dark magic and werewolves; the forced moon cycle change, I mean. But we ran out a while back, killing some boobries. They have a bad habit of dying out at sea, so we lose the silver."

"Wait, I have an idea," said Volganin.

"Is this your idea of a prank?" said the musketeer, rolling his eyes.

"No," she said, and cringed. Her idea of a prank was when her sister Ripper would hold her down and rip out her feathers. Ripper found it funny, at least.

"We're not holding your tortured otter here," said the officer.

The otter continued to scrape off the tar.

"I will be back," she said.

"You have an hour," said the officer. He reached up onto an hourglass and turned a small one over. "Otherwise, we will file charges."

"Fine," she said. She departed to Lund and Mageirissa's room. She waited for some vigorous activity to subside before knocking on the window.

She was met by Mageirissa, who wrapped herself in a blanket and opened the window.

"Oh, hey, Bird," she said. "Sorry, we were having a social visit."

"You were having sex," Kingfisher said. "I'm not that naive. I'm an adult swamp monster."

"Right," said Mageirissa. She yanked her left braid to her front, gasping as the decorative clip at the end swung into her breast. "What do you need?"

"I think Fade took a circlet from the Academy. Made of silver," she said. Lund hastily laced up his trousers, not as out-of-sight as he believed. A sudden and sad curiosity seized Kingfisher, as she wondered if she could learn his transmo-grification magic, and become a human woman.

"He picked it up from the massacre site," Lund said. He walked over to Fade's bag. "He left it and his grimoire with me. Want it on your head or hand? Claw?"

"Head," she said. Lund crowned her. She thanked him and circled the inn to the constabulary.

She opened the door to find the officers frozen in shock.

"It's me," she said, wondering if the crown was somehow enchanted.

"Where did the otter go?" asked the exasperated officer.

"You were watching it," she said.

"What kind of prank is this?" said the musketeer.

"This is a serious investigation," she snarled. "I'm trying to solve a crime. You watchmen can't even watch an otter."

"It vanished," said the officer. "An illusion. Or the hypnotic song of the siren."

"It attacked me," she said, showing the wounds on her feet.

"You're under arrest," said the officer.

Knocks echoed through the room. The watchmen turned to face the door to the cell block. Fade opened the door and raised his hands.

"Loganev's notes and my translation vanished from my desk," he said. "And the cell was unsealed. Obviously."

"Fade, are they treating you well?" Kingfisher said.

"Coffee's terrible. Decor's worse. But our work was almost finished before my elbows slammed into the table and several nights of translation vanished into thin air. Which still leaves us with more proof that I've been doing my job than any of you. Any progress? Where are your leads? Suspects? Or anything against me?"

"I'm sorry," said Volganin. "I thought I had our killer, but they vanished."

"I'm not mad at you," Fade said. "You've been working. You've been hurt."

"Back in your cell," said the officer.

"She's one of my patients," he said. "Not until you've allowed me to bandage her up."

"This filthy monster will be one of your cellmates, soon," the musketeer said.

"What are you charging yourself with?" asked Fade.

"That's it," said the musketeer. "Charge him with insubordination. Hold him for that."

"Anyway," Fade said, opening a medical cabinet and grabbing a bottle and roll of cotton. He dabbed Kingfisher's wounds with the purified alcohol. She made a humming noise to push through the pain as her scales knitted together and the alcohol burned. She looked outside, up at the clocktower.

The musketeer aimed at Fade.

"Go ahead and fire," Fade said. "The gun is empty."

"How did you manage that? You didn't cast anything," said the officer.

"So, let's work through this…" said Fade. "If I didn't cast a spell, and something magical happened, it wasn't me. Check your powder horn."

The musketeer set down his gun and shook his horn. "Empty."

"The Whirlwind," groaned the officer. A phantom ache shot up his back.

"Yes?!" called a voice from the cell block. "What the fuck is wrong?!"

The officer opened the door to confirm her presence. A hanging heraldic emblem obscured her, an escutcheon rather than the typical cartouche of a lady. *A Pantheon rampant argent attired cendrée on a field gules, on above of which is an argent aurora.* The shield was bouched to the viewer's left, with a rest for a lance, which must have been its origins. She was not a noble, but every participant in a joust must have their arms. Kingfisher felt a tinge of envy.

The officer ducked inside to see what she was up to, alerted by vague straining noises. He tapped on the bars, and Cunigunde became visible. The Sylphide was doing calisthenics, hanging upside down, her feet locked around the bars.

"What are you doing?" the officer asked as she approached.

"You think my stomach just looks like this?" she said. She pulled herself up and glowered at the officer through her legs.

"Someone has been moving about invisibly," the officer said.

"Right, so that narrows it down to a wizard or an elemental," the Whirlwind said. "And air elementals are best at it. So, me. The problem is, I didn't do it. I've been here."

"I only have Fade as a compromised witness, and your

word," he said.

"My word is all you need," she said, delivered with the sharp edge of a threat.

"Your word is worthless," said the officer.

The muscles in her arms and back rippled as she slammed her feet down on the ground.

"I will shit you into your wife's mouth," she hissed.

"Starshina?" the musketeer called out from the main room. The startled officer glanced towards the door, just as Cunigunde's arm reached through the bars. She relented as the officer moved out of the cell block.

"There's your proof," whispered Fade, a slight raise of the chin pointing towards the desk. He reached out and pocketed a package meant for him, delivered from Mirror-Makers' Lane.

"Where?!" snapped the officer, struggling to understand.

"This wasn't hypnosis. Your hourglass is empty," said the harpy. She nodded her head towards the clock tower. "Only twenty minutes have passed."

"Wait," said the officer. "If this was some type of… time magic… Why would the sand move? I mean, in the frozen time?"

"Scale," Fade suggested. "To see in frozen time, you would need to let the particles of light hit your eyes. Same goes for breathing air."

"The spell needed to consume the black power," Kingfisher added. "So, the sand also began to move. And, briefly, anything the size of the cap, presumably."

"Hey!" shouted Cunigunde, red-faced and hanging upside down. "You talking about time magic? Huuuh?"

"What do you know about it?" asked the captain.

"Can't use it. Neither can gnomes," she said, punctuated with a grunt as she sat up. "One of the side effects of immortality, you and time only meet in passing. Salamanders can cause time to accelerate. But only accelerate."

"What about an undine?" asked Kingfisher.

"The water nymphs might be able to cause time to flow in reverse, maybe a second or two. Water has that affinity for currents and flow, time and tide. And perhaps, freezing. But I've never seen it, except to shorten the path over river and sea. And that may be a working of distance, space."

"How powerful would they have to be?" asked Kingfisher.

"Extremely," said Cunigunde. "*Maybe* in a tower, surrounded by helpers and heaps of materials. Out in the wild? No. Never heard of anything like it."

"The cost involved in catalyzing a time stop would be insurmountable," said Fade. He had never come across a successful attempt at time travel, but institutions of Arcane Philosophy jealously guard their secrets from spies and the common press. The best anyone had done, to his knowledge, was dredge up Devils from the primordial past, or accidentally conjure forth some creature from a distant planet or the far future. He supposed, however, that reliable control of time was such a dangerous art that wisdom and sanity would necessarily conceal its existence. And how would he, of all people, know if such temporal adepts were constantly at work, rewriting history with their alchemy of ages?

"Honestly, it's the kind of thing a human would be better at," Cunigunde said. "You things get absolutely ravaged by time. You're like grapes in the sun. You get wrinkly but you taste good."

"Stop talking about eating people!" shouted the officer.

He threw the empty powder horn at the cell. Cunigunde caught it.

"I don't actually eat people," she said. Then she added under her breath, "But humans aren't people."

She smiled and worked the straw from her naatsit's band. She transubstantiated the dry straw and the powder horn, she tossed it back, letting it skid to a stop in the door.

"Wait," said Kingfisher. "What about that... that woman? Severin?"

"Oh, her? She's gone. Been gone for a while," said Cunigunde. "Though, then again, I guess *when* and *where* wouldn't apply to a time wizard. But she wasn't anything special. I mean, magically. There were things should do with her tongue that were... wow..."

She stopped for a moment, leaning her elbow on the crossbar, and letting her head drift off whimsically in her hand.

"Gun?" Fade prompted.

"Oh, right, but she was young, only in her forties, not enough time for that kind of mastery, and she wasn't dedicated to the craft. She's a money person."

"Accountant? Banker? Investor? Economist?" asked the officer.

"Look, I just get money and give it to people for things," said Cunnigunde. "I don't know anything about it. But it could be a thing of Old Chaos."

"Old Chaos?" said the Officer.

Fade explained that the elements each have their higher form, the old or deeper Chaos. For Earth, there is *Azoth*, the perfect and primal matter and its unmaking, the universal substance and solvent. For air, there is *Æther*, the rarefied field between the stars, and their material make-up. For Fire, the *Astra*, the luminous heat of the sun and stars. For Water, *Æon*, the Abyss of Time, the nature of flow and stasis. And then the perfect, united chaos, *Apeiron*.

"So, it would be a super-mermaid," said the musketeer.

"The Seventh Sun is a junk heap of possibilities," Cunigunde said. She made a ball gesture with her arms, before she had to reach out to keep herself from slipping off the cell's bar. "The first sun was beyond us. Pure thought, pure possibility. It laid the rules. You know, effects have to have causes, things are finite, that kind of thing. The second sun narrowed what was possible, so there was just magic. Five elements. That was a rootless mess, the sun had to change. Third sun had no magic. The fourth tried magic again, chaos structured by order. The fifth sun was ruled by physics, but mutable. The sixth sun was unknown to us because we're still dealing with its fallout. I was told it was a battle between good and evil, where your so-called gods came from. The horrors who rip their way out of the watery Vorago were lost warriors, the broken and vengeful bits of the loser gods, just as the Devils of the Infero are this world's failed eidolons. Whatever happened, it led to our age. The continents broke apart, smashed together, and the gods broke apart again. The didn't-happens became did-happens, the never-could's became could-have-been's. Artifacts, out-timers, magic, physics, and bits of all the prior epochs boiled up like a seven-day stew. Or washed up on our shore, like the wake of a shipwreck. Every work of alchemy leaves behind lees and dregs."

"So," Fade said. "Was there a sun where the gods or beings had control over time?"

"Perhaps," Cunigunde said, rolling from a handstand to a seat on her bunk. "I wasn't there. We weren't. Sylphs are older than humanity, but the sagani weren't the first elementals. Before us were Thunderbirds, whose descendants are rocs and simurghs and other great birds. The salamanders are the degenerate remains of a race of dragons. The drakes of this age are a pale shadow of what they were, lap dogs to wolves. The gnomes are but the severed fingers of the titans. And the sea was once ruled by the ketea — god-whales, sharks with teeth like spades, turtles with shells like islands, and the endless squids called krakens. The ketea have the blood of the Leviathan, who swims outside the flow of time."

"What happened to them?" Kingfisher asked.

"Overthrown and diminished by the gods. They still live,

in their descendants and on the fringes of the world," Cunigunde said.

Kingfisher looked out at the city of ice and wood. She
thought of the Pridvornov estate, and the blue streaks and
strange horns of Ludmilla Orlova, and asked, "Now, when
you say fringe of the world, how fringe?"

Chapter 19: Allopatric Speciation in Subarctic Vicariants

Kingfisher's first line of questioning involved the death of Viktor Ragnavich Pridvornov. She first flew to the Losian Lighthouse, the primary navigation tower of Northernmost. Its crystal peak housed a shallow bath of mercury, a nigh-frictionless bearing surface for its rotating lens. It was rumored that Viktor Ragnavich had not only manufactured the reflective pool, but used it to scry through the timestream and project his soul through the beam of cold light. The lighthouse preserved the mummified corpses of sharks and squids that wash-up on the rocks below, their bodies twisted into mockeries of human priests, oracles, and monks. Spooked by the silver-eyed keeper, she decided to ask around Lund's team of medical investigators and Mageirissa's herbalists. The hospital's iatrochemical operation occupied a long stone hall of the Merchant Court, one of the fortress depots near the port. The chamber was originally used for gunpowder manufacturing, so it had the proper equipment, ventilation, and fortification, and was occasionally used by the Office of Pratique during quarantines. It was in the stone town, built after the Midwinter Fire of 2397. A floral perfume masked the acrid, medicinal work. Two old herbalists melted butter of iris, the purified oil of orris root, in a cauldron as a fixative for pellets. It was easy enough to procure, as potpourri was a common craft in this city of rotting fish.

"Viktor Pridvornov. Martyr of science," Volganin asked Lund as he pulled the Whirlwind's velvet sample from her pouch. "Was he killed for his research?"

"No," Lund said. "I believe he died in an experiment. But I don't know much about the man. He was a student of the abstract, physical laws of arcane philosophy, while I am a naturalist."

"You don't wear clothes?" she asked.

That felt wrong, but he carried out the practice around Mageirissa, and it may simply be too cold for the lifestyle in Northernmost.

"Oh, no, I travel the world, studying the anatomy of animals and plants. You have heard Fade call himself an anatomist and physiologist? He specializes in man and sagani, while I look at the entirety of nature, and make comparisons. He's one of the finest young surgeons I have ever met, while I specialize in comparing traits and making analogies across the animal kingdom. In my field, we have begun experimenting in transplanting modified animal parts into men."

"Does it work?" she asked.

"On hands and eyes," he said. "I earned my doctorate on a paper comparing the anatomy of apes and men, and how to modify the heart of a chimpanzee or orangutan for use in humanity."

"Why those animals?" she said.

"Because they are related to men," Lund said. "Or so it would appear. I was inspired by the Ganwe of Deep Cannaria, who spoke of a Brother Monkey and Grandfather Ape. They believe that mankind is descended from apes, through the intervention of Father Sky and Mother Sea. When our priests claim that all beasts were created by the gods, their own kind and species, they were utterly baffled. 'How can you look at a monkey and not see a kindred of man?' What surprised me was that there are no apes in the Windward Isles, and none in Zephyra, Hesperides, or Favonia. So where did they get the notion of the ape? The Volim servitors? Petty Fujin thralls?"

"Divination," Kingfisher suggested.

"Perhaps," he said. "As good of a guess as any."

"Could that be what Viktor was studying?" she asked. "Humans are good diviners. Can you die by divination?"

"Perhaps," Lund said. "Thaumaturgic experimentation is tremendously dangerous."

"There are parts of time you shouldn't look into," Mageirissa said, walking over with a mortar and pestle in hand. "The tribes of Moga practice divination but use special herbs and pixie-mushrooms to fly out of our body and look across the world and the suns. We even have priests that specialize in following the racer stars. We are trained in centuries and centuries of tradition, and still, some people come back wrong, terrified or filled with malicious spirits and the voices of strange stars."

"Like what? What voices?" Kingfisher asked.

"Other stars have other worlds, and on some worlds, there are elementals. Many worlds are filled with an evil race of earth elementals called the Conformers, religious fanatics who want to purge the cosmos of fleshy life, so the world is only stone-life. Gnomish wizards have contacted them and traded knowledge, and hide the existence of all other Thieran life. We have met the Drifting Dreamers, air elementals like great leathery balloons with a dozen batwings, and Violet Ghosts, formless fire elementals. Sometimes, in dreams, they drift down to us to study a 'solid-home,' and displace a shaman to their cloudy, windy world without land, nearly the size of the sun."

The notion of fire elementals without form awed Kingfisher. Though she was admittedly no scholar of stoichiology, she had read that the Sagani were, like all creatures and things, composed of a matter and form, an elemental aspect and sidereal flesh. The pure elementals and their demi-elemental offshoots like ghouls and grey-elves could simply control the ratio of hylic form to material body, unlike humans and harpies. Those violet creatures must have been true ghosts, the wandering forms of dead stars. Perhaps this Pridvornov was some sort of astral necromancer.

"What do you think he contacted?" Kingfisher asked.

"Pridvornov? If he was practicing divination, perhaps a god," Mageirissa said. "If he truly disappeared, as his brother says, and was not possessed and driven into the sea… it would have to be a god."

"Why?" Kingfisher asked. "I don't disbelieve you. I just want to understand."

"He was meddling in time," she said. "See, my form of magic is not based on elements and alchemy, but ritualism. We have to do the same thing across time and space, across the ages."

"Tradition over science," Volganin suggested.

"No, it isn't just something to be repeated because it's always been that way. It is powerful *because* it's repeated," said Mags. "If people walk down a path for hundreds and hundreds of years, it becomes easier. We wear it down. We keep it clean. It's a channel. But we do not channel just through lines of force. We channel across time and space. It's how we connect to our ancestors, the wheel of life, and the Great Devourer. The Well-Trod Path of our people."

"It makes sense from what we know of the Law of Conduction. We have carved our runes and signs into the memory of mankind, into the very heart of Nature," Lund said. He paused, lost in thought, recalling the gorgon reefs of the deep sea, with millennia of petrified creatures rising from the black chasms of the Vorago. One grows faint when looking down into millions of years, history reaching a vanishing point.

"Tradition," Kingfisher said. "Like my knighthood? Am I… am I actually tapping into something?"

"I think so," Mageirissa said. "But imagine starting your own kind of order, out of nowhere, with no tradition. It wouldn't be well received. Dealing with time through novelty is a risk. Especially if you plan to travel. That's when the gods intervene."

"Hubris?" Kingfisher said.

"Paradox," Mageirissa said. "Creating a contradiction in time's flow is incredibly dangerous. Nobody may break the cycle of causality. Something must fill that gap. And who may do that but a god? That's why we cannot break our rituals. We do not want such powers to fill the cracks."

"Gods are good at filling in the gaps in our understanding," Lund said. "But they must retreat against the tide of enlightenment. Gods of thunder and lightning have faded against the understanding of aerial excitation and material charge. Gods of earthquakes died away when gnomish geurgy mapped the world's long-shifting plates. But a temporal paradox is beyond human ken, truly impossible, incomprehensible. So, such a god has unfathomable mystery and majesty."

"Would a god of time always be around?" Kingfisher asked. "Or would it only come into being when you made it necessary?"

"There is that niggling question, and the risk of humanity's Greatest Work," Lund said. "Of course, once a god of time *is*, it will always and forever be."

"Eternity," Kingfisher said. "The Great Leviathan. There used to be legends of sea serpents wrapped around the world, but it's a globe. But I guess there's one around the cosmos, around the beginning and the end of time."

"I'm afraid so," Lund said. "I had always hoped it wasn't real."

"What is that?" Mageirissa said. "You have a god of time?"

"A god before the gods," Volganin said. "Primordial non-creation, or pre-creation. Formless matter, space without time. Or the motion of time. It swam from its Eternity into the small river of Time, wounding its eye by the change in pressure. Like some fish die when they swim from freshwater to salt. Or perhaps by the spears of the Titans of our Sun. But that story doesn't make sense to me. So, uh, its wounded eye became Los, its rigid horn became Urizen, its time-grayed scale became Incano, and, perhaps, its body's reflection became Rahab, the 'small' sea monster goddess, and mother of the ketea. These gods escaped into our cosmos and set it into motion. The Aeon of moving time, cycles, age, and progress and change and potential."

"Oh," Lund said as if still reeling from some horrible revelation. "Those migrating fish. Oh no."

"What about them?" Kingfisher asked. Her head snapped to face Lund. Her stomach rumbled, and the mention of fish reminded her that she hadn't eaten today.

"No, that was a perfect analogy. And I hate it," he said. "You can't raise a child, it can't grow. In in a timeless place, I mean. I think the Leviathan of Eternity came into Time to spawn."

Kingfisher wavered on her feet in discomfort.

"So… what do you do against a pre-god god?" asked Mageirissa. "If Eternity is your enemy, what do you do?"

"I don't know," Kingfisher said in despair. "I was hoping to start off fighting a big snake or crocodile or wolf. But then I get a dragon, an ancient elfin warlord, a naval conspiracy, and a god of time. It escalated so quickly and I don't know what to do."

"Well, you don't have to do it alone," Lund said.

"Thanks," said Kingfisher. "But the *one elf* still crushed us and a mercenary company. I don't have hopes for the time god."

"What would they even be like?" pondered Mags. "Prophets are madmen for a reason. Casting the mind into the future disorders it, ages it, dements it. Something outside of time would be unimaginably foreign to us."

"Maybe… maybe it goes both ways," Kingfisher said. "I mean, we might be ants to a god, but ants are scary. Sometimes people even get stung to death by those Lentoran fire ants."

She nodded towards the amber sample, with an orange ant captured in its death throes.

"Gods are omniscient, omnipotent," said Mags. "At least, when you've reached that level of divinity. This is no petty household god or tutelary spirit. Eternity would require an infinite lord."

"Right," said Volganin. "Maybe. But gods always seem so human in the stories. Even Urizen was wounded by Orc, and Hedran was born from Incano's splitting megrim. Maybe Eternity is powerful enough to hold eternity, but only that powerful. Imagine having to keep every book ever written in your memory. And multiply that by a billion billion."

"That capacity to completely embody your role is what separates mortal and god," said Mags. "Spirits become concepts. And the other way around. Even a shaman should be born a bit strange and big. I had a full set of teeth."

She smiled.

"Right," said Volganin. "But Eternity was wounded and bleeding into our Time. Imagine being a fire god with one hand in the sea."

"It sounds like you have a plan," said Lund.

"No," she said. "Just a notion. If Eternity was wounded, then we're the infection. The poison. The little animals in the wound."

"Are you suggesting that we sterilize Thier?" he asked. "I'm not getting the actual suggestion here."

"No, just, we pull Time and Eternity apart and close the wound. Or… hole… time hole," sputtered Kingfisher.

"What could do that?" said Lund, opening his pocket notebook.

"I don't know," she said. "You're the magical doctor and the shaman. But if you know what can do it, I'll quest for it."

"Well, we'll try to think of something," said Mageirissa. "But even if there was some artifact from back then, from your Aquilan gods, I don't know how to fend off the wrath of a vengeful eternity."

"Maybe it's not evil. If my talon was stuck in a bee's nest, and it miraculously came loose, I wouldn't want to come back to attack the bees. Especially with a bear around," Kingfisher said.

"What does the bear represent?" asked Lund.

"Oh, uh, well, unforeseen... problems..." Kingfisher mumbled, her voice trailing off into shrill birdsong.

"Was the beehive something that happened to you?" Mageirissa asked.

"Yes," Kingfisher said, then quietly added, "Bears are scary."

She looked around, backed up, and retraced her steps in memory.

"Are you reliving your encounter?" asked Mageirissa.

"Loganev said something about the Pridvornova women," Kingfisher said. "There was only one member of the family left. A posthumous bastard. He said the family was small, with a bad habit of going missing. Said they were witch-like, mutated, with strange experimentation or something. Maybe arcane experiences. Maybe... Your families have ogre and undine blood. Maybe the Pridvornova's have Leviathan blood."

"How far back was Viktor Orlov?" Mageirissa asked.

"A hundred and thirty, a hundred and forty years ago?" Lund said, hastily scratching what he knew of this Leviathan. Its children were Rahab, symbolized by sulfur, the salty, Writhing Deep, and Taphthartharath, the malevolent spirit of Mercury, the matter of decay and change. "Not sure."

"Oh," Kingfisher said. "Not long enough for... generations... and... oh."

"If this was a family prone to those oddities you mentioned, what if Victor was born to be a time traveler? Like Mags, with her alarming baby teeth. Or what if he made the agreement? A pact with Eternity? Or was forced into it, to complete a causal circle. Imagine, someone contacting you to sign a contract that has retroactively applied to your ancestors," Lund pondered. "Perhaps he was collateral for his siblings."

"Brother," Kingfisher whispered, as everything fell into place.

"What if we are groomed by the gods?" Mags wondered aloud, her voice distant and shaken. "Forced into castes, bred like cattle or dogs… What are nobles and royals? What am I to Moga? A priestess or a pet?"

"They're on the throne," Kingfisher said. "Ludmilla Miluvna Orlova… née Pridvornova. Mother of the reigning imperator. And she's here."

"Here?" said Lund. "In Northernmost? How?"

"I might have let her in," said Kingfisher, with a nervous chuckle and a shift of the eyes.

Chapter 20: The Tall Man

Fade's stomach stirred with apprehension as Lund, Mageirissa, and Kingfisher filled him in on the details of the Privornova family and the question of Eternity. The watchmen worked quietly, as if in a daze, filling the Constabulary with a stifling stillness. They were armed, twitchier, and frequently glanced inside the cellblock.

"This is the longest year of my life," Cunigunde declared, out of the blue.

"Were you aware of your imprisonment?" Lund asked.

"No," she said. "No, I mean it literally. The Long Year. I was born in 5 *Anno lupi coronandi*. Can you understand the enormity of two millennia and over two centuries?"

"No," Fade said.

"Year after year after year. When I was born, the priest-king Yasnatar celebrated his second year on the throne of Arada, Noanbaniapli was building the Heavenly Pillars in Eurus, and Arcadiano Hirtus was a child in a petty Loberan kingdom that would become the Hirpan Empire. Kalon Zeondotus was writing his first poems. The Kiric peoples were still a single tribe along the Illoc, with no mutterings of the brothers Van, Illo, Tsokan, and Dan."

"Turns out the Brothers Kir never existed," Mr. Fade explained. "They're a folk etymology, explaining forgotten borrowings of the Olarians. *Van* meant south, *Dan* meant north, *Tsoka* was the sound of horse hooves, and *Illo* is obviously the river."

"Well, I never saw them," Cunigunde said. "But what I'm getting at is, that same calendar, year after year, that has some potent ritual power. There are two extra days this year. One every fifty years. One unique to history. That disruption to our reckoning of Time and this push by this Orlova woman can't be coincidental. It's electional astrology."

"So she will strike soon," Kingfisher said. "Am I right? If she needs some astrological alignment, that narrows down her window of opportunity."

"If I am correct," Cunigunde said. "I usually am."

"All we have to do is interfere, then," Kingfisher said, finally feeling a twinge of confidence. "Harry her."

"Yes, it is what you do best, daughter of the storm winds," Cunigunde said. "But I would also not hinge everything on delaying one empowered with mastery of Time. It is hard to judge the nature of one born from such an unnatural union."

"Her *nature* doesn't matter," Kingfisher objected. "It's her plot. Her ambitions for this city. Even if she lacked Leviathan's blood, she would scheme to reclaim this birthright. It weakens them, the empire, when they have a rebellion in their midst. That might be it. The calendar, the currency, the Crown- they're trying to reckon the new world."

"That's still her nature," Cunigunde said with a smile. "It's inescapable. Your only choice is to either fall flat or tumble through that fatal velocity."

"No it isn't," Kingfisher said. Fade sucked air through his teeth, knowing that Kingfisher had handed Cunigunde a knife to use against her.

"It is funny how we use this word," the Whirlwind said. "Both for the naked state of the wild world, and for ourselves, at heart. That is where people struggle. The two should be in harmony, but people hide their true nature from the truth of Nature. They build up this mask of civility, this armor of civilization, suffocating themselves. Don't those pauldrons weigh heavy on those shoulders, constricting those beautiful wings?"

"They protect me," Kingfisher said. "They remind me of who I want to be."

"It is artifice," Cunigunde said. "Tear it down. When your nature sings the same song as wild Nature, you dance as one. Your will, your self, works the world. It's wonderful. You do not lose yourself. You achieve a universal grandeur."

"I will," Kingfisher said. "I will be part of something greater. I am a Knight of-"

"This dying empire built by Man to lord over Man," Cunigunde said. "That face of yours would look so beautiful, framed in undone hair and stained with the blood of your kills."

Kingfisher wanted to hiss and snap at her, but that would play into the monster's games. Instead, she raised herself upright, standing tall and proud as a Protector of the Homelands. It pained her knees.

"Dame Kingfisher," Fade said. "What is a chimera, but a creature of possibilities and volatile natures?"

Kingfisher's head snapped towards him, quizzically.

"You have the freedom and might of the bird-of-prey and the wisdom and will of womankind. You are the storm and the raging sea," Fade said. "It is in your nature and your power to transcend. Even you, Whirlwind, know the sublime awe of the tempest."

Kingfisher nodded, unable to say anything through her tightening throat. The Sylphide looked down her nose at Fade, willing to concede the point.

Captain Rhee stepped into the jail and unsealed Fade's cell.

"Mr. Fade, please gather your belongings and step outside the cell," he said. "You will be permitted to keep your blanket."

"What about me?" Cunigunde asked.

"You will also be permitted to leave," he said. "As no evidence could be gathered against you for the killing of Lem Loganev. However, according to the ancient pacts between the Severnayan and Hyperborean Peoples, any further offenses against the citizens of Northernmost, no matter the degree or severity, may result in a sentence of permanent exile from its limits."

"Sure," Cunigunde said.

She bent the bars of the cell and slipped out.

"Why did you…" Rhee muttered.

He held up the sealing ring.

"Fuck you," she snapped, and stomped out through the jail room's door.

One of the officers in the main chamber stepped in front of Cunigunde.

"Wait wait, I'm going to have to ask you to wait for a moment," he said, nervously eyeing his captain. "Please don't force us to—"

"You and what actual army?" Cunigunde scoffed.

The pantheon skull erupted from her back, freshly-harvested heads and ancient charms rattling against hook, prong, and chain. Her fury instantaneously softened and she looked out the glass window.

"Why's it dark out?" she asked.

She pushed the sweeping charwoman down and opened the door. The window was occluded by an ironclad coach drawn by a quartet of camels. To Cunigunde's eyes, the driver was a black smear against the black carriage, small and bundled in a coat, and smelling of petrichor and steel.

She looked back into the Constabulary as a trio of men in heavy watchcoats approached, warlock rifles slung against their shoulders.

"Are they with you?" she asked.

Captain Rhee picked up a pistol of his own. Cunigunde's eyes shook. She tilted her head and swung to lock eyes with Volganin.

"Don't do anything rash," she said, with a motherly tone that caused Volganin to pull back in alarm.

Rhee swallowed and cleared his throat. "Please cooperate."

Two of the men in watchcoats entered the constabulary. One stepped forward and pointed at Fade, Lund, and Kingfisher.

"Enter the coach," he commanded. He raised one of his sets of handcuffs, a tight pair armed with acupuncture needles and lodestone nails to suppress a mage's flow of yliaster. "Hand your bags to my assistant, they will be stored safely. Cooperate, and everyone goes home safely tonight. No need for the wise man's cuffs."

"To which office do you belong?" Lund asked, with a gentleman's untroubled tone of authority and propriety.

"I am Valerian Popov of the Extraordinary Commissariat for the Defense of the Homelands," he said. He pulled a gilded hellhound's skull from his belt. "No more questions."

Kingfisher's chest heaved against her armor. Queens were supposed to be tranquil and pretty with orders of noble knights, or scary and pretty with legions of goblins and devils. The Dowager Queen was scary and pretty but now she had sent the taxmen after her, and Kingfisher had no idea how to handle that.

"What are they going to do to us?" she whispered to Fade. She shrunk down, folding her quavering legs.

"Don't give them an excuse," he whispered back, setting his hand at the nape of her neck. She swayed towards him, and tightened her wings against her chest like a feathery mantle. The men seized Fade and Lund's bags and stored them in the rear of the coach.

Fade turned towards Cunigunde and handed her a boiled-leather pouch.

"What is it?" she asked.

"A gift," he whispered. He pointed at his eyes. "Don't open it here."

She nodded and turned the case over in her hands, before slipping it into her hollow.

Popov unlocked and opened the ironclad coach's door. Lund entered first, then Fade, who tried to position Kingfisher near the door.

Mageirissa and Cunigunde stood under the Constabulary's sign.

"Shaman," said Popov. "You may depart to your homeland. You have served the nation well. No reason to further involve yourself with foreign interference."

She hung her head, closed her eyes, and chanted something quietly in her obscure Pokinutinese dialect. An existential smallness oppressed her, a rare feeling for the bulky Barvaci. Her tongue had no true alphabet, barely noticed in the shadow of the Tsokiri Empire. She had no love for the westerners and their blackened city, but no animus either. They had simply swallowed up her valley with a swipe of a surveyor's pen, and nothing had changed. He had ignorantly stepped into this national conflict with their incomprehensible political rivalries and spycraft against the Aquilan nations. She thought of her family and wondered if they would be targeted. Or perhaps, never learn that their daughter and sister lay dead in the White Meska.

She looked up at the sky as the back of the stage coach slammed shut. A blue bird drifted against the sun-silvered storm clouds.

"I will go with him," she said. She inhaled sharply and a cruel combination of fear and cold struck her in the throat. "I'll go with them."

"Then get in," Popov said. She did, sitting alone on the forward and right side of the carriage. Cunigunde began to follow her up. Popov placed a gloved hand on her arm.

"You are not wanted, Hyperborean," he said.

"Your unsatisfied wife disagrees," she said.

He slammed the door shut, locked it, and knocked on its side. He remained on the street, while the other two commissars held onto bars welded to the outside of the carriage.

"Mademoiselle Cunigunde… the Whirlwind," he said. "Do

not concern yourself with the intricacies of mortal affairs."

"Oh, I don't," she said, and she began to walk to the Alchemist's Isle.

"Do you have a purchase to make?" Popov asked. "And what may I call you?"

"Gun," she said. "To both."

Her attention turned to a decrepit stone tower with a conspicuous gap at its crown. A local guild filled the space with an astronomical clock.

"There should be a silver bell here," she said. "Did they move it?"

"I don't know," he said. "It was likely melted down."

"Ah," she said softly. "So they forsook our truce."

"What do you mean?" Popov asked.

"Nothing," the Whirlwind whispered. "It does not matter. Not anymore."

She turned, grabbed Popov by the hand, and twirled him as though dancing.

"What was that?" he asked, grabbing for his shoulder-slung rifle and backing away.

"Ah, have you never sung of the circle dances of old? The women in white turning on the mounds?" she asked. He nodded, and a strange timelessness shorted the passage to Gog the Gunsmith, with Popov huffing and posing questions as she moved. She ignored most of them, and entered the shop, with Popov on her heels. She announced her triumphant returned to Mr. Gog and tossed him a large black pearl that screamed when it stopped rolling.

He handed her the rifle, built to her specification, and her jacketed bullets.

"What are these?" Popov asked with a smile that surprised him. A giddiness overcame him, and he recalled his days as a young scout sneaking ice wine and prostitutes into the company tent.

"Prototypes," Gog said. "I worked hard on it, but it was her idea."

"Feel free to replicate the design," Cunigunde said to Gog. "Spread it around. I want to see what modern man can do."

"Are you an engineer?" Popov asked. "Did you know Mr. Loganev?"

"No," she said, looking down the sight. "To both. I'm a traveler and a warrior. I see ideas here and there and put them to use. I find solutions to failures, but it is not my vocation. What do you want? To stare at my ass?"

She waved at Mr. Gog and left the shop.

"No," he said, punctuated with an unbecoming laugh. "Our government wishes to offer the previous proposal by the Combine."

"Dragonslaying?" she said as she jogged north. "What's your problem with this lad?"

"He's an enemy of the state," said Popov, half in a whisper, half the huffing of an older man forced to run through slush. He paused to collect his thoughts, fighting against the euphoria. "Leader of a nearly independent port. It's a threat to the integrity of the Homelands."

"Sounds like 'the intricacies of mortal affairs,' there," she said. "So, I kill him, and you people leave?"

"No, no, no, we will come in force, once he is no longer a threat to the fleet," he said. "We will reintegrate this rogue province."

"Dragon fight, storm, invasion, rebellion, repression," she listed. "Lots of people are going to die."

"They're traitors," Popov said. "They've put themselves in danger."

"Ah," she said. "Alright. If that's all it takes to justify it."

Her jog broke out into a sprint when the edge of town was visible, and soon she was running through the snow. Popov was winded with a stitch in his side but kept moving in some dance-drunk haze. His joints ached, but there was an unsettling, childish joy in it. The cold no longer bit at him.

In the snow, she stripped off her tunic and spun around in nothing but her strips of red leather.

A great white stag emerged from the forest, as massive as a bull moose but with the slimmer head and branching antlers of a red deer. Beyond the gigantism and albinism, its jaws more closely resembled that of a borzoi, long and wolfish. It turned as it approached, and a flap of feathers revealed its bulky, fluffy torso to be wings dotted with twinkling silver stars. The ferocious animals approached each other, and Cunigunde ran her fingers up its neck and giggled.

She waited for him to approach. She breathed deep, and Popov noted that her face briefly seemed weathered, with purple bags under her eyes. Sickly almost, but it faded with each gasp until she shined like the snow. She turned away, as if ashamed.

"Are you ill?" he asked.

She looked back at him with a haggard face, and vomited blood tainted with soot. She wiped her mouth and jaw clean with a handful of fresh snow.

He touched his head, a foreign object, and nearly swooned from the meaty odor. His body was numb and distant. His mind drifted into fog and fairy-dreams, his eyes heavy and desperate for a warm bed.

The Sylphide closed her eyes and breathed deep. The wind picked up, and blew away the illness and signs of age.

She was beautiful again, Popov though. *In her element.*

"I feel sort of sick too," he said. His teeth clattered, and he looked around to find his bearings. "I shouldn't be here."

"Who are you now and where are you going? What is the color and the curl of the hair that you're growing? What started black or brown always ends up gray, who's the man that you are at the end of the day?" She recited.

He doubled over, his stomach bubbling. He wanted to laugh despite the instinctual terror, the foolishness of a drunkard. He remembered these symptoms, from divers and explorers in poorly-pressurized diving bells. This was the rapture of the deep.

"I've got a confession to make," she said. "I ordered the gun because I was nervous."

"Why?" Popov asked, looking up at her.

He squinted hard, trying to force the enchantment out of him.

"That town poisoned me," she said.

She pet the pantheon, stretched and looked up at the sky. She exulted in the virgin air, her pinwheel hair clip buzzing and her horsetail braid whipping.

"Mr. Fade helped, ripping the metals out of me, but just a bit. That whole city is rotten. The air is filled with soot and metal. It was killing me. I've been bluffing, mostly, with bursts of a failing strength. Living under a glamor. Of myself, but still a glamor."

"Was that the poem?" he asked. "To end the glamor?"

"To begin the new one," she said.

Popov watched the hollow on her back spread like a cloak of shadow. He saw himself turn and the simulacrum's coat smeared across the air like rolling charcoal and his chest was burning and splitting like a rotten log on the hearth. His heart was in her hand, ruptured when it scraped against his spine. His ribs poked through his chest wound like a child's incipient teeth. That mewling maw swallowed him up, his nerves only registering a cold inside and outside as everything dropped away from him. The following right-hand uppercut liquidated everything in front of the ears, faster than pain could scream up his nerves.

She harvested the corpse. The coat and hound's head would help with the deception. The face's leather and the dried heart would strengthen the glamor. The liver was just good eating. She led the pantheon to what remained.

"Humans wish for strength to swoop down from on high," she said to the Pantheon. "Go and ask the hare if there are saviors in the sky. The eagle is magnificent on seal and shield, but a nightmare to the mouse in the open field."

The Commissariat let Kingfisher, Fade, Lund, and Mags sweat as they rolled to the northwest. An empty seat lay next to the Shaman, and she gestured to Kingfisher to move up to it. Kingfisher shook her head and sunk into her wings, despite how awkwardly she sat.

As they approached the Narrows, a meter-tall figure appeared in the empty seat, wearing a subtle plate under the same black coat as the men. The gauntlet on her left arm carried a cruel gnomish weapon, a powered circular saw. A fake beard of coins and bone beads hung from the helmet. She removed it and shook her backcombed hair out. The unruly shock of jet matched her large black eyes.

She was a rare sight. Only one in seven dwarven births are female, and gnomides tend towards interior affairs, managing a polyandrous hall. When you find a lone gnome adventuring in the world, it's almost always a fertile male leaving a hive to become a husband in another region, a natural drive to prevent inbreeding, or a surplus sterile male pushed out of a failing colony. This gnomide crafted her pearly skin from polished marble and white agate, and a frost of clear diamond decorated the dangerous quills erupting from her scalp. Her horns were typically female, nothing but a pair of nubs above her bat-like ears.

The seamless construction of the armor worried Fade.

She was powerful enough to warp the metal with each movement, with no need for articulation.

Humans have many aphorism about the magic of diet – "the herbs make the witch," "you are what you eat," "the lord's domain is proved by the plate" - but this is the concrete truth of the Pharyes. Unlike the other elements, the earth freely provides an endless variety of minerals and physical and folkloric properties to choose from, allowing gnomes to alter their bodies and minds. The dwarf-lords have a reputation towards greed for fine jewels and precious metals, but such wealth literally makes them stronger, wiser, and greater. For this reason, gnomes either become mad masses of shapeshifting clay filled with hundreds of sundry jewels with a dozen persona, or stodgy conservatives holding on to the same set of arms and armor for fear of losing their very essence. A body almost completely composed of the fine, metamorphic crystals of marble and the prismatic edges of obsidian, demonstrated something altogether mightier, a level of self-control akin to a woman who could command her body on the cellular level. She was still able to transform into the beasts of the field and sea, even after purging herself of the humble, and vulnerable clay.

And that softness and high-melting point would prove useful against dragonfire.

"So, what are we going to do with you?" asked the gnomide.

"What's the issue, madam?" Lund asked. "What is your title?"

"Just call me the Tall Man," she said.

"Tall Man?" Mageirissa said. "You're the Tall Man?"

"Yes," she said, flashing her teeth, their orange the only hint of color on her. "One shouldn't have an accurate code name."

"Gerana Nikneveny," Kingfisher said.

The gnomide glared at the harpy as though she had been slapped.

"Kingfisher," said Nikneveny. "What's your game?"

"I didn't torpedo the *Imperator Dragomir*," Kingfisher said.

"I never suspected you," Nikneveny said. "We searched your belongings when you boarded. You had no explosives, nor the magical catalysts or capacity. Neither means nor motive."

"Why did you kill Loganev?" Kingfisher said.

"I didn't," Nikneveny said. "Nor did my men. How inconvenient. I wanted to question him. The dragon is moving against us. I believe it destroyed the *Dragomir* and had Loganev killed."

"Your ship makes sense, but why Loganev?" Kingfisher asked. "He electrified the town. People liked him."

"It perplexed me as well. Unexpected, too. Until I read his notes. He was designing cannons," she said. "Or rather, the firing mechanisms. Anvils striking mercury fulminate. Dragons were once a terror to the armies of man. Even ballistae and catapults use easily foiled wood. But those cannons, they will even fire back if scorched by dragon breath, like a trap. Dragons are no longer the kings of war. Now is the age of artillery."

"Galbasi," Fade said. "General Aurélien Galbasi. He and Loganev had a string of correspondence."

"Soft-hearted Lem and the conquering revolutionary. Both engineers. Visionaries," Nikneveny said. An almost wistful look crossed her face. "It must have eaten at him. No wonder he stayed here, in self-imposed exile. Sitting on the secret of this disease."

"He knew?" Fade said. "He knew about the hydrargyrism?"

"Lem was a fierce opponent of slavery," she said. "Ashamed of the Saganarchy. He feared what his people could do, knowing that a liquid metal was so easily spread in a population of humans. Imagine… imagine the temptation of that power. Chains running in their veins."

Fade's gray eyes dulled, chilling Kingfisher to the bone. He crossed his arms, clawing at his shoulders. She slid her left-wing over his back when he slouched forward. His hand tapped on her single finger, before sliding into his frock coat, to trace the lip of a glass bottle that once held surgical ether.

"My sympathies, Mr. Fade," said Nikneveny, with cloying artifice. "Theobard is a husband by arrangement, but I haven't spoken to him in a century. You were brave to return to the Polar Sea."

Fade said nothing and continued to trace the lip of the empty bottle.

Lund examined his frightened companions, and leaned forward, to take the lead.

"Ah, Dr. Lund," Nikneveny said. "A landed gentlemen. You know the danger of these upstart free-traders, of course. It's not about aristocratic pride. It's about the rot of the market. Without the honor of the nobility and the might of the Throne, the state begins to sell off its institutions. The Mayor has already devolved his power to companies and guilds. But what do these merchants know of duty and chivalry? They will rob the North of its wealth and flee at the first opportunity."

"What do you need from us?" Lund said with well-mannered professionalism. He decided not to bring up the fact that the Throne hired foreign mercenaries to do their dirty work, or that the Imperators were descendants of robber barons. "None of us are aligned to the dragon or your regime. We're not going to fight for you, or against you."

"We're going to need you to also sit on the nature of the Contortions," Nikneveny said.

"No," Lund said with a subtle shake of the head and

peaked fingers. "We have a duty as medical professionals. Oaths and pledges to the common good. And, in any case, we've published our findings, circulated letters. It's done."

The coach turned up a steep incline.

"As I feared," Nikneveny said. Fade watched the gnomide's detachable digestive system squirm against her stomach, a hideous hive of burrowing maggots frothing with *aqua regia* and primal greed. "We will have to accelerate the integration of Northernmost. Unless you would join us. Make the cure our effort. Indeed, we could provide alchemical guilds, charters, stipends, titles… knighthoods. This could be mutually beneficial."

The prospect of funding briefly pulled Fade back to reality, and he glanced at Lund.

"As I said, we will stay apolitical," Lund said. "We are two foreigners and two outlanders. This is between the Veche and the Throne of the Fallen. Release us, and we will conclude our work here, and depart on the first available ship."

Lund looked around again. Fade burned cold, and the threat of Chernograder retribution silenced Kingfisher and Mageirissa. They let the landed gentleman of Murmur speak.

"No working of wills is apolitical. No question of ethics," Nikneveny said. "The war and the state draw us in. What we want doesn't matter. The winds of change are blowing from Merovy and Vankir. Fire rises to the horizon from a thousand petty rebellions. If we fail here, the Homelands will fall apart. And we'll be eaten by the empires of Aquilo."

"I don't wish to sound cold, but it's not my nation," Lund said. "Not my empire. Not my duty."

"I know," she said as the coach struggled against an incline. "Which is why I could have you arrested as enemy agents, and press Ms. Barvaci and Volganina into our service. Desertion would carry the death penalty. Imagine how she'd hang. Too light to break her neck; instincts driving her to fly.

It would take hours."

Kingfisher hopped to her feet, digging her talons into the flooring. Fade's untrimmed fingernails bit into the coach's upholstery.

"I'd rather serve the dragon than the eagle," Kingfisher said. "Even if he is evil, a beast in a tower is more tolerable than a treacherous gang of sneaks, thugs, and otters."

"How simplistic," Nikneveny said. "You–"

"I know what I am," Kingfisher said. "And you know what? Simplicity beats a complicated plot. You think you're a spider in the web, catching flies. But guess what? I'm a bird of prey diving in with a big dumb rock."

Kingfisher slashed at the gnomide, trying to grab her. Nikneveny's simulacrum collapsed in a pile of sand and pulverized limestone.

"Foolish," Nikneveny's voice said. Someone rapped on the front of the coach, and Lund flatly noted that she was the driver. Fade screamed in pain, and his chest stung like an asp bite and the warpath of a thousand angry bees. A connection unhitch with a leaden clank. A sickening lurch punched them in the stomach, and the coach rolled down the hill.

Fade tore at his shirt and wiped the blood from his tattooed chest, boiling it away to complete his hungry spell. He transubstantiated the hardness of the ironclad carriage door and its locks with the fragility of the vial. The glass struck the corner of the carriage, just the point of weakness he needed. He pushed all of his strength into one solid kick. The hardwood and steel shattered and slashed Fade's leg. A spurt of blood mixed vaporized upon contact with the stray yliaster impulses of his now exposed venation. As the door cracked open, Fade pushed Kingfisher up and out of the carriage, blowing her clear with the last of his strength.

"We're tumbling towards the Meska!" Lund called out as he reached for the stored note bags. The shaman grabbed the unconscious Fade and pulled him close.

Lund pushed Mageirissa and Fade in front of himself, wedging them against the corner as he transformed into a skinny walrus. The blubber encircled and sealed up their bags. As they hit the riverbank, a blast of wind broke the forward-left wheel. It snapped under its weight, and the coach 's floor collapsed, opening up in the freezing water. Mageirissa and Fade slammed into Lund's wall of blubber, using his tusks as a handhold. The hasty transfiguration warmed the walrus' surrounding, but the water devoured the heat. Kingfisher swooped in and carried Fade to the shore, while Mageirissa and Lund had to swim.

The camels were far gone, beyond the hill, and nobody had the energy to pursue. Magierissa stripped off her anorak and tried to clean Fade's chest. He sweated blood from a tattoo of chains and skulls, done in kraken ink and powdered meteoric iron.

"This is a slave tattoo," she said, dumbstruck and horrified.

Lund turned his heavy head and tried to slip next to the others to warm them. A dozen mysteries of his friend's past clicked into place, though it didn't show on his face. He changed his skin back to a man, but the effort winded him, and he fell to his knees in agony. Unlike the easier transformations between two forms found in lyncanthropes and those who wear enchanted hides, his more flexible shapeshifting relied on his knowledge of comparative morphology. In his panicked haste, he misaligned the bones in his hands, feet, and leg joints, which swam in gelatinous connective tissue.

"Hey!" cried a man from the top of the hill, an old man with a rasping bellow like the roar of a great cat.

Kingfisher trained her eyes on him.

"The innkeeper," she announced. "It's the innkeeper. Shura."

"Is that his name?" Lund said, distracted by the attempt to stem Fade's blood loss. "Never got it."

"It was on the sign," Kingfisher said.

The icy winds halted, and a dry warmth washed down the hill as he approached. The change was potent, reinvigorating. Lifesaving.

"Shura, is that you?" Kingfisher said. "I mean, the warmth."

"Yes," he said, with a wry smile. "A bit of salamandery, nothing special, passed down from a great-granny. But Shura was my father. My name is Erazm."

Chapter 21: The Knight and the Dragon

Lund and Mageirissa cleaned and closed Fade's wounds and tucked him into Kingfisher's bed. Erazm Makarov helped move the surgeon's things to the harpy's room, and said he would try to keep the heat off them.

Kingfisher perched on the headboard and maintained a solemn vigil over Fade until Lund assured him that he only needed rest. The debris had punctured the tibial artery but missed the sciatic nerve, sparing him the nightmare of neurological divination and the surgical binding of nerves and arcane venation.

After an hour of attending to Fade, making sure he was warm, and singing to him, Kingfisher went to the window and unlatched it. She had learned to push up the frame just enough that it did not lock, balanced on the nape of her neck before she slipped out and let it fall shut behind her. She flapped up towards the Mayoral Tower. It was an easy ascent, as the bizarre black iron radiated heat and directed a rolling cushion of convection up towards the Posadnik.

She rose to the open upper chamber. The portal was some thirty meters wide, and half as tall. The dragon's six necks coiled against each other, each ending in a half-serpentine, half-lupine head. They met in a crocodilian body, its batlike wings bearing a reddish underside painted like a setting sun. Their green-tinted copper scales plated red hot flesh and shimmered with orange light and the roiling air of a mirage. Their front claws were iron scythes tempered in a forge. The chamber must have stood twenty meters tall with a radius of thirty, and the Mayor filled up half of its volume when they raised its heads. While Kingfisher briefly relished the heat of the draconic body, the intensity soon grew uncomfortable.

"Sorry for the intrusion," Volganin said. "But it's a state of emergency."

"Oh, that harpy, isn't it?" said the Mayor.

The Mayor rose up, revealing the *gromovoi znak* – the six-spoked wheel mark of thunder- tiled across the floor. Kingfisher had interrupted the dragon's pious meditation, and one head still gazed into a sacred flame. The athanor burned with the astral oil of the Salamanders' Core, a caldera where the charred friars pooled the celestial grease which rains from the Sun-heated corpse of the Rotting Eclipse, what may be a dead god locked in an erratic orbit through the heavens. She wondered if this coveted fat motivated the band of ogres to invade the Mayor's city. They were often locked in wars over such exotic meals, such as the ever-growing divine excrescences under the Hypouranid plains.

"Dame Kingfisher Volganin, knighted by Sir Eol," she said.

"Ah, Zmei Mednayevich, Elected Posadnik of Samyy Severnyy," the Mayor said, echoed through two heads. "What is our emergency?"

The other heads conversed with each other in brief snippets of Acthnician, a language like serpentine sibilance and steaks hissing and popping on a grill. Kingfisher could not tell if the heads were truly different people or if the Mayor also talked to themself under their breath.

"A gnomide named Gerana Nikneveny, a bureau chief for a special commissariat, is in town, plotting your downfall," Kingfisher said. "That slaughter in the north, near Hyperborea? They were trying to recruit an ancient dragonslayer, before turning back to entrench for a war against this town. It was a plot by some Skeironic noble pretender, a Waylander prospecting company, and Chernograd. I think the Queen Mother is here, too, with some kind of time magic…"

"Is that their design?" the Mayor said.

Two heads said it flatly, as if expected, while another's lips smugly curled. One hissed in icy fury, and one nearly roared in fiery outrage. Fear gripped the last one, which darted about the chamber in paranoia.

"Oh, far worse than I thought. I feared they were bolstering their naval presence here, hoping to provoke me to attack. To drive me into the sea with their cannons… But this is far more dangerous and daring… Thank you for coming to me with this. What do you want?"

"Nothing but fair play," she said. "Outlanders fear you, but not your citizens. I haven't even heard whispers. My only question… did you kill Lem Loganev?"

"No," the Mayor said through all of their heads, one calmly, the rest snarling or growling with indignation.

"You must have known of his cannon designs," she said. "A weapon against dragons."

"Yes," said the Mayor. "Loganev and I shared a common disgust with our peoples' pasts. What have we done to earn absolute dominion? Our legacy as slavers and draco-tyrants?"

"I understand," Kingfisher said. "I more than understand. Please, let us settle this. Peacefully."

"Peacefully?" the heads roared, hissed, and laughed incredulously. "They had their chance at peace. I gifted them a century of peace. And yet they infiltrate and intrude and scheme to conquer. And what does the conqueror know but fire and force?"

"Please, I understand your anger," Kingfisher pleaded, before hopping up with a flutter of wings and shouting. "But think of the crossfire! You'll burn down the whole town! Blow it up! They've filled it with gunpowder and pitch barrels!"

"What?" said half of the heads.

"Sailors were unloading and carting around barrels of pitch, or marked as such, at least. I…You can't use your fire against them," she said. "I think they've trapped the town."

"Poison it is then," said the Mayor. "Like the rats they are."

Kingfisher yelped and fluttered her wings as the dragon gathered itself up, putting its full weight on its elephantine limbs. Its spreading wings baked the air. The frill on its tail went erect, ready to steer itself towards the Imperial Naval Yard.

"Stop. Stop!" Kingfisher pleaded, but the Mayor ignored her and took to the sky.

The dragon spiraled above the tower, with each beat of their wings quaking through Kingfisher's body.

She remembered that strange pulse in the water, as the *Imperator Dragomir* sank. She had explained it away as a tertiary blast, perhaps delayed by a bulkhead or some other circumstance. But no, it came from that stone anchor. That second, iron anchor in a crate confused her, but perhaps it was intended for a vessel at the yard. It was the least of her concerns.

It should have been her main one, she thought. That stone anchor was a blood lure. Erazm's distant draconic ancestor had summoned the Mayor. What was Orlova conjuring up from this churning abysm?

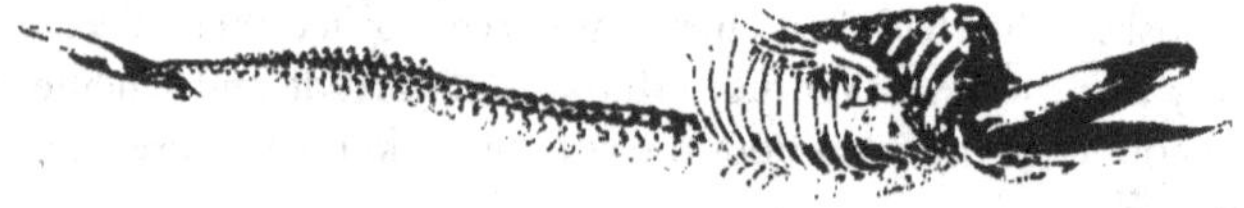

Erazm Makarov led Lund and Mageirissa downstairs and announced to his customers that they needed to get their families and friends and leave town. There was a moment of disbelief before the old brick of a man leaped up on a chair and caught himself with the other foot against the bar.

"War's coming, friends," he said, a burst of hearth-heat rolling from him. "Has been for a while. Get your family and spread the word. Head out and spread out. I better see all of you back here next week."

One old Hookman dug in his bag for some coins.

"Forget your tabs and inn-dailies, they're on me," Erazm said. "Elena, close up and grab Rita's kids. I'm heading out."

Erazm left the *Eternal Flame*, and Lund and Mags followed, though Lund doubled back to unscrew and pocket the gauge from the samovar's economiser engine. The Innkeeper's flesh glowed white, with orange and red flickering at the edges. The glamor burnt away, and Lund and Mags estimated the man beneath to be in his early thirties, perhaps late twenties. Average height but wide, with coppery hair and eyes. He had the build of a strongman, fat over muscle, slightly out of practice.

"What?" Mageirissa said. "Which is the illusion? The old man or this?"

"This is me," Erazm said, as he crossed the street. "The Sagani got away with it, but men have to start aging or people ask questions."

"How?" Lund asked.

"Back at the Academy, there was a ritual. To magnify the properties of metals. We wore these silver crowns, you know, the metal of curse breaking, and tried to cure that early phase of the Convulsions. But it magnified the mercury, too. There were a hundred and sixty of us. Most of us went berserk, and blew the place away. But those of us with saganic blood survived. The three gnomes, then Iszt, Milla, and I. You know how ancient alchemists tried to get immortality and power from drinking mercury?" Erazm explained.

"Yes," Lund said.

"Yeah," Erazm said. "I hope I'm not *immortal* immortal, I don't wanna watch Lena… but… well, I only aged to this in a century."

Erazm knocked on the Constabulary's door.

"Hey, Captain Rhee," he shouted into the door.

Chesti answered for the Watchmen.

"What's the emergency?" Chesti asked. "Oh, hey Doctor, Lady Barvaci. The carriage ride wasn't so bad, then."

"Don't ask," Lund said.

Captain Rhee approached from the back office.

"Some Chernograd bureau and the Imperial Navy's plotting an attack on the harbor," Erazm said. "The queen mother is back in town despite the ban."

The Mayor's choral roar echoed through the center of town, and their swiftly-moving shadow eclipsed the sun.

"And that's happening," Erazm added. "I'm not your boss, but... evacuate, south to north."

Rhee arrived at the door and nodded with a "Yes, sir."

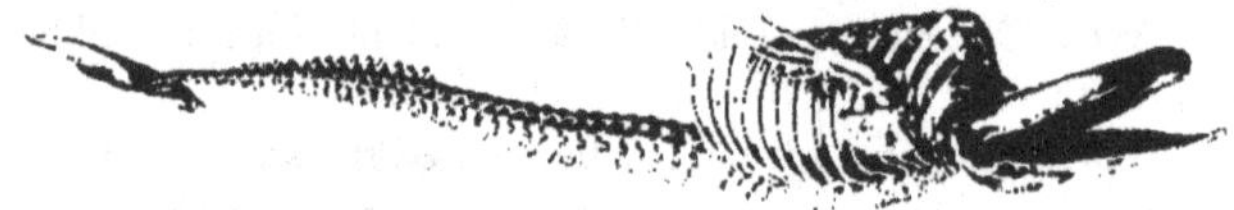

Blood and steam filled Byeol-i's foggy memory as she stuffed leafy tar into a grease-lined vegetable-lamb and wrapped it in a canvas bag. She had seen Gangcheori kill and devour a man and a kaftar, swallowing them whole. The ancient salamander protected her. She knew that for certain. The Hyena-man tried to drown her, and Pander pulled out a gun. That memory was too fresh and dramatic to forget, even for her. But she feared for her life when all this plotting was over. She was a loose end, and she wondered if Gangcheori would test her memory, probe her mind with their conjured creatures of consciousness, and see if she truly forgot what she saw.

She consulted her notes. Eun Injeong had asked her for rockrose, currant, aloe, and sticky nightshade, to be added to an offering of asbestos and tungsten. The puzzle pieces of Gangcheori's plan snapped into place, and she sprung to her feet and ran to the tunnel beneath the Hwagasari. She came to the alcove where the metal statue's massive haunches sunk into the earth above the steam canals, nearly slipping into the water on the slick stone.

"Byeol-i, you've returned," said Gangcheori as it rose from

the water, barely visible in the darkness. A brass dome sat below the Hwagasari, leaking a metallic smoke that sparkled like pixie dust and crackled with working yliaster.

"What is this?" she asked.

"The asbestos and herbs you helped gather," Gangcheori said. "I'm purifying the Hwagasari, removing its bane of fire."

"If the Mayor finds out—"

"The Mayor has left the tower," said Gangcheori. "Now is the time to strike. Byeol-i, I need you to awaken the Bulgasari. We have no time to spare."

She approached the paw of the idol. A golden skin grew across its stony hide, a rapid transmutation fueled by the yliaster of an ascendant dragon.

"Shed your dress," said Gangcheori. "Hurry."

Byeol-i's heart fluttered, but she did as she was told.

"Let me bless you with the mists of a dragon," Gangcheori said. The salamander exhaled a blue-white haze that clung to Byeoli's exposed skin like morning dew.

She thought of the vegetable-lamb in the package. A pathetic chimera that grew from the earth, eating away at the grass around it. They will starve or overheat without their master, the gift oats and shearing razors of their stable shepherd.

Are the grateful, unto the slaughter?

"Now, approach the statue," Gangcheori commanded. "Touch it."

"Will it kill me?" she asked. She did as she was told, but her legs trudged against the mire of her apprehension.

"I won't let it," Gangcheori said.

"Will it hurt?" she said. Her fingers hovered above the transmuting stone flesh, shaking.

"Yes," said Gangcheori.

She pressed her hand against the idol, which was said to draw up any metal that touched it, melting the weapons of legions into its metallic flesh. First came a twinge in her palm, then an itch, and a burning. A thousand pins slid from her skin, a million sharp pricks, one for every nerve ending, the acupuncture of hell. Her palm shredded under the torment, as the guardian awoke and drank the mercury in her body and the reactive burst of arcane power. Her blood filled the groves of the quincunx symbols, and she watched her guardian feed upon her.

The Bulgasari awoke as she collapsed, both the tunnel and her arm shattered and cracked. The breathy dew filled her broken body with yliaster, a heavenly water soothing her burning wounds.

She screamed after the initial shock wore off, and Gangcheori covered her with another burst of draconic mist. The wounds on the rest of her flesh closed, with nothing more than red dots quickly scabbing mauve. A rolling wave of revulsion churned her stomach as Gangcheori's lingering healing spell devoured the blood on her destroyed arm. The pain was excruciating, but it was the thick muscles and coppery scales that drove her to tears.

"Thank you," said Gangcheori as they slid into the hole left by the vacating Bulgasari. "We will both be dragons soon."

Black nails dug into the stone tunnel as Byeol-i pulled herself up. She slipped on her dress, grabbed her bag, and stumbled into the courtyard and the dimming light. A mighty splash and a foamy spray erupted from the Narrows. The Bulgasari's paired tusks, rising from a strong underbite, briefly resembled a brazen walrus swimming upside down. The metal juggernaut sank into the Narrows, walking on the river bottom, a scaly hippopotamus marching to war.

Gangcheori had already disappeared, lying in wait for its moment of opportunity. The other members of the Jooga gathered, an uneven chorus of whispers and shouts, with nothing in between. Byeol-i's head was clear, for the first time in her life. There was no fog, only pain. She ran to the coast, fastening her belt, and dove into the water above the guardian's great shadow.

The distance singing stopped, and Fade was back in the loamy darkness. His eyes burned after the surgery when the Lord of Dust plated his eyes with reflective, metallic flesh. It was his master's idea of a gift.

Fade was relatively lucky. The first test subject had gone blind. Fade called him the boy, although he was only eight fortnights younger than him. He was short and even skinnier than Fade, with a delicate beauty. The boy was Lentoran, and Fade knew nothing of his tongue. The boy cried more than he spoke, and after the botched surgery, he rarely left Fade's side. He was bullied by the other slaves, knew of no other speaker of his language in the oil pits, and lacked the life skills of a long-term blind man. Only Fade treated him with patience. Fade was in his debt, his night vision coming at the boy's expense. He led him around the bunkers and tunnels by hand, drew symbols in his palm, and tried to teach him the Tactile writing of Pharyean. But the double language barrier proved too much.

The boy crawled into Fade's bed at night, in that cold northern underworld. The boy played with Fade's hair, and embraced him, and dared to kiss him, eventually. The boy gave Fade his first intimate experience, following a cascade of wet kisses from neck to navel. Fade could not bring himself to reciprocate in kind but kissed and fondled his bedmate until he shouted something in Lentoran and shook in Fade's embrace.

One day, the Lord of Dust asked if Fade wished to take the Lentoran as a slave. His life would belong to Fade if his 'dear apprentice' would provide for him. Fade nearly jumped out of his skin at the proposal, and said no, hoping to drop the matter.

By the end of the week, the boy had disappeared. The Lord of Dust never explained what happened to him, and Fade realized that he had killed the blind Lentoran with that refusal. His execution often played itself out in Fade's nightmares, in variations. Was he led to his death by someone pretending to be Fade? Did he die ignorant? Did he realize the deception too late? Did he die thinking Fade had betrayed his love?

His next partner came into his life at the beginning of his third and final year in that pit of horrors. She was a displaced Eurian, black-haired, swarthy, but with pale green eyes. She was quiet and demure, and as frightened as the rest of them. Her small frame made her unsuited for the mine labor, and Fade feared her purpose in this hell. She had become sick, and Fade nursed her back to health, learning her name. Pleyone.

One night, exhausted after excavating a pit of bones from estwhile epochs and dissecting goats, Fade settled in his chamber to clean himself. Pleyone entered and finished washing him and took him to bed. He learned from the pattern of fine green scales that she had some arcane heritage. In hindsight, he knew he should have stopped, but his lust and loneliness made him stupid over those three nights. She was beautiful, and like the boy, loved to play with the rapidly spreading gray streaks in his hair.

She did not come back for a fourth night. Fortnights later, he saw the products of those nights, reptilian homunculi-things. Several jars and vials held the beautiful Eurani. The Lord gave Fade her bones, and act as though the whole affair had been a reward.

That was the cruelest part of his life in the Lord of Dust's tunnels. His master treated him not as a slave, but as an apprentice. He expected gratitude for his teaching. As though Fade had made a diabolical pact. The other humans and chimerae in the pit were disposable, meant to toil, die, and fill the cabinet of cadavers. But Fade, the Lord said, was special, his prized pupil. And Fade was good at it. They made break-throughs in the science of anatomy and reanimation, the mapping of nerves, and the arcana of the mind and the soul.

The Lord of Dust explained the four stages of the Great Work. That one must begin in chaotic darkness, reveling in rot, until you are truly prepared to escape the dredge heap. To hatch from its blinding shell.

Soon, one must wash away the putrefaction, polishing the primal matter with cold water and the caustic spirit of hartshorn, coughing amid the dross and miasma and the trimmed away gangrene. And one must do this all in moon-light, the veil of silver. Only when the primal matter is clear as glass can one see the dawning sunlight, the yellow stage of wisdom. One must turn to the learning of older generations, the yellow of ancient pages and the fingernails of sages. But all this labor, too, is a prison, the life-stealing obligations of li-brary and laboratory.

His dusty master whispered in conspiratorial tones of the final stage, the Redness that few ever reach. The freedom of the true innovator, the unfettered philosopher. This climax was the transmutation of the Stone, the end of the Work, the marriage of the red king and white queen.

The Lord of Dust said that such mastery would bring freedom, that Fade would rise from that mine in golden glory, a phoenix reborn. But there would be fire, blood, and agony.

He remembered the pain as his master sliced his wrist with a bronze sickle, dripping his lifeblood onto the skull of what seemed to be the skeleton of a deformed child, or unknown ape. But the Lord said that these were the bones of a primor-dial man, a cousin ten million generations removed – and there was nothing more suitable that the blood and suffering of a modern man to revive such a wretched wight. The Lord of Dust led him deep into the underworld, into the Inferno where magma pulses like blood. In the horrific heat, the offerings of human grease began to boil. The bone rose and danced and knit themselves together with unnatural flesh like char and thickening tar. The stronger the Devil, the more ancient a host it can bind to its resentful will. The Infernal Lords dwell in the petrified bones of primordial lizards, but their numerous spawn and slaves can only bind themselves to small, long extinct mammals. A breed of man, even one lost to the crushing epochs, is the most prized of bodies for the imps.

For finding such a complete skeletal host, the Lord of Dust earned three questions from the grateful imp. This devilspawn's domain assumed knowledge of animals, vegetables, and minerals. The Lord of Dust asked questions about human flesh and subtle metallic poisons.

He graciously allowed Fade to ask about ancient plant life, almost as a joke. But Fade paused for a moment, and the serious young man asked a serious question. And the imp answered.

The devils were the failed creations of the world, those species that had withered from the tree of life. Those rotten fruits sank to the depths of Thier, their flesh turning to dust and their bones turning to stones. Their souls, or some echoing ghosts., cling together. After millions upon millions of years, those faint traces of animal volition eventually congealed into an alien awareness. Something spiteful towards that which survived, that which the gods or fates chose to live. What frightened Fade most was knowing the power of spite to keep one moving. The power of hate tinged with ambition, a drive to tear down the masters and winners, rooted in a rich soil of worldly resentment. Society had deprived the poor son of a draper of any other chance to study. That knowledge sickened him to this day. What he learned in that darkness gave him what he needed to impress the housecarls and earls of the world, and he hated himself and the Master and all the world's lords for that.

He heard ghouls whisper in the depths, women of crematory smoke whose voices crackled like guttering bonfires. They spoke of the invisible threads of life, the power of marrow and blood and the visceral flora. They held demonstrations.

And Fade spied ghosts in the Lord's gray flames. He could still hear them, at night, in the silence. That was the greatest horror in this cosmos. That it never ended.

Fade felt someone play with his hair again, and he mumbled a question he could barely recall, something about why Kingfisher had stopped singing. But the harpy didn't have hands. His attendant smelled like peat moss and pine needles, wassail, and wet leather. He reached out to touch the fingers, and delirious said, "Mum?"

"Hey kid," said the Whirlwind, with a mocking motherliness.

"Oh no," muttered Fade, still too tired to open his eyes. He dreamily imagined that he would be reinvigorated, but the pain killers deadened his adrenal production.

"What's wrong?" she said.

He found himself on her lap, with a fox tail around his neck.

"If you're here to kill me, just do it," Fade said. He tried to point at his forehead and succeeded on his third attempt. "Crush the front."

She picked him up and slid his limp body onto her lap. His head settled on her left breast.

"Ah, laying with the does," she said with a laugh.

"They're lovely, thank you," he mumbled.

"You're pale," she said. "More than usual, you gray Waylander bookworm."

"Oh, that's terrible, coming from you," he said. "Albino… hey… did you open the package?"

"I didn't have time," She said. Her free hand slipped towards her hollow, and she called forth the case. Her finger traced the branded seal of the ophthalmologist, and opened the package. It was a pair of temple-framed, deer-horn glasses with teardrop loops at the end for a red ribbon. Cunigunde paused and examined the thick lenses, holding them up to her face.

"The ribbon has a button clasp," Fade said. "And there's a matching quizzing glass."

She tightened the ribbon around her head and buttoned it, happy to avoid pulling it around her antlers. Her twitching ears played with the frames, until she let the spectacles settled on her face.

"Two pale bookworms," he mumbled.

"Heh," she chuckled, and bounced him on her knee like a child, forcing him to sit up straight.

Fade's eyes snapped open and he yelped, "Where's Kingfisher? What—"

"She flew off to speak with the Mayor," she said. "Brave creature."

"Gun, promise me Gun… I know you're going to do something… something violent soon," he said. "It's who you are. But don't hurt her. You can kill me, eat my heart do whatever you will. But swear on your mother's name that you won't… won't hurt Kingfisher."

She grabbed his hand, and played with his limp wrist, before intermingling her fingers with his.

"I swear on my mother's name," she said.

"Alright then," he said, about to nod off. He tapped his head. "Ready to die. But I'll haunt you good."

"Do you love that thing?" she asked.

"King? Yeah," he said.

"What about me?" she asked playfully.

"What? Why?" he asked

"You have a massive erection right now," she said. "It might be worse than the blood loss."

"Oh no," he said. He tried to cross his legs, but gasped and shook in agony as he raised the leg several centimeters.

"I was teasing you," she said. "I am the skald, after all."

"You're comely," he said. "But not her."

"It's fine," she said. "You're not attractive."

"Ow," he said.

"Short, thin arms, scholar's body," she said, tapping on the frame of her spectacles. Fade restrained himself from laughing at her magnified eyes. "But hey, this horn after a horn of mead could be fun."

Fade yelped and snapped upright on his good foot after she flicked his penis. She stood up to catch him and raked her fingers across his tattoo.

"I know what this is," she said, examining its fine details for the first time. She never realized he was so young.

"You said that you dreamed in that hawthorn," he said. "Of what?"

"I think so. But maybe I dreamed that I dreamed," she said. "Mostly of home."

"I'm sorry," he said.

"I know you think I deserved it," she said.

"Yeah," he said. "You've murdered a lot of people. We don't matter to you. I still know it's miserable. Captivity. I missed my mother and father. You miss your sister."

"What is this?" she said, burying her chin into his shoulder.

"Sympathy," he said. "These are basic social interactions, Gun."

"Why did you commission these?" She asked. She folded

the glasses and returned it to the case.

"I have a duty to care," he said, finally unfolding his legs. "Anyone with an affliction. Swore to Hedran, Ours, and In-cano."

"Was it mere duty?" She asked.

"No," he said quietly.

"I killed a man less than three hours ago," she said. "You're not going to win me over."

"You did?" he said.

"I ate his liver, Fade," she said. "And I'm about to go out there and kill a lot more. The dragon. The Queen's dogs. Sailors and watchmen and townsfolk who get in my way."

Fade stumbled towards the door, bracing himself on the knob.

"What's one more then?" he said.

And even he was surprised to feel the knife against his jugular.

"Don't be stupid, Fade," she said.

"I have a duty to care," he said.

"I will kill you if you don't move, Fade."

"Yeah, I see the knife and the monster holding it," he said. "Kill me, kill the dragon, kill a thousand other people, and then sit alone in the snow and ashes and wonder why nobody looked for you."

She pressed her other hand against Fade's ear and raised the one holding the knife to match. Fade's heart started to pound, burning away the drugs in his system.

He screamed as she swept his injured leg. She caught him with her off hand and tossed him on the bed, the stuffing of Rahab's hair moss barely softening the blow. She glowered down at him until her eyes shook, raked her lips with her sharp teeth, and stormed out of the room.

Chapter 22: Sovereignty

Kingfisher tailed the Mayor, partially hoping to somehow slow it down, partially because it was an easier path than the cold air. She needed altitude to see as the fog rolled in. She flapped her wings and tried to map out where the Bureau's men had placed those barrels of pitch. She spotted one of the troika carriages on Royal Isle, hidden behind one of the Academy of the Northern Lights' remaining walls. It had been well hidden, pushed into a storage shed. However, there was a crack in the roof, and her fisher's eyes could spot fine differences in aquatic blues and grays. The hole was too unnaturally black for the sunlight, even as the storm clouds gathered above.

She circled and found an undisguised carriage in Ogre-Back, and a likely cache near Cannery Row, if she correctly read the clusters of circular impressions and fresh drag marks. She completed the circle around the mainland in hopes of catching the heat rising from the Mayoral Tower but dived to the rooftop of the Constabulary as she spotted Lund and Mageirissa.

Lund called to her and held up the pressure gauge. Kingfisher hopped to the ground as he handed it to her. She fumbled with it, and Mags tied it to a talisman on a leather strap, wrapping it around the clawed thumb on Kingfisher's left wing.

"Air pressure gauge?" Kingfisher asked.

Lund nodded.

"To track the storm? See if the Mayor or the Whirlwind or the Queen are manipulating it?"

"No," Lund said. "Watch if it spikes. It's not just a barometer, but an anemometer."

"Sudden buildup of air in the gauge," Kingfisher said, puzzling it out. "The Whirlwind?"

"The barometer might catch the Whirlwind, but if the Queen stops time for everything but the air, the aerometer should surge as time flows normally again," Lund said. "I hope."

"I hope so, too," Kingfisher said. "You're evacuating people, it looks."

Mageirissa nodded yes, and added, "Makarov just left, too, up the row."

"I'm going to the shore, maybe get the citizens out," Lund said.

"And I'll find Fade, and hopefully send my spirit out, keep us all in touch," Mageirissa said. "I'll have to find a protected place, though."

"Alright," Kingfisher said. "We need to move. Goodbye."

"Goodbye, Bird," Mageirissa said, hugging Kingfisher.

Lund nodded and tucked a loose lock of hair behind Kingfisher's ear, kissed Mageirissa, and departed south, transforming into a giant bat. Kingfisher flapped one street north to wrap around the Mayoral Tower and its lingering heat. A storehouse to the northwest erupted in flames, with heavy smoke rising over Merrowlight Road and the neighborhood known as Vila's Bones.

Terrible beasts rampaged through the northern corner of the neighborhood, forcing townsfolk and militiamen to flee back into the chaos. An elven unicorn crashed through barrels, the powder blackening its shaggy hide. One man tried to light the rampaging *Indrik* on fire with a torch but lost his nerve as the five-meter-long rhinoceros charged in his general direction. It was soon joined by a pair of pantheons, who tore at dead horses.

Kingfisher found the Mayor in the clouds over the bay, as ironclad vessels turned their cannons and elephant-tusk harpoons against the firedrake. They were dragonfighters, covered and insulated with ceramic and wards and capable of pumping water through its body to extinguish flames. They lacked sails, depending on boilers, and the well-drilled sailor-covens practiced a form of collective crewing magic derived from rituals of siegecraft. They disguised themselves in Polar Sea ice, trading most of their maneuverability for protection and a low silhouette.

Kingfisher swooped closer to Merrowlight, finding only a sprawling wreck. It was more than a fire. The cannons had been sabotaged, their wheels smashed, and a pile of broken firearms lay in the street, snapped in half. She found Popov on the roof. He darted away from the spreading fire and leaped the entire block of buildings to the Stone's Throw neighborhood.

She dove down to him, from behind. He spun and smacked Kingfisher's legs out of the way, and grabbed her by the armholes of her cuirass, forcing her to the ground.

"Stay away from me," he commanded, with more annoyance than authority.

"Where's the Tall Man?" Kingfisher demanded. She threatened him again with her claws. Popov crouched down while pulling Kingfisher up, pivoted on one foot, and hurled the harpy into the sky. Popov leaped four hundred meters in the air, where he stopped. He raised his right hand and made two stirring motions as he bellowed like an elk. The thick clouds churned around his position, and the eye of this storm moved with him.

"Cunigunde!" Kingfisher screamed.

Kingfisher heard a distant, feminine "What?"

"Cunigunde!" she repeated.

"Yeah, can barely hear you, Big Nose!" Cunigunde said as she flew away.

"Don't do this!" Kingfisher screamed as the wind picked up.

"What?" Cunigunde shouted back, and the rest was

drowned out by the cyclone.

The wind stuttered. Cunigunde noticed as well, turning towards the Academy's position. She became invisible, and rose upward into the sky, dragging the eye of the storm with her. Kingfisher beat against the winds, sweeping down to the Academy of the Northern Lights.

The harpy stalked down the route she had traced with Fade, noting that someone had opened the septic tunnel. A trail of water led to the central hall. Kingfisher pressed against the wall, yet still felt a shift in the air. She ducked inside.

She then found herself pressed against the wall. A strange breeze and a whistle of the aerometer followed, and she was ducking back inside, with only a sense of déjà vu for her trouble.

A woman blinked into being before her eyes.

The lady stood with the willowy, imperious glory of a demigoddess, a hiltless black bastard sword in her left hand. Her right forearm was bandaged. A gossamer, celestine dress rolled out of a silver breastplate like mist and winter's cold rain, all covered by an immaculate polar bear coat. Her cheekbones, jawline, and forehead, already pronounced, were further defined by paralleled tiger stripes of fine, iridescent scales the same glacial blue as her eyes. She wore her platinum blonde hair in a flat side braid, doubled over, and impaled on three pairs of hooked horns growing in lines above her ears. She wore a more a subtle tiara, marked only with practical morion gems, as smoky quartz clouds the gaze of diviners and mental dominators. Even if you didn't know she was the queen-mother and dowager empress, you would assume she was the monarch of some icy empire.

She had not aged a day since sitting for her portrait.

"Your Imperial Grace," Kingfisher said.

"Dame Kingfisher," she said. "You attacked me before."

"You're going to destroy this town," Kingfisher explained

with hesitation, quite confused at her erased actions.

"This is my town," she said. "I was born here. My family ruled here for generations. I don't want it destroyed. This is a matter of safety."

"The people don't want you here," Kingfisher said.

"The people don't know what's good for them," said the Dowager Empress, a layer of ice slipping over her queenly calm. "They have allied with Merovy. Do you know how dangerous is it to have an enemy empire with access to one of your major ports? Backed by a dragon? At any moment, the Leviathan could break through."

"Don't you want that?" Kingfisher asked.

"No," she answered, with a subtle shake of the head. "Of course not. Eternity has an affinity for ice and cold stone and dead stars, the most stagnant and still things. It is strongest here, near the North Pole. It's one reason why the Sylphs are born immortal. They survived its presence by noticing the winds as it churned and writhed."

The Queen Mother pointed her sword at the pressure gauge on Kingfisher's wing.

"Clever, but it wouldn't have worked for long," said the Queen Mother.

Kingfisher blinked, and the sword was at her neck. Then it was sheathed, with nothing in between.

"The dragon has extended the Thaw. The Leviathan is stirring, waking in the warming, changing water. Only one fragment, one small scale, is present in our world. But still, it is a threat."

"And how do you intend to solve it? Kill the dragon?" Kingfisher said.

"Yes," said the Queen Mother. "And send much of the population south. This land must be colder. Stiller. Stagnant. The Leviathan must be contented. Sleeping."

The Dowager Empress gazed into the abyssal blade of

Wartime, her long amazonian shashka, half-saber, half-backsword. As the story goes, her grandfather carved it from a black tooth of the Leviathan's shadow – as a human's shadow had width and breadth, the higher order being cast a shadow with depth and substance. Kingfisher recalled the legendary dwimmerlocks, the witch-warriors of the elementals, and the ancient nobility of mankind, and strange pacts with things dreaming in the corners of the map, lingering from prior iterations of the World.

"You're going to drive them out against their will," Kingfisher said. "It's your town by birthright, but it's their town, too."

"I know," she said. "Some sacrifices must be made for the good of all. The world is a war, everyone looking out for themselves, nation against nation, tribe against tribe, man against man, a sea of hostility."

"Then you should have convinced them," Kingfisher said.

"I've tried. Nobody is going to sacrifice themselves for the greater good. Nobody will vote against their own current interests," said the Queen Mother. "They speak of independence, yet they still use our coinage, unwilling to commit to their words. They wish to trade but don't want the taxes which pay for road and port. They want our navy protecting the seas but are unwilling to offer them shelter. It's a shame, returning to the fold would only strengthen the value of their money, in the long term. But they think only of 'right here' and 'today.'"

"Is that true?" Kingfisher said.

"Is this a town you would wish to live in? This ugly new order of squabbling and capital? It was better, in the shadow of the eagle. If I am remembered as a tyrant, so be it. This is my empire, my people. By both birthright and burden. Do we blame the surgeon for drawing blood to save a life? What if we kill one to save dozens? A hundred to save millions? Such thought experiments make the displacement of a few thousand to save all of the cosmos a non-question."

"No, but–" Kingfisher started.

She defensively raised her talon. The Queen instead embraced it with a smile.

"Someone must seize the reins of the rampaging beast of fate. Someone must guide us to the future, no matter how immediately vile. Let it be the corrupted granddaughter of Eternity," said the Queen Mother.

She pulled the claw closer to her hip. Kingfisher's rough, scaled toes felt the attenuated indentations of stretchmarks beneath Orlova's thin dress.

"We were both born unwanted monsters, Dame Kingfisher. Let us die necessary evils."

"I didn't expect this," Kingfisher said.

"I hope I've convinced you that I didn't want this to come to violence. Ladies must use our gentle words and subtle propriety," said the Queen Mother with a gentle smile. "But how can one contend with a dragon?"

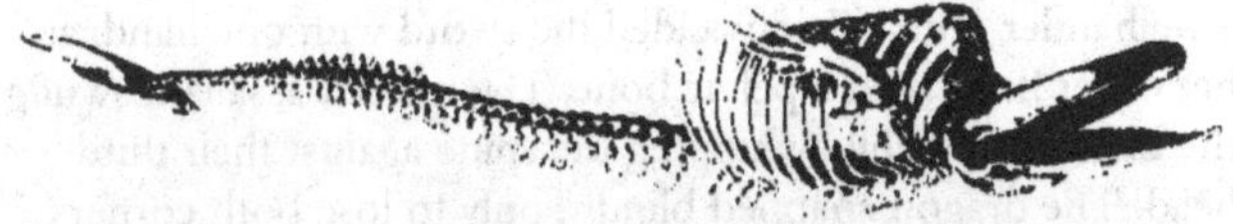

The Mayor's six heads unleashed a torrent of flame over the Imperial Naval Yard, destroying its wharves and the stockades and magazines along Whalebone Quay. The dragon channeled a spell of rust through their hands, attempting to rapidly oxidize the ironclad ships below, though they found some expected resistance as the designers had engineered an expensive alloy to ward off such rustwork.

As the Mayor tilted to dodge a cannonball, a bolt of red lightning tore through their right wing, and the descent of the Whirlwind carved it off at the scapular joint. Cunigunde bellowed like an elk at the center of cyclonic winds, dug her hooks into the exposed joint that was bound there by its molten discharge, and sent a lightning-rod javelin through the base of the Mayor's tail with an off-hand toss. As the first second of her attack ended, she slammed her Atgeir, *Werbel*, into the base of the Mayor's leftmost head. The whirring adamant spirals ground through its bronze scales, digging into the flesh and bone until vertebrae met vertebrae and heat met cold air, staining the storm clouds with a stream of rusty steam.

The dragon hissed and shook like a boiler on the verge of bursting, echoed by the water below as they left a trail of glowing blood. They whipped their necks about, trying to muster up another volley of fire or poisons. The spine of its first neck was soon ripped from its back, with a verdurous hook piercing its nervous cord.

The death of the head jarred the dragon's senses and the loss of the wing sent a cold shock rippling through their side. They turned their rightmost remaining head to face the attacker, only for its eyes to meet the swing of a flamberge Zweihänder. The villain wielded the sword with one hand, as her other hand held a pelvic bone. The unseen assailant swung the blade again while whipping the spine against their third head. The dragon snapped blindly, only to lose both corners of their mouth and half of that tongue to the backswing. The carved black tooth of some abyssal ancient penetrated the base of the third neck. It tried to keep their fourth head straight and spray poison backward into the face of the foe, but a vacuum enveloped that head, bursting its eyes and eardrums and boiling away the poison into a harmless green flakes. To punctuate the torture, a nerve-rattling scream sent a thunderbolt through their second skull.

As their third head died in as many seconds, the Mayor decided that this was easily their worst day in office. They beat theirs remaining wing and tried to maneuver with its weakened tail, only to find its soft flesh shredded by a dust devil of shrapnel. Its uniquely uninjured fifth head gathered up enough yliaster for another blast of flame, but it decided that stopping its fall was more important than revenge. It flash-heated the waters of the drain between the Losian Lighthouse and Royal Island, building a cushion of steam. The viper-reins rippred from their hide as the invisible creature returned to the swirling clouds. While slowed, the boiling burgomaster crashed against the sands and stones of Students' Beach, leaving a streak of glass in their wake.

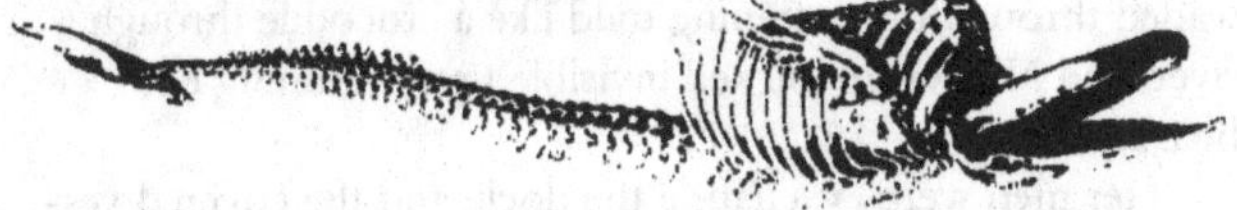

Lund flew towards the flame, beating against the rising winds. He marveled as the dragon fell apart within seconds after dodging a cannonball. He briefly supposed that some exceedingly fine chainshot or grapeshot had done the deed, but an elkish bellow and a chorus of sharp whistling betrayed the true culprit. Three heads were destroyed in a flurry of blows and bolts, and Lund watched the great salamander crash into the Narrows.

The commonfolk at the harbor were already fleeing, though hindered by their higher-than-average age and infirmities. Lund had not expected the Mayor to be so bold and reckless, but perhaps a dragon will always act draconic. Perhaps the best he could do was to keep the sailors and men of the Bureau from harming civilians.

As Lund looked down at the Naval Yard, the seaside silt bubbled up to smother the flame and bury the gunpowder magazines. Nikneveny guided her men through the smoke with the blast of a goat horn, a primitive complement to her brace of flare guns. After three soundings, she decided not to push her luck as a stationary target and sent her hellhound skittering forward into the muddy street.

The hellhound only vaguely resembled a dog. The infernal synapsid was more like an up-jumped naked mole rat with canine pretensions, with skin like black leather and sprawling, powerful forelimbs capable of tearing through permafrost and flesh. Its eyes were red beads in a shovel of a skull, its tusks and whiskers recalling a starved walrus. It had been bound to her service, like many lesser devils enslaved by their gnomish foes, with branded runes, Sepia tattoos, and golden stakes. It waded through the softening mud like a crocodile through a river, and Nikneveny turned invisible upon donning her bearded helm.

Her men were evacuating the dock, and the covered vessels moved to the shore of the Royal Island. Sailors scrambled on the burning wharf. Lund counted at least five obviously dead men. One screamed as Lund's giant bat form descended. He reverted to humanity and landed beside the sailor. The dockworker was too weak to move, covered with burns. Lund cut the most restrictive parts of the man's clothing and used the cleanest portions to cover the burn.

"Hey, you two!" Lund called out to two able-bodied sailors. One had severe bruising across his chest, visible to his neck, and the other's forearms and palms showed signs of defensive burns. "Take this man to Kiril's Infirmary. Keep his upper body elevated, watch his breathing."

"We're under orders," said the bruised sailor, with a dreadful distance to his voice. "Royal Island."

"That's dragonfire. You're poisoned," Lund said. "All three of you will be dead by night if you don't move."

The defensively burnt man clearly knew it was a lie but nodded and asked his attendant's name.

"Dr. Gustavus Lund," he said. "Blame me."

The men looked at each other, and the burnt man.

"You can possibly face a firing squad or certainly face that dragon," said Lund. "Move."

They nodded faithlessly, and struggled to lift the moaning, gasping man, but soon found a steady march despite their wounds. What surprised Lund is that this was unspoken permission, and other sailors formed an evacuation route of injured along the yard. One dock worker, a burly man who resembled a blue-eyed Erazm, picked up a civilian woman who must have been in her eighties, and joined the procession. Some of the locals saw this break in the line and joined to help the sailors under a makeshift truce.

Kornov Street, Harpooned-Head Way, and Whalebone Quay cleared after the initial strike, along with the Merchant Court, from what Lund could see. They witnessed the attack firsthand. Lund focused on Timofiev's Main and Rose Hat Road. The Main had the Civilian Arsenal on Neszo Hill, where Captain Rhee oversaw the distribution of firearms to the militia and other locals. One of the watchmen lay dead in the snow, killed by a powder horn explosion. Lund decided that it might be better to double back, smaller and faster.

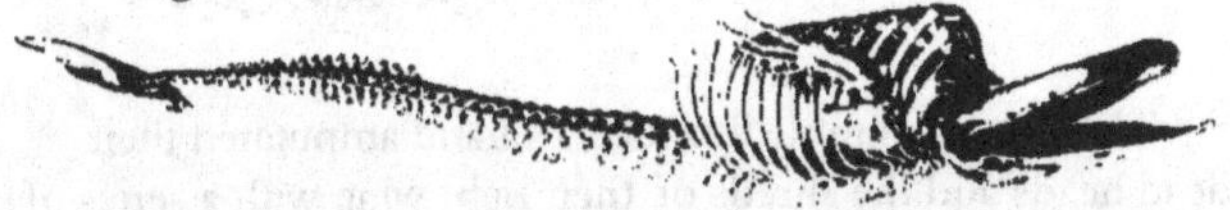

Mageirissa found Fade on the floor of his room, still in his long underwear.

"What are you doing?" she said. "There was an evacuation."

"I think someone came in and saw the bed empty," he said. "And left. I dozed off."

"Get up," she said. She walked over and threw his trousers at him.

"No," he said. "It hurts. And the Whirlwind kicked me."

Mageirissa picked him up, sat him on the chair, and forced the trousers up his injured leg.

"Alright, alright, I can-" he said, before grunting as she picked him up under the shoulder and yanked the trousers up. "Ow, ow, watch the rise!"

"The what?"

"The rise!" he groaned. "The measurement between the inseam and the waist. It...ah..."

"The crotch," she corrected.

"I didn't..." he whimpered as he put on his coat.

"I've delivered babies," she said, and rolled her eyes. She supported him so he could hop on his good leg, and he grabbed his grimoire case and the driving whip. The stairs took some effort, but they made their way outside and turned towards the Tower.

A faint roar rolled down the rows, and Fade broke off towards the Academy of the Northern Lights, hopping and conjuring his crow from his black ink.

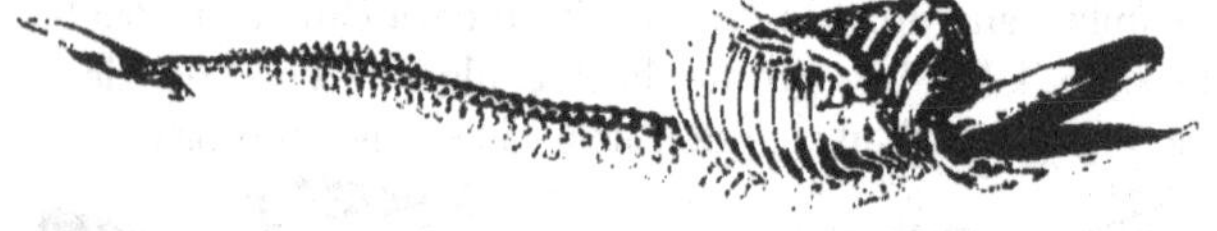

The Mayor stumbled to their feet and amputated their dead heads and the shreds of their right wing with a series of internal blasts. They similarly cauterized the wounds on its fourth and third head. It was nothing, the dragon thought. Only one head and its red pearl must survive. It must bathe in blue flame for hours to heal this damage, but it could be undone. It only needed the fuel. And the Queen Mother had barrels of pitch, if the harpy was to be believed.

The Mayor searched the sky for signs of the sylphide. After the initial terror, they realized this must have been the Whirlwind, the Kingavila. At one point, the wind abruptly sped up, and the Mayor spun their heads around, exhaling a gout of flame.

It was nothing.

"I am the hunted, I am the played," said a soft female voice, a whisper on the wind. "I am the hound and the hart and the flayed."

The dragon found nothing with their three heads and began to sniff the air for an invisible creature.

"No no no, smell is on the wind," said the voice. "Answer the riddle."

The dragon crashed forward, deeper into the courtyard of the Academy.

"That's not an answer," the voice teased.

"Show yourself," bellowed the dragon.

"Game," she said with a click of the tongue. "It's a game."

The dragon spewed a sticky venom over the court.

"I seal and slough from the burning bark. I bind ancient beasts in the fluid dark. In the rising cry of the meadowlark, I blacken the road yet go white with a spark. A mound and a toss in the open park, I am the pool that murders the shark."

The dragon paused and said, "Pitch?"

"Good boy," said the voice.

The pale woman became visible, covered in a cloak and high boots of red leather. The dragon moved back, readying a narrow pillar of fire, and breathing a wall of black smoke. The sylphide laughed and pointed at a storage shed with a hole in its roof, before vanishing again.

The Mayor wondered what she was up to, how she had trapped the pitch barrels. The dragon speculated that it was reinforced with a secondary explosive, but while the concussion might injure a dragon, the spreading flame would do nothing but help. Perhaps it had been transubstantiated into an explosive that would not leave a lingering flame. The dragon decided to watch the shed and look for how the Queen Mother's forces planned to use it, climbing to the southern walls.

The sea roared, the tide rose, and water rolled over the campus. The Mayor soon faced a colossal beast from the drain, pulling itself ashore with a dozen groping tentacles, each as wide as felled timber. A thousand hooks led to a black beak and a body thrice the length and mass of a blue whale. Both great creatures screamed, and fire met water.

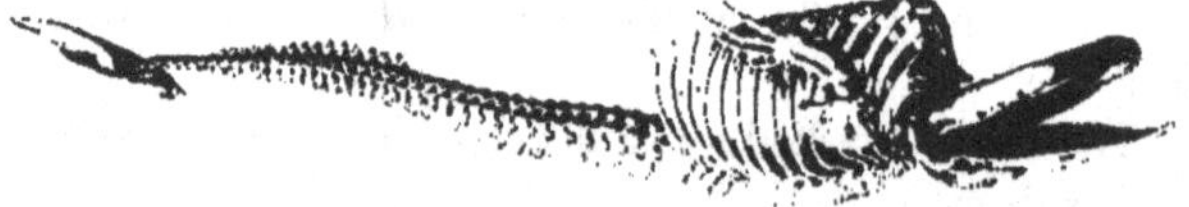

Steam rolled into the base of the observation tower. Ludmilla Orlova looked concerned and annoyed, but Kingfisher enjoyed hot mist and rain.

"The dragon is here," said the harpy.

"And the ketos," said the Queen Mother. "Dame Kingfisher, it's time for you to leave. It's dangerous."

"I am a knight of the homelands and the realm," the siren said. "If I must die for the good of the people and the nation, so be it."

"Which people? Which nation?" asked the Queen Mother. "Thank you for your aid and concern, but this is outside of your oaths. I am your queen, you are dismissed."

"But I must still protect the weak and innocent," Kingfisher said. "And technically the women, but–"

Her heart skipped a beat as the building shook with a scream like a rutting elk in a hurricane's eye and all the Wild Hunt running down a devil.

"I think the fairer sex is doing fine," Kingfisher continued. "You know, someone should protect the men. They tend to be the ones on the front."

"Indeed," the Queen Mother said. "You would make quite a nurse, delivering supplies, lifting the wounded, and carrying them to safety."

"I'm a knight," Kingfisher pronounced as she unbent her legs and puffed out her chest.

"Yes, but that's an anachronism, I'm sad to say," Ludmilla said. "The homelands will need nurses when the war comes."

"Yes," Kingfisher said. "Sure. I'm an anachronism. But we're fighting against time."

Kingfisher beat her wings and rose in the air.

"I'm going to keep your men *and* the Northmen from getting roasted or drowned or smashed to bits," she vowed, bestowing her sharp features with a hawkish nobility. "I can't stop any of you. But mind where you are."

The Queen Mother watched the strange siren leave through a hole in the window, and continued her thaumaturgy, making up for lost time by making more time.

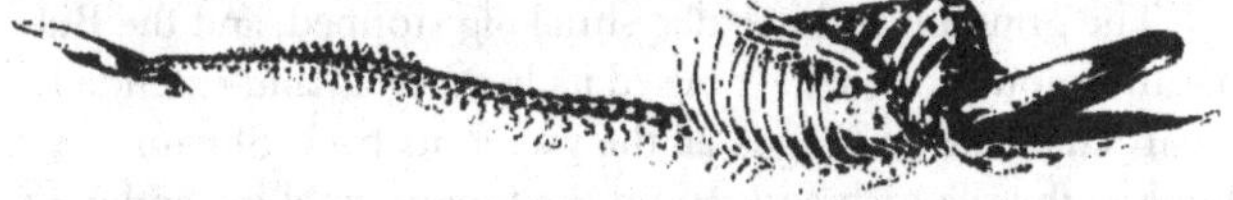

Byeol-i pleaded with the Bulgasari to halt its march while struggling to keep her balance and her head above water. Her hands grasped at its mane of iron wire but paid for momentary stability with cuts across her fingers. She twisted her sash and looped it around the Bulgasari's left tusk. She stood up and leaned back, using the tension of the silk to maintain her footing. The guardian did nothing to stop her, as it could not directly harm a child of the Jooga, but it did little to keep her from drowning as it charged forward.

She did not expect the Bulgasari to maneuver so well in the Narrows, but its raw strength propelled its stony mass forward, towards the Imperial ironclads at the mouth of the Narrows.

"Stop!" she screamed. "You're going to get me killed!"

The Bulgasari dove and Byeol-i let out a pained gasp as the icy cold soaked her bare legs. She closed her mouth and eyes and tried to protect her hat and bag. The water hit her chest like a hammer blow, and the panicked shouts from the sailors as they rapidly shifted from the aerial arc of the cannons to manning the harpoons terrified her.

The Bulgasari turned its head and opened its mouth. Byeol-i yelped and pleaded as the guardian swallowed her. A horrifying metallic scream echoed through that cavernous darkness. She held on for dear life but soon noticed that the Bulgasari did not actually have a gullet. The mouth was decorative and ended an arm's length past a pendulum uvula. She reached out to grasp its chain, only to recoil at its heat. It smelled like jasmine, hinting that it was a censor for herbal working. It must have been her family's contribution to the beast.

The grinding and metallic shrieking stopped, and the Bulgasari's mouth opened. It raised its head again and extended its articulated iron tongue all the way to its back. She unhooked the silk sash and ran up the tongue, sobbing and panting. She came to a stop against a steel beam and doubled over with a stitch in her side, coughing and trying to spit out the flavors of the forge - wet wood-smoke and metallic soot - and wipe the water from her stinging eyes. Her ears rang once more with a cacophony of iron fatigue and snapping beams as the Bulgasari resumed its transformation.

The Bulgasari wore the ironclad destroyer like a turtle shell. The beast's tendons of volcanic stone continued their attachment with a sound like cracking whips and breaking hawsers. Byeol-i gasped as they erupted from the deck and grew into the cannon's sponsons.

She saw the soul of its plot as the ironclad titan settled below the waterline and fired a cannonade at the Mayor under the Imperial banner. She reached down and touched the head of the Bulgasari with her scaled hand and felt her mind drift into the programmed consciousness of the guardian. She had been prepared, she realized. That was the primary reason that Gangcheori placed that entity in her. Not a mere protection against the kaftar, but to widen her consciousness, and train it for handling constructs of arcana and metallurgy. If the Mayor had not forced its hand, what other training did the august imugi have in store for her and the Bulgasari?

In that instant of paralyzing fear, a psychic shadow darkened her vision, a looming and hungry ghost.

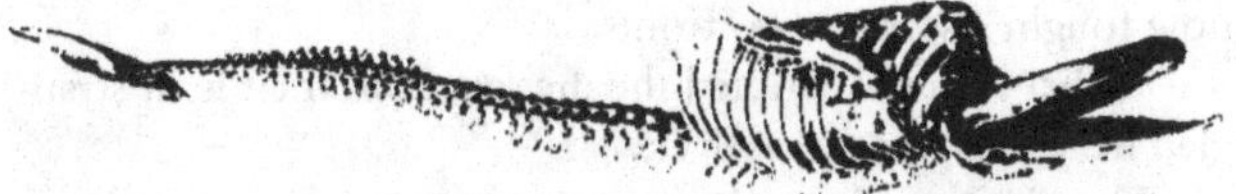

The dragon struggled with the arms of the great ketos, biting and slashing through the veil of steam, trying to shield its faces and vulnerable necks with its remaining wing. But it knew it was at a loss. It is nearly certain doom to fight an elemental in its native chaos, the ancient ones even more so. What the Mayor boiled and stripped away was rapidly restored by the sea, salt pouring into the dragon's wounds for its struggles. Behind the squidlike head, this ketos' body was too thick to find a vulnerability, a bulky form like a seal or walrus covered with rough scales and smaller, ceaselessly beating flippers shaped like the tails of a dolphin. Those tentacles could be bitten through, but an arm for a head was an abominable trade. The Mayor rather wished they contended with one of those Ketea which resembled an oversized turtle or a serpent.

Water rolled over the south of the Royal Island, washing away much of the Students' Beach, and sealing the dragon's wounds into clots of char and withered scales. It sucked the water's heat in an attempt to dam the flooding, but the rapid flow washed away any attempt at an icy barrier.

Just as the Mayor found their footing against a pillar, ready to twist their way out the ketos' grasp and voraginous energies, cannonballs smashed through their left front leg and the base of the column. The dragon collapsed to the ground, quickly and painfully followed by the stone roof supported by the pillar.

As the Mayor resigned themselves to death, lighting carved jagged runes through the air, a declaration of war. Cunigunde fell on the ketos with a whirlwind, ripping water from the sea monster, and dragging its innards into the storm. The ketos struggled to pull the dragon deeper into the sea, but it now fought a war on two fronts.

"What is this?" shouted the dragon from their least strangled head, despite themselves.

The Whirlwind simply screamed in response, quieted only when she ripped a peel of raw cetacean flesh from the back of the beast. Between the loss of scales and the bite wound, she had room to hack away at the ketos with her singing spear, spraying herself with a blue mixture of abyssal blood and salt water. A wide cut sliced through four tentacles, and the Mayor managed to pull back far enough to anchor three of its legs against the wall.

The disparity in scale was enormous. Cunigunde was a mouse to the dragon's cat, while the dragon was a house cat to the ketos' leopard. The rotating vertebrae of her spear whined and wailed. The flutes and hollowed spirals binding her leathers whistled and screamed like a squadron of great hawks tearing at prey. The gray horizons droned with her cyclonic force. The sylphide cut through the three struggling limbs still wrestling with the dragon and vanished into thin air. The ketos retreated beneath a violet cloud of blood. The dragon poisoned the waterfront with its venomous breath and ran deeper into the island under a hail of bullets. It turned its head to retaliate, but its breath hit a wall of rising, wet earth.

The Sagani held that the world was created by the stirring of the molten Inferno, earth intermixed with fire, and the formless Vorago, the blue-black blur of sky and sea. These are the dark deeps that Yliaster cannot reach and cannot define, leaving them in a state of primal chaos, a place of dynamic matter and the abyss of space and time. The world of Thier was born in steam. And one day, rather than the Vorago enveloping the Inferno, the sun shall reach for the core of the world, smothering the Vorago, and all will be annihilated in filthy steam. This wave of bubbling mud turned the battle of three great Sagani into an apocalyptic quartet.

The pygmy, it thought, as caltrops dug into its feet, and the refreshed ketos crushed the shoreline beneath its blubbery bulk.

Makarov spotted Fade as he stumbled and struggled against the tide of the retreat and came to support him. They watched as the old knight Kazimir rode a white camel in his old leopard helmet, shouting for the Severnayans to come into the sanctuary of the House of Wisdom, and directing the foot traffic with an ashwood staff. The blind oracle was at the door, divining injuries. The acolytes established a ramshackle triage center.

The oracle looked up briefly, and nodded at something, before telling her attendants to race to a burning building. Mageirissa's spirit appeared to Fade. She pointed at herself, and then the Tower, mimed a "sleeping" gesture, and then flew into a row of houses as a vaporous specter.

"What were you looking at?" Makarov asked.

"A ghost. They're at the Academy," Fade said. "Kingfisher and the Queen Mother."

Makarov snorted bullishly. The pair ran and hopped despite Fade's fatigue. He clenched his jaw and powered through it, and they were soon at the covered bridge, with Fade's familiar scouting for Kingfisher. She dragged away a fallen sailor as the dragon rampaged, pushing through a wall towards the Royal Forest to escape a rising tide and an animated pool of sucking mud and lancing stalagmites. Kingfisher placed the sailor in the boughs of a tree and turned to follow the crow.

"Fade!" she cried and landed on the wall above him. "Why did you come here?"

"I knew you were here," Fade said.

"You divined that?" she asked.

"No," Fade said. "It was the bravest and stupidest place someone could be at the moment. Where's the pitch?"

"Remember that storeroom near the septic tunnel?" Kingfisher said.

Fade thanked her as he began to run, trying to power through the pain. However, the scent of hot, freshly-turned earth stunned him. It was the scent of intense geurgy; soil tormented by rapid magical change, the overheated dust sprayed out by stones dissolving into soft mud.

She swooped down to pull Fade over the walls. A crack of gunfire alarmed him, but it was at Cunigunde, who wrestled with Nikneveny and her hellhound in the mud. The Whirlwind punched through the gnomide, but Nikneveny slipped off into the rippling earth. Nikneveny sent a tremor out, ordering the hellhound and her men to flee as she fired an evoker-culverine. The smoke consolidated into a flock of gray birds with sharp crescent wings. This was the Flock of the Dead, the Sluagh na marbh, a host of a faerie-magpies enchanted by feasting on the dead of battle and carrying away the ensorcelled spoils of war. Their skull had shifted towards a haunting, human quality, but these ghost-snatchers had nothing but contempt for the living. The five-hundred bird swirled around the sylphide, slashing at her bare flesh. The Whirlwind screamed and the men retreated north, pulling away from the rampaging elfin warrior and the wall of sweltering heat marking Makarov's approach to the Academy gate.

The sailors briefly marveled at the raw output of Makarov, without any apparent sign of spellcasting. His hands remained in his peacoat's pockets as icicles melted and piles of snow sublimated away. He consumed nothing but the tundra that blackened into ash under each footfall.

Erazm said nothing but a firm announcement of his station as a recovered Nikneveny rose from beneath the shattered tiles in the center of the campus, "There are two dragons in Northernmost."

And the dead trees exploded in tongues of blinding blue and the statue of Hedran wept tears of liquid metal. The Mayor bathed in the ambient heat, while the ketos screamed in outrage as its hundred-meter arms stopped their assault on the walls.

Three of the Extraordinary Commissariat's men struggled with the central hall's door, kicking it in and crawling inside as the last man's coat burst into flames. Nikneveny let out a shrill wail as her skin hardened like ceramics, forcing her into the earth. She burrowed off the campus, leaving a trail of collapsed tiles and porcelain flakes.

Kingfisher used the sweltering heat to drag Fade right to their destination. Fade felt for the pitch with his ghostly carrion crow, rapidly heating and bubbling under Makarov's pressure, and put his training to work. The Queen Mother's working had already consumed more than a third of the pitch.

"May I ask why?" Kingfisher whispered as they set down on the wall above the shed. "Why the pitch?"

"There are several types of pitch, asphalt, tar, resin. But this is the secret distillation of the Pharyes and the Yaogah of Favonia. They call it stone oil," he said, as the crude petroleum bled from the barrels, ready to flood from the collapsing shed. He called down to Makarov. "Stop the heat!"

Makarov let out a grunt of confusion, but turned his attention to the main hall, thinking that Fade and Kingfisher were overwhelmed. The violent arrival of the ketos through the southern wall forced him inside, the foaming waves drenching his heels.

Fade tossed his stolen whip down at the archway, letting it snap and twitch like the severed tail of a lizard, to keep out any approaching soldiers. Its coating of linseed oil ignited in the heat. It would be easily dispelled, a simple bit of necromancy on the oiled leather, but Fade wanted all the time he could get.

He closed his eyes and breathed deep, rubbing his hands with the linseed oil. He thought of his reedy body, the oily patches of his face and palms and the stores of fat in his viscera. His necromantic art was dangerous and self-consuming, and needed to be guided with scientific knowledge and the precision of a surgeon's hand. He had to burn only fat without atrophying his muscle or leeching his blood and bones. He thought of the cold-eyed ghouls and their transparent skin, smoke and wisdom pouring from their mouths. He thought of his master in his diabolical helm, a fossilized beast with an avian beak and twin horns jutting from a brow that swept back in a serrated wave of petrified bone. He thought of primordial remains and novel notions.

He opened his eyes and turned to look at Kingfisher, who watched him with bated breath. The corner of his mouth flick up, in spite of himself. Perhaps they weren't so different, searching for signs of life in dead ideas. He wondered if he should lean over-

"What does oil have to do with time?" Kingfisher asked, her straightforward question spoiling the imagined mood.

"Oh. It's ancient life. Plant matter. Crushed drown by the weight of a billion years, perhaps trillions and trillions across the Suns," Fade said, channeling yliaster through his signet ring, a Philosopher's Stone. He could not think of her. He had to work. His attention spread out through the oil and tar, rich with primordial power. It was the ultimate and most ancient alchemy, processed through a putrefied blackness into a purified *albedo* and a refined golden flow that ultimate erupts into the red fire of action. This deathless vitality served as a medium for devils, eidolons, and ghosts alike, the verdant might of a jungle distilled to a glistening liquid. Fade had long wondered if harnessing its power and burning it all away would purge the world of its primal devils – or perhaps transmute Man into something diabolical. "It's the oldest organic thing in the world. It's also, fortunately, dead."

The crude oil rolled along the mud, animated by Fade's skeins of yliaster, and slid over the water.

"You saw me animate those corpses in Hyperborea. All those complex nerves, thews, and muscles," Fade said as the pitch rolled up the hall, conodont elements biting into the walls like pitons. "This simple dead mass is nothing."

Kingfisher marveled as the coruscating blackness slid into the ketos. The sea monster screamed, its arms wrestling with limbs of twisting tar.

Fade and Kingfisher both flinched as mud splattered across the wall and the observation tower.

"What the fuck are you doing?" Cunigunde said, hanging in the air above Fade, mud dripping from leather as she became visible. The bone-deep cuts inflicted by the Sluagh's wings were slower to close than those of mundane blades, and she had to physically press her left biceps to the shoulder until the muscles and skin reattached with a sucking, slurping sound.

"The world has changed," Fade said, as if delivering a eulogy for an age. "The dwarfs discovered it, but humans are *finding* it, all across Thier. The stone-oil. It's earth that flows like water. It burns and blights the air. The black blood of the ancient world."

Cunigunde's eye widened as the ketos writhed under the

oily assault, releasing its limbs to pull away, but finding its flesh moored and bound to the sand and mud. The abyssal beast stopped struggling, and either fell dormant or died.

"I don't like how easy that was," Fade said.

"Necromancer," Cunigunde whispered. She knew how to pull air from the water, how to breath beneath the waves; but this choking darkness poisoned her imagination with terrible possibilities. Her eyes quaking, the Whirlwind looked at Fade with disgust and horror, and flew higher, out of reach.

She mumbled, and added, "I'm getting that dark-elf," before disappearing once more.

Kingfisher looked at the hall.

"Close it up with the oil. When I'm through the gap," she instructed, as she took to the air. "Thin it. Keep her from using it."

"I'm not going to trap you in there!" Fade blurted, breaking the cold control of his show of force.

"Trust me," she said and dove inside.

Fade withdrew the oil from the ketos' body and sent it squirming to the hall, the pitch painting the wall like the hulls of a ship.

Fade closed his eyes and hoped he could live with himself if he lost her.

"Trust her," he told himself, and the hall was black as night.

The Mayor turned back to the fiery glow of the Academy, soaking in the blissful heat as the Tall Man's retinue scattered. In that brief moment of rest, Gangcheori struck, its radiance disguised by the roiling wake of Makarov. The Mayor nearly blacked out as the lesser salamander bit into their chest, digging for their cintamani with fire and fang.

Gangcheori relished the taste of the dragon, their hot blood rolling down its lapping tongue. The fresh flesh was delightful, far better than the severed heads it swallowed up on the beach. The imugi only stopped when the Bulgasari fired another cannon, smashing into the back of the dragon. The gilded guardian dragged itself ashore and charged through the forest. It thrashed and smashed and drew up the metals of the earth.

Gangcheori pulled back and shouted for the Bulgasari to strike, stripping the copper from the stunned dragon's scales, the iron from their blood. And yet the guardian idol stopped dead. The Mayor stumbled and pulled back, and Gangcheori ordered Byeol-i to charge.

Byeol-i said nothing, and the Bulgasari stood still. She threw her bag to the ground, at the dragon's feet, and wiped the feverish sweat from her brow.

Gangcheori hissed and struck again at the dying Mayor. The dragon pleaded with a simple, repeated "Stop," as their consciousness drifted.

"It was always about you, wasn't it?" Byeol-i said. "You've thrown us into the fire of your ambition. Your hunger."

Gangcheori struck again, and the Mayor fell to the ground, their last head smacking into the fractured earth. A tantalizing aroma rose from that last gasp of heat, a smell like crackling fat. The imugi was mad with hunger, a desperation born of famine, a thousand years of want. Gangcheori flew into a frenzy and snapped at the Mayor before turning towards Byeol-i's bag. It ripped the canvas open and swallowed the hide in one bite.

The imugi paused and choked. It shook and slapped its throat against the ground. It glared at Byeol-i with a look of betrayal, pleading as the tar sealed its mouth. It tried to burn it away, but it simply liquefied and slid further down his throat.

The imugi twisted and swallowed against its better judgment, compelled by a terrible appetite.

"I'm sorry," she said. An unseen hand touched her shoulder. "We can't do this. We can't help this invasion."

Gangcheori whipped its head forward, knocking Byeol-i down and scalding her forearm. The Mayor kicked at the imugi with their working leg, cutting the writhing serpent deeply. If the great firedrake was at their full strength, it would have split the lesser salamander in two. A quick bite and crocodilian thrash of the head broke off a long section of Gangcheori's tail. A rusty haze swirled from the Mayor's luminous teeth as they croaked out a call for aid, the imugi's blood evaporating upon contact with the blazing copper.

Byeol-i screamed in terror as Gangcheori shrank and wrapped its bleeding body around her scaled arm. She feared the imugi would crush her like a constrictor, and the heat on her flesh was a needling agony, a brutal tattoo, a burial in burning sand.

The soul of Mageirissa hovered above the Mayor, and the dragon was aflame, a rising blue conflagration that consumed trees and tar and gunpowder.

"Ogre woman! What are you doing?" Byeol-i shouted from the ground, half-herself, half-Gangcheori. The salamander rooted its psyche in the gaps in her mind.

"A bit of regression," Mageirissa explained, playing the island of calm in the situation. "The Mayor will die at its current size. Too hard to sustain. Too weakened by that serpent's treachery. Don't worry, I am good with children."

Byeol-i suddenly needed to eat as Mageirissa worked her strange magic. The shaman's astral body raised an egg in one hand and a small torch in the other, in sympathetic affinity with the birth and renewal of a salamander. The egg blackened, hollowed, and cracked. Byeol-i wondered if the cruel sorcery of the ogres consumed others people rather than tax the shaman's body and implements.

The dragon burnt and broke apart, leaving behind a charred, winding spine. It writhed, twisting serpentine, reborn like the phoenix. The small salamander panicked, and briefly fled towards a rotten fallen tree on fresh legs. It halted as the stumbling Byeol-i approached.

Kill it, you treacherous whelp, Gangcheori said in her head. *Smash it with the Bulgasari's paws.*

She picked up the Mayor and held them in her opposite hand. The salamander newt crawled up her arm and sat on her shoulder, cooling itself to her comfort.

What are you doing? Gangcheori said. *I did everything for you. At least rip out its red pearl and take it for yourself.*

Byeol-i waited for Mageirissa's spirit to drift closer to her, uncertain of the astral body's senses The nurse reminded her of the recent medical efforts, which spoke of contamination of the port by leaching metals and the pollution of alchemical industry. There was a solution here, Byeol-i realized. The Jooga had a bargaining chip.

"The Bulgasari doesn't have to be a weapon," Byeol-i said. "It can purify the water and the earth, pulling out the mercury. Gangcheori, I'm sorry, but we're going to do this the right way."

Politics is never the right way, Gangcheori thought to her. His astral form writhed against the cage of her skull. *Compromise, bribery, back-room deals. I liked you better without the memories.*

"No strength or seniority," she said. "So, you're going to have to talk through me. Think of it as part of the amnesty. It will protect you from reprisal... Ogress, tell whomever you're with that we have the Mayor and a way to sink their ironclads. And this solution for the tainted soil."

She climbed up on the Bulgasari with her human hand, and guided it back to the Narrows, with Mageirissa cautiously watching its trail. The senses of the shamaness' astral body, more sensitive to arcane forces than corporeal eyes and ears, were soon overwhelmed by a terrible power rising from the tar. Mageirissa had never felt anything like it – it was as if the crackling roar of a burning forest echoed up through a chasm for a million years without ever losing strength. It was catastrophic and overwhelming, a tsunami of primal power.

It was Infernal.

Kingfisher flew into a firefight, with Makarov heating the battlefield from his position behind a statue, and the black-coated men of the Commissariat resorting to a three-man rifle line behind an overturned table. They struggled with their new loading cycle, as their muskets and pistols relied on a two-part chemical system rather than black powder, dangerous to use against a dragon. Kingfisher didn't have time to take in the sights and avoided all of them. One of the sailors glanced up at her, but her eyes were searching for the Queen Mother.

A powder blast shook the Academy, the pressure wave smothering the screams of men. An abrupt silence cut the tumult short, and Kingfisher found herself a meter back from her prior position. The Queen Mother was there, rolling back her side's sudden loss.

"What is it?" Ludmilla Orlova hissed at the approaching harpy with a sharp mixture of pain and frustration. A purplish-red soaked through her bandaged arm as she tried to support her ketos cousin with desperate blood rites. She had a new tool in her arsenal, a belt of grenades.

Kingfisher swooped down and seized her.

"What are you doing?!" the Queen Mother snapped as the harpy pulled her from the room and past her fighting men.

"Come with me, found a safe place," Kingfisher mumbled

as she moved, trying to maintain the momentum of the swoop with a sharp turn, a tactic used when yanking beluga sturgeons out of rivers and onto the banks. Kingfisher experienced a strange temporal stutter and gasps in the airflow into her nose, but the Queen Mother realized that she couldn't undo the harpy's grip on her breastplate. Her fingers briefly tried to pry off the talons, but she knew it was a futile gesture, and slaying the harpy with a stab would drop her to the ground in the firing arc of the Severnayans. She instead simply frozen everything but herself and Kingfisher, bullets hanging in a mirage as the thin pitch around the building sublimated into yliaster. She pulled the chord on one of the grenades and tossed it at Makarov's position.

Lumilla Orlova nearly swooned, overdrawing on her resources. She wondered if she had already burned through the pitch, or if the dragon's men rolled the barrels into the icy harbor.

Kingfisher brought the Queen Mother to a stop in front of the statue of Viktor Pridvornov. Ludmilla looked upon her uncle with a strange awe.

"This was the last statue they installed before it happened…" she said, sadly. She put her uninjured hand against her temple, suppressing the emotion and faint ache with pressure. "Martyr of science…"

Kingfisher sent a sharp gust of wind into the far room. It forced the door shut, and the grenade stuck against the pitch, thickened into a wall within frozen time. That level of precision proved too much of a strain for her, and she stumbled to the ground as she tried to glide to the far wall.

"What is the meaning of this?" the Queen Mother demanded. She turned and approached with a paranoid unsheathing of Wartime, ready to skewer Kingfisher if she attempted to attack. "Are you trying to distract me?"

When Kingfisher rolled over, the black blade was beside

her jugular.

"Did you move the grenade towards my men? Is that why you sent a gust through the door?" she said. "If one of them dies, you die. I am no fool, Dame Kingfisher."

"I am," Kingfisher said as she covered her face with her wings, sealed her nose, and generated a vacuum against the glass door.

A painful disturbance struck through Ludmilla's chest as she pushed against the flow of ages. At first, she wondered if this was the Leviathan, awakened and fighting her. But no, it was the harpy snatching her heart and scratching at her lungs, stilling the air so she could not breath in this elongated moment. The bird-woman proved far more cunning than she looked, Ludmilla thought, before she choked on the dead calm.

The Queen Mother burst the dam of time. Kingfisher's collapsing vacuum cracked the door as she rolled out of the way, forcing Makarov through it. The grenade went off, but rather than sending shrapnel into Makarov, the pitch absorbed most of the blast. The three men dove as the shock of the grenade slammed against their makeshift pavise. Two of them stayed to turn the table, while one glanced inside, raised his rifle, and joined his Queen.

Kingfisher studied the Queen Mother's face. She had perfected the steely royal mask, but a relieved glance at her rifleman confirmed that she knew what had happened. Makarov shouted as Kingfisher dug her claws into his coat.

She gestured towards the fire-extinguishing runes on the archway and said "Fireproofing magic. Sailor, your wise man's cuffs."

"You bitch… you sold us out," Makarov said. "I sheltered you."

"Silence, dragon," Kingfisher said. "This is what knights do."

The sailor approached Kingfisher with a look of apprecia-
tion and confusion. She ignored his face and focused on his
woolen coat and the mites inside. The other two sailors entered the room, shedding their coats.

"Well," said the Queen Mother. "I think we're done here."

One of the sailors stepped outside and shouted in alarm.
Lund forced him back inside, stolen pistol in his clawed hand,
with a horrifying visage slowly shifting from mite to man as
the wards reversed his karcist transformation.

The floor gave out beneath Kingfisher, and her talon was
forced into the earth as it bubbled with crude oil. Kingfisher
screamed in agony as an unseen force crushed her breastplate
and rolled her wings in the black pool.

Nikneveny burst from the ground in fury, her porcelain
skin streaked with the bubbling oil and cracked by the heat.

"She's setting you up!" the gnomide screamed as she
placed her pick against Kingfisher's heart, the metal dilating
around the sharpened point.

The room sapped her magic as she rose from the ground
to the level, but the fury in Gerana's steely muscles let her drag
the struggling harpy towards the leg of the dining room table,
shielding herself against Lund's pistol shot.

"She came with Makarov," Nikneveny spat. "Fade has you
surrounded. Leave the room, freeze it, get out."

"She's not with me!" Makarov shouted.

He pushed himself to his feet, but a twist of the pick kept
him from charging the gnomide.

Lund pointed the pistol at Nikneveny in panic, allowing
the man in front of him to close the gap and wrestle with him.
As they pulled away from the antimagic wards, Lund fired the
weapon and swung an ursine arm at the sailor, knocking him
to the ground. The other man backed up and fired, and Lund
was a bleeding bear in the door frame, huffing and puffing.

Nikneveny watched the transformation in shock but managed to beat Kingfisher's cuirass with her pick to continue the threat. The harpy kicked reflexively, the oil sticking to her wings inciting a raw, animal panic. Kingfisher bit her lip with enough force to break the chapped skin, hoping controlled pain would overcome the primal drive to fly. The stifling tar aggravated this survival instinct into a hellish torment.

Ludmilla Orlova could only let out a quiet gasp as the third sailor slapped the wise man's handcuffs on her wrists.

"I'm sorry, your grace, but I need you to release the harpy and sit down," the sailor said, pulling her own sword on her.

His eyes glistened with the hint of tears.

"Who are you?" Ludmilla Orlov asked the sailor, in the same uniform as the naval detachment. She watched Gerana's face for a hint of triumph – was this yet another betrayal?

"Fade?" Nikneveny asked. Her clear befuddlement reassured Ludmilla. She still had one friend in the world.

"Release her," the third man said, prodding the sword against the queen's bandage.

He moved to block her final escape route from the room and to distance himself from the two remaining sailors.

Light poured in through the widows, and the pitch pulled away from the glass. An eerie, rising whine echoed through the roof, followed by a smashing foot, as Cunigunde broke through, holding Fade.

"Alright, sea monster's dead, dragon's fucked, wrap it up," Cunigunde said.

"You've lost your magic by entering here, too," said the Queen Mother.

"So, I'm still an athletic marvel with a polearm that can grind the skin off a dragon," bragged Cunigunde with a wry smile. "Listen to the kids."

"Wait, that's Fade," Nikneveny said. She pulled the pick from her captive's chest. "Who's this?"

Kingfisher breathed a sigh of relief and examined the

third man now that she had a moment to think. He was young, maybe early twenties, with dark blond hair. She hadn't seen him in such a lively state for a long, long time.

"Arkady Sergeyevich," he said. "The night janitor at the infirmary said that you saved my life."

"You pulled through?" Kingfisher squawked with astonished joy despite the crude oil dripping from her hair and feathers. Her voice cracked, and she shifted from one foot to the other with a hop. "I saved someone?!"

"And he threw his life away," said Nikneveny.

"I understand," Arkady said. He saluted the Queen Mother and placed his pistol against his head.

"Hey, hey kid, don't," Makarov said as he sat in a chair at the table, struggling with his handcuffs. "Fuck the bureau, stay in a free city. You have a good heart."

"My duty to my savior and my empire conflicted," Arkady said, his voice cracking. "Shall I?"

"Put the pistol down," the Queen Mother said. "You're dishonorably discharged from my service and exiled to this port."

"This is treason, Ludmilla," Nikneveny whispered. "He should be shot."

"I'm tired, Rana," Ludmilla Orlova said.

She lost her stiff, refined posture and slumped in a chair.

Her voice sounded both unnaturally old and young when she added, "I wish Lem was here. He always knew what to do."

"Yeah," Erazm Makarov said. "Well, you had him killed."

"It wasn't us," Nikneveny spat.

"I was not yet here," Ludmilla said.

They all looked at Cunigunde.

"I was cleared by the legal system," said Cunigunde with a pumped fist. "First time's a charm!"

"I... I think I know who did it," Kingfisher said in dawning horror. "The Merovene party. The three Summit members."

"We cleared them," Nikneveny said. "They all had alibis at the time of Lem's murder. They were all seen by the patrons of that theatre bar. And heard."

Cuingunde bared her teeth and clicked her boots.

"No," Kingfisher whispered, shaking her head as she put the pieces together. "Legrand… he brought me in under a glamor. I looked like… I think the name was Mignard. I was stupid."

"So, this was a Merovene plot," Nikneveny said.

"Lem was used and thrown away," Makarov whispered.

"I was used," Kingfisher said under her breath.

"I was used!" Cunigunde screamed. "They literally fucked me!"

"Beg your pardon," Ludmilla said as Cunigunde stormed out of the room, still screaming.

"The Summit as a whole? Galbasi?" Fade suggested. "Who do you think ordered it?"

"Uncertain," Nikneveny said. "I'll have to launch an investigation. And reprisal, if possible."

"I'll go," Fade said.

"What?" Nikneveny said with a baffled grimace, exposing her second set of orange canines. "You? Avenging a gnome?"

"Avenging someone who tried to make up for old sins," Fade explained. "And I always needed an excuse to go into the ossuaries and catacombs of Achille. The dungeons of the Old Order."

He looked over at Lund.

"I'll have to speak to Mageirissa about it," he said. "She's never left the Homelands. But if you need a spy… I might have the right talents."

"I will go if you order me to, your grace," said Kingfisher.

"Do you wish to?" Ludmilla said.

"Yes, but…" Kingfisher mumbled.

Ludmilla drew her sword and tapped Kingfisher on the shoulder.

"I hereby task you with the quest for justice, for the death of Lem Loganev, for the deception of your trust, and for the safety of our national interests," said the Queen Mother. "Rise, Dame Kingfisher."

"Thank you," said Kingfisher.

"Rana, take her out of the library and fix her armor," Ludmilla ordered. "And ward it from geurgy. That's always been a problem."

Gerana ground her orange teeth but hopped to her feet and pulled Kingfisher outside to work the metal, accompanied by the two loyal sailors. Lund followed them outside, changing from a tired-looking bear to an exhausted man.

"So…" Fade said, tapping at the table.

"Right, let's hash this out," Makarov said with a clap that demanded they get down to business. "We're staying a free city."

"You're cutting all ties with Merovy and any nation hostile to the Throne," she said. "You will continue to service the Imperial Navy and will pay for the base's reconstruction with tariffs."

"Fine, the Mayor did it, but they can't last," Makarov said. He pointed at one of the men and mimed a pen and paper. "Our low tariffs make this port worthwhile. Strangling us will start this all over again."

"No imperial taxes or levies," she said. "It will all stay here. But we shall command all rights to the White Meska outside of the Severnayan Province, and profit there."

"Alright, reasonable," Makarov said.

He began to write out the terms when the sailor gave him a parchment, inkpot, and quill.

"Yeah, we're wizards, but what is this shit?" Makarov exclaimed as the quill struggled with the cold ink.

Ludmilla pulled a fountain pen and well from an ivory case and pushed it across the table towards Makarov.

"Your tastes only grew grander," Makarov said.

He undid the clasp and finished his shorthand.

"When was the last time we talked?" she said. "Seventy-five years ago?"

"Yeah," Makarov said, pausing to think. "2474 or 5. Sounds right. Wow, yeah."

"Children?" she asked.

"One," he said. "Elena."

"Is your wife?" she asked.

"She passed away," Erazm said. "She was sixty-seven. Not too young… I suppose. I would ask, but your family is rather well known."

"Fair," she said.

"Did you want this?" he said. He gestured broadly. "This…"

"I was always going to be this," she said. "No use wasting time on daydreams and possibilities… This brings us to my primary point. The Thaw has to shorten. Back to the natural cycle."

"Longer winter will kill us," he said.

"The long Thaw might kill us all," she said. "We can't risk it."

"We will have to put it to a vote. The Mayor won't be happy," he said. "Unless you've done something to it."

"It fled the battle," she said. "I don't know its fate. How about this? You will have the entire province ruled from this city, *re juris* rather than *de facto*, with complete trade and fishing rights to the Polar Sea, the White Meska unto Kastorin, and all the River Mutny."

"I would also send out prospectors, looking for tin," Fade said. "A tip from one Polybius Pander. Might be profitable, tide you over until a solution can be found."

"I see," said Makarov. "This might prove sustainable. We want freedom, but the terrain is poor."

"Imagine an entire continent of this," Ludmilla said.

Makarov laughed.

"I'll propose this to the city council," Makarov said. "And tell them we have your assurance."

"For all the good that will do," she said. "What if they say no?"

"That's democracy," he said.

He chuckled again, nervously. She leaned in.

"I'm scared, Erazm," she said. "I don't want this world to die. And I don't want Northernmost to die. I was born here. But if I have to choose... no, there is no choice."

"But how much time do we have?" Makarov said. "Decades, centuries?"

"We only have right now," she said. "When you're in a mine, do you know how many times can you accidentally strike the support beam? Your pick only makes a dent, a hole, a few splinters. Miner after miner doing the same thing, day in, day out. You may not be the one to make it fall. It might not be your responsibility when it all collapses. But still, shouldn't you stop?"

"Don't speak in aphorisms," Makarov said. "We need hard numbers. The council will demand to know a time."

Ludmilla's eyes dulled, as if the century caught up to her.

"Don't speak to me of time."

Chapter 23: This Mortal Armour That I Wear

Kingfisher waited for the meeting to end, testing out her new armor. Instead of the male cuirass beaten into shape by slamming into stones and walls, this breastplate was fitted and firm, altered to repel magic and blades, enchantments fed by heat and sweat and blood loss.

She tried to fly to the tower, to watch for Fade, but the crude oil in her wings forced her to flutter and hop her way to the top. She hoped she could glide down, but her wings were already strained, and each act of exploration uncovered a novel ache in yet another muscles. Lund departed to find Mageirissa soon after, while Nikneveny attended to her troops and recovered her hellhound. The dragon could not be found on Royal Island, with no signs of a recovery pyre.

Cunigunde appeared on the wall, not far from Kingfisher. She looked down at the corpse of the ketos, still massive after losing a third of its water. She watched her dark reflection in the oil spill.

"Hey," Kingfisher said. "Thank you."

"For what?" Cunigunde said.

"In the end, you sort of did almost the right thing," Kingfisher said. "Likely on purpose. Right?"

"Fuck you," Cunigunde said.

"You could have killed thousands of people," Kingfisher said. "You bombed the storehouse, sure. But you wounded the Mayor just enough, struck at Nikneveny, just enough, fought the ketos, just enough. Violent, but you were strategic."

"Yeah, fairy tale endings are possible if there's a fairy hauling tail across the city," Cunigunde said. "I'm your fairy godmother. You're welcome."

"Yeah, it's not a fairy tale," she said. "A lot of sailors were hurt, and I can see fires in town. And I'm not sure about that ketos."

"Fuck him," Cunigunde said. "Are you not into this knight thing anymore?"

"I'm sort of a real knight," she said. "I have a royal mission."

"Yeah, good," Cunigunde said. "I thought you were always a knight. But I guess it comes from the outside. Not my world."

"What world?" Kingfisher asked.

"We are warriors of two worlds," Cunigunde said. "You're the knight, the adorned and apprenticed, the forged and favored. Chivalrous, armed, and armored by lords and gods and society. I'm the barbarian. Not ironclad, but muscled, naked but for the leather of the wild and the heat of blood. I was a killer born. Like a god, I am. You're a weapon, made for the use of others. Is that what you want to be?"

"I *want* to be made something for others," Kingfisher said with an affirming nod. "Anything. I understand how confident you are. I'm already a third of the way through my lifespan. And this is all I've done."

"Yeah, too bad," Cunigunde said. "But this was a pretty good run."

"You think so?" Kingfisher asked.

"Yeah," Cunigunde said. "How about I snap your neck now, end on a high note?"

"No," Kingfisher said. "No thank you."

"Alright, but I better not catch you complaining about peaking young," Cunigunde said. "That's so annoying. 'My twenties were the best years of my life, what happened?' Well, because you're a drunk who married a drunk, Tara."

"Ah," Kingfisher said.

"I guess I'll go to Merovy with you," Cunigunde continued. "She was from its northwest. I gave that woman a hair clip, maybe I'll get it back."

"When was that?"

"About 2280."

"Human? She's dead."

"I'll get it from her family."

"Are you that petty?"

"It's humans who have disregarded the gifts of elves."

Kingfisher decided not to talk to Cunigunde. The Sylphide eventually grabbed her and flew towards Fade.

"How did the meeting go?" Kingfisher asked.

"It's certainly not as heated," Fade said. "They've hammered out terms. But it's going to be tabled for a vote, and messengers to Chernograd."

"Ludmilla has a gate in and out of her palace," Kingfisher said. "Should speed things up."

"She has agreed to stay here. The Tall Man is coming with us," Fade said. He looked down at the oil slick and sighed. "Let's get you cleaned up."

Arkady Sergeyevich followed them out, hiding behind a popped collar and downward glances. Cunigunde gifted him with a solid gold band and a ruby the size of an apple. Fade told him to stick around, in case they needed a sailor.

Mageirissa's projection guided them to the House of Wisdom, where she returned to her flesh and rose up from a pew. Lund took up the rest of the seating, having bandaged wounds, translated some Murmurish, set a broken arm and accelerated its healing, and passed out from the stress of shapeshifting.

"Dame Halcyon Volganina," Kazimir of Staraya Stolitsa said.

Kazimir rose from healing a broken leg with a touch of his hands and an orison to Grodna and his mother Incano, the gods of bone formation.

"Many spoke of your valor."

"Thank you," said Kingfisher.

"Your wings," the old knight said. "They're covered in oil.

This doesn't smell like whale oil. Fresh asphalt."

"Yes," she said. "I'm sort of worried about it, but how is the city? The fires out?"

"We've sent two dozen and two men from the naval yard and storehouse to the crematory, three citizens," he said. "The fires are out. Could have been worse if the oil was allowed to spread. We will need some time to adjust to new politics, contending with a hostile navy."

"I think Makarov and the Throne are sorting something out," Kingfisher said. "We have to have faith."

"I suppose so," said the Knight of the Old Capital. "But something has been troubling me… that Mignard woman. She has the talents and blessings of the Paladins of the Ivory Court. But no faith. She hates the gods and the order of things. No rituals, no spirits, no elemental blood. What is empowering her?"

"I'm going to Merovy," Kingfisher said. "I'll ask her."

Fade purchased soda ash, natron, and tincal of the Rasayanas from the dry goods store, and met Kingfisher at the banya. They rented a room for hours, a deep basin, and liters of hot water, at a steep cost. They stripped down to their underwear, Kingfisher sat in the steaming, basic water. She swished the lather around the tub, Fade loosened the oil from her feathers. It took an hour and a half.

They spoke of their families, and what ports they traveled to. Fade explained what Merovy and Achille were like now, from his second-hand knowledge. She spoke of its age of chivalry and darkness, battles between horned knights and vampires enthroned in elephant howdahs, undead armies clashing in the shadows of pyramids under the cover of red mist. Its courtiers wore masks and took new family names to hide from curses and the retribution of ghosts. Merovy was one of the few places in Caunias, Aquilo, and the Septentrine Empire where humans did not cremate and pulverize their dead. They were tithed to the lords, before their recent downfall.

"And before the vampires, the founder of the kingdom was descended from a sea creature, called the Quinotaur. I thought it was a ketos, but what if it was the Leviathan as well?" Kingfisher said.

"A city built on death and eternity," Fade said. "We have to go, don't we?"

He helped her out of the bath. She asked him to cover her wings with towels. He turned to adjust the steam and filled the room with a hot, white haze. He peeled off his wet clothes.

As the steam cleared, the pair sat across from each other in the small room, a meter apart. Fade had covered his waist with a towel, exposing his slave tattoos, a pair of chains crossing his torso from shoulder to waist around a circle of Pharyean runes. The chains crossed over his heart, through the eye sockets of an ancient lizard's skull. Kingfisher had wrapped a body towel around her retracted wings. Another hung from her knees, covering her shins and feet.

He was surprised to see that she had pulled the tie on her wet chemise, letting it fall beside her.

"Let the steam seep in," he said, not quite knowing what to say or where to look. "We'll dry it off later."

Kingfisher thought of Cunigunde's confidence, and how she held herself. Shame was a human obsession. She only knew guilt. She pulled her wings back even further, until it began to hurt, and pushed her bare breast forward.

"Do I look good like this?" she asked.

Fade caught his breath and wiped his face dry.

"Yes," he said. He stood up and pulled the blankets off her wings and knees. "But you look wonderful like this."

There was a moment of hesitation and slow breathing before she ripped off his towel with her mouth.

After a week of preparation and recuperation, Kingfisher, Fade, Lund, and Mageirissa waited for the crew of the Murmurish freighter to finish loading. Nikneveny anticipated that the Summit expected Tsokiri reprisal for interference, espionage, and the murder of Loganev, so a vessel from neutral Murmur would be the best way to enter Merovene waters. She would come alone–along with crates of dirt and the covered portrait of Ludmilla–as her Commissariat had neither an external operational apparatus nor mandate. She had secured an independent room and was clearly irritated that Arkady Sergeyevich was asked to come aboard as a deckhand and Kingfisher's squire, largely for his protection and the get him out of the country.

Cunigunde appeared beside Kingfisher as the final barrels were rolled into the hold.

"Politics is boring," she whined. "Listening to that council made me want to tear my hair out."

"They let you into the council?" Kingfisher asked.

A tall woman in peasant's clothing approached. The movement caught Cunigunde's eye.

"She was security, with her might and weapon of bone," said Lumdilla Orlova. "The Bookhangers' metal beast has taken the role of the draconic protector, at least until the Mayor can recover. The holder of its command was convinced to split its mastery among five other members of the city government, as a matter of security. Good politics, the Jooga got quite a deal out of it. They're manufacturing more automatons, small lions which leach the mercury from the soil."

"So, everything finished?" Kingfisher asked. "Will you be returning home?"

"No," she answered. "I will be staying here. At the old estate and the summer palace. And perhaps looking further north, towards the polar ice. The Leviathan cannot be allowed to wake."

Nikneveny stood at the end of the ramp and raised her head to acknowledge the Queen Mother. "It won't, your grace. We must depart soon."

"Farewell and a safe return," said Ludmilla. "Do what you must in the name of the Homelands."

"I will," Nikneveny said.

"Me too," said Cunigunde the Whirlwind. "And whatever else I feel like. Thieving, reiving, light arson… Ah, I miss Merovy."

She flew to the topmast, helped the men with the rigging, and conjured up a favorable tailwind with a blow of her horn.

"I might be out of a job," Kingfisher said.

"Eh, they'll need a spotter," Fade said with a shrug. "Her eyes are rubbish, even with the spectacles."

"Well, all aboard that's going aboard," said Lund.

Mageirissa looked at Ludmilla and bowed her head. Ludmilla nodded back.

"Your grace. I'm sorry I never spoke to you," Mageirissa said.

"Thank you. I don't know who you are," Ludmilla said.

Mageirissa nodded again and chuckled nervously, before bowing and picking up her bag. Lund and Mageirissa carried their luggage to the vessel, aided by Arkady, who kept his head down amid the royal discourse and the presence of the Sylphide pacing along the berth.

Fade bowed to Ludmilla, handed her an envelope in silence, and returned to Kingfisher's side. He slipped his bag over his shoulder, picked up the harpy's small trunk, and played with the hairs on the nape of her neck.

"So, you ready to be our guide?" he asked.

"Yeah," she answered. "It will be good to be out at sea again. Hopefully, this one won't blow up."

"Hopefully," he said, as he followed her up the ramp.

He watched the sailors pull its clanking chains up like a drawbridge, imagined the castles and old knights of legends, and leaned in to kiss the one beside her. She drifted aimlessly in thought, looking up at the crow's nest, but his touch was a pleasant surprise.

Fade looked back at the wharf and up to the great tower, with a hint of suppressed worry.

"Everything is going to be fine," she said, and nuzzled up next to him.

"We're sailing to a city of death and revolution, in the heart of an enemy empire," he said. "But for once, I believe it."

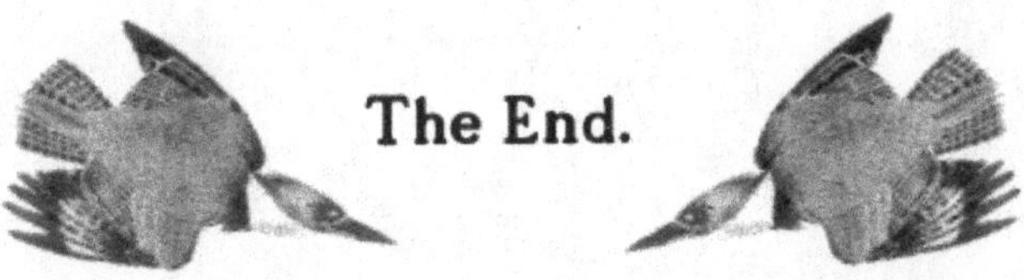

The End.